FINDING HOME

Rollin' On Series,

Book 1

EMILIA FINN

All rights Reserved. No part of this book may be used or reproduced in any manner whatsoever without written permission, except in the case of brief quotations embodied in critical articles and reviews.

This book is a work of fiction. The names, characters, places, and incidents are products of the writers' imagination or have been used fictitiously and are not to be construed as real. Any resemblance to persons, living or dead, actual events, locale, or organizations is entirely coincidental.

All songs titles, lyrics, film titles, trademarked statuses and brand names mentioned in this book are the property of, and belong to, their respective owners. Emilia Finn is in no way affiliated with any of the brands, artists, musicians, or songs mentioned in this book.

This Book is licensed for your personal enjoyment only. This Book may not be re-sold or given away to other people. If you would like to share this book with another person, please purchase an additional copy for each person. If you're reading this book and did not purchase it, or it was not purchased for your use only, then please return and purchase your own copy. Thank you for respecting the hard work of this author.

An original work of Emilia B Finn. Finding Home copyright 2017 by Emilia Finn.

ISBN-13: 978-1544999227

ISBN-10: 1544999224

Finding Home

Rollin' On series, novel # 1

By Emilia Finn

To E, Love Me.

Other Books written by Emilia

The Rollin' On Series

Finding Home

Finding Victory

Finding Forever

Finding Peace

Finding Redemption

Finding Hope

*

*

*

Coming in 2018:

The Survivor Series

The Inamorata Series

Table of Contents

Prologue

November 17, 2013

"McTavish Wines, Kit speaking. How can I help you?" I answer the phone with a huff and I wonder where our receptionist is. My workload is insane right now, and I just don't have time to take calls that aren't even meant for me.

My eyes narrow at the almost silence. No one speaks, but I can hear them. They're … crying? Crazy or not, that tone is familiar to me. "Dad? Daddy, is that you?"

"Kit, honey," he chokes out.

"Daddy, what's the matter?"

"Can you come? Please. Can you leave work?"

"What happened? Where's Jack?" Tears immediately spring to the surface and spill from my eyes. My dad is the strongest man I know. If he's crying, then someone is dying. Oh god! "Daddy? Tell me now, please, what's wrong?"

"I … honey, I have cancer."

He… "What?"

"Leukemia. The doctor says I have leukemia."

"You're sick? I didn't even know you were feeling unwell..."

"Can you come? Please?"

"I'm on my way now. I'll be there in a minute."

1

Kit

Saying Goodbye

Five Months Later.

I scan the crowd in front of me as revulsion rolls through my belly. 'Mourners' that aren't mourning at all, all stand around and watch me with the eager gazes that scream of greed and excitement.

A hundred sets of eyes track my every move, a decent turn out of family, though only a very few are genuinely in mourning and here to support me and Jack. The other ninety are simply enjoying the attention and hoping for some big will reveal. Spoiler: there won't be one. Assholes.

I turn my head slightly and look behind me, to the open grave dug into the almost red dirt, and the coffin sitting on the blue straps that will eventually lower him into the ground. The person inside is... was... my best friend.

He was also my dad.

The timber coffin is as plain as they come, because it's all I could afford. Today's service is at the graveyard. There will be no church portion because I cannot afford it. The flowers on top of his coffin, I haggled over a few days ago because although I want the best for my dad, I can't afford to buy extravagance that will only be buried. I'm not flat broke, but I know the next few years of my life are going to be expensive.

My dad was a single parent, and although I moved out of home a few years ago, my younger brother Jack, who's still only fifteen, is still in need of a guardian, a home, and money to put food in his belly.

Once we leave here today, he'll come live with me.

It wasn't a discussion we had. It was just kind of assumed by all parties. Not that I mind—he is my baby brother after all.

I struggle to speak past the lump in my throat, but after stalling as long as possible, I begin to read the eulogy and remember my dad's short life. I'm not really present in the moment. I'm speaking on auto, reciting the words that I hastily scribbled together late last night. It's the first time I've ever had to read at a funeral. Actually, it's the first funeral that I've had to participate in at all, and I'm literally shaking in my boots.

My best friend Casey says it's shock; I guess she's probably right since I can't seem to warm up either. Case stands a few feet to my left, trying to lend her strength, trying to be here for me but still maintaining a respectful distance.

But her distance leaves me front and center, and largely alone.

I hate it here. I hate these people looking at me. I hate that he died in the first place. I look to my right, to Jack standing there with his tough guy attitude, but I can see his devastation. He's a fifteen-year-old orphan after all, and I can't entirely blame him for the asshole attitude he's adopted.

As I look around at the crowd, I see loads of familiar faces; very few who have ever supported us though. I see my dad's brother, with a scowl on his face and a five-day-old beard. I guess my dad's funeral didn't warrant shaving, or anything more than casual jeans and flannel. My Aunt Renee cozies up to someone half her age while she blubbers and sniffles into a tissue, but I see no tears in her eyes.

My cousins wear expressions of boredom, with their iPhones in hand and short skirts that barely cover their ass cheeks.

My dad had six siblings; most of them are here and waiting for this to end so they can get down to the business of drinking and bitching. It's a hobby of theirs.

My boyfriend's mom and dad are also here, standing in the back and at least appearing to be genuinely sad for me. They're decent people; his mom has helped me a lot this last week, lending a shoulder to cry on when needed. As someone who cries no more than twice a year, this is unchartered territory for me.

But I don't see my boyfriend Max. I'm not entirely surprised he isn't here. His mom wears a sheepish expression, telling me she knows of his absence and she doesn't approve, but not enough to do anything about it. Like I said, they're decent people, but they're enablers, and I hate that they've allowed him to be this person; the kind that doesn't even attend the funeral of his girlfriend's dad. He's been distant the last few weeks, as if my dad's sickness had been a nuisance for him, and I've been so busy that I just don't have the time or energy to care.

I don't know how we became these people, so indifferent toward each other now that I'm not even torn up that he isn't here.

But that's a problem for future Kit.

I continue reading from the notes in front of me, knowing the words are just shallow crap that in no way describe him, his life, his accomplishments, or how much he'll be missed.

My eyes flick away from my notes when I hear a small commotion toward the back; my Aunt Renee argues with her sister, Aunt Lisa. I don't really care whether they get along, but I do wish they'd shut the hell up. They can't keep their shit together for the five minutes it takes for me to read this. This whole service, cheap as it is, will take less than thirty minutes and then Janine, Max's mom, has offered to host the wake in their home.

I accepted, though I'm embarrassed this will be when they meet my extended family. But again, I don't actually care that much. Max and I seem to be on the tail end of whatever *this* is, so I don't really have to worry about impressing his family for much longer.

On the surface, they're nice enough people, but Max and I have been together for about two-and-a-half years now, and while pleasant on the outside, I haven't gotten to know them very well. No one really made a huge effort to get to know each other, and I guess subconsciously, everyone knew this wouldn't last. We're just not a good fit.

I finish reading my bit and refold the paper I wrote on, then the funeral director starts a Kenny Rogers favorite of Dad's, and he hands me a rose to drop in on top of the coffin. I walk up to him, and although I want to tell him how much I love him, or how much I'll miss him, all I can obsess about is hopefully not tripping and falling in with him. Grief and exhaustion can make a girl think weird things.

I throw the rose in and it hits the coffin lid with a sickening thud. Should I have done that differently? Surely I could have done it so that we wouldn't hear it land? I don't know … maybe I should have bent lower and gracefully placed it in? But if I got closer, it would be my luck that I would fall in. I hate that I'm overthinking this.

The funeral director asks all mourners to make a single line, take a rose, say their goodbyes to my dad, and give their condolences to my brother and me.

I stand there and accept hugs and pretentious words from assholes who don't mean a thing they're saying. This portion takes a long time, but I soldier on because the last few people are people that I actually want to see. Casey steps up to me with eyes that are pink and puffy from crying. I know she genuinely cares. She's been my constant support through all of this and I adore her. She and I have been best friends our whole lives. She'll miss my dad as much as I will.

Next in line is George, my dad's good friend. They met as business associates, and although George seems to be quiet and standoffish to others, he and my dad really hit it off. He's a good guy, and another I know is genuinely mourning today.

A few days ago, I asked if he'd mind reading the eulogy, but he respectfully declined. Turns out he'd buried his mom earlier this year and is, understandably, still a little raw from that. Even though I really, *really* didn't want to do the reading myself, I can't blame George for declining.

He gives me the warmest hug I've had in days, wipes my tears away and kisses me on the forehead. "I'm sorry, sweetheart. Truly. I'll miss him very much. You give me a call anytime. Don't be a stranger."

This kindness almost breaks me, but I hold it together. I don't have time to fall apart.

Casey stands beside me as she hugs Jack, but his posture remains stiff and he doesn't return the hug. The music changes, catching everyone's attention, and we all watch the director as he walks over and flips some latches.

He starts lowering my dad into the ground.

Hold it together, hold it together, hold it together, no, no, no, no, pull it together.

Nope. I break.

Watching a loved one being buried is so unbelievably hard. It's so final. They're officially gone. I can't stop the tears or the wracking sobs ripping through my chest as I watch him disappear lower and lower into the ground. Casey moves to my side immediately, holding me together when all I want to do is break into a million pieces. The time it takes to lower him seems to last forever.

I'm officially broken.

~*~

Casey, Jack, and I drive together to Janine's home for the wake. I don't want to be here, since my dad isn't either, but it would be pretty rude to saddle Janine with my family and not actually turn up.

When we arrive, Jack immediately takes off into the yard, and Case and I walk into the dining room in search of Janine. "Wait." She grabs my arm. "Did you speak to Max today?"

"No ... We haven't talked for a few days."

"He's here." She indicates over my right shoulder with a look that I can't decipher. I mean, it would make sense that he's here. This is his home after all. I turn in the direction she's looking to find him standing close to who I assume is a waitress.

We'll call her Fake Boob Betty.

Janine must've gone all out and hired caterers for today and while I appreciate the effort, I know it's because she wants to keep up appearances. She wants to appear the saint for volunteering her time and money to help me – the poor girlfriend.

Everyone who knows us, knows Max and I come from different sides of the tracks. I'm the chick with a single dad, and that single dad is *just* a manual labor worker.

The waitress flutters her lashes and giggles obnoxiously. I can't even blame her. Objectively, he's a very handsome man. In a very preppy, snobby, but beautiful and attentive way. And she, while trying to appear as though she wants to get back to work, has her boobs thrust out so far, I fear that she might fall over. Perhaps she's hoping she does, straight onto Max's dick.

He looks up and our gazes lock.

His eyes say *busted, buuuuut I don't really care*. He takes a step back from Betty, but as he turns to walk away, he looks back at her and says something I can't hear and touches her arm. She blushes and hurries back to the kitchen, and I roll my eyes.

He walks toward us with his pretty smirk and arrogant eyes. "Hey Kit. What's up?"

"Max." Casey greets him with narrowed eyes. She likes him much less than I do, and I think she's equal parts worried and excited that I might hit him with a chair. "What've you been up to? Didn't see you there today."

"Ah yeah, soz." He actually says *'soz.'* Not sorry, but *soz*. I feel like I'm going to fall over from the momentum my eye-rolling causes, but instead Casey and I remain silent. The awkwardness is a tangible presence and makes him squirm. "Yeah anyway, me and the guys got in pretty late last night, well early … this morning … I guess, and I slept in a bit. I'm actually still feeling a little off, so I came in here looking for something to eat …"

At some point in a woman's life, months or years after breaking up with someone, you get that feeling in your stomach, the revulsion as the question flashes through your mind, 'what was I thinking by dating him?' Max and I are still together, and yet the revulsion hits me hard. Max is a legit douche.

And he still hasn't answered for missing my Dad's funeral.

Case looks like she's about to use my imaginary chair to beat him with, so I ask if she wouldn't mind taking a walk around to check that everything's okay. I remember my extended family are here; all in one place, which hasn't happened for about fifteen years, and I don't want any drama. Casey knows everything about everything, but she also knows that Max is a dick and I can tell she doesn't want to leave my side.

I give her a literal shove and send her away, and as I turn back to Max, he grabs my arm and pulls me in to his chest.

I go, because I'm an idiot, but also because I need comfort and I figure he'll do for now. I move in and try to tuck my head under his chin, but he angles his face to bring his lips down on mine instead. As his tongue snakes out, I pull away and jerk my elbows out of his hands.

I'm not even that angry at him. To think this tiger would change his stripes simply because we're at a wake was foolish, so I simply turn and walk away. I can still smell the cigarettes on his breath and the perfume on his shirt. Fucking pig.

I catch up to Casey as she circulates and she reports all is well, then an hour later with barely simmering drama that's bound to explode soon, I decide it's time to wrap this circus up. Everyone's been fed and watered, and it's time for them to go home and back to pretending my brother and I don't exist.

I haven't seen Jack since we walked in, and after a lap of the house and rooms, I head outside to search for him.

Voices can be heard near the back of the house, and as I approach, I listen to my Uncle Mark theatrically telling a story about 'times gon' by.' Several of my cousins sit around in a circle, half drunk and giggling and passing around a joint. Classy.

I search the faces of the dozen people sitting around, then I finally spot Jack. And the beer.

In. His. Hand.

A fucking beer!

"What the hell's going on here? Who gave him that?" I storm forward and snatch the bottle from his hands and glare at everyone. "Jack! We're going. Move it."

He starts to stand, but stumbles and catches himself against the wall. "He's drunk?" My voice comes out at such a high screeching decibel, surely only dogs can hear me. "What the hell is your problem? Why would you give him a beer?" I grab his arm and start to steer him away.

He's only fifteen, but several inches taller than me and much heavier, so I can't move him if he doesn't want to be moved. Thankfully, he can walk, and mostly in a straight line. He must've been chugging the beer to get this drunk in such a short time, which means he's bound to start vomiting soon. Gross.

I lead him through the garden, hoping to god none of Max's family see this. I'm so embarrassed and feel like I'm already failing at my new role as parent. My first day on the job and my charge is drunk.

Fuck. My. Life.

Case spots me as I round the corner and starts walking toward us, but I'm pulled up short when a firm hand grabs my arm. "Don't go yet," Uncle Mark slurs. "Have a drink with me. We can catch up."

"No, we're going home now. You should too."

"Please, honey, I never get to see you. Spend some time with an old man. I buried my brother today." He starts to sniffle and his eyes are red. Nope. Not going to happen, especially today.

"No, I'll see you later. I'll call you next week." Lie. I'm not calling him next week. I'm not calling him ever.

Casey and Jack stand back and watch me, and as I approach we start walking toward the front of the house where Case parked her small Toyota hatchback.

Jack continues to stumble, and furious, I shove his head low as he gets into the car, probably rougher than necessary, but frankly I want to beat his ass. We exit the estate drive north toward my house in town, and I watch over my shoulder as Jack busily texts and sways with the movement of the car. It's a busy conversation. He's typing, waiting, reading, and typing again. Back and forth the conversation continues and the longer it goes on, the more my temper spikes.

Fortunately — or unfortunately — I don't have to wait too long. "Kit." His voice is thick and he slurs his words. "Shannon says we should come to Aunt Lisa's room tonight. Everyone is going over and catching up."

Shannon is one of my cousins, and Aunt Lisa's daughter.

I snort sarcastically. "Absolutely not. I have no intention of going over there, and neither are you."

"Yeah, I am," he argues petulantly and probably half a second away from stomping his foot. "I'll walk if I have to."

"No, you're not. And I'm not going to argue about it."

"Why the fuck not? Don't be such a bitch."

"Because they're trouble, Jack! And because you've been drinking. What the hell did you expect me to say when I found you drinking? Move over bro, and pass me one? You're fifteen for chrissake!"

"So what? I can do whatever I want. Especially now. Dad's gone, there's no one left to tell me what to do."

I feel for him, I really do, but getting drunk with those troublemakers is not the answer. "No. You're living in my house now, so you'll do as I tell you. We're going home."

Casey watches me from the corner of her eye, pity mixed with approval. Thank god. At least she's on my side.

But then the realization hits me and my hand literally comes to my chest as it throbs with pain. Casey is the only person on this planet who's actually on my side. Mom died when I was little, Dad's gone. All my extended family are idiots. That just leaves Jack and me, and he's definitely *not* on my side at the moment.

In fact, he and I haven't agreed on much in years. He's been so bitter for so long, and with Dad being a single dad with only the 'baby' at home, Jack's had free reign for a long time. I love my dad dearly, but in this moment, I'm so angry at him for leaving me in this mess. Not only a teenager to look after, but one with a giant chip on his shoulder.

It doesn't take long till we're rolling into my driveway, and as I climb out, Jack jumps out and starts walking away, back in the direction we just came.

"Where the hell are you going?"

He looks back toward us like I'm stupid. "Aunt Leesi's, I just told you."

Is he kidding?

"And I told you, no you're not. Get back here."

"Later losers," he shouts back and keeps walking, his swaying mostly under control now.

"Fuck!"

Casey puts her hand on my arm and walks me toward the front door. "Come inside for a bit. Give him twenty minutes to walk it off. You can't argue with him when he's been drinking anyway. He won't listen."

Fuck.

We go inside and Casey flicks on the kettle. That's her solution to everything. Had a bad day? Cup of tea. Stubbed your toe? Cup of tea. Lost your virginity today? Cup of tea. I chuckle under my breath at that last one. Good times.

She looks up when she hears me, but I just shake my head and walk away smiling.

After going to the bathroom, I walk back to the kitchen to find Casey setting out cups for the tea while she hums softly. That girl is my own personal jukebox. She and I share a serious love of music, and I don't think I remember a single moment of our friendship where she isn't humming, singing, or playing music. She isn't particularly gifted, but she's consistent and I figure it must relax her.

It definitely relaxes me.

She spots me and turns around to pour the tea and hands it to me, then she walks to my pantry and grabs some cookies for us to dunk. She's here often enough; she needn't ask where something is, or for permission.

"So, big day huh. Are you okay?" She has the kindest, greenest eyes a person can have, and right now they're shining with sympathy.

"Yeah, I'm fine. Tired though. Have to go get Jack, then I plan to go straight to bed. I'm exhausted. Do you think we could tie him to his bed or something, to stop him trying to sneak out later?" I'm joking. But if her answer is yes and it could be done, I'd be open to this being a serious question.

"Yeah, not sure that'll work. I'll hold the rope for you though, and we can try." She winks at me. She totally would too. "Do you know where Aunt Skank is staying?"

I smile at Casey's words. She isn't far off the mark, and my cousins didn't fall far from the tree. One of them, Aunt Renee's daughter, we've dubbed Rita the Dick Eater. I think we're pretty damn hilarious.

"Yeah, that one on Main Street. The one the name starts with A. I'll know it when I see it."

"All right, saddle up. Let's get it done."

Case stands and grabs my empty cup and takes them both to the sink, then she rinses them and sets them in the drainer. She's a clean freak and I love that about her. We're soul sisters for that reason alone.

About thirty minutes after Jack took off, we're back in the car and headed for Main. He's had enough time to walk to the motel, but I keep my eyes on the road just in case. I don't see him though, and as we pull into the motel I see a crowd milling around in the parking lot. I roll my eyes as I realize they're all related to me.

Way to keep it classy guys.

I spot Rita and Shannon, as well as a bunch of my other cousins, then I see my uncles Mark and Peter, and Aunt Lisa. Renee must be in a room. I don't see Jack anywhere. We park the car and get out, and Shannon spots us. She walks toward us with a couple beers outstretched in offer. "Thirsty?"

Yeah, that's a firm no.

"Jack's here," she says when we continue to walk by.

"Where is he?"

"Pretty sure he's gone to take a leak. Room thirty-nine."

"Yeah thanks." I brush past her and her offering, and Casey follows as we work our way through the crowd. We enter room thirty-nine to find Renee watching TV with a cigarette in one hand and a vodka mixer in the other, then Jack walks out of the bathroom with a fresh beer in hand.

"Oh, for fuck's sake." This is ridiculous! Don't these people understand supplying a minor with alcohol is illegal? "Get in the car, Jack. We're not staying."

"Why not?" he whines. "Just let me stay. You can go home. I'm fine."

I'm so damn frustrated by this shit. These people are supposed to be family. They're supposed to be the adults in this relationship. They're meant to remember I buried my dad today, offer me a shoulder to cry on or a meal train to help ease Jack and me into our new living arrangements. But they're doing none of this. Instead my aunt sits to the side and watches us like we're the day time soap I feel I'm a part of, and the rest of my family do nothing but undermine what little authority I have and offer Jack a place to drink.

"Get in the car, Jack, now."

"No, I want to stay here."

I take a deep breath and attempt to find my calm. "It's been a big day for us, let's go home."

"No-"

"Jack, get in the fucking car!"

Casey grabs my arm and pulls me away. "Let's go. You can't physically force him, and he doesn't want to leave." She shuffles me outside and we head back to the car with heads hung low. She's right, I literally can't force him, so we silently make the drive home and I continue to take deep breaths in an attempt to keep my tears at bay.

I'm so torn. I don't know what to do. I don't know if I should leave him there. My first official night of this shit new parenting job can be drummed up as a big fat fail.

"Come on," Casey says, unlocking my front door and holding it open for me, "let's get in our jammies and we'll go to bed. I'll stay here tonight and we'll sort Jack out in the morning."

With my tired mind and body exhausted and unable to come up with any other options, I nod my head and walk toward my room as Casey walks to my freezer and takes out the tub of ice cream and some spoons.

I strip down to my underwear and switch the TV on in my bedroom, then I climb under the covers as the opening music for Pride and Prejudice begins. Trust Mr. Darcy and ice cream, and they'll get a girl through anything.

Casey climbs into the other side of my queen bed and we snuggle in, but before I doze off and forget, I send a text to Renee.

Have him at my house no later than 8am in the morning. I will not come looking. If he isn't here on time, I'll have the police escort me to room 39.

I get comfortable and let Elizabeth Bennett and Mr. Darcy lull me to sleep. I have shit to take care of tomorrow, then I go back to work on Monday. Life must go on for those of us who have a mortgage to pay.

2

Bobby

Club 188

June 7, 2014

I close the side gate at my mom's house and my shoes crunch along the gravel pathway as I head back to my car. My phone vibrates in my pocket, and when I check the screen, I smile at my brother's name.

Aiden: Where are you? Guys are heading to 188. Wanna come?

Not many Friday or Saturday nights go by without a text from one of my brothers looking to party. I don't mind though. I've got two younger brothers and a best friend, and they're the best anyone could ask for. Everywhere we go, you'll find the four of us together; me, my middle brother Aiden, my youngest brother Jim, and my best friend Jon, and where one goes, the rest go.

Me: Yeah what time? I'm leaving Moms now, she needed help with something. Where are you?

A: Is she okay? Why didn't she call me?

M: Calm down, Nancy. She needed help hanging a shelf. She's not dying.

I mock his overprotective ways, but know for a fact we all worry and make sure she's happy and comfortable.

M: What time? I ask again

A: We'll come over to yours at 9. And Jim will drive. He's DD tonight, and he's bitchin' about it.

As a group, we rotate designated driving duties so there's always someone safe and able to drive, and the rest of us can have a good time. It's a good system that works for us, although the DD of the night usually complains about it.

M: Okay, see you in a few. Pick up a pizza on the way, we can eat before we go.

A: K, see you soon.

It's a bit after seven now, so I head home to shower and relax for a bit before the guys arrive. Bar 188 is a new nightclub in town that opened a month or two ago. It's pretty nice, fancy, compared to other clubs in town. Maybe just because it's new and clean and not run down yet like the other local club. But either way, the music is top notch, the drinks top shelf, and the other clubbers are there for fun, not looking for trouble.

An hour later, the guys noisily walk through my front door. I head out to meet them and find them in the kitchen, passing around drinks and laughing amongst themselves. I've showered and shaved and dressed in my favorite dark blue jeans and black button-up, with the sleeves rolled to my elbows. Aiden slaps me on the shoulder and offers me a beer.

"Hey B. How was Mom?"

I walk toward the pizza on the bench and flip the lid over. The delicious smell of pepperoni and melted cheese waft my way and I suck it in like a starving man.

"She's good. Wanted some shelves installed. They turned out pretty good, if I don't say so myself." I wink at him and smile. "Which I do. She cooked some chicken thing, so I ate with her before I came home."

"You ate already?"

I look up at Aiden with my eyebrow raised. I don't understand the question.

"Then why'd you ask for pizza?"

Ummm. "It's pizza. Who doesn't want pizza?"

"You're a fucking pig. Better watch yourself, or you're gonna get fat," he teases.

Jon laughs with him. "He's right, you know. Can't maintain this many calories a day and still stay hot." He leans in and steals the slice of pizza straight off my plate.

Jim thinks these assholes are pretty funny, but I'm not worried. I'll get the last laugh when his punk ass is sober as a nun and chauffeuring us around later. I walk to my fridge and grab a bottle of water, then I shove it at his chest, pushing him back a step—just a friendly reminder of his DD duties tonight. I grab another slice and take a seat. I plan to enjoy this, then I plan to enjoy a night out with my boys. And hopefully, maybe I'll get to enjoy some girls too, if we find any interested parties.

"Alright guys, let's get moving." Jon stands long after we finish the pizza. "188's has been getting bodies through the door, and I don't want to be standing in any lines tonight."

Mirroring his actions, I stand too and grab my wallet, phone, and keys, then we all wander outside and pile into Jimmy's beat up truck and head to town.

It's a warm spring-like evening, and the breeze is relaxing on my face as I gaze out to the street. The music is turned up, but it's a shame his old car stereo is crap and the sound is tinny. Still, it gets the job done and we cruise to the soothing bass of a new song on the radio.

Next door to the club is an old furniture store and behind that is a parking area that no one really uses outside business hours, and as expected, there're only a couple cars in the lot. Jimmy pulls in and we all jump out, eager to get the night started. The four of us head to the front entrance and I smile when I catch sight of the bouncer. Mike is an old school friend and he was always cool. It's nice to see a friendly face.

"Oh shit, not the fearsome foursome," he jokes loudly when he spots us.

I lean in and return his rough hug. "How you been Mike? It's been a while.

"Good Bobby, I've been good. Just started bouncing here not long ago. It's a good gig. Good boss."

"That's great. How's Becky?"

Mike and Becky have been together for a long ass time, probably at least ten years now, since I recall them dating back in high school.

"Holy shit, man, she's pregnant! We're having a baby. We found out last month, and she's due in the new year."

"That's awesome, Mike, I'm really happy for you."

"Thanks man, I 'ppreciate that. Hey, tell your mama Becky and I said hi." I nod that I will, and he opens the door for us. "Alright, in you go guys. We're about half full now, should be at capacity within an hour or two. Enjoy yourselves, and have a drink on me. Ask for Casey at the bar, she'll hook you up. She's good people." He winks and after a round of fist bumps we walk through the heavy door.

Once inside, I stop and look around. We're standing near the front door still, which is actually kind of near the back of the club. Most of the interior is black—leather lounges and stools, dark-stained tables and a dark bar. It's a two-story club, with a mezzanine level above and people dancing and hanging out on both levels.

The downstairs bar runs the length of the room, with stools perched all along the front and about half of those stools occupied with singles and couples. Behind the bar are five bartenders, glass shelving for all the liquor bottles, and a mirrored wall, reflecting the whole club back at me.

The mirror is handy to see the barmaids' asses as they work and the faces of those singles sitting on the stools.

The lighting is low, so the room isn't dark, but not light either. Above us, attached to the ceiling is some kind of light show that has beams and dots shooting around the room on a constant loop.

"Let's get a drink," Jon says as he walks past me. We all follow him and I watch our own approach in the mirror's reflection. He flags one of the bartenders—they're all chicks except one—and she heads over. "What can I getcha, boys?"

"Are you Casey?" Jon asks her, almost shouting over the loud music to be heard. She quickly looks to her left, but swings her gaze quickly back to us.

"Nah, I'm Lindsay. How do you know Case?"

"We don't. Mike just told us to ask for her. Told us she's good people."

"Oh yeah, she is. She's cool. Hey Case!" Lindsay shouts over the music.

Casey is a tiny chick at the end of the bar, pulling a beer for another customer as she smiles and chats, but looks up at Lindsay's call and nods. She places the full glass in front of him then she turns toward us, but stops again in front of another girl.

Casey's cute. She's short, maybe five and a bit feet. Her body is tight and she fills her skirt and tank out nicely. She has a short haircut. What do they call that, a pixie cut? It's cute though and reminds me of a tiny fairy.

But the girl she's speaking with? She's something else. While Casey's cute, this other woman is a siren, *my* siren. I can't tell how tall she is since she's sitting, but her legs are long, as is her torso. She's wearing a black dress that fits her like a second skin but seems to flare from her hips. The skirts sit loosely on her legs and my fingers tingle with want to feel the creamy flesh of her thighs. Where Casey's body is tight, this girl's is a little less so. She's not big, but she's bigger than Casey. She looks good. She has long dirty-blonde hair that stretches down past her shoulder blades. It's wavy and looks soft as silk. She has large eyes, probably larger than normal, but they suit her. I can't tell the color since its dark in here, but from this distance I'd guess light. Green or blue to go with her other fair features.

Casey speaks quickly and squeezes her friend's hand, then removing it with a soft smile, she turns and heads toward us as she checks us out. She's not shy at all, not looking away when she's caught looking. She simply smiles and drags her eyes over each of us slowly.

Brave little thing. I like her instantly.

"What's up?" She stops beside Lindsay with questioning eyes.

"These guys asked for you, I guess they think you can pull a beer better than I can." Lindsay winks and at the call of another customer, she walks away. Oops.

"Don't worry, Lindsay's cool." She answers my unspoken thoughts. "So, what can I get you boys?"

"Three beers." Aiden orders, then looks at Jim. "What do you want, man?"

"Just a soda."

"Are you desi?" she asks him. When he nods, she takes a glass and starts filling it. "Desi's drinks are always free at 188. Here you go, cutie." She passes his drink across the bar and I roll my eyes at the cutie comment. Jim doesn't need the encouragement.

She gets busy pulling three beers and I study the club around us. "Are you guys local?"

Aiden nods. "Yeah. We're local. I'm Aiden, and these are my brothers Bobby, Jon, and the desi is Jim."

"Brothers, as in actually related? Or as in *bruthas*?" She smirks and taps her hand to her chest in a weird gang symbol.

"Both." Aiden laughs. "Me, Jimmy, and Bobby are brothers from the same mother. Jon has been our *brutha* since kindergarten."

"Cool, nice to meet you guys. I'm Casey. I don't have any siblings at all, but my *sistah* from another mister is over there." She points toward the siren again. This girl just got more interesting. If those chicks are as close as me and the boys, then I think I'll be making friends with Casey just to get to know her friend.

She notices my scrutiny and raises her brows. "You're Bobby, yeah?"

"Yeah …"

"Well, that chick you're staring at, that's Kit. And she's my best friend. She's a good girl. Are you trouble?"

I like that she's protective of her friend. Kit. Nice name. Looks like I have to get past the tiny warrior before I can get to her friend. That's okay. A good friend is important in this world.

I turn back to Casey and smile my most charming smile. "No ma'am. I'm not trouble."

"Ma'am? Jesus, I'm not forty, don't call me ma'am. Besides, you look like you're older than me."

"Sorry, I'll just call you Tink, then." I thought my nickname was clever, but when she narrows her eyes, I hurry on. "Or not. I'm twenty-six."

She passes our beers over and continues with the evil eye. "Twenty-six. Thought so. Kit and me, we grew up together as well. We're twenty-five. Well I am. She turns twenty-five in a few months."

"Cool. Your friend Kit, she expecting any company tonight?"

"No ... she's not. You looking to keep her company?"

"Yes m-- yes." I quickly correct myself and a huge grin transforms her face. I feel like a puppy that she just taught a new trick.

"Okay well, she's drinking vodka and orange, in case you were wondering." She winks and walks off to serve another customer. Is that approval from the tiny warrior? Fucked if I know. The guys chat amongst themselves, checking the room out, checking the girls out. They see Kit, but keep their eyes to themselves. They heard my interest, and we never poach another brother's girl. Jimmy might joke about it, and he might tease me or the girl, but he'd never actually poach.

I can't help as my gaze continues to sweep past her, back to her, over and over as though she was a magnet, and on the last pass our eyes lock as we're both caught staring.

Those eyes. Such big windows to her thoughts. I reckon Kit would be a terrible liar.

I hold her gaze, refusing to waste the opportunity to read her and after a minute, she catches herself, blushes and looks away. Not as brave as Casey then.

3

Kit

Stop staring at him!

I can't believe Casey talked me into coming out tonight. She can't even stay with me because she has to work the bar. She wasn't supposed to work today. We'd planned a girl's night out, but she got called in last minute when another bartender called out sick. Not that Case really minds. She loves her job and it feeds her extrovert tendencies.

I tried to get out of coming since our plans were squashed, but she insisted I come anyway. I haven't been out in months, and she's determined to socialize me again. Like I'm a puppy. I've been so busy getting Jack to actually go to school and not sneak out at night, I haven't had time for much else. He has a sleepover at his friend Michael's tonight. Usually I'd be suspect of this, but I know Michael's mom and trust her to hold the fort for the night. Hopefully. He's in safe hands, and since I'm getting a worry-free night, Casey is demanding I take advantage of it. I, on the other hand, am not feeling the party vibe. I'm on my second drink and am patiently awaiting that happy buzz drinking used to give me. I'm feeling extra self-conscious since I'm sitting at the bar alone. I'm not one of those girls who can do that, and it's slowly killing me inside.

I'm also feeling pretty disgusting with how I look. I'm wearing a dress that I used to love, but in the last few months I've been so busy with work and Jack that we've been eating crap and I haven't step foot in a gym. That lethal combination landed me with an extra fifteen pounds or so, and I feel like my dress is showing those pounds in all the wrong ways. Casey assures me I look fine, but I don't feel it.

Sigh.

I really need to get back to working out and eating clean. It's not even about getting skinny, but more that living like this is leaving me lethargic and weak. Just another thing to add to my already overfull to-do list. Add it between work, getting Jack to actually go to school, and corresponding with estate lawyers. For at least the hundredth time this month alone, I curse my dad for being so unorganized. No will. No money. Plenty of debt.

Pulling me out of my pity party funk, that feeling of being watched buzzes just below the surface of my skin. I look up to find Casey speaking to a group of guys — good looking guys — and she must be talking about me because they're all looking my way.

She speaks about me like some proud mom speaks of her angelic toddler; she's the best friend anyone could ever have, even if a little embarrassing. I look away and pretend to mind my own business, even as I bite down my own jealousy that she can meet a group of guys three seconds ago and already be chatting and laughing with them. She's so outgoing and just not scared. Me? I'm scared of everything.

She moves on to serve others, but the feeling of being watched continues, so I keep staring into my drink. I can't handle one on one attention tonight. Frankly, I just want to finish my drink and then head home. My bed is screaming my name.

Despite my intention to mind my own business, instinct has me looking up again for the hundredth time. My eyes catch on a guy's and the way he smirks at me has the blush rushing to my face.

He stands with three other guys, and I hate that they're a group formed on the foundation of good looks. No uglies allowed.

I can't help the way my eyes eagerly search and catalogue him. His gaze is so intense, like he's trying to read my thoughts, and he doesn't look away because he was caught staring back. He's quite tall, at least several inches over six feet. He's wearing dark jeans that hug his thighs in a way that makes me want to touch, just to see if they're as hard as they appear, and a dark button-up with the sleeves rolled to his elbows to show off nice tattooed forearms.

His broad shoulders strain the shirt and have me wondering just how far the tattoos on his lower arms stretch. The lighting is too dark in here to see any of the inked details, but I certainly wouldn't mind a closer look.

What? No, you don't!

I feel myself blush and quickly look back to my drink. I'm such an idiot. Not even a little bit smooth. Then without giving myself permission to move again, my eyes are drawn right back to him and my entire body goes into a panic. I suck my stomach in and hold my breath as he walks toward me with an upturned lip, like he's trying hard not to smile.

Fuck, fuck, fuckity, fuck. My eyes dart around the bar in search of rescue. Casey, where the hell are you?

I look back to him in a panic, then away again; I can't maintain eye contact. His stare is too intense, so instead I focus on my hands. Hands that are holding my now empty drink glass. Dammit! I don't even have a drink to focus on. I can see his shoes in my peripherals, standing entirely too close. Or maybe not close enough? *No!* He smells good too, damn!

"Kit?" he says my name in a deliciously deep voice, and the personal greeting has me whipping my head up. Why would Casey tell them my name? She's the biggest stranger danger advocate I know.

Flustered or not, I can't help but catalog his features up close. His moppy dark blonde hair hangs long enough that it brushes the collar of his shirt and slightly curls at the ends. His eyes are a deep, dark, chocolate brown that has my instincts warring. I want to stare into them forever, but at the same time, his stare is too intense that I can't stop myself from looking away.

I realize that I still haven't said anything back yet, and I blush again. Oh, my god! He can leave now. I'm thoroughly embarrassed.

He seems entertained by my inner turmoil though because he's still here, and his smile is getting bigger. Bastard. Very sexy bastard, but a bastard nonetheless.

"Um, yeah, hi. I'm Kit," I croak out. *Frog in my throat, frog in my throat!*

"Hey. I'm Bobby," he says with the crooked smile of the devil himself. He puts his hand out for mine and I take it. This couldn't possibly get any worse than it already is, so what's a sweaty palm between friends. Not like I could have discreetly wiped it first, anyway.

He points behind himself. "Those are my brothers." I look toward the group; two of them are almost as big as Bobby, but with more military type haircuts, and the third could be Bobby's twin, but he's smaller. Not small. But smaller.

They all meet my gaze and wave, flashing identical devil grins. Yep, brothers, alright. I nod my head to acknowledge their friendly waves.

"Can I buy you a drink?" Bobby continues, drawing my gaze back to him as his deep voice floats in the air between us. "Pretty girl like you, sitting here all alone, I figured I better stake my claim before some other dude does. I see guys looking at you, and I wanted to get in before they do."

Stake a claim? What is he … wait, he called me pretty? Bobby sure is confident. And so unbelievably out of my league. "Umm, nah, no thanks, I'm good …" I stammer and point at my glass, then I drop my head when I remember it is, in fact, empty. Idiot.

"Here you go, babe." Casey suddenly drops a fresh vodka orange in front of me and a beer in front of him. "I'll add it to your tab, Bobby." She winks, and she's gone again, just as suddenly as she arrived. Bobby has the smile of a satisfied fat cat, and I glare at Casey's back. Traitor.

"Well Bobby, thanks for the drink." I lift my glass and we tap them together.

We sit in silence for a minute, and the pressure for me to say something clever and witty is suffocating. Bobby doesn't look at all uncomfortable though, and again I curse my lack of confidence.

"So … Kit, you're twenty-four?"

"What the h … Did Casey give you my entire biography? How long did you guys talk? And why did you talk about me? I don't even know you!"

"Whoa, slow down, speed racer." He chuckles. "You're a feisty one too, aren't you? I can see why you and T are best friends."

Oh, my god. She really did tell him everything. Wait. "Who the hell is T?"

"Haha yeah, your bestie Casey. Tell me you don't think of that cartoon fairy when you look at her. What with the five foot nothing height and pixie haircut. Have you ever watched that movie?" He moves in closer and his aftershave fills my senses as I suck in a deep lungful of air. "But I don't want to talk about her, I want to know about you. So far, I know your name and that you have a birthday coming up in a few months, although I don't actually know when. And I know that you and Casey have been bff's, *for like, ever*," he finishes in his best girly voice.

He's a funny dude, I'll admit that much. I'm trying not to smile and encourage his teasing, but I think he knows he's won me over, for now. "Okay, yeah, fine. I'll play."

His smile grows huge. It's a nice smile. He has mostly straight teeth, although not the artificial straight that braces will give you, like mine, just the nice straight a lucky person can be born with.

"My name is actually Catherine, but my *friends* can call me Kit." I give him a narrowed glance, indicating I haven't actually added him to my 'friends' list yet. He continues to smile, as though it's a sure thing. It probably is. "I am, in fact, twenty-four, my birthday is in December. And yes, *Casey*," I emphasize her name with a pointed look, "is my best friend. We've known each other for as long as I can remember."

"Okay, great." His smile is so pretty. "But I already knew all that, except the December part. Tell me something else."

"Ummm, alright." I tuck my hair behind my ear as I think. "Something else… Oh, I'm an accountant."

"An accountant?" His face pinches as though he just ate a lemon. "You absolutely do not come across as a numbers chick."

This almost sounds like a deal breaker to him and I laugh. "Yeah, you kind of read that right. I hate my job. I love the company I work for, they're great, but I really don't like doing the books. It's boring."

"So, why do it? That's a lot of years at school to do something you don't like."

"Yeah well, I figured that out after my first year, but I was already in, and family expectations dictated I pursue something corporate."

"Ah, I see. Your family a bit stuffy huh? That sucks."

"No actually, not my family, my boyfriend's -- ex-boyfriend!" I correct when Bobby's head suddenly whips up. I haven't seen or heard from Max since the day of my dad's funeral, except one text he sent looking to hook up. I ignored it, and he never tried again. That relationship kind of resolved itself, and his ghosting me definitely made my life just a little simpler. It's better than a dramatic break-up.

"Yeah, his family was kind of pretentious and I guess I wanted to measure up," I tell him, but it's like he wasn't listening, because his next question is, "but just so we're clear, he's an ex, right?"

"Yeppppp," I draw the word out with a laugh, and his eyes light up. Bobby steps back in again and lowers his head closer to hear me speak. It's not that loud in here, but I like him being this close, so I don't complain.

"So, if you could choose a new career, what would it be? What do you want to do, family and social expectations notwithstanding?"

I enjoy the feel of his breath fanning the loose strands of my hair and ticking my neck, and I hope he doesn't notice the goosebumps that race down my arms. "Hmm, to be completely honest, I'm not sure. I'm not good at many things. While accounting is boring as hell, at least I can do it, you know. Perhaps that's why it bores me?" I ponder aloud. "Because there's no challenge?"

He pulls back a little to look in my eyes. "Well, what do you like to do in your spare time?"

Oh geez, I can't tell him that. I can't mention that I basically spend all my time managing my teenage brother or coordinating lawyers. That's too heavy for a guy looking for a good time in a club. "I like to read books, and I used to enjoy running. Not that you can tell by looking …"

"Don't do that," he snaps, surprising me with the intensity of his glare. "Don't put yourself down, not in front of me."

"Well, I just meant—"

"No, just don't. I think you're beautiful, Kit. Really, I do." He takes a strand of my hair between his fingers, his gentle touch contradicting the hard tone of his voice. "And I assure you I'm not the only guy tonight thinking the same thing."

We sit quietly for another minute and I try not to melt to the floor in a puddle of mortification. I'm not sure how to come back from this. The guy just told me off, for crying out loud. I feel like it's time for my exit, so I begin mentally preparing myself and try to think of something half decent to say to leave the guy with a less awful impression of me, but just as I'm about to speak, Bobby abruptly smiles, "Alright chatterbox, no need to talk my ear off. I'll tell you about myself, you only had to ask once."

4

Bobby

Who the hell was that?

Well geez, man, you could've complimented her without yelling at her. I can't believe I just did that. Way to ruin the mood, you fucking idiot.

The message might have been correct, but the delivery was awful. This beautiful girl next to me is hotter than fuck, but the sadness and self-consciousness in her eyes dims her light. And I know down to my bones that she wasn't always this withdrawn. I could see the fire when she wanted to murder her best friend for talking about her. And I can see the way she sits, slumped in as though she's not quite comfortable in her own skin. I'd bet my shitty car Kit has gained weight recently.

I know in my gut I need to get to know her, and I can tell she's getting ready to split, so I fall back on my trusty friends: cockiness and humor.

"So, about me … hmm, I don't know, you've really put me on the spot here …" Her eyes light up at my teasing, thank god. I think I really hurt her when I snapped, and I'm sorry for it. "Okay, so, you've already met my brothers, sort of." I indicate over my shoulder, but I watch her face as her eyes twinkle and a small smile grows. "What?"

She hesitates to speak for a minute but then asks, "Brothers or bru—"

"Brutha's?" I interrupt her, pressing my fist to my chest. I smile when she giggles.

"Casey already used that one, huh?"

"Yeah," I chuckle, "but the answer is three of us are actually related. Me, Aiden and Jimmy, and then there's Jon, who I've known as long as you've known Tink. He's my best friend. They all are."

"Cool, I can definitely see family resemblance. Even Jon could pass as related. I guess after so long together, you've all taken on similar facial expressions."

"Yeah, same way that you and Tink use that same lame ass bruthas joke."

She giggles and looks down at her drink. Every now and again I get a glimpse of shallow dimples, but only when she smiles big, and it's like a punch to the gut, in a good way, every time I see them. "Hey," she playfully scolds, "Casey and I are funny as hell. Just ask us."

"Okay." I move another inch closer and play with a single lock of hair that sits on her shoulder. "To continue my riveting life story, I'm twenty-six years old, I have a January birthday. I'm a personal trainer and so are the guys, well except Jimmy. Jimmy builds houses as well as train, but he comes to the gym after work every day to help out. And unlike you, I actually really love my job... What else? I don't have a girlfriend, ex or otherwise." I smirk at her. "I drive a Rav4 that's almost as old as we are, but it's a beast and probably won't ever die. My mom is awesome and raised us alone, since my dad died when I was a kid. She's the strongest woman I know ..." I wonder what else I should add, but stop when Kit moves an inch away to put distance between us again. Talking about my mom when I just met a girl? Rookie mistake. Time to steer back to shallower waters. "I have no illegitimate children or baby mamas floating around." Shallow waters? Oops. I'm losing her, so I thrust my hand out. "Come dance with me." It's not a question.

She hesitates and looks at my hand, then at her drink, then back to my hand again.

Come on Kit, take my hand.

She looks back to her drink, stares for a long second, then finally picks it up and drinks it quickly. She places the glass back on the bar with a cracking sound then she takes my hand and stands up. *Thank god!*

When fully standing, with her beautiful warm hand in mine, I realize she's much taller than I thought. Maybe five-nine? Not as tall as me, but in heels, she's not far below my eye level. I like it.

While Tink is cute, Kit is hot, and she's calling at me on every level. We stand for a minute, hand in hand, looking into each other's eyes, and I wonder if she can feel what I feel. I turn and lead her onto the dance floor. I look back to the guys still standing at the bar. Jon's chatting with Tink, but they're all looking our way. The guys smirk, and Tink's eyes follow our every move.

We reach the center of the floor and I spin her around and place my other hand on her hip. She puts her hand on my shoulder formally and I frown. This all feels a little too high school for me, like we're nervous at prom, so I let go of her hand and grab her hips with strong hands and yank her body against mine.

The force behind my move forces a yelp from her plump lips and her hands move up around my neck; and what do you know, she and I fit perfectly. She's a little stiff for a minute, but it doesn't take long for her to relax and she places her head on my shoulder. Her fingers thread through the hair at the back of my neck, and fuck me if that doesn't feel amazing. We haven't said a word since we left the bar, but that's okay. I'm happy to just feel this, whatever this is between us.

The DJ plays a song by the Goo Goo Dolls, and Kit and I continue to slow dance in the middle of a packed club. As each new song begins, I find we're not really listening to the music anymore, and we aren't changing our step speed or position to match whatever song comes on next. We're in a world of our own, and frankly, I don't want to leave.

After a while, I move my head back so we're still connected from hips to chest, but so I can see her pretty face. I've missed it. "What's your full name, Kit?"

"Catherine Maree Reilly."

"Nice. What's your favorite color?" She looks at me again, wondering about my strange question, but plays along.

"Pink." She blushes. "And orange, not burnt orange, but bright orange."

"Okay. You mentioned reading. Who's your favorite author? No, wait! Before you answer, let me guess." She smiles up at me, willing to let me play. "Bronte?" I guess, but she continues looking at me, not confirming nor denying. I'll assume that's a no. "Hemingway?" She's still silent. "No, okay, hmm, who's that guy who writes all those books?"

She smirks.

"Nicholas Sparks?" I ask. No ... "Nora Roberts? You seem like a romance book type of chick."

She smiles and I take that as confirmation, so I continue along that theme. "Ooh I know." I lean in close to her ear. "Are you into that Fifty Shades chick? Are you freaky, Kit?"

She blushes a deep red and my dick stirs at her unintended confession.

"Okay, let's backtrack." She blushes deeper, so I add, "no, I mean back to classics. Jane Austen maybe?"

Her eyes flash and I know I nailed it. "Ah Jane Austen, okay. So, the next part is easy, your favorite book is Pride and Prejudice?"

She laughs, and I fucking love that sound. And those dimples — I kinda want to lick them. Weird, right?

"Well, you're quite knowledgeable on romance authors, Bobby. That's ... different," she laughs. "For such a big guy. You're mostly right," she continues on. "I actually read and love all of the above. And if you'd asked me a year ago, I would have agreed Pride and Prejudice was my all-time favorite. I still love it, a lot."

"Okay. Let's continue." I smirk and tuck her love of books away for another day. We continue to slow dance and I luxuriate in the feel of her hips under my hands. Every now and again I stretch my fingers around and I get to feel her ribs, or the top curve of her delicious ass. I'm pretty sure she can feel my half erection against her stomach, but she doesn't seem to mind and she doesn't mention it. "Favorite food?"

"Chocolate." She smiles. "And cheesecake. Oh, and pizza. Ugh, so many choices." She laughs.

I get it though; I really like all of those things too.

And on we continue.

I ask about pets, cars, dream holiday destinations, and millions of other seemingly unimportant questions. I love that she's relaxed around me now; no more stammering, blushing, or clammy hands. She has a spunky, funny personality and I love being on the receiving end.

A little while later, conversation slows down again and she leans heavy against me, like she's getting tired. I take her hand and lead her off the dancefloor and back to her seat. I look around for my boys, and I find Aiden and Jimmy dancing with a group of girls. Jon sits at the bar with his eyes on the bartenders. Well on one bartender in particular.

It's getting close to one in the morning, and I can tell Kit's beat. She doesn't seem to be a veteran clubber, and one a.m. is late for someone not used to it. The club closes at two so I have a little over an hour left with her. Just as I can tell she's not a regular clubber, I can also tell she's not a one night stand kind of girl. I had come out tonight looking only for a good time, but Kit's not someone I can take to bed once and never see again.

I'm feeling conflicted. I'm not one to look for long term, but Kit is too good for short term. So where does that leave me?

She must take my silence for disinterest, because she starts looking through her purse, and I'm pretty fucking sure it's not for a condom. She pulls her keys out and looks at me. "Well, I had a nice time Bobby. Thanks for introducing yourself, and for the drink. And for the dance ..." she rushes on as shy Kit makes a reappearance.

I don't want either Kit to go yet.

"Where are you going now?"

After a short thoughtful pause, she holds her keys in front of her, almost like a shield. "I'm going home."

"How are you getting there? You can't drive. You've been drinking."

"I'm okay. I only had three drinks tonight, and the last one was over two hours ago. I'm good to go ..." She smiles shyly at me, then she puts her hand out to shake mine. What the fuck? Back to the awkward formal phase again? That won't do. I take her hand and tug her against me.

"I'll walk you to your car."

She stares for a moment, breathing my air, then with a sigh, she nods and we start walking toward the exit. I catch Aiden's eyes and nod to let him know I'll be back in a minute. I keep her hand in mine as we exit the club and walk toward the same furniture store parking lot that Jim parked in. She isn't walking particularly fast though, as though she wants to prolong this as much as she can, and honestly, I don't want her to go either.

She points out her car, a decent not old but not new hatchback, and I smile when I realize it's parked right next to Jimmy's Jeep. Small world and all that. We stop in front of the cars, and she hesitates. I'm not sure if she wants me to kiss her and if she's just too shy to initiate it, but this might be the only chance I ever get.

I take a step closer, testing her, and I smile when her eyes flash with excitement. My fucking pleasure. I place my hands on her hips again, and she presses her chest against mine. She's so soft and warm, in all the best ways. "It was a pleasure to meet you Catherine Maree Reilly." Our lips are only inches apart, and I can practically taste the strawberry lip gloss on her lips.

"I really enjoyed meeting you too, Bobby … Wait. You didn't tell me your full name."

"Kincaid," I murmur and breathe her in. "Robert Kincaid. My mama didn't give me a middle name, I guess she didn't love me enough."

Her smile is back, and I thank the angels for it. "Well Robert-*I have mommy issues*-Kincaid, thank you for the good evening. I really enjoyed it."

I laugh at her joke, but stop quickly when I notice her hooded eyes and the way she watches my lips. Forgetting everything else, I move in and close the gap. At the first touch, she's hesitant, so I hold her tighter to me, and lick her bottom lip. She opens hers on a gasp and I get my first real taste. Electricity shoots straight to my toes and I wonder if she can feel it too. She tastes as amazing as I expected, and I can't help but kiss her with all the intensity I have. I know I should reel it in, I know I'm coming on really hard right now, but she doesn't seem to mind, and after her initial hesitation, she meets my tongue stroke for stroke.

I back her up against the Jeep and press my body to hers, and I enjoy the feel of her from thighs to tongues. My hands roam her delicious curves, and hers grip onto my biceps and shoulders, working her way up and down my arms. I feel as though my mouth is making love to hers, and I physically ache at the thought that I won't get to experience the real thing tonight, possibly ever. I'm determined to make this last and savor her for as long as she gives me.

Naturally, though, as though some bitter fate has a grudge against us, we don't get long, because some assholes thirty feet away wolf whistle and act like fools. Are they fucking kidding me? Is this high school, where kissing is an offense worth mocking?

I look up at three guys and the overwhelming desire to wring their necks courses through my veins. Kit looks up at them too and instantly stiffens. She goes from warm and limber, sexy Kit, to stiff and pissed off Catherine. She's either scared of these guys, or she knows them. Neither of those options sit well with me.

Kit lets out a filthy stream of swear words, and before I have a chance to even speak to them, she's gone from my arms and charging forward.

Whoa!

"What the hell are you doing here?" she demands loudly. I jump forward and grab her by the arms to stop her attack. I mean, she's not tiny like Tink, but I'm still not letting her attempt to take on three guys.

I hold her back against my chest, and I turn my attention back to the trio. Asshole number one is just as unhappy at seeing her as she is of seeing him, because he swears too, then asshole number two stops short once he sees Kit charge forward. "Oh shit."

I keep her in my arms, but I'm not sure who I'm protecting anymore. Her, or them?

With a weary sigh, she turns back to me and places her hand on my arm. "You should go now, Bobby. Thanks for a good night."

She's dismissing me? Yeah, that's a hard no from me.

"I'm not going anywhere. Do you know these guys?"

"Um, yeah, I know them. It's okay, you can go," she says softly, then she turns and shouts when asshole number one turns to bolt, "Jack! Don't you even think about it."

"I'm sorry, I have to go," she hurriedly adds only for my ears, then turns and walks toward the guys. "You three, get in my car. Now!"

At closer inspection, these men aren't men at all, but boys. Late teens by the looks of it. They're big fuckers though. They're big, and outnumber us both, yet they still do as they're told and walk toward Kit's car. I don't feel comfortable leaving her. My brain is screaming at me not to, but she's not leaving under duress. If anyone is scared, it's them.

If I could see this all as an outsider, it would almost be comical the way three large guys pile into her small car. But it's not comical, and I just can't let her go that easy. Rushing to her, I put my hand on the door frame to buy myself more time. Just another second.

Her eyes lock onto mine for a moment, but I don't see feisty Kit anymore. Sexy Kit is gone, and even authoritative Kit is hiding. Now sad Kit looks back at me.

"Hey, so, can I call you?" I ask softly, knowing that privacy is futile, but doing my best to speak only to her.

Surprise flares in her eyes, as though it's shocking to her that I'd be asking for more, before she locks it down quickly. "Ah, I'm not sure …"

One of the assholes in the back laughs at my rejection, and everyone turns to glare at him. His laughter stops instantly and sinks back into his seat.

Good. Sit the fuck down, asshole.

"I'll see you later," Kit murmurs, then she puts her car into drive and leaves me standing alone like a punk. Once she's out of sight, I realize I still don't have her phone number.

"Fuck!"

I rush back to the club double time; the fire in my eyes has people moving out of my way. Mike is still on the door and steps aside to allow me entry without saying a word; he can tell I'm on a rampage and he's smart enough not to stand in my way. When I walk inside, I catch Aiden's eyes, then instantly gauging my mood, he taps Jon's shoulder, and they meet Jim and me in the center of the dancefloor.

Aiden frowns and looks around the room. "What's wrong?"

"Who the fuck is Jack?"

His eyes snap around the room again. "Huh?"

I push past him and head straight to the bar, where I know I'll find answers. I make a beeline for Tink, and she spots me and heads over, faltering when she spots my volatile mood. "What's wrong? Where's Kit?"

"Who the fuck is Jack?" I demand again, and Jon puts a firm hand on my shoulder.

"Watch it, B," he says low, but with heat.

Tink isn't offended by my tone, but she is wary. "Ahhhm, Jack. How do you know Jack?" she hedges. "And where's Kit? You haven't upset her, have you?"

"Kit," I spit out angrily, "just left with three big ass guys."

"What?" Aiden explodes.

"I thought she was a nice girl," Jimmy murmurs. "Not a three at once kinda chick. Fuck, didn't see that one coming." He doesn't sound offended or upset, just genuinely mystified that he'd read her so wrong. We all look at him, speechless at some of the dumb shit he says. I have to remind myself that he's young.

I look back at Tink, who still hasn't said anything, and I glare.

"Look," she sighs and sets her hands on the bar, "the three guys, was one of them Jack? Is that why you're asking who he is?" When I nod, she lets out a low whistle. "Okay yeah, she's fine. She's safe. Jack on the other hand, is in bigggggg trouble."

Then it hits me. "Is Jack her ex?"

"Max?" She laughs. "Not even a little bit. But, like I said, she's safe. Just let it go."

"Let it go? Can you give me her number? She forgot to give me hers." Lie. A useless lie, because she can see right through me.

"No, I can't give her number out, I'm sorry. I'm sure you're a stand-up guy, Jon says you are, but I just can't. I'm sorry."

I stand there and stare for a long pleading minute, but she doesn't crack, so with no other option, I walk away and head home. I feel sick to my stomach.

I had something, and then I lost it.

5

Kit

Extracurricular Activities

It's been three weeks since the night at the club, and I still have so many mixed emotions when I think about it.

Embarrassment for how I left Bobby standing there. I'm fairly sure he thinks *good riddance and dodged a bullet* after the mess he was witness to.

I'm also tense with sexual frustration at what could have been. The kiss we shared shook me to my core, and I swear my lips still tingle when I think of it. And I think of it often.

Embarrassment again that Bobby's probably already forgotten me, or at least filed me away in the *could've been fun, but so glad I didn't get involved with that craziness* file.

Back to a sexual ache when I remember his hard chest against mine, his hard thighs against mine, those delicious biceps under my fingers. That tongue stroking mine. Ugh, I need to stop. I need to let it go.

Then I move into red hot anger at Jack and his friends. I drove the boys straight home after leaving the club that night.

First, I dropped Calum off and wasn't even sorry that I woke his parents in the middle of the night.

Once they realized what was going on, they turned their anger on him too. They promised to speak to Michael's parents the next day too, to express their disappointment at the lack of parental supervision.

Next, I drove to Michael's house and slammed my fist down on the front door for the full five minutes it took for someone to answer. Eventually, Michael's mom swung the door wide and I watched as her face transformed from anger to surprise and then finally settled on embarrassment when she spotted the boys standing sheepishly behind me.

"I just found the boys in town hanging around outside Club 188. Why weren't they inside your home? I trusted you could keep a few teenagers safe for the night."

It felt a little weird that I was only a few years older than the teenagers we are speaking of, and yet *I* was scolding *her*, but frankly, I don't give a damn. I'm half her age, and apparently more responsible because I can assure you they wouldn't have snuck out if they had a sleepover at my house. In fact, they have had sleepovers at my house, and everyone was where they were meant to be.

"I'm sorry. They were here when I went to bed at eleven thirty. I thought they were settled in for the night … Did you at least have a nice time out with your girlfriend?"

"No," I responded simply, then turned to walk away. "Get in the car, Jack."

The boys seem shocked that Mrs. Kolby was apologizing to me. I hated to undermine her authority in front of her kid, but damn if I cared in that moment. I was pissed that I couldn't trust anyone to keep Jack under control for one fucking night.

Jack didn't argue. He just followed me quietly and got in the car. He didn't speak because he knew when the time came, my anger would burn.

I took five minutes to collect my thoughts. I thought through every action and consequence and I made sure I could and would back it all up. It's a ten-minute drive home and half way, I finally spoke up. "You're grounded. And you've lost all sleepover privileges until I say otherwise."

Jack snorted at that. "You can't ground me. You're my sister, in your twenties, and you're supposed to be fun."

"Wanna bet?" I asked simply. "I'm not kidding. No sleepovers, not until I can trust you. Once your grounding is finished you can have friends sleep at our house, where I can keep an eye on you. No parties until further notice. When that ban is lifted, you can go, but I'll be dropping you off and picking you up, since you can't be trusted to return by curfew. This isn't a negotiation, Jack. It's law. *My* law. If you have a problem with it, if you argue or backtalk, you'll also lose phone privileges."

"Yeah right," he scoffed. "You can't take my phone. You won't get your hands on it."

I simply sighed. I may be his sister, and I may be young to be a 'parent' to a teenager, but I'm not stupid. I didn't need to physically remove his phone to suspend phone privileges, I just needed his charger cable, which was on my kitchen counter at home. He'd get maybe another twelve hours of battery life, if he's lucky, then with no charger, voila, no phone.

The next day he came searching for his charger. It took him that long to realize his loss and that my silence on the matter wasn't conceding defeat. He was pissed, royally, loudly, annoyingly pissed, but that was fine with me, because I was pissed too.

A week later, once his attitude cooled and with no further incidents of sneaking out or being a shit, I returned his charger and he actually thanked me. It was a nice week; no phone, no visitors and no social outings. We hung out, we talked, we watched TV.

Now three weeks later, he still has his phone privileges and I'm ready to lift the grounding. He's still a bratty teenager who literally seems to enjoy arguing and rolling his eyes, but he's stayed out of trouble and that was enough for me.

After walking in on him one evening as he sat frustrated at the kitchen table, I realized he's been seriously struggling in math at school. He was surprised by my offer to tutor him, but I was so much more surprised by his polite acceptance.

He was wary at first of adding more 'school' after school hours, but we've been having fun with it, and we're enjoying the quiet hours we spend each week hanging out without those outside interferences.

He has a quiz in class on Monday, so the extra work will be put to the test soon. I hope I've helped him.

As a reward for good behavior, and the fact it's a Friday night, I've allowed Michael and Calum to sleep over tonight. And since it's in my home, I feel comfortable that he and the other two boys wouldn't be able to get up to no good. I felt it was important to reward his hard work during tutoring and his attitude adjustment, so I ordered pizza for everyone and let them have the living room and big TV to themselves to watch a few movies.

Some might think it was a lame treat, but I feel like these boys simply need down time. I refuse to be the *cool* parental figure and allow them to drink and party, and instead I'll provide them with quiet and security. Some people want to be friends with their kids these days. Whatever, that's on them, but I don't think buying their affections with fun and excitement is the way to go. Maybe I have the edge on this because I was a teen not long ago? Or maybe I'm full of shit and screwing everything up. Who knows, but I'm comfortable with my decisions today — they're working for us.

I'm currently sitting in my kitchen, working on my laptop. Its end of tax season, and the work is piling up. I have enough to keep me in the office for hours more every day, but I'm not that person anymore. I need to be here for Jack, so I bring the work home instead. The boys are in the living room watching one of the newer X-Men movies. I don't get guys and action movies or why the fight scenes get them excited, but whatever. Whatever works for them.

I get some of the draw, I guess. I have a semi-secret crush on UFC champion fighter Rhonda Rousey. I just think she's so badass for doing so well in a sport that was previously dominated by men. I saw her on Ellen one time, and she seems really friendly. Rhonda, that is, not Ellen. Well Ellen too; she's amazing.

"Have you guys been to that new gym in town?" Michael asks the other two excitedly. "I started classes there last week. The guys that run it are supposed to be pretty awesome. I haven't met them all yet, just the one so far. We should open our own gym one day ..."

I roll my eyes. If Michael follows through with anything in his life, it'll surprise me.

Calum and Jack answer that they haven't heard of it. "But I don't think I can go. I haven't found a new job since the news agency ..." Jack used to stack papers at a news agency, but he was only employed on a casual basis and when he needed a few weeks off when Dad was dying, they never added him back to the roster when he returned. I thought that was pretty shitty of them, but there's not much to do about it. "I don't have the money to pay, and I can't ask Kit."

Thankfully, since I'm sitting at the counter, not the table, they can't see me from the living so they don't realize I'm listening, but this conversation has my attention. I'm all for something that'll keep him busy after school while I work.

"How much is it?" Calum asks.

"I dunno, my mom pays it. Maybe like fifty bucks a week? But you can work for them to pay fees. Like mop floors or clean machines, that sort of thing." I roll my eyes again at Michael's tone of voice; I doubt that boy would ever mop floors or clean up behind others, not when Mommy Dearest is there with an open purse.

This news is exciting to Jack though, because his voice perks up. "I could do that. I have nothing better to do most days. Kit and I have things to do on Mondays and Saturdays ..." I know he's talking about our tutoring sessions, but I guess he's too embarrassed to admit them to his friends. He also *forgot* the Thursday night tutoring that we do too. "But the other nights I could go. Shit! But I'm still grounded."

I'm actually all for this plan for Jack to work and train, so I stand from my stool and walk toward the living room. "Jack, I heard that, stop swearing." The boys pale as I walk into the room, and snap their mouths shut. I kinda like that I have this fear/respect thing going on. Makes me feel a little badass myself. Fear probably isn't the best way to inspire obedience, but, again, whatever. It's not like he's scared for his life — although, there've been moments — mostly just for my approval I think. "What are you guys talking about?"

No one volunteer's information, they simply sit and try to wait me out, so I silently stand with my hip against the doorjamb and decide to play their game. It takes a minute, but eventually Jack gathers his courage. "So, Mike was saying he goes to this cool gym now. He goes to classes after school, and I thought I might ask them if they have any work going to pay for membership fees. Mike said that I could mop and stuff in exchange for class time. … anyway it sounds kinda cool. I was going to ask you what you thought."

"Okay…" I bounce my hip off the wall as I think. "That sounds interesting." Jack lets out a deep breath of relief. I frown and turn to Michael. "What days are classes?"

"Well, they have classes every day, and you can go to whatever ones you want. I've only been a couple times so far, but I'm going again in the morning. Maybe Jack can come too…?"

Jacks eyes light up for a moment, but then dull again. "I can't go straight to class yet. I have to ask them about work first, plus, I'm grounded."

I really like this newly responsible version of him, so decide to give him a break. "Actually, Jack, I was coming in to talk to you. I'm really impressed with how things are going lately … So, I'll tell you what. If you keep it all up, I'll take you to the gym tomorrow to sign you up. I'll help you talk to them about working, but whatever you can't earn, I'll pay the rest. I'm officially lifting your grounding."

The smile on his face reminds me of five-year-old him on Christmas mornings from long ago. He looks stoked with the news, and it makes me happy that I made him happy. I like that the thing he wants most is to work. He has to work to earn class time, then work during class to get fit. I couldn't be happier with this turn of events.

"I'll take you there around ten tomorrow. Sounds good?"

He nods enthusiastically and his smile spreads from ear to ear. Sadly, I realize just now that I haven't seen that lone dimple in a while. Sometimes it's hard to remember that he lost a parent too and that acting out was likely a cry for help.

"We can talk to them together and we'll see what's what." I bounce my hip off the wall one last time, then I look to Michael and Calum. "Do you guys want a ride too?"

When all three boys nod their heads yes, I nod mine too. Sweet; my work here is done.

Jack clears his throat as I turn to leave. "Um, Kit, so since I'm not grounded anymore … some kids from school are having this party tonight, and I thought maybe …"

"Nope," I say, popping my lips on the 'P,' then I leave the room with a smile as big as Jack's as the guys laugh behind me.

~*~

The next morning after the boys plough through enough pancakes to feed a small army, I stand in the kitchen and I listen to Michael and Calum call their moms to ask for permission to go to the gym.

It's only a short drive across town, and we still have plenty of time before we have to go. I'm wearing my favorite white denim cut-off shorts and a black tank that says 'I don't always roll a joint, but when I do, it's my ankle'. I get a real kick out of wearing tops with jokes on them, especially watching people try not to stare but almost bend over backwards to finish reading before I walk by.

My hair is tied up in a high pony, and I've left it to its natural curl, better known as frizz. I brush my teeth, and with a swipe of mascara, I'm good to walk out the door.

"Saddle up boys, we're leaving now," I yell out as I walk by Jack's bedroom and I hear the guys assing around. I hear a loud thump, and then the door opens. Jack and Calum walk out laughing and I look inside to see Michael on the floor, groaning and swearing. He doesn't appear seriously injured, so I tell him to buck up, stop swearing, and get moving.

In the car, my music cuts out when I get a phone call ringing through Bluetooth to my speakers. It's from my office so I accept the call. "Hey Maree. What's up?"

"Hey Kit. I haven't caught you at a bad time, have I?"

"Nah, I'm driving. What's up?"

"I just wanted to ask you about the Bundling account … The deadline is coming up fast."

Michael continues giving me hand directions to the gym and I keep one eye on him, one eye on the road, and continue to speak to Maree. And this here, this is exactly why women are the superior species. Multi-tasking at its best.

I pull up at a gym, noting signage that reads *Rollin' On* and chuckle. Clever name. I assume it's a play on the jiu jitsu style of martial arts.

We're in an industrial area at the edge of town with a bunch of large sheds all lining the road. Most of them have roller doors lifted and open, although Rollin' appears to be the only gym. The business next door is a glass cutting place and on the other side is a mechanic.

I continue to speak with Maree, but the guys are getting antsy while they wait for me to finish up. "Maree, just hold on a sec, okay?" I turn to the backseat. "Jack, I'm just going to be a few more minutes. Do you want to wait here for me, or do you want to go inside and I'll be there in a minute?"

"Come inside." Michael answers for him. "I'll show you around while we wait."

With the decision made, all three boys hop out and start walking inside. I pick my phone back up from the holder and switch to regular mode. "Hey, I'm back. But I only have a couple minutes ..."

6

Bobby

Well, you fucked that up

"Get the fuck out of the ring and cool off!" Jon snaps as he pushes me back against the ropes. I've been a miserable bastard for weeks, and the guy I was just sparring with is currently laid out on the canvas. He thought he was being clever taunting me, but he got a little close to the truth when he mentioned me needing to get laid. It immediately brought Kit back to the forefront of my mind—a topic I've been trying to avoid, but she's been there since the moment I saw her tail lights fade into the darkness.

I can't stop thinking about her, or her eyes. They haunt me. They're so big, the color shifting like a deep ocean. They communicate so much: desire, heat, anger … sadness. Since my last moments with her left me with images of sad eyes, I just can't seem to shake her.

Every night when I close my eyes to sleep, I see her. She's branded on the backs of my eyelids. I'm not proud to admit I've rubbed one out at least once daily with the vision of her fueling me. Call me crass, but it's the truth. She's the sexiest woman I have ever seen in my life and I can't stop thinking about her. I have an almost magnetic need to see her again, but have no way of contacting her. I've been back to the club a hundred times in hopes to either see her or convince Tink to hand over the goods, but I've achieved neither. Tink is one tough fucking nut to crack. But at least she assures me Kit is safe and sound. Small reassurances will have to do for now.

I pick up my water bottle and rip out my mouth guard, swishing and guzzling to get the taste of blood out. I've been going for a few hours now, and I have class in about forty-five minutes. I have to clean up and prep.

I pick up my shit and start walking toward the locker rooms. I grunt a pissy *Hi* to anyone who catches my eye, but mostly I just want to get to the shower without talking to any fucker.

Despite my attempt to get through without stopping, I spot something in my peripherals and my feet come to a sliding stop. I don't even know why I looked that way; it's not like anyone was being rowdy or making a scene, but the hair on the back of my neck rose and my head turned without my conscious permission.

It takes me a moment to understand, but the three guys coming in the front door look familiar and I don't know why. I look from one face to the next, to the next, and when I spot the third guy it hits me. No. Fucking. Way.

Nope asshole, not my gym!

I turn in their direction and when they spot me steamrolling their way, they transform from three laughing motherfuckers to three scared as piss motherfuckers. Good. They know what's good for them.

And what's *not*.

Before anyone has time to blink, I have *Jack* pinned against the wall with my hand solidly holding his shoulder and his feet balancing on the tips of his toes. His eyes are wide as plates and I can see I'm scaring the dude. Good.

I remember thinking that night at the club that these guys are teenagers, and I wasn't wrong, but I assumed eighteen or nineteen or so, but now, with my face in his in broad daylight, I can tell he's much younger than I thought. Maybe fifteen or sixteen. I loosen my hold a little. I don't want to go to jail today.

"Who the fuck are you? And who are you to Kit?"

Jack doesn't answer me, he simply swallows noisily as his friends stand to my right in shocked silence. When a full two minutes passes with my face in his and my breath coming out on adrenaline fueled pants, I loosen my hold. "You and your goons, get the fuck out. You're not welcome in my gym."

"But - "

A strong hand clamps down on my arm, and I look to find it's Aiden. He attempts to loosen my hold on Jack, but the adrenaline firing through my body means no one will move me without my permission. Aiden looks to the guys, then zeroes in on one. "Michael? What's going on?"

His easy recognition has my head whipping back and my eyes narrowing. "You know these fuckers?"

"Well, I know Michael. He's new here. Been coming to the MMA classes. Next class starts at eleven, so I ask again, what the fuck is going on?"

"Bobby?" I hear her voice, and my whole body tingles with awareness. Without any conscious thought, my hand is gone from Jack's shoulder and I'm facing the complete opposite way, looking at my dreams and realizing my memory did her no justice.

Fuck! She's so much more beautiful than I realized. She's wearing sexy little cut-offs that show off tanned legs that go on forever, and a cute tank that highlights her sexy shoulders. I scan the writing that stretches across her tits and I want to laugh, but I'm far too tightly wound right now to do that.

She's here. She's back!

It's like I've lost all control of my body, because I don't know how it happened, but I suddenly realize I've moved and I'm standing within inches of her. I can feel the warmth radiating from her body, and I know with the combination of sparring and adrenaline, I'm pumping a lot of heat her way too. Her hair is up today, and her long thin neck is screaming at me to bite it. Her chest is rising and dipping with fast deep breaths, and I hope she's as happy to see me as I am to see her.

Time stands still as we stare at each other, but the moment is broken when someone clears their throat. Wouldn't you fucking know it, but its asshole number three, again. Timely bastard that one.

She takes another big breath then steps back from me, breaking the electrical current that was running between us. Does she feel that too?

"Bobby? What's going on?"

I think she's trying to be commanding, but mostly she sounds breathy. I want to groan at the images flashing through my mind.

I've got nothing though. I don't know what to say; my mind just can't get past the fact she's here.

"He just came over and shoved Jack!" Asshole number two — Michael — whines. "I don't know what his problem is, but he says we can't train here, which is bullshit though, since my mom already paid fees."

I don't give a damn whose mama paid fees. This is my gym. I turn to give that entitled shit a piece of my mind, but Kit beats me to it. "Michael, don't swear! And stop whining. You're fifteen, not five!"

She looks around at our small crowd, realizing that we're not alone, and realizing that Aiden's here too. Recognition flares in her eyes and she smiles tentatively. "Hey …" she begins, but it's clear she doesn't remember his name.

Understanding, he replies, "Hey, it's Aiden. And I've just realized you're Kit, from the club."

"Yeah. So, you wanna tell me what's going on?"

"Ah, well, I'm not entirely sure, to be honest …" He looks to me with a lifted brow, and my stomach drops out. Shit, I guess I was the instigator here. Fuck, fuck, fuck. What did I do?

"Well, ah, so, I wasn't sure who these guys were. But I realized they were the ones who upset you the other night … I've been wanting to get in contact with you, but Tink isn't giving, so … I wanted answers." This is the point I realize I sound lame as fuck.

Her eyes are starting to get angry. And then she confirms it. "So you decided to start pushing around a kid?" I don't know if she actually wants an answer, but fortunately — unfortunately? — I don't have to wonder for long. "Did he say anything to you? Backtalk?"

"Umm, no …"

"Did he say anything at all?"

"No …"

I'm the one who can't maintain eye contact now, but still, I can't help but notice how fucking hot she is when she hits her stride.

"Did he start *anything*? Did he shove you back?"

"No."

Fuckkkkk, may as well just step into this tidy little grave I dug for myself.

"So, three kids walk in, minding their own business, and you decide to start shoving?"

"Well …"

"Yes or no?" she demands. I look over and find a shit eating grin on Aiden's face that I want to smack right off. Mom wouldn't approve though, and I mentally roll my eyes.

Shitttttt, I'm in trouble. "Yes'm."

"Do you think you're a tough guy, pushing around my kid brother?"

What … *what*?

"Your kid brother?" I sputter. I look up at him and sure as shit, he's smiling and I see that fucking dimple. Well there it is, the noose is tied and I'm a goner. There's no coming back from this.

Dismissing me, she walks past me and over to Jack. She grabs his arm and looks him over. I didn't actually hurt the little fucker, and once she realizes that, she cools off. A little bit. "I don't think it's a good idea for you to train here, okay? Some of their other members seem to have … anger problems."

Train here? Other members? I realize she means me, and I chuckle.

She whips her fire eyes back my way, and I shrink back a little. This mother hen can be scary! "You have something else you want to say?"

Ouch. She can cut me down like the best of them.

"Ah, just that I'm not a member here. This is actually my gym. I'm part owner, and just about to run the class that he's here for."

Kit drops her head in defeat and I'm sorry to see it. Aiden speaks up, ever the peace keeper. "Actually Kit, Jack's welcome here, and I'm taking that class today. Bobby's been training for hours already and needs to rest."

Jack coughs awkwardly. "It's just that, I was hoping to work for you guys to earn class time."

"That's okay," Aiden says. "First week's free anyway, so we can sort the details later."

I smile internally. We absolutely do not offer first week free. I don't mind though, he's smoothing feathers, and if it means I get to see more of Kit, at least long enough to dig myself out of the shit, I'll spot the week for them. Hell, I'll pay the kids classes for the next ten years if she'd agree to meeting me in the dark parking lot again.

She looks at Aiden with suspicion, then at me with anger. Like first predicted, I can read her eyes like a book. She wants to say yes for Jack's sake, she wants to say yes because she's intrigued and interested in me, but she wants to say no because she's pissed and she's a proud woman.

After another moment, she releases a big breath and her shoulders relax as she turns back to Jack. "Okay then, if you're comfortable here … then you can stay."

He looks at me with that dimply shit eating grin and nods, then he and his goons walk away to prepare for class. He's a gutsy fucker, and now that I'm getting a clearer picture, I like that about him. I have a million questions though. Why do he and his friends listen to her? Why is she with them in the first place?

I keep watch from a distance as Kit looks around our gym, and I feel immense pride at what my brothers and I have achieved here. We've been slogging it out for years trying to create a successful fight gym. We now have several contenders on our roster and I love that we have a hand in training such amazing athletes.

Kit spots the bench near our reception area, and pulls out a laptop and gets comfortable. She must be working. She reaches back into her bag and pulls out something small. I realize as she puts them on that they're glasses, and she looks sexy as fuck in a sexy librarian way.

I start walking toward her, and my movement draws her attention. Her eyes flare in panic and she rips the glasses back off again, and disappointment swells inside my gut.

"So..."

She twirls the glasses between her fingers, and she silently looks up at me.

"You're still here. Good to know you're not just a figment of my imagination." I'm trying to joke. I'd be willing to dance on an elephant just to get her to talk to me.

"Yeah, I'm here while Jack's here. Can't leave him, can't trust him to stay put, can't trust you not to beat him up."

Okay. She's still pissed. I read that loud and clear. "Look I'm sorry I pinned your brother. I didn't even realize you had a brother. I told you all about mine but you didn't mention yours. I remembered he was the guy who upset you at the club, and with no other way of getting answers I decided to get them from him."

"What answers though? Why do you care? I'm surprised you even remember me!"

Surprised I remember her? I haven't stopped thinking about her! "I asked for your number, but you didn't give it to me. I asked Tink, but she wouldn't give it to me. I went back to the club hoping to see you there. I haven't stopped thinking about you in three weeks, not since I first saw you." I move closer so my legs almost touch hers. "I can still taste you on my lips..."

I know I'm showing my hand, but this girl doesn't see her own appeal, and I refuse to play games.

Her eyes flare in surprise, and while I'm sad that she isn't told this daily, I'm thrilled that I seem to be the only man on her radar right now. She licks her lips and I follow the movement with my eyes. I can't look away from her. I wonder if she'd be open to giving me another taste right now?

Probably not.

"So you own this place? I thought you were just a personal trainer?"

"Well, I am a PT, *and* I own this place. I'm in partnership with my brothers, and this is our full time job. Mostly we're a fight gym and we train athletes to go pro, but we run beginner classes for kids like Jack too.

"That's cool." She tosses her glasses down onto her laptop then she re-crosses her legs. "Pretty good accomplishment for guys your age."

I bask in her praise. Willing to go buy that elephant now if it could guarantee more. "Yeah well, the four of us have always been in the fight scene. We spent most of our time in a gym anyway, it was the logical thing to open our own."

"Yeah?"

"Yeah. We started in my mom's garage actually, just training ourselves. Then other friends wanted to get into it, then their friends … and that's how we grew. People didn't pay. We just had a group kitty kind of thing to buy mats, bags and gloves, that sort of stuff, or people brought their own. Eventually we outgrew the garage, and it was around the time I came into a bit of cash, so all the stars aligned and we found this place."

That cash is actually prize money from my own fights. I won the UFC heavyweight title three years ago, and I used those winnings to buy this place. I also won it again last year, so I'm training to defend my title in December. I'm not sure how she'll react to this, so I don't tell her. Not today. "So anyway," I hedge. "What've you been up to? How've you been?"

Her intense eyes meet mine, as if gauging the seriousness of my question. No worries Kit, I'm not asking for idle chit chat—I truly want to know. She must be satisfied because she closes her laptop lid and turns her body fractionally my way. A positive sign, I think.

"I'm … good. I've been good. Busy at work. Busy at home." She sighs. "I'm kind of drowning in life right now …"

I frown. She looks as though she almost regrets sharing so much, but after a moment bolsters herself and looks me in the eye. Challenge maybe? Maybe judging to see if I want to know about the heavy. I do.

"Is there anything I can do to help? Or my boys? Not that I can help with your work, I'm not really a numbers geek like you are." I smile at her, hoping to make her smile too, and thanks to all those beautiful angels wherever they are, because I get a glimpse of that dimple. I want to collapse onto my knees and worship her, I'm that happy. I've never thought about a girl this much before, never wanted to make one so happy, and I never cared all that much if they liked me— beyond a quick roll. Kit's different, so different, and I don't know if I like it, or if it terrifies me.

"Umm … there's not much you can do." She stops and thinks for a moment. "Well actually, yeah, keep Jack in your classes. Teach him discipline, teach him respect. Don't worry about exchanging fees for work. I mean, make him work, but I'll pay the fees, that's fine. In fact, it's probably a good investment ... Oh, and please don't beat him up anymore. Maybe just let him spar with kids his own age, you can supervise from outside the ring ..." Kit is smiling her dimply smile, full of sass, and my heart thumps in my chest.

That's an easy wish to fulfill. That's my job, and I'll do it. But I still have so many questions. Why is she so involved with Jack? Why would she pay the fees? Where are her folks? But I don't ask, yet. I don't want her to run. Not now that I've only just gotten her back.

I look in the direction the boys walked. "Jack's a big dude. How old is he?"

"He's fifteen."

I nod. That's right. She already mentioned that when she was setting me on fire with her eyes and anger.

"He's huge for his age. He could go toe to toe with any of my pros on size alone. When you're not watching, maybe I can put him in the ring with Aido, or even Jimmy."

I'm joking, sort of — *he really is big.* She whips her eyes back up to mine, ready to rip me a new one, again, but relaxes when I start laughing. This mother hen wouldn't hesitate to rip my eyes out if I mess with Jack. That's cool; I really like this assertive version of her.

I'm half tempted to get up and watch Jack train. I want to know if he's a big uncoordinated mess, or if he can handle himself. But if I'm choosing between spending time with Kit, or watching her kid brother train, well, that's a no brainer. I'm parking my ass and soaking up every second she gives me.

This is such a strange concept for me; never, in the history of ever, have I been this taken by a single girl. I've never been the commitment type. Not that I'm a commitment phobe or anything, just that I've only really spent time with 'one night' kind of girls in the past. But Kit, she has all my cylinders firing and I can't get enough of her. I feel as though we each have magnets under our skin, and that mine are pulling me toward her. Only her. Mom used to tease me that this would happen one day, when I'd no longer treat a woman like temporary fun.

Kit is worth so much more than that though. She's more precious than that.

Shiiiiit, I'm in trouble.

And yet, I'm smiling.

7

Kit

I'm not like ... her.

I can't believe I'm sitting with Bobby again. I can't believe what I walked in on earlier!

This whole ordeal since I walked through the gym doors has been surreal. To walk in on someone ready to pummel Jack. Then to find out that someone is Bobby. *Bobby!* The man that I see in my dreams at night. The strong broad shoulders that I drool over. The tattoos that I haven't stopped thinking about.

Mind. Blown!

But, what the fuck? I was ready for heads to roll. It didn't matter that I wasn't sure whose head — Bobby's or Jack's. I know firsthand that Jack is no angel, so he could have easily landed himself on the receiving end of fists with his bad attitude and smart mouth.

I was fully prepared to hear the whole story before I started rolling said heads, but I swear I felt my brain explode when I realized Bobby was here.

When he admitted to zero provocation, then add my lingering sexual tension and work stress, I saw red. Bobby's head it would be. But no, the mind fuck doesn't end there, because once Jack was organized, not only hasn't Bobby forgotten me, but admits to have been actively looking for me.

What the hell kind of warped universe is this where someone like him is interested in someone like me? He's a personal trainer and business owner. His body is his income, and he maintains it to perfection.

No wonder I felt so many delicious muscles under his shirt when we danced. His solid, sexy, broad back under my hands. Or those rock-hard thighs pressed against mine when we kissed. My wayward thoughts have me licking my lips again, and just like last time, his gaze zeroes in on them. Interesting.

But for someone like him to be into someone like me, the poster child for unfit. I'm a numbers geek who sits down all day and enjoys cheesecake far more than I should. I'm an emotional eater, and emotions have been going crazy the last few months. Since my dad's diagnosis I've stopped working out, had to deal with lawyers—which is still ongoing, organize a funeral, and try keep my teenaged house guest out of trouble. Add in tax season and a carb craving teen, nutritionally balanced meals have been replaced with fast, easy, and filling. All of this has resulted in flabby arms—which I not so lovingly call my chicken wings—and a squishy paunch at my midsection.

I hate it. I really, really hate it, but I feel so overwhelmed with life, I just can't find the light yet. I don't know how to fix it.

I wasn't always like this. I used to run track at school; I enjoyed it a lot and maintained that habit daily for many years after graduation. Running used to be my escape, where I could regroup and find my calm. But now, fifteen, possibly twenty pounds heavier, and I feel too heavy to run.

And the cycle continues.

I feel disgusting in my own skin. I've lost my passion for life. I used to be witty and clever. I'd never back down from a challenge and was never shy. But now, I just feel so dull.

I can be assertive at work, because I'm confident in my abilities there. I can be assertive to, and for, Jack, because I'm his ambassador now. I'm the only thing standing between him and a mean world, and I need to do what I can to soften the blow.

"So, what do you think?"

My eyes snap up to Bobby's. "Huh?"

He smiles. "I asked if you'd like a tour. I can show you Jack's class; it goes for an hour and a half, so we have a little time before he finishes." He stands and holds his hand out for me. I know he's looking for a yes, so I place my hand in his—and there's that electricity again—and slide off my stool. I let go once I'm steady though. I feel walking hand in hand around a gym is just … too much.

Kissing in a dark parking lot is one thing. But broad daylight in front of his brothers and clients. And Jack. That's a nope.

I turn to organize my laptop and stuff, and as I pack it all away Bobby grabs the shoulder bag from me and motions to his receptionist.

"We can store this here if you like? It'll be safe."

I look to the young girl behind the desk and note that she's maybe a couple years older than Jack, perhaps eighteen or nineteen. She's average height, maybe five foot seven or so and she's really very beautiful. Her hair is about shoulder length, although it's hard to tell because she has it in a pony, and her body looks amazing. She's toned all over, her muscles long and lean, her olive skin making them look even nicer. She has kind, brown eyes, and a reassuring smile so I nod okay. He steps to her and passes it across the desk.

"I need you to guard this with your life, Izzy." He winks at her, and she smiles. He turns back to me. "Don't worry. Izzy's got your back. She's a beast in the octagon, no one would dare cross her."

"She's a fighter? No way! She's tiny."

My mind is spinning. Izzy is so badass. She appears to be one of very few women in this gym, and she fights. And she's good?

"She's small but she's mean. And a hard worker. She well and truly earned all credibility around here."

I can't help but look back at her. I'm in awe. As I turn. I realize she's watching us, too, and our eyes meet. She smiles and winks at me.

"Isn't she scared? To be training with men. In such a physical sport?"

"You don't strike me as the type to judge or put limitations on what other women can do."

"Not at all. I'm not saying she *should* be scared, just that *I* would be. I idolize women like that. Rousey, Holm, Tate, Nunes. They're awesome and super brave."

"Wait. You know Rowdy?"

I laugh at his reaction. He's lit up like a Christmas tree, like a little kid in a candy store. "Well, I don't know her personally."

"Ha-ha smartass. I meant you know who Rhonda Rousey and Holly Holm are?" His smile is so big, it looks almost painful. "If you're a fan of the UFC, the women's league even, what about Izzy surprises you so much?"

"I don't know. I guess it's just that those other fighters are just on TV, you know? Completely removed from my real life. But she's right here in front of me, and I suddenly realize how scary it must be. It's not that other chicks can't do it, just that someone like me couldn't."

"Well that's just not true at all. I think you could fight. You have the body for it. You're tall, good muscle tone, and your arm and leg reach is awesome. It'd do amazing things for your confidence. You should totally train."

Is he teasing me? Is he implying I need the exercise? Is that all this is about?

Maybe now that he has a side-by-side comparison of me and Izzy, the difference is impossible to ignore, and he realizes that he's slumming. The humiliation burns, and my eyes start to sting. I immediately look away and get ready to run.

"Whoa." Bobby grabs my chin and turns me back to face him. "What's the matter? What did I say?"

"It's nothing. I'm okay." I snap my face out of his hand before the stupid tears fall. "But I do have to get back to work. Could you please tell Jack I'll be in the car? I … have to make some phone calls. To the office."

"No Kit, stop. I'm asking you, what did I say wrong? You were fine a second ago. Then I bring up training and you shut down on me? I'd never pressure you. You don't have to. I just meant, you *could* do it. You can do anything you wanted."

"No, it's not that. It's just …" I look back toward the front desk. "I just don't understand why you're even talking to me."

His forehead creases in confusion. "What do you mean?"

"I mean … I'm not like Izzy, okay? I'm not like any of the girls you'd be interested in. I know I need to lose weight, it's just …"

"Wait. Who said you needed to lose weight?"

"Well you said I sh—"

"Learn to fight. Yes, I did. For many reasons, but not as a veiled insult to you. Listen to me, Kit," he takes my hand in his, and he ducks his head to meet my gaze, "I know fighting, I know the human form, I know weight loss and muscle building. And I know, just from the small amount of time I've spent with you that you're uncomfortable in your own skin. But I've also seen the fire in your eyes. So this leaves me thinking fighting could be a great fit for you."

"Okay, but all that aside, I know I'm not like Izzy or the other girls you'd usually date …"

"First, I've never dated, at all, so you can't say you know anything about that. Next, I don't want you to be like 'those girls;' I like you exactly the way you are. I didn't suggest training so you could lose weight. I don't know the *you* from last year who may have been a bit skinnier, I know this version of you and I really want to spend more time with her.

"I suggested training because I honestly love the sport and want to show you how good you could be at it. I wasn't lying when I said you have the body for it. You could blitz your divisions because not many chicks are as tall as you. In a fight, your competitor would be the same weight as you, but she'd likely be shorter and stockier. No one could touch you because your reach would keep them away.

"And finally, *please*, stop putting Izzy in with 'those' girls. She's practically my baby sister. She *is* Jon's sister. Literally. We grew up together and you're putting weird images in my head. So just …" he shakes his head as though to dislodge the weird images. "Stop it."

I can't help myself — I start laughing, "Sorry. Maybe I should still go sit in the car. I didn't mean to imply you were an ass. And I didn't mean to make things weird with Izzy." I'm still giggling at his facial expressions. Jokingly, I start to turn around to walk toward the exit, but he grabs me and puts a strong arm around my shoulder and steers me back in the direction we were going.

"No, you'll stay here. We haven't finished the tour yet, and we haven't seen Jack in action." Bobby leads me through a doorway, bringing us into a large gymnasium type area with rubber mats on the floor. A class works on bag drills along one wall, and then I spot Jack with Calum, and Michael near them, training with another young guy.

We walk towards the back wall, then Bobby stops. "We can sit here and watch, or," he smirks, "I can show you my office."

I start laughing again. So cocky. "We'll sit, thanks."

He makes a big production about being disappointed and slides down the wall until he's sitting on the floor. Still laughing, I join him, and although I didn't mean it, once I sit I realize our bodies are touching. I can feel his warmth run all along the side of my body, from our shoulders and arms to a flashfire where our thighs touch.

No way in hell am I moving. I couldn't do it inconspicuously even if I wanted, and frankly, I don't want to. It feels nice. It feels even more amazing because we're both wearing shorts — me in my cut-offs, and he in what must've been his training shorts — and we're touching skin to skin.

My whole body has become hyper sensitive and I can feel wisps of my own hair brushing against my neck and shoulders from where it escaped my ponytail. I can feel his course leg hairs against my smooth legs. His large, strong shoulders against mine. I can feel my own chest rising and falling, and I almost feel winded, as though I've run a race. I can smell him, manly and sweaty, but not in a gross smelly way. I kind of want to run my nose along his chest and neck. I want to taste him. I want to lean into him the way I could the first night we met and we spent hours dancing.

My eyes drag along his body; legs, arms, chest, neck. Eyes. Bobby's lips are turned up in that shit eating grin of his.

Oh. My. God.

I've been caught leaning into him, practically ready to mount him here and now and my blush burns me from the inside out.

8

Bobby

I want to know more

She's so fucking cute.

She's trying to be discreet, but I can tell she's totally into me. And fuck if that doesn't make me happy.

I almost fucked it up. Again. She thought I was calling her fat. No way. Not in a million years. I think she looks amazing just the way she is and I hope she comes to accept it. She's hot! I especially love when I see her eyes spark, and I'll fight every moment I can to put it there as often as possible. I genuinely think training would help with that. I know the confidence a person can gain when they train the way we do.

She's gone quiet, introspective, and when our eyes meet, she blushes head to toe. I'd kill to know what she's thinking right now, but although that blush is hot, and although I'd love to take her shirt off just to see just how far it spreads, I show mercy and change the subject. "So, you're into Rhonda Rousey, huh?"

Kit wipes her hand across her cheek as though trying to wipe away the blush, then her big eyes meet mine. "Yeah. I mean she scares the crap out of me, but if she wasn't as tough and intimidating, she'd totally be my female fling."

I want to impress her, so much, and I'm so thankful for Aiden scoring us passes to a Rousey fight last year. "I've met her."

Kit's mouth opens and closes like a guppy fish. Finally it's my turn to surprise her, and her wide eyes and floundering mouth tell me I hit the spot. "No fucking way?" she whisper-shouts and I laugh.

"I totally have. We're not besties or anything, and she probably wouldn't remember me, but yeah, I scored all access passes to a Rousey fight last year, and I got to meet her and her competitor. She's actually really cool. And humble."

"No fucking way," she repeats softly, making me smile. Her swearing is a strange turn on. "That's so cool. I can't believe you were at that fight. Can you believe that went right till the third round?"

"You watched it?" I mean anyone can say they're a fan, and that fight was big in the media, but for her to have actually ordered the pay per view and watched it, that's hot!

"Yeah, it was an amazing fight. Me and the guys ordered pizza and had a fun night watching-- "

"Whoa up. What guys?" I'm back to demanding answers, but I just can't help myself. I feel all kinds possessive over this girl, and to hear of other guys physically hurts me.

"Yeah, the guys … the usual at my house."

I narrow my eyes at her, and she laughs. "The guys, as in Jack, Michael, and Calum," she explains.

"Jack, is your brother. Michael, his annoying whiney friend. Is Calum the third guy that rounds out Jack's trio of assholes?"

She stops laughing and narrows her eyes at me. "Yes, Calum is Jack's friend. He's actually a decent kid."

"Okay," I laugh. "I'll be nice. So just you and those three though? No other guys?"

"Yup. Just those three."

"Okay cool. You may continue your story."

She laughs. "Gee, thanks. Anyway, Jack's always been into watching the fights; that's how I knew training here was really important to him. After having him and the guys over for so many fight nights, I started paying attention, learning stats, backing favorites. Now it's become tradition. We hang out, eat bad food, and argue over the results."

She looks toward Jack as he kicks the pads that Calum holds. All three kids are huge for their age, and not nearly as uncoordinated as I expected. Jack attempts a high roundhouse kick. He can get leg up high, but the force of his kick is pushing himself back rather than the pad. That's cool. We can fix that.

He needs to engage his core and chamber his leg better. But for the first day, that's really good. Some of the other new guys can't get the height at all, and when they try, end up falling on their asses.

Kit and I watch in silence for a while and I take mental note on all three guys' abilities. I know this is my job, and I would do it anyway, but since it means so much to Kit, I'll be paying particular attention to Jack and his friends to make sure they keep up and behave. Anything to make Kit's life a little easier. I watch now as it's Calum's turn, noting he's not too bad either. He and Jack make a good team, their mass and experience similar, and they can read each other and work well together.

I hate myself for what I have to ask next, but I need to know. I brace myself and try my best to soften my voice, trying to soften a potential blow. I sigh. "So, I know we don't know each other well, and I don't want to push you for information, but … since Jack is in my gym … I have to ask."

She sits up straighter, stiffer, and I wince. I don't want to do it, but I can't help the situation. I need to know who's in my gym.

She sighs in defeat. "Go ahead."

"Why are you so involved with Jack's day to day life? Don't misunderstand me, I get he's your brother… but why are you bringing him to a gym, why are you paying his fees? Why are you hosting fight nights for him and his friends? Why are you so involved with getting his ass home when he's busted for partying?"

Kit sits silently for a while, and I worry I've asked too much and that she'll shut me out again. I hope she doesn't. I want to know her, on several levels. Eventually she sighs and looks up at me. "Jack lives with me now. He's my responsibility."

"Where are your parents?"

"Our mom died when we were really young."

"I'm really sorry to hear that. What about your dad?"

Taking a deep breath, she answers with a shaky voice, "Dad … died in April."

"April? As in … shit."

"Yeah, as in, a few months ago."

"Jesus, Kit. I'm sorry. Do you have other family around?"

She surprises me again when she lets out a bitter laugh, "Yep, loads." But the bitterness behind her words tells me they're not the kind of family she wants around. "Nope, just me and Jack. And Casey," she finishes with a smile.

So she's alone in this world, and taking care of a rebellious teenager. No wonder Tink is so protective of her. And now I understand a lot of that night at the club when Jack was busted. It explains why she was so pissed, and why he was so compliant. There's nothing I can say that won't sound like the cliché *I'm sorry for your loss* rubbish, I just can't find any words to convey my true condolences. Eventually I simply ask, "Want to talk about it?"

"Nah. Not much to talk about. Plus, it's not very good first date material." Kit's smiling again, albeit shyly, but I know a deflection tactic when I see one. I'm happy to oblige though. Anything to make her smile.

"First date? You think our first date consists of sitting on a sweaty gym floor, watching other guys work out?"

Kit turns her head against the wall lazily. "Would you prefer I watched you train instead?"

"Well yeah, of course, that'd be okay. I'm kinda awesome."

"And humble too." She smiles. "That's such an attractive quality in a man."

"Yeah, humble might not be the word most people use to describe me."

"Maybe I can watch you sometime, make sure you're not underselling your talents."

"You'll see me, don't worry. We'll be seeing a lot of each other from now on."

She lifts a brow in question and smirks. "We will?"

Now I've caught her again, I won't be letting her escape. "Yeah Jack will need supervision, you know, so he doesn't sneak out."

"Or get beaten up … by you?"

I laugh. "I promise not to beat him up. I mean, I'll still hit him and stuff, but you know, only for training purposes. Or if I find out he's giving you trouble. But don't worry, I have plans for you, too. Once you're trained up, Jack would never dare cross you again."

Her eyes grow. "But --"

"No buts. I'd like for you to at least try it."

"Try what?"

Kit's head whips up to face Jack. He scared the crap out of us both. "Nothing --"

No way am I letting her out of this. "Kit's gonna start training here too."

"Doing what?"

"Fight training, like you guys."

I worry that his reaction, if negative, might hurt her. He might think it's uncool that his sister pursue training. I'd hate for one single frown from him to discourage her and make her doubt her abilities. "Really?"

When Kit gives a small nod, Jack's eyes light up. "That's so cool! So, we're both in?" He looks at me in question. In the last hour, I'd completely forgotten about our confrontation today. He probably still thinks I'm a psycho with anger issues.

"Yeah, you're both in. I'll walk you both through your class timetables later. I'll also need you to head to reception and speak to Izzy and fill out paperwork."

"Umm, I'm not sure how it works here with fees ..." He scratches the back of his neck nervously as his dimple pops. "But, I can work double hours to pay for us both. I know it'll be expensive for two people to train, but I won't complain, I'll work hard."

Kit and I both stare at him in shock. I know he's given her trouble in the past, and she definitely didn't expect his generosity or concern over her finances. Most teenagers wouldn't give a shit about that stuff, and are too selfish to work for their own benefit, let alone for someone else's. My opinion of him just jumped several notches. "Ah, that's okay, Jack. Like Aiden said, first week is free, and then we'll work out details later. It's not a big deal." Standing, I hold my hand out to him. "Anyway, I know we kinda got off to a bad start. I'm Bobby Kincaid."

His eyes bug out of his head, and too late, I realize my mistake. "Bobby Kincaid? Holy shit, you're Bobby Kincaid, UFC heavyweight champion?"

"Jack!" Kit scolds Jack, then stopping, she looks at me. "Huh?"

"Umm--"

"Kit! He's Bobby Kincaid, reigning champion for the last, what, three years?"

It's my turn to be shy, and not because I'm not proud of my accomplishments. Usually I'm a very proud man, but in front of Kit, I suddenly worry what she thinks. Would she approve? Would she think I was just some meathead fighter?

"Holy shit!" she repeats Jacks words. "I mean, I knew your name, you told me at the club, but I didn't … Holy shit! You're kind of famous. I heard them talking about you on TV. I never made the connection."

"You two know each other?" Jack squeaks. "Like actually knew each other before today?"

"Yeah, I met Bobby at a club a few weeks ago. So did you, sort of."

"Ohmyfuckinggod, you're the guy from the parking lot? HOLY SHIT!"

A few heads to turn our way and Kit blushes. "Okay, that's enough." Time for him to pull his head in before he embarrasses his sister. More. "Head over and see Izzy. Get your paperwork started, we'll be there soon."

"Yessir." He instantly turns on his heel and bolts away from us.

"So …. You're kind of a big deal huh?"

I turn back to her and smirk. "Well yeah. I told you that from the start. Remember, you teased me about being humble …"

She smiles. "Yeah, you did try and tell me. You didn't mention … specifics though."

"Yeah ... Is that a problem for you?"

"Not at all. It's none of my business," she says as she looks away. That doesn't sit well with me though. I want it to be her business. I want to be her business. "So, you weren't joking when you said I should train?"

"Not even a little bit. I think it would be great, and it comes with the added benefit of you getting to spend more time with me."

"Ha, I just love how down to earth and unaffected you are."

"Well, my mama taught me not to be conceited. She says it's unattractive ..."

She laughs. "She's right in most cases. But, somehow, you make it almost endearing."

"Why thank you. I'll take that as the compliment you never intended to give. But yes, I really think you should train. It is a special kind of therapy and helps a person in so many ways."

"How many days a week would I need to commit?"

"As many as you want. As many as you can. At least three ..."

She bites her bottom lip as she thinks. "Okay. I could probably fit in three, especially if Jack's here too. Then I won't have to worry about what he's up to."

"Is he really that much trouble?"

She sighs. "He has been. He's been a lot of trouble actually. The stress of this last year alone has me feeling like an old woman. It sucks being in my twenties, and feeling like

I'm a hundred. But he's really started to come around in the last few weeks. Who knew grounding him and taking away all communication to the outside world would reset him? His shitty attitude is getting better. He's studying and behaving in school. We've had no more sneak out attempts, nor has he been drinking or doing anything else like that.

"I mean, I know one month of good behavior doesn't make for a reformed kid, but it's a good start."

"Wait, you ground him? How? He's huge. Physically, you couldn't stop him from anything he wanted to do."

"Ha, well don't tell him that! I guess he chooses to do as he's told. He bitches about it, but I think he craves the discipline and routine that we have together. My dad was a good man, but I guess he was tired the last few years, and as a result, Jack had free reign to do whatever he pleased. I'm sure it was fun at the time, but all it really accomplished was a giant chip on his shoulder and bitterness. I see that chip slowly shrinking now."

"Good, that's good. Listen Kit, I'm sorry about your dad. I know that sounds kinda lame, but I mean it. I know what it's like to lose a dad."

"Thanks. I appreciate it. I'm sorry you lost yours, too. My dad, he was a good man. A really good man. He was my best friend. We used to talk every single day. He was my biggest supporter, no matter what my goals were. He would brag obnoxiously to anyone who would listen about Jack and me."

She peeks up shyly through her lashes. "When he was sick, he was transferred to a bigger hospital in the city for treatment. Jack and I couldn't get up to see him for a week because of work and school, but once we arrived, the nurses, who we'd never met before, knew us by sight. He must've flashed pictures all over the place and talked about us non-stop." She giggles. "Those poor nurses, probably run-off-their-feet busy, but they stopped and listened to him. I'm very thankful to them for that. He must have been very lonely there by himself …"

Kit's voice shakes as she gets stuck in memories that are still quite fresh, and all I want to do is hug her. I feel a little selfish, like I'd be hugging her for my own benefit, that I would be the one gaining comfort, but I can't help myself. Stepping forward, I pull her to me. Her head rests on my chest, her nose pressed to my neck, and at first, she seems a little surprised, but almost immediately relaxes against me. She needs this too. I want to give her someone to lean on, and I want it to be me.

We stand like that for a few long minutes as a couple curious looks come our way, but everyone remains respectful and keeps their distance. Eventually she pulls away, avoiding my gaze and attempting to discreetly wipe tears and boogers on her arm. "Shit. I'm sorry, Bobby. I didn't mean to get all depressed on you."

"Hey, it's okay." I turn her chin toward me, forcing her to look me in the eye, "Don't ever be sorry. I'm glad you told me about him." I lean forward and kiss her on the forehead, lingering, and I feel her release a big breath. "I'm sorry I'll never meet him."

"Thank you, Bobby."

"You're welcome. Come on, let's get you guys signed up. Then I'll finally, *finally* have your phone number!"

She smiles at my dramatics. That's better.

9

Kit

What was I thinking?

It's Monday. Two days since we signed up to Bobby's gym, and tonight will be my first class. It's safe to say I'm freaking out and seriously reconsidering my life choices. I don't know what I was thinking. Temporary insanity? Sexually frustrated stupidity?

Logically, it's probably the comfort I feel when around Bobby. I haven't received a hug that good in … forever. And it definitely felt nice to lean on someone else for just a moment. But I can't believe I spilled my guts to him the way I did. I'm so embarrassed.

I guess I've been so busy, I never realized how much I missed my dad. When it hit me the other day, I had no choice but to hold on for a minute. I'm so glad Bobby was there and didn't make it weird after. I would have died if he had.

Now it's D-Day, and I'm scared out of my brain for what tonight will bring. Jack, on the other hand, is psyched to go back to class, and hasn't stopped talking about it.

Normally, I'd be happy that he's happy, but today his excitement is fraying my nerves. I have a little over an hour to go till class starts and I'm tossing up whether I should eat now, since I haven't eaten in hours and I don't want to pass out from starvation at the gym. Or if I should attend on an empty stomach, for fear I may toss my dinner all over the floor. And I know I'm overthinking this, but I can't seem to switch it off. Kill me. Kill me now.

Since I'm already going crazy, let's also add worry about what to wear. I know, I know, it's a gym, not a fashion parade, but seriously, I don't want to look like trash.

I try on half a dozen different pairs of shorts; some too long, some too short, some too tight, some too warm. Who knew this would be so friggin difficult? After a lot of frustration and hair pulling, I decide on a pair that have a yoga pant type roll at the top. They're short, but not indecent. Pulling on a super sturdy sports bra and simple black tank, I stand in front of my full-length mirror and declare myself good enough. Exhaling a huge breath, I turn away and leave my room. "Fuck," I mutter to myself, then louder, "Let's go, Jack, we're leaving now."

"I'm ready, Kit. I've been waiting for you. Here I got you a bottle of water." Smartass. He knows I'm freaking out.

"Yeah, thanks, alright." We walk outside and to my car, and as Jack hops into the passenger seat, I realize I have to pee. Damn nervous wees, gets me every time.

Fuck, fuck, fuck. "Fuck, fuck, fuck." Fuck, FUCK! What have I done? To further my stalling tactics, I may or may not be driving the scenic route to the gym.

"Kit, you missed the turn." He laughs. "Stop stalling."

"Shut up, I didn't miss it, I just wanted to check something out, up here, at the …" I trail off hoping I sound convincing. I don't, because he continues to laugh.

"Kit, quit it. Get our asses there already. Unlike you, I want to go!"

"Shit Jack, stop swearing! You make me look like a terrible authority figure."

"You just swore then, when you got up me for swearing, you said shit."

I sigh. Shit. "Okay, sorry. I'll try to stop, but I'm not kidding, you *have* to stop. You're fifteen and not allowed. At least I'm an adult, I can do whatever I want."

Jack just rolls his eyes at me. Whatever. We pull into the gym parking lot, and since it's normally only a ten minute drive, my scenic route only bought me an additional three minutes or so. Damn.

As soon as I park the car, Jack's out and rushing toward the front entrance. That's okay, he can go in. Maybe I can slink back to my car and wait for him to finish?

"Don't even think about it Kit, get inside now!"

I groan.

Resigned to face my doom, I follow him in, and as we cross the threshold my eyes adjust to the lighting. It's still really bright outside, so the inside of the gym is a little darker. I look around and see the ring to my left, and two large guys sparring.

When I look closer, I realize it's Bobby and Jimmy, and I'm suddenly rooted to the spot, unable to look away from two very virile, very sexy strong men sparring. Jack stops beside me and watches as well—probably for different reasons than I am though.

"They're so cool, aren't they?" he asks, and before I can even answer, Bobby distractedly drops his arms, and Jimmy strikes out with a solid right hook. Bobby takes it on the jaw and instantly drops to the canvas. I rush toward the ring before I even consciously realize it. "Shit Bobby, are you okay?"

He's not unconscious, and already attempting to stand again. Jimmy wipes tears from his eyes as he wheezes with laughter. "You got distracted, man! Suddenly Kit's in the house, and you drop your guard. Suck it, lover boy. Told you she'd come."

"Shut up, Jim." Bobby quickly stands again and offers his gloved fist, "Let's go again. I owe you a trip to the canvas."

Jimmy laughs. "No thanks. Another day maybe. We have to get ready for classes anyway." He turns away from Bobby and heads our way, then parting the rope and easily climbing through, he stops in front of me. "Help me undo my gloves, Kitty Cat?"

Normally I'd cringe at someone calling me that, but from Jimmy, it's kinda sweet, plus I'm enjoying his friendly banter. I start ripping the Velcro open but then suddenly he's gone, and Bobby's in his place. "You can take your own fucking gloves off, ass. Get lost."

Jimmy continues to laugh as he turns and walks away, then I turn back and find myself face to face with a sweaty and testosterone pumped Bobby, and my momentarily forgotten nerves come back full force.

Part nerves for the class I have to endure very soon, part nerves because Jack just walked away and left me to fend for myself, and part nerves that I can't explain. My heart pounds so loudly I'm sure everyone can hear it, and I look down as my face warms with embarrassment.

Bobby uses one of his gloved hands to lift my chin. "Hey." He smiles and his eyes flitter across my face. "Glad you made it."

"Hey. Are you okay? That looked like it hurt."

"Nah, Jimmy doesn't hit hard. Didn't hurt at all." Whether it hurt or not, I can already see the swelling on his jaw. His slightly scruffy, chiseled jaw that I kind of want to lick ... "Are you excited for your first day?"

My eyes snap up to his as I jump back to reality. I swallow heavily. "No, not really. Kind of wetting my pants, actually."

He laughs and shakes his head. "Alright scrapper, let's get started. Looks like Jack's sorted. Jimmy's running his class today." He steers me by the arm in the opposite direction that Jack went, and we walk through a large set of double doors to a room where the floors are completely covered with rubber mats. Before I step on the mat, he stops me with a hand on the arm. "Shoes off."

I look down to see he has none on; I don't know why the sight of his bare feet embarrass me, but they do and I blush, because I'm a hopeless weirdo. I quickly flick each shoe off, then I look up at him questioningly.

"Okay, so today I'm just going to evaluate you. See what you can do, see your flexibility, that way I can place you in the appropriate class."

"So, it's just me and you?" My heart pounds heavily in my chest and nervous bile rises up in my throat. This can't be real. This can't be happening.

Bobby smiles with a giant grin that I simultaneously want to wipe off, but also keep there permanently. "Yup. Just you and me. So you'll need to warm up first. Go over to the wall and select a rope, then come back over here and we'll get you started."

My face is calm and composed, but my brain is screaming at me, *not a jump rope!* "Are you skipping too?" At least if he were doing it too, he'd have less opportunity to watch me make a fool of myself.

He grins. "I'm already warm."

I grumble under my breath as I walk to the wall. I hate him already. Pretty face and big muscles be damned, I hate Bobby Kincaid and wouldn't even be sad if he was hit by a bus tonight.

"Did you say something?"

I turn back and growl under my breath when I spot his shit eating grin. I hope he teaches me how to hit soon. I feel like it could come in handy. "No."

"Okay," he laughs. "So I want you to do three rounds of three minutes. In each rest period, you'll do ten sit ups and ten pushups."

I balk. "You want sit ups and pushups *in* the rest period? When do I actually get to rest?"

"Better move fast then, huh." He looks at his watch then looks at me as if to ask *you ready?* I glare at him, but I position myself with the rope before I decide to strangle him with it.

"Go."

I start skipping, and immediately feel the burn of humiliation. I hate it and feel mortified. My whole body is bouncing and jiggling in all the wrong ways. I stop.

"What's the matter?"

"I really don't feel comfortable doing this while you watch. Can you skip too? Or you could leave the room?"

He looks at me with a stupid grin. "No, I'll stay, I'm quite comfortable watching."

I narrow my eyes.

"Okay fine," he laughs and runs to the wall. "I'll skip too." He walks back and stands beside me, then using a remote control, he sets a clock that hangs on the wall. "Are you good now?"

No! "Yep."

We start again, and pretty fucking soon I realize three minutes is a long ass time. I keep catching my rope on my toes, or on the floor, or on thin air, and keep having to reset. Bobby hasn't stopped once. Show off.

I look up to see fifteen seconds left on our first round, and Bobby speaks—not out of breath at all. "Okay, remember, ten sit ups, ten pushups. You have a minute between rounds, so the sooner you finish your reps, the sooner you get to actually rest. Ready?"

No, I'm not ready. Despite my pleas, in spite of me, the stupid the clock beeps. Instantly Bobby drops to the floor, already halfway through the pushups before I even hit the ground. Shit. I struggle through, doing my pushups on my knees, but at least I do them. I flip over, letting out a whoosh of air when I land on my back and work out my sit ups.

I'm panting and sweating when I get up, and I'm thoroughly pissed when the clock informs me I get no rest during this round. The clock beeps again and I scramble to get my rope ready.

The second round doesn't seem so bad. I stumble less often, but I'm running out of breath. I find it easier if I focus on something. The first round I was counting the bricks on the wall, but this time I watch Bobby. His movements are so fluid, so smooth, so controlled. He isn't out of breath at all, and I envy his fitness. He must feel my gaze because he looks up and into my eyes, and smiles.

"Like what you see?"

I do. Very much. I can't answer him though; both because I'm embarrassed, and because I can barely breathe anyway. The clock beeps again and we're back on the mat for the wretched *rest period* torture.

I finish my set with fifteen seconds left to rest. Wooh! But I sigh when the third and final round begins and I start stumbling all over again. If Bobby notices, he doesn't say anything. I'm too stubborn to not finish though, so I push through and get it done. What feels like twenty minutes later, the buzzer goes off and we drop for the final set of pushups and sit ups.

My arms feel ready to fall off, and my stomach cramps every time I try sitting up, but I'm pleased with myself for not dying, and not whining—out loud.

"Good job. Go grab a drink of water and hang your rope. We'll stretch, then get started."

Get started? I feel ready to finish.

Like a good, obedient girl though, I trudge over and hang my rope, then come back and start to guzzle my water.

"Whoa. You'll make yourself sloshy and sick. Small sips."

Silently planning his death, I follow him back to the middle of the matted area and sit when he sits. We face each other and he stretches his leg out to the side and shows me how to stretch certain muscles.

Thankfully, due to years of running, I know how to do this part, and know which muscles I need to stretch. I'm pleased to find my flexibility is still pretty good. I make sure to stretch my groin muscle out, remembering when I hurt it years ago during a soccer game. I'm stretching it while on one knee and the other leg bent in front of me, pushing my pelvis forward and actually enjoying the stretch when I swear I hear a loud swallow.

My eyes snap open to Bobby's blank face staring at me. His dark hair hangs long and over his brows, and sweat sits beaded on his forehead and lips. I watch him watch me for about twenty seconds before he comes back to reality and his eyes come to mine.

Boldly, I smirk. "Like what you see?"

He looks almost embarrassed, but covers it quickly by jumping up and heading to a stereo in the corner. He turns it on to some rap stuff and I can feel the pulsing energy in the room. I'm ready to start hitting stuff.

"Okay, so we'll start some pad work. You'll need to put on some gloves -- you probably don't own gloves, do you?"

"Nope."

He pushes his own black with white gloves toward me. "Here. You can use mine." His gloves are pretty beat up, with a giant spider on the top, but the leather cracked and worn. I pull the first glove on and try to ignore the creepy spider before I give myself a panic attack. As soon as my hand is seated inside the glove, I internally wince at the feeling like I've plunged my hand in a warm, sweaty bath.

I don't show any discomfort though. I refuse to be a girly girl and look like a wimp. I get the first glove on and the Velcro fastened but then find myself stuck on how to get the second on …

I don't want to ask for help, but … I'm not sure what else to do.

Bobby doesn't give me time to ask. He walks back and grabs the second glove and holds it open for me. "Usually you'd put the second glove between your ribs and arm, shove your hand in, then use your teeth to do it up. That's how you'll get it off too."

Noted.

He finishes the Velcro, then looks down at me with a small lopsided smile. We're standing less than a foot apart, and despite the heavy rap music, stinky soggy gloves and the fact I probably look a mess after the initial torture, I still enjoy the closeness for moment. Not exactly romantic, but nice all the same.

Too soon though, he steps back. "Okay, these are called Thai pads," he says, holding up two rectangle pads that span his forearm as he slips his hands into some handles on the back, "I want you to jab with your left hand, jab again, then hit with your right hand. So, left, left, right. Okay?"

I feel like he isn't actually looking for a verbal answer, so I just position myself in front of him and get ready to hit.

"Go."

Bolstering myself, I bunch my muscles and strike out. Left, left, right. I thought I'd feel badass after that, but nope. That felt sloppy. Damn.

"Alright, so we have to fix a few things. First, feet. I want you to stand in your fight stance. So," he gently kicks my feet into position, "left foot forward. You're right handed yeah?" I nod. "Yeah cool, so left foot forward, right foot back. Feet shoulder width apart. Don't let your stance get too narrow, or you'll just fall over as soon as someone hits you. Put more weight on your back leg, but not too much, sort of like sixty/forty. That way you'll be able to lift your front leg easy for a quick strike. Good, try again."

Left, left, right.

"Better. Now arms. Keep them both up high, always. Always protect your head. When you strike out with one, the other stays behind to protect your head. Your hitting arm will strike out from your head, then straight back to continue protecting it. I want you to extend your arm out to me, yeah like that, and see how your shoulder is now protecting your jaw and face while your hand is gone? That's good. Try again."

Left, left, right.

"Good. Now hips. All your power will come from your core and the swing of your hips. Hit with your left, and your left hip will swing around too. Imagine you have a karate belt on, you know how the loose ends dangle a bit? So you want that belt swaying side to side with each strike. And because you're swinging your hips, your feet need to follow too. Like this," he says and shows me. He strikes out fast and I watch his hips swing. I don't catch everything though, his movement much too fast.

"Do that again?"

This time I watch his feet, and I note when his hips swing, his foot twists in the direction of his arm. He strikes again and again and I watch the way his shoulder protects his head. I can hear the air whistle each time he strikes, and I can see the power behind each one.

"Okay, I think I got it," I tell him and stand ready to try again. I take a moment to make sure my feet are spaced correctly and in the right position. I lift my arms to where he showed me they should go, and my heart stutters at the look of approval in Bobby's eyes. He raises his Thai pads again and I concentrate on each strike. Instead of a sloppy slap like last time, this time each of my strikes results in a deep *thwump* sound. I'm impressed even with myself. There's that badass feeling I was looking for.

"Good," he says, "really good. Try again. We'll do this thousands of times in the future, literally, until your muscle memory knows it perfectly. That way, eventually you won't even have to think about it, your body will just do it. There's a saying that goes something like *don't fear the man who has practiced a thousand strikes once, but the man who's done one strike a thousand times.* Bruce Lee said that, and it's true. So, we keep practicing. Try again."

Time seems to both fly, and standstill as we keep practicing. After a while, my arms feel like jelly, not helped by the pushups we did at the beginning, and I'm ready for a break. Fatigue has my previously okay punches declining into downright crap, and Bobby notices so calls time.

"Go take a break and grab a drink. We'll come back in a few minutes to work on some other stuff."

I don't have to be told twice, and practically sprint to my water. My poor arms struggle to lift its measly weight but I make sure not to guzzle this time. Bobby walks toward me with his own water bottle and we stand drinking in companionable silence for a minute. Although tired, I'm enjoying the hot flow of blood through my muscles, and the energizing music blasting through the sound system.

"You're doing a good job," he says. "You're a good student. I don't have to repeat the same thing over and over again. Fast learner. I like that. I told you you'd be good at this."

"Ha, yeah, thanks." I continue to sip, and between panting breaths, I wipe spilled water off my chin. "So what's next?"

"Next is legs. We'll practice kicks. Then we'll stretch and be done for today."

Oh, thank god!

"Alright," Bobby throws his water bottle to the floor. "I want you in your fighting stance again."

I know this is a test because he gives no hints to what exactly he's looking for. Thankfully we spent the last forever in fighting stance so I remember easily.

Left leg forward, right back, legs not too narrow, slightly more weight on the back leg. I position myself and lift my arms to protect my face. I look up at his face triumphantly.

"Close. Spread your legs wider," he says with a wicked smirk, and I narrow my eyes at him.

"No seriously," he laughs, and kicks my feet apart, "shoulder width. Okay good. Now I want you to do a roundhouse kick, to my rib area. Show me what you got."

Hesitating for only a moment, I kick my leg out and although I reach his rib area, it hurts my foot like hell. I also lose my balance and barely stop myself from falling.

"Alright. First, you want to kick me with your shin, not your foot. Let me show you on the bag. Come over here." He walks toward the row of boxing bags hanging from the roof, not looking back to see if I followed. I did. Of course I did. He gets in his fighting stance and his leg whips out at super speed and knocks the bag to the side. He shows me again, slowing the movements down. His shin does in fact hit the bag. He keeps kicking while talking. "So you want to strike your opponent with your shin. Your foot will break long before your shin does. Secondly, all kicks are to be chambered through your knee, so however high you want your kick, you need to lift your knee first. Watch."

I watch as he lifts his leg to his side, and he stops his movements with just his knee in the air. His kneecap is at his chest level. "When you have your height, you flick your leg over and out and hit your target."

His leg slams into the bag with a deep thump and again the bag whips out to the side. "Your turn." he says and points at the bag next to his.

I face my bag and make sure I'm standing correctly. I attempt to copy what he did, but again, I almost fall over and the kick is weak and sloppy.

"Slow it down. We're looking for quality technique right now, not power or speed. Those will come later."

So I try again. I find my fight stance, engage what little stomach muscle I have and lift my knee. Once I'm happy with my height and catch my balance, I flick my leg out the way I saw him do, and my leg hits with a satisfying thump. I look at him and I'm smiling from ear to ear, on the verge of breaking out in dance.

"Good job! Now do it again."

So I do.

"And again."

And I do.

On and on we go until we both feel confident with my technique, and eventually he stops me. "Okay, come back over here and we'll work your kicks on a person." He picks his pads up and straps them to his forearms again, then places one near his rib area.

"Again," he says. "Remember, I want quality, don't worry about your speed or strength yet."

Nervous again now that we're face to face, I try and concentrate on what I'm doing. I strike out and fumble it. "Shit!"

"That's okay. Try again, slow the movements down, concentrate."

I take a moment to prepare myself. With deep breaths, I find the correct stance, hands up, flex my stomach, lift my knee, and flick my leg. Thwack!

"Good! Again." And on and on we go.

After a while of consistent, decent quality—albeit slow—kicking, he stops me and throws the pads on the floor. He lifts his arms above his head, leaving his whole body unprotected.

"Alright, now kick me without the pads. You'll find it feels completely different."

I hesitate, unsure if I really should kick him. I'm not scared of purposely hurting him. He's a professional after all, but I'm sure I could manage to hurt him by accident; by kicking him in the balls or doing something else equally stupid.

Shit, shit, shit, shit.

"Kit, go ahead," he encourages. I concentrate and make sure I continue with the quality kicks I was doing a minute ago. I make my movements slow, ensuring good aim, and flick my leg out. It hits him squarely in the ribs with a deep thump noise that I'm immensely proud of. His smile is matching mine, and I can't believe how happy this is making me.

"So good, Kit. Well done. Okay, keep going. I want you to practice both legs though, front and back. Keep it up, keep it slow, aim good."

And so we continue on. I'm not sure how many kicks later, maybe fifty or so on each leg, when he stops me. "Alright, we're almost done. I want five more …" I begin to nod and position myself but he continues speaking "… I want five more. At full power. Give it everything you got. I want to see bruising on your shins. Remember to keep the movements slow, follow through with your hips, and kick me as hard as you can while maintaining correct technique."

"One!" he demands, and I kick out. I feel a satisfying thump. Yeah, that was a good one.

"Two!" And I kick again.

"Three."

"Four."

"Okay last one, babe. Leave everything you have on the mat. Never walk away from a training session with fuel in the tank or you'll regret it. Let's go. Five!" he growls and I gather everything I have left and channel it into my hips. I lift my knee, roll my hip over, and release my leg. Without conscious permission, I release what could only be described as a battle cry as my leg flips out. It connects with a solid thump, and Bobby releases a small noise of his own.

"Good! So so good! I'm proud of you. I told you you'd be good at this!" I laugh as he grabs me in a quick hug, then he releases me with a big stupid grin on his face. "I told you. Sit down and we'll stretch out. Then you're all done for today."

I sit on the floor and stretch both legs straight out in front of me and bend my upper body over them.

He looks over at me as he does the same. "How do you feel after that?"

I smile and nod softly. "Good. I was really scared to come here today, but I'm glad I did. It sucked in the moment, but I'm glad I came."

"Good. How did you feel about those kicks? You're pretty tall, I reckon you could get them much higher."

"Yeah, I didn't feel like I was fully stretched out. I could go higher."

"Cool. We'll work on that then. You're going to be unstoppable. Your reach is amazing, and just the basics we worked on today show that you have great potential."

His praise is starting to embarrass me so I look to the floor, pretending like my current stretch is the most important thing in this world. "Yeah thanks. I had fun."

"When will you come back?"

"Ah I'm not sure. You said three days a week, yeah? So maybe I'll come Monday, Wednesday, and Friday, and Jack can go to classes on those days too."

"Okay." He nods slowly. "That works."

I frown at his distracted answer. "What days do you come in?"

"I'm here every day."

"What days do you train for yourself though?"

"Every day I get a few hours in for my own development."

"A few hours. As in at least three? Everyday? Shit, Bobby, I just did that one hour with you and I'm exhausted. You do a couple hours for yourself plus running classes? You must be super fit."

"Yeah, I guess. This is my job, I'm used to it. As I get closer to a fight though, my hours increase. Closer to six or seven hours a day plus classes. I don't get much down time for a couple months before a fight." He looks up at me, almost shyly, which is strange on his usually arrogant face. "Actually, I have one toward the end of this year …"

"Like a real, professional fight? Like on TV?"

"Yeah, on TV," he says quietly and looks up at me. It's so weird seeing Bobby shy.

"That is so cool!" I gush. "Can I bet on you? Like is that allowed? Are you allowed to bet on someone you know or is that frowned upon because people might assume we have insider knowledge?"

He laughs softly at my yammering. "Yeah, you're allowed to bet on me. Probably shouldn't bet on me to lose though, it might be considered fight fixing if I do actually lose."

"Will you lose?"

"No." He laughs. Ah, there he is. "Probably safer for you to just not bet. Save your money."

I nod, but the smile can't be wiped from my face. "Okay."

We continued stretching as we spoke and I realize I'm all done. I don't actually want to leave though, and in an effort to maximize my time with him, I start all over again.

"So, ah, Kit," he starts, and I glance up at him. His hesitance is back. It's so strange to see on someone usually so confident. This is the same guy who walked right up to me at the club and told me he was staking a claim.

He doesn't get to finish what he's saying though because Jack walks in, followed by Jon, Aiden, and Jimmy. Geez, they make a formidable group — the other guys, not Jack. I can't really see him in any way other than baby brother.

They walk right up to us and stop; the older guys with various cocky smirks. Jack's smile just seems to indicate an endorphin high.

"How'd you go, Kitty Cat? How was your first lesson?" Jimmy asks, and his voice is low and smooth, his lips sporting a wicked smirk that lifts a few notches when I hear something akin to a growl come from Bobby's direction. I look toward him but he's already schooled himself.

"*Kit* went well," he says with extra emphasis on my name, but then his features brighten as he continues. "She really did well. She's a fast learner and didn't complain once — out loud. She kept up, and her reach is amazing. Seriously, she has potential."

I look back down to my shoes as my face burns from his praise. I mean, everyone wants to be complimented, but I have no idea how to receive it graciously. I know my embarrassment is obvious though because all the guys chuckle.

"So, you'll come back, Kit?" Jon asks.

"Yeah, I guess. I said I'd be here on Wednesday, and that I'll commit to three days a week. Jack and I will both train the same days."

"Sweet!" Jimmy says enthusiastically. "So that means you're family now. Welcome!"

"Jimmy!" Bobby snaps and hops up from his seat on the floor, but before he moves any further, Jon pushes Jimmy by the shoulder and leads him toward the door.

"What?" Jimmy complains as he's being shoved away. "I meant the Rollin' family! Geez, don't be so friggin sensitive, people!" His voice trails off as they walk through the door.

Aiden chuckles, then his eyes meet mine. "Well, I'm really glad you enjoyed your session, Kit. We hope to see more of you and Jack around here. Although Jim failed spectacularly, the sentiment remains the same, welcome."

"What are you guys up to now?" Bobby asks after Aiden leaves.

"Gotta go home. It's a school night," I reply, somewhat sad at ending the night, but at the same time, too scared to accept anything more for today.

"Okay, yeah, school night, forgot …"

"What about you?" Jack asks. "What are you doing now?"

"Um, classes are finished, we're closing the gym now, so I'll be heading home for some dinner."

I think I know where this is leading, so I rush out that we must go. I feel bad at the implied rejection, but I'm terrified of venturing any farther out of my comfort zone tonight, plus, it really is a school night, and Jack and I still need to eat.

"Okay, well I'll walk you guys out." Bobby says and puts his arm out as if to say lead the way. Jack walks ahead first, and then I follow and Bobby walks right next to me. He doesn't speak, just walks with me, but I enjoy the intimacy. We approach my car and I beep the doors unlocked. Jack hops into the passenger seat straight away with a quick "See you later, Bobby."

Bobby stops beside me, standing close. "So I'll see you Wednesday then?"

"Yeah, I'll be here." I nod shakily.

Last time we were in this position, in a parking lot, in the dark, he kissed me. I haven't stopped thinking about it since it happened. Will he kiss me again? I can't help but stare at his lips, which aren't much higher than my line of sight.

He must notice my gaze because suddenly his shy persona is replaced with the confidence I met that first night. His lips curl into a beautiful smirk, and suddenly my hesitance is gone too. I very much want him to kiss me. He doesn't though. He leans forward, his chest brushing mine as he reaches past me and opens my door. "Drive safe, Kit. I'll see you soon."

"Okay.... Thanks for the lesson, Bobby. I enjoyed it, really. Even when I was calling you horrible names in my mind."

He chuckles then drops a soft kiss on my cheek. "See you later. Sleep well."

After I get in my car, I keep him in my peripherals as I pull out and circle toward the exit. Too soon, I'm on the main road and he's gone.

Goodnight Bobby. I'll be dreaming of you.

10

Bobby

Bad news

July, 2014

It's Wednesday morning, and I've just woken with a raging hard on, again. Sighing, I sit up in bed, itching to touch my dick, but knowing it's a poor replacement for the real thing. I haven't been able to get Kit out of my mind, not for a single moment since I met her.

I've thoroughly enjoyed spending time with her these last few weeks, even if we only get to see each other at the gym. I want to spend more time with her. So much more time.

Kit's been a little hot and cold since day one, but not in a cruel way. I feel for her, I know she's confused. She wants me, I'm sure of it, she just doesn't want to want me. When I thought she was indifferent toward me, I was hurting, I thought I'd lost her–not that I'd ever had her–but after our shared kiss, and spending time together, I was sunk, desperate to make her mine.

When she wasn't giving any go-ahead vibes, I thought all was lost and I was doomed for the friend-zone, but then I saw her obvious want for me to kiss her that first night after training. I realized then she was interested, just scared. I can work with that.

As long as she isn't saying no, then I'm more than happy to be patient and help her feel comfortable, which is why I've been cool, training her, being her friend, but not pushing. Despite my best efforts though, I'll be fucked if I can erase the images of that warrior princess training. It's the sexiest thing I have ever seen.

I've seen chicks train a million times before, but it's never, not once, affected me the way watching Kit does. Forgetting for a second the sexy shorts she wears, and the tops that show off her beautiful arms and shoulders, I focus on the way she trains.

She doesn't complain, she doesn't argue, and she tries– and exceeds my every expectation. I knew she'd do well training with us, but she has a natural talent that even I couldn't have guessed. My interest in her is now both personal and professional, and I truly hope I get her both ways.

Realizing that thinking about her fighting isn't helping my morning issue, with no other option, I stand and walk to the shower to hopefully relieve some tension. I know it won't truly satisfy my hunger for her, but hopefully it'll take the edge off.

During the day, I've been trying to stay distracted, to keep thoughts of her at bay, but now I welcome it. If I'm going to do this alone, I'm going to enjoy the view burned to the backs of my eyelids.

I flick the water on and wait for it to heat, then I step in and just stand, enjoying the sluice of water pounding my always sore muscles, watching as the steam fills the bathroom. I close my eyes and enjoy the smooth sensation of the warm water, and without a conscious decision to do so, my mind has already conjured a vision of Kit standing in the shower with me. In my mind, she's standing in front of me, her soft breasts pressed against my chest, smiling, her eyes dancing.

I grab my dick in one hand, holding it tight and start moving up and down. I imagine it's her hand, her velvety soft hand, and I imagine her other hand cupping my balls. In my mind's eye, I'm bent down and suckling her nipples, giving each one the attention it deserves. My mind conjures the soft sounds of her pleasure filled whimpering and my cock jumps from the thought. I sweep her up and slam her against the wall, entering her in one smooth move. No need for condoms in my fantasies, or much foreplay, I guess.

I'd give anything to actually feel the real thing. I want to know how she feels, how tight she is, how warm, how soft. I bet she feels like … heaven. In my head, I'm pumping into her, slamming her against the wall with every thrust, and I'm imagining the sounds she'd make. I imagine she's coming and tighten my hand to simulate her heat clenching around me, and with a short growl, I come, too. I stand there, panting and tingling, trying to catch my breath, and as soon as I come back to my senses, I feel a loss at the fact she isn't actually here with me. I'm pissed off with myself, with the whole situation. I want her, so fucking bad.

My dick is still swollen and throbbing, not even close to satisfied, but at least I get to see her later today. It won't help my dick, but being near her soothes me in other ways, so there's that. With nothing else to be done, I flip the water to cold and let it shred my body. Cold showers fucking suck.

~*~

A few hours later, I'm back in the gym and on the mats with Aido and we're working on a few submission drills. These moves are derived from the Brazilian Jiu Jitsu martial arts, a favorite of mine.

It's important for a martial artist to perfect every portion of an MMA fight — the standing, the take down, and the locks — if you want to be successful. A lot of fighters will be an expert at one, but only okay at another, and if your opponent, who perhaps specializes in BJJ gets you on the floor, no matter how awesome you are at stand-up sparring, you're a goner.

The guys and I have all formally trained in several forms of martial arts, and all have graded to various belts. Aido has a black belt in BJJ and a green belt in Kyokushin karate. Jimmy and I each have a black belt in Kyokushin karate and colored belts in Judo and BJJ. And Jon has a black belt in Judo and a purple belt in BJJ. We all started out in karate and a casual MMA class when we were young, and after a few months, we each found what appeals to us, and pursued those with a passion.

Somehow, we all knew owning our own gym together was the plan all along, and so we now combine our knowledge and provide a rounded MMA experience for all of our students. It works really well for us to further our own knowledge and skillset too, because while I specialize in stand-up combat, Aiden will help me with the ground and pound portion. Essentially, we all plan to master each martial art and grade for black belts in each. You could call it our ten year plan.

"Concentrate!" Aiden snaps, surprising me out of my thoughts. He has my back and already has me wrapped in a choke hold before I even react.

"Fuck!"

"What the hell man? You let me have that. You need to concentrate or Thomlassen will own you." Thomlassen is my opponent in December. And he's a pussy.

"Not fucking likely. Let's go again." He releases me and we go back to starting position. We slap hands and bump fists and restart. We circle for a minute, searching for an opening, and suddenly Aiden pounces and is almost behind me again. His arm is already snaking out, but I dodge and evade, barely. We continue circling and I charge him, coming in low, attempting to take his legs and flip him to his back. As soon as I have my arms around his hips though, he sprawls, dropping his body weight and pinning me to the mat. Again. Fuck the fuck.

He flips his legs around while still pinning me down, and on his revolution of my body, he slips his arm under mine and pins it at a ninety-degree angle. I wait it out a minute, assessing my position, wondering if I can escape, but we both know I can't.

He adds pressure until I feel the sting in my shoulder. Knowing I can't get out of it, I tap my palm to his leg twice. Instantly he releases my arm, and we both flop to the floor, breathless.

"What's your problem man? You're better than this."

"Fuck you, Aiden. You're the expert. If I beat you then you're not doing a very good job."

"Bullshit! I know you, B. We've been doing this forever. Doesn't matter who you're sparring with, we both know you're better than this." He stops as his chest heaves from training, and looks at me. "What's on your mind?"

He's my little brother, but he's always been so much more mature, more caring, and more fatherly. The four of us have always felt comfortable talking to each other. About anything. Nothing has ever been off limits, so when he asks me what's on your mind, he isn't looking for a generic brush off, he's looking for facts.

For some reason, though, this is the first and only topic that I've ever choked on the words when trying to get them out. Something about Kit is different. It's like my body knows it, my soul knows it, but logic is still playing catch up. I can't force the words past my tongue, so instead I continue staring at the floor and picking at imaginary lint.

"Shit man, are you okay? What is it? Is Mom okay?"

I feel terrible for worrying him, especially when the real explanation is so much simpler, "I'm fine, Mom's fine. Calm down. It's just that … well." I continue to pick at the mat nervously. "You see … it's … fuck!" I shake my head. "It's girl trouble actually."

I look up with an embarrassed smile on my face. I expect him to laugh at me, even tease me, but he doesn't. "Is Kit no good for you?"

Trust him to arrow straight to the point.

"Nah, she's good. So good." We're discussing her personality, her soul, no innuendo at all.

"Okay … she's not interested?"

"I'm not sure. She can be a bit hot and cold."

He scowls. "She's playing games?"

"Nah, no games, she's not like that. I think she's just kind of …" I consider my words, "world weary. Like she knows the world is an ugly place, and she's just … tired, I guess."

"Is she trouble?" I shake my head. "Is she *in* trouble?"

I shake my head again. "No, I'm not sure, I don't think so. She just has a lot of stress in her life now."

"So where does Jack play into all this? Why does she bring him to training? Why did she fill out her own credit card details when filling out our paperwork?"

His attention to detail doesn't surprise me in the least. I don't know if I'm betraying personal trust by telling Aiden, but I trust him not to blab. This is his gym too. "Their dad died a few months back. Their mom died when they were little. It's just the two of them left now, and Jack lives with Kit."

Aiden winces. "Shit, that's rough. To be orphaned so young, both of them. I can see why Kit's tired and stressed. To be playing mom at her age, to a teenager nonetheless. That's rough."

"Yeah, and from what I can gather, Jack doesn't make it easy on her. Arguing, sneaking out, drinking. That sort of stuff."

"Alright, well we can definitely help with that."

"Yeah, she thought some formal martial arts training would help too. Discipline, routine, respect—all stuff we can teach him."

"So this is what has you distracted?" he asks with a teasing smile, "You have the hots for a chick, a chick who has a complicated life and a teenage kid."

"I feel like the hots isn't the right description for it though. I feel something, deep inside me, like I *have* to get to know her, I *have* to be near her. That's crazy, right? I mean, I met her one night at a club and we danced. That's it." It's like I'm begging him to tell me it's crazy. To validate the warring inside me. "This isn't who I am. I get with chicks, we mess around, and I leave. That's it, no attachments. And this thing with Kit is literally making me sick to my stomach when she's not around. I can't stop thinking about her. Literally! What the fuck?"

"Whoa. Calm down." He chuckles. "Just slow it down. It doesn't have to be all or nothing right now, you know? Just spend time with her. Get to know her."

"That's easy for you to say. I want to spend time with her, but between me barely being able to stumble over my words with her around, and her scared to add more complications to her life, we're not getting anywhere."

"So just start small. Spend time here with her training. She won't panic thinking it's more than it is, it's just a training session after all, and you can both talk and hang out. Let it happen naturally. But for god's sake, calm down man!" He laughs again. "You're my usually unflappable big brother, and you look like you need to pop a Xanax right now."

I scowl at his smartass remarks, though, a Xanax could probably help right now. "Right, well since I got that off my chest, let's roll again." I smile and lunge at him.

~*~

It's nearly time for Kit and Jack to arrive, and I'm sparring in the ring with Jimmy again. Thinking about Kit again. I can't help but sigh at my hopelessness. I need to get my head back in the game. I snap back to reality at the same time my head snaps around from a clip to the jaw. I'm so fucking sick of Jimmy getting through my guard lately. Aiden's right, I'm better than this. And if I continue sucking, Jimmy's ego's going to inflate, and that can't be good for anyone.

I turn back, hands raised and charge him with a flurry of body punches, a kick to the outside thigh, and then an uppercut, which snaps his head up.

Good. He needs to know who's boss. He resets himself and licks his bleeding lip. Tasting the blood, he looks me in the eye and smiles a wicked smile and although he's my baby brother, I know this won't be a one-sided fight. Squaring off again, we bump fists and start trading jabs. We're circling and I have my back to the front doors when Jimmy says, "Ooh, hey Kitty Cat!"

Without conscious permission, I spin around to catch my first sight of her for today, when suddenly he kicks the back of my thigh and I slam to the canvas. Instantly he's on my back and has me in a choke hold. Fuck!

Desperately trying to recover, to not look like a total bitch in front of Kit, I don't tap. I refuse to tap.

His arm tightens around my neck and restricts my breathing. I have no choice but to tap out or be put out, and being put to sleep in front of Kit is a million times worse, so I furiously smack the canvas twice.

Jimmy rolls off me as my head snaps up in search of Kit, and he lays on his back, wheezing and breathless from laughter. "She's not even here, B!" He hiccups on his words. "But fuck that's an awesome tool for the rest of us to have now." He wipes tears from his eyes while still wearing his gloves. I look around to see that half the gym saw that shit, and they're laughing their asses off at me. "Assholes!" I spit at them all, but that only causes more laughter. "Get up. Let's go again."

We start again and I'm determined to stay focused. I've had enough of looking like a fool for today. About twenty minutes later, we're still sparring, hitting our stride and we're both doing well. My body is feeling warm and limber. Conditioning has been good lately, and while I'm taking a lot of hits and leg kicks, it's not hurting. Jimmy comes in with a body, body, head combo that I deflect easy enough, then as he pulls back he starts laughing again.

"Well, hey there, Kitty Cat."

Nope. No way in hell am I falling for that bullshit again. "Fuck off Jim, hands up."

"No really, she's here." He continues to laugh.

"Stop fucking around! Fight!"

Our audience is back, everyone has stopped and are watching, waiting for Jim to make me a bitch again. Nope.

Fed up with talking, I just start throwing jabs. Left, left, right. Instead of covering properly, he continues to laugh and he parries my fists away like he's swatting a fly. "Hey Kitty Cat," he giggles. "Come over here, talk to me."

"DUDE!"

"Umm, hey guys. How's it goi --" I don't hear the rest of Kit's sentence because Jimmy clocks me in the jaw. My head snaps around painfully and bells ring in my ears.

"Fuck!" I yell in a high pitched girly tone and every fucker in here laughs at me.

"Alright. Time!" Jimmy says, giggling like a teenaged school girl as he hops out of the ring and starts walking toward her. "Hey girl, you sure you don't wanna join my class today? Bobby won't mind. We're working on grappling today, and I need a roll partner." He winks at her. A fucking wink. Prick.

He's physically much taller than her and speaks to her as though he's a mature grown ass man, when in reality, he's barely even legally allowed to drink, and definitely younger than her. Apart from Jack, he's the baby of our group. "I mean, I'm happy to teach you some moves, since Bobby's lacking."

I jump the ropes of the boxing ring and I stalk forward and shove Jim away from her. "Fuck off."

This seems to be a reoccurring theme on her training days now. Jimmy thinks he's a funny fucker, and I vow to shut him up next time we're in the ring.

I grab her by the arm gently and start steering her away.

"Hey Jack," I throw behind me when I notice him standing there, then, softer, "Hey Kit, let's get started."

I'm fucking ecstatic to see her. I've been waiting all day for this, and I want nothing more than to get away from all the assholes still laughing at me. The highlight of my life these days is the hour I get three days a week while she and I work out together. I should have put her in a class ages ago, but I don't want to share.

Kit lets out a soft sigh and I look down at her, realizing that she's not nearly as excited about our time together tonight as I am. Her face is stony and worried, her brows pinched and her lips set in an angry pout.

I don't ask yet; we need privacy first. I continue leading her until we enter our training room with all the mats on the floor and the hanging bags along the wall, and just on the inside of the doors I stop her with my hand on her chin, and force her look up at me. "Hey, what's the matter?"

She pulls her chin from my reach and turns from me.

"Hey." I take her chin again. "Talk to me."

Her eyes begin to water, then she snaps her face away again in anger.

"Kit, talk to me. I'm freaking out over here. Please, honey. Are you okay? Are you hurt? Is Jack okay?"

"I'm fine," she snaps angrily and swipes away a traitorous tear. "I'm okay, I'm not hurt, Jack's fine … Jack … is Jack."

"What's that mean? Is he giving you trouble?"

She looks into my eyes for a moment, and I worry she won't talk to me, but then she nods softly. "Um, yeah ... I was called to pick Jack up from school today. He's been suspended for the rest of the week .... for fighting."

I don't like this at all. I'm worried that she thinks training with us will encourage him to fight, when, really, it's the opposite. A trained fighter knows to avoid a fight at all costs. We teach mental strength to enable them to walk away.

"I can talk to him. We don't allow our students to fight outside the gym."

"No, it's okay, it's my problem, and I'll fix it."

"It doesn't have to be your problem alone. I can help, as a friend, as his trainer."

"No, let it go. Can we start training now?"

I don't know how to help her right now. I don't know what to say to make her feel better, so I start the timer and pass her a rope. I can't do anything about this right now, so I start skipping too.

Tonight, we worked on five strike combos ending with an outside thigh kick. Kit trains with a single-minded focus and potent anger. I'll let her work it off tonight, but we'll be talking about this at some point. Fighting while angry will only result in hurting herself; when you get angry, you get sloppy. You end up kicking elbows or hip bones, or rolling wrists and hyperextending limbs.

I help correct her technique and show her alternate combos, but other than that, we don't speak. I hate this distance between us but I'm glad we're at least physically in the same place while she's feeling this way.

I can be her safe space. I'll always be her safe space. I'll let her work it out of her system, and I'll be here to catch her when she comes down.

Our hour passes by pretty quickly, so I send her to a hanging bag for finishing drills—front kicks, knees, roundhouse kicks. Fast reps without strength to cool her body down.

I've been thinking about what she told me for the last hour, and although she asked me not to get involved, this is still my gym, and we do actually have a *no fighting outside the gym* rule. I can't let this pass just to save her feelings, or Jack will just keep doing it.

I tidy the room and pack our equipment away while she does her drills, then walk her out. We find Jack standing at the front door, and now that I'm specifically looking, I notice the coloring on his jaw, and his knuckles are torn up. I'm not happy with him for fighting, but mostly I'm pissed at him for upsetting Kit. As we approach, I just look at him, then turn away and lead them outside to her car. I close her car door behind her and watch her drive away, then head back inside.

I need to find the guys, and we need a team meeting, now.

Jon and Aiden spar in the ring, and Jimmy watches and verbally corrects them. I look at the timer and when it buzzes less than a minute later, I step up to the ring. "Hey guys. We need to talk."

We rarely ever 'talk' in a serious team meeting kind of way, so I instantly have their full attention. "Who had Jack's class tonight?"

Jimmy raises his hand. "I did. Why?"

"He got in a fight today at school. He's been suspended for the rest of the week."

The guys let out their disappointed remarks, since we all know not only is he in trouble at school, but now he's in trouble with us.

Since they need the whole story, I tell Jimmy and Jon what I told Aiden earlier. They deserve to know, so that we're all on the same page.

"She didn't tell me specifically, but I assume he'll have to stay at home, since she has to work, and I reckon that's gonna be stressful for her and will probably compound the bad behavior. If he's bored and unsupervised, he's bound to find more trouble. So I propose we have him in here tomorrow and Friday. He can work. He can sweep, clean, stack, all that shit that needs to be done. That'll be his punishment from us, and that'll save Kit the worry of him being home alone."

"Who was he fighting?" Jon asks. "Do you know why?"

"I don't know. Kit wasn't very talkative tonight."

Jim nods. "Okay, well I think it's a good idea having him here. It'll keep him out of trouble while she works -- Shit. I didn't upset her when I was joking earlier, did I? I was just playing."

"It's cool. I don't think you upset her. I, on the other hand, am pissed at you. But don't worry, I'll work that shit out of you tomorrow. I'll show Jack what happens when someone messes with me. Or when they mess with Kit."

Jim smiles. "Don't be jealous because your girlfriend wishes she could see me naked."

He skips out of my reach when I attempt to hit him. "She's not my girlfriend. Dick."

"So she's a free agent then? Good news."

Aiden, the ever mature one, steps between us before I go ape on my idiot brother. "Did you already ask Kit about sending Jack here tomorrow?"

"No, I wanted to talk to you guys first. Then we'll call her."

"Okay, well it's agreed, so go call her."

"Ah, about that … I was hoping you'd call."

"Me? Why? She's your girlfriend."

"Well, firstly, she's not my girlfriend," I repeat and Jimmy continues to laugh. "And second, she likes you, she'll respond to you differently than if I call her. Please?"

"Fuck. Okay. What's her number? You pussy." He walks toward the front desk. I rattle off her number as he picks up the phone. I've never actually called her, but I've typed it into my phone a hundred times then chickened out at the last second, so I know it by heart.

Jimmy continues to snicker about the fact I know my non-girlfriend's phone number by heart. Asshole. I walk toward the front desk and I lean against the wall as he waits for her to answer.

"Hey Kit, its Aiden Kincaid, from the gym. Sorry to bother you …"

…

"Yeah everything's fine. Listen, Bobby told us about Jack fighting …"

…

"I know, yeah I know, sorry …" Aiden runs his hand through his hair. "But Bobby's right, this is our gym and we have rules. We don't allow fighting outside the gym …"

…

"What? No, we're not kicking him out! Slow down, hon. Everything's okay. It's just that, it's our rule, and since he broke it, he needs consequences. We thought, since he can't go to school for the next two days, he can come in here and work. Some good honest labor. Wiping down equipment, sweeping floors, that sort of thing …"

…

"Yeah, we understand you have to go to work, and figured you didn't really want him staying home alone anyway."

…

"Honestly it's cool …"

…

"Okay, cool. Drop him in on your way to work, and pick him up on the way home. We'll keep him honest in the meantime. Okay, yeah, good night, hon, see you tomorrow."

Aiden lets out a big sigh when he hangs up. "Fuck, I think she almost started crying when she thought we were gonna kick him out. I feel like a prick for worrying her. By the way, although I told her it's gym rules, you're in big fucking trouble when you see her next." He walks away laughing, but I don't even care. I'm just glad there'll be a next time.

~*~

I wake up Thursday morning with my usual Kit-induced raging hard on and head to the shower to fix it. In the past, I've never been so caught up on one woman, and hooked up with women often and freely. I was never in a girl drought, and never required so much self-maintenance, but since I met Kit, I've been with no one. There is no one else.

My dick's in a constant state of pain since knowing her, and though I absolutely don't regret meeting her, I wish I had a better solution for these blue balls. I finish up in the shower and hop out, wrapping my towel around my hips and head to the sink and mirror to shave. I'm excited I'll get to see Kit this morning, if only for a minute. It's terrifying how much I miss her already, considering I just saw her last night. And she's not actually my … anything. She's not my girl, no matter how much I wish she were.

I intend to speak to Jack today, to demand he pulls his head out of his ass. I don't like the defeat I saw in Kit's eyes last night, and I intend to help any way I can. That means Jack and I will be having an unpleasant chat today.

Realizing I've been staring into space, shaving cream in one hand, and a razor in the other, I shake my head free of distraction and get started.

Later, I walk into the gym to see a few of our regulars working the bags. I stand for a minute watching them one by one, and note that they're all doing really well. They have good form, good technique. They work hard, come in often, set goals for themselves and reach them. I'm impressed with them all—except one guy, Timms, on the bag furthest from the door. I used to have such high hopes for him. He has amazing potential, but he's become lazy, not hungry for it. It's like he's only here for appearances these days. He's got no power behind his strikes, and his feet are sloppy. He doesn't care anymore. And since he doesn't, neither do I. He pays his fees so he can train here, but I won't invest my time with him anymore, and neither will my boys.

It's not uncommon in my job. People sign up with big enthusiasm but don't back it up. Instead they come in just so they can snap a selfie. A quick photo op in front of the mirrors with the bags surrounding them, then they leave again. It takes hard work to become a successful fighter, and if they won't work for it, well, there's not much I can do.

I continue walking toward the ring and find Aiden doing a PT session with a kid named Stephen. He's a cool guy, about seventeen or so, and brings plenty of enthusiasm to the ring, and the hard work to back it up. He's awesome at stand-up combat but struggles with grappling. They're working on takedowns now, and then Aido will coach him through submissions. Stephen has competed in a few local fight nights and dominates until he gets to the ground. We intend to help him with that, and then he'll be a machine. He has a promising fighting future ahead of him.

Jon is walks in the door a few steps behind me, since neither of us have early sessions today. I actually don't have any clients for another hour and a half, so could have stayed home, but I wanted to be here in time for Kit and Jack.

"Hey B. How's it going?"

"Alright. You busy today?"

"Nah, not really, I have four privates, plus groups. Definitely not too busy to be riding Jack."

"Good, so we're both on the same page. Kid needs to sweat."

"Definitely. There's no call to stress Kit like that." His eyes grow stormy for a moment. "She's all he has. They need to be a team, and at the moment, she's carrying them. Fifteen or not, he needs to step up."

"Agreed -- "

"Well, hey there, darlin'. You're a fine sight this early in the morning."

I swing my head to the door, then to Timms when I realize it was him speaking. To Kit. He was calling Kit darlin'.

The.

Fuck?

I look back to the door and watch Kit and Jack pause as he begins swaggering their way.

Nope. No fucking way. I charge across to intercept.

To give credit where credit's due, Jack steps in front of Kit and blocks her from Timms' view. Good kid.

"Hey there, you're Cat, yeah?" He peeks at her around Jack's broad shoulders. "I've heard about the pretty new thing working out around here."

"Timms! Get back to work."

He looks over at me, surprised to see me there, surprised that this is even an issue. "Coach, hey. Just saying hiya to my friends."

"Nope, bags now. Or you can do thirty on the treadmill. Your choice. Either way, get moving."

He looks at me through narrowed eyes. He looks to Kit, or Jack actually, since he's significantly bigger than her and blocking her from view. Then he huffs out a breath and walks toward his bag in the corner. We watch silently as he shoves his gloves inside then storms past us and out the front doors.

"Dick." Jack and I both say quietly, and surprised by the other, we both look up and grin. I feel like we could actually be friends if he weren't such a shit to his sister.

Silence descends on the gym as everyone awkwardly stands around in Timms' wake, then Kit steps out to face me.

She's so beautiful, it hurts my chest.

She looks different today from how I've ever seen her before. I've seen her glammed up at a club, and I've seen her sweaty and rumpled at the gym, but today she's wearing a skirt suit thing that looks so grey it's almost silver, her hair in a low bun, and she has those sexy as fuck glasses on. Her skirt sits a couple inches above her knees, and she's wearing heels that make her already long legs appear as though they go on forever. She has fire engine red lipstick on, and the glasses just make her beautiful big blue eyes look bigger and highlights her long lashes. I should be stoked she's here in front of me, but I'm again struck with a sadness; I can't help but wish she were mine.

"Hey Bobby," she starts shyly, "umm, I'm sorry about my shitty mood yesterday. I won't come to training like that again."

I smile. "It's cool. I'm glad you came in rather than stew on it at home alone."

"Okay, well … thanks. Jack has something to say to you guys, then I'll be going to work." She looks to her brother. "Jack?"

"Yeah, okay …" He takes a deep breath. "Okay, I'm sorry for fighting at school. I know the gym rules, and I'm sorry for breaking them."

He's clearly being forced to apologize, and I work hard not to smile at the bulldog being led around by the chihuahua.

"And …" Kit prompts him with a raised brow. I love that this sassy pants can control men, men that are significantly bigger than her, and all with a look of the eye. She has the same effect on me. And my brothers too, apparently.

"And thank you for letting me work my punishment off here, rather than kicking me out."

"Good." Kit says quickly, then she looks back up at me. "I have to go to work. I'll be back about five-thirty, maybe six to pick him up. Thanks for letting him work here. I appreciate it." She turns back to Jack and glares. "We'll grab something for dinner on the way home. Don't screw around, do as you're told." And with that, she spins on her sexy high heels, and walks out.

I quickly look at Jon, then I tell Jack to stay put and I run out after her. I'm desperate for just a moment with her. "Hey, wait up." I'm amazed that she got so far so fast, especially in heels.

She spins around at my shout. "Shit!" She presses her hand to her chest. "Jesus, Bobby."

"Damn, I'm sorry. I didn't mean to scare you. You okay?"

She lets out a deep breath. "Yeah, its fine. I was daydreaming. What's up?"

"Nothing. I just wanted to say hi. Walk you to your car?"

"Oh, sure, it's over here." She turns again and I fall into step with her, trying to get close without crossing the creeper line. I don't want to be a creeper; I just want to be near her. A lot of the time. And maybe touch her some, or just watch her sleep …

Woops, there's that creeper line.

I struggle to think of what to say, unsure of where we're at in our 'thing,' so I try for easy chit chat. "How do you feel after training? Sore?"

"Ha, yeah, I'm dying actually. My thighs are so sore, it hurts to sit and get up. And my arms feel like they're going to fall off. Struggling to remember why I come here, actually."

"Yeah, a new workout will do that to you, but soon it won't hurt so much. Don't quit on me yet."

Her eyes turn from laughter to fire in a heartbeat. "I won't quit," she snaps, "I'm not a quitter."

I frown at her words. Her mood changes are crazy fast and lethal. I know there's more to her statement, but now's not the time to ask hard questions. We're standing in a parking lot and she's rushing off to work. If I broach it, she could easily brush me off and shut it down. I need to get her alone, and we need time.

"Come to dinner with me, Kit."

Her head whips up, confused by my 180 topic change. Eh, I can do it too. "Is that a question? Or a demand?" she asks after a moment. "I can't anyway. I have to go to work."

"Ha jokester." I step closer. "I'm asking you. Come out with me Kit. Please? We can grab dinner, go for a walk. Just hang out, alone … together."

She bites her lower lip for a long minute as her eyes flick back and forth between mine. "I don't know, Bobby. I'm not sure I'm the best dating material right now. My life is complicated. And, I don't trust Jack to stay home alone."

"Your complications don't bother me. I'm looking for a date, nothing more." That's a lie. I want more, so much more. "As for Jack, he can stay at the gym with one of my brothers, or one of them can go to your house."

"Like a babysitter?" She balks. "No way. Jack would never agree to a babysitter, and I could never ask your brothers to do that."

"Not a babysitter. Just a friend. A responsible friend who'll keep him out of trouble. Jimmy would be happy to do it." I gleefully throw Jim under the bus for my own gain. This is his payback for yesterday's stunt. "He's always playing Play Station, so why not do it at your place?"

"I don't know, Bobby …"

"Come on, it's just dinner. We can eat and hang out, no big deal. Jack will be fine. You have my word."

She smiles, not fooled by my puppy eyed pleading, but I don't even care because then she nods. "Okay, dinner. One time, as long as Jimmy doesn't mind."

"Deal!" I pounce. "Does tomorrow night work for you?"

After a long minute, she finally nods again. "Yeah okay … Tomorrow night." The look on her face tells me she's scared, but she has a small smile. We'll be okay. There's absolutely zero reason to be scared where I'm concerned. I'll never hurt her. Never. She, on the other hand, could tear me down easier than anything ever has before. And that terrifies me.

We walk the last few steps to her car, and she turns back around to face me. "Alright, so I'll catch you later. Thanks again … for everything."

I smile, then surprising us both, I brush loose strands of her hair behind her ear. "It's my pleasure, Kit. Have a nice day. I'll see you this afternoon."

I watch as she gets in and buckles up, then with a last smile, she turns her head and drives out of the lot. I'm fucking ecstatic and can't stop grinning like an idiot, my smile so big I can feel my cheeks stretching. I walk back toward the gym entrance and pass a few guys who work out here. They look at me as though they think I'm crazy. I probably look crazy, but whatever, I won't fight it. I'm happy. Today's definitely a good day.

I walk back inside, then remember my earlier irritation when I find Jack standing where I left him. Good, at least he can follow instructions and stay put. I look around and find Jon working with a client at the bags, but he looks up at me and nods, passing supervision of Jack over to me. He's clear across the room, but he was still watching over Jack until I came back.

I walk over and stop in front of Jack, my grin, gone. My good mood, gone. "Right. Come with me."

I don't want to be an ass, but he has to know there are consequences for breaking rules. And for making Kit's life harder. I intend to talk to him about the fighting, but not for a few hours. I'd rather make him sweat for a bit first.

I walk toward the cleaning supplies closet then I pass him a roll of paper towels and a spray bottle of sanitizer. "Take these to the weight room. I want to you wipe over all the equipment. Everything we touch with our hands, I want you to clean. Everything we touch, period, you clean it. Then head to treadmills, rowers, that sort of stuff, and clean all that. Then come back and find me or one of the other guys, and ask for more instructions."

"Yes, coach." He walks away with his head bowed low. He's not happy about it, but to his credit, he doesn't complain.

I don't have to follow him and watch to make sure he's working; everyone here knows, if you're using that spray bottle, then you're being punished. He'll be kept accountable, so I head toward my office. I have a PT client due in soon, so I have to get ready. When I'm finished, I'll find Jack and we'll have that chat.

Before I forget, I quickly pull out my phone to text Jimmy. He's working on a construction site today, so I can't ask him in person.

Me: *Hey Fucker. You're hanging with Jack tomorrow night. Bring your PlayStation.*

Jim: *The fuck you talking about?*

M: *I'm taking Kit out to dinner. You're hanging with Jack so she doesn't worry about him.*

J: *Why me?*

M: *Because you thought it would be funny to flirt with Kit and make me look like a bitch.*

J: *Clearly I didn't damage your image if she's still going out with you.*

M: *Yeah well, I'm kinda awesome. It's a curse.*

J: *Fuck you, Pussy*

M: *Cool comeback bro. Anyway, tomorrow night. I'll get you her address. You'll need to be there by 7pm.*

J: *Fuck. How do you know I didn't already have plans?*

M: *Do you?*

J: *...*

J: *Fine. I'll be there at 7.*

With a smile, I throw my phone down and don't bother replying. I know he's not actually mad; he just likes to argue for the sake of it. He's in, and although he doesn't always appear so, he's responsible. I trust him to take care of Jack. No hesitation.

I get changed and head out to meet Eliza, my first client of the day. She's a thirty something mom of twin boys, whose husband works long hours in the city. She says she wants to learn how to fight, but she's yet to don a pair of gloves in this gym. Mostly she stretches and walks on the treadmill. Whatever. She continues to come back with a smile on her face, and despite her lackluster training attempts, she looks good, so I doubt she's complaining.

A little over an hour later, I walk her out again, then I spot Jack across the gym. He watches me with a goofy grin on his face as he continues to fold massive piles of clean towels.

I frown at the dreamy face he makes. "What?"

His blue eyes, just like his sister's, look away from the front door and stop on mine. His dimple pops as he smiles up at the side. "That chick was hot."

I look back to the door that Eliza just left through. I mean, he's not wrong. She's beautiful in the traditional sense, but she's not for me. She's tall and thin, but I tend to like strong and sassy. I find I'm attracted to the long, dirty blonde hair types, with the big innocent eyes and the spine to snap at me every time I annoy her. I'm attracted to Kit. Full stop.

My stomach hurts at the realization that there's no one else for me. Just a chick who doesn't really give me the time of day – except the hour that we train together. Fuck I hope tomorrow night goes well.

Jack's nervous fussing brings me back to reality. "Okay Jack. Let's talk."

He sighs. "Right, well, I know the gym rules. I know I'm not allowed to fight outside of the gym. I'm sorry for breaking the rules."

"What happened?"

"Nothing. Just an asshole from school was being a loud mouth." He runs his hands through his hair again as he looks everywhere but at me. "Look, I know it's against the rules. I'm doing the punishment, and I'm not complaining. Can we just drop it?"

If he wasn't so desperate to not tell me, I might have let it go. But now I'm more curious than ever. I know he doesn't want to tell me, but I want to know. I have to know. "We can't drop it. So speak."

"Fuccccck. Okay," he rubs his hands over his face in frustration. "This guy I go to school with was talking shit ..."

"About what?"

"About who," he corrects me angrily. "He was talking about Kit. Talking crap, so I shut his mouth for him."

Instantly I'm pissed off. Pissed at the asshole for talking about Kit, and pissed for Jack for getting into trouble – from school, from me, from Kit – all because he was defending her.

"What was he saying? Why would he say something about someone he doesn't even know?"

"Well, actually ... he does know her. His name is Chris, and his girlfriend's name is ... Rita."

"Okay ... I still don't follow you."

"Rita's my cousin. Our cousin."

"Oh. Right, okay." How strange. "Why would your cousin's boyfriend talk bad about you or Kit?"

"Well, Rita, she's not really a good person. They don't get along. Our family all have a problem with Kit since ... since my dad died."

"Okay, so your cousin's boyfriend picks a fight with you at school? Why?"

"Well, he wasn't really trying to pick a fight. He was mostly talking shit about Kit. Saying how I should come live with them instead. With my aunt, that is."

"What the fuck? Why?"

"I don't know, really. I mean, I kind of get along with them. I've done some shitty things to Kit since living with her, drinking with Rita and them and stuff like that, which Kit tried to stop me from doing. I don't have a problem with them, not really, but I'm not stupid, I know they're bums. I know Kit's the only one who'll do the right thing by me. Make sure I stay in school and out of jail. That sort of thing."

Good kid. "Does Kit know about this? Does she know it was Chris that you hit?"

"No. I didn't tell her."

"Why not?"

He shrugs carelessly.

"So she's punishing you for standing up for her?"

"Well, yeah, unknowingly."

Shit. I'll have to fix this. Can't have the kid being punished for doing the right thing by her. Even though fighting is against the rules, I won't be telling him not to have her back.

"I feel bad, you know. I was pretty horrible to her, the ah, the day our dad was buried ... and plenty of other times since." He sighs. "I've been pretty horrible for a long time, Bobby. I've got a lot of making up to do."

I'm glad he's realized his actions hurt her. Though, I'd bet everything I own that she's hurting so much more than even he knows. She's like a fortress, locking her emotions up tight and putting on that brave front.

"Okay, well, if it means anything to you, I think you did the right thing. As the gym owner and your trainer, I need you to continue your punishment for today, but as Kit's friend, and yours, I feel you did the right thing and want you to always have your sister's back. I mean, don't hit everyone that pisses you off, but always stand up for your family and yourself. Kit's your family. So tomorrow, if you wanna, you can shadow me or one of the other guys and help with classes and stuff. It's better than cleaning."

His smile almost splits his face. "Really?"

"Sure."

"I get to shadow Bobby-fucking-Kincaid while he trains?"

I chuckle. "Yeah, but stop swearing like that. Kit will kill us both. One more thing. What are you guys going to buy for dinner on the way home tonight?"

He studies my face for a long moment, as though that was the strangest question he ever heard, but eventually he smiles again. "Pizza. We always get a loaded pizza."

These are my people. "Alright, get back to work. When you're done here, I need you to organize the front desk, inventory our stock—wraps, gloves, that sorta shit. We sell those, but I've got no idea what we have left. Come find me if you need help, or when you're done."

"Yes, coach." He turns away with his rag and spray and a big smile. Shaking my head, I look at my watch and note my next client is due in about thirty minutes. I head to my office to look over my session plan. I need some space to think about my next move with Kit.

11

Kit

A Twist

Later that afternoon as I sit at my desk, I stare at my computer screen with my head in my hand and my eyes glaze over. I'm alternating between dying from boredom and considering taking a nap, and running on adrenaline dumps and probably never sleeping again when I think of Bobby asking me out.

I'm going out on a date. Tomorrow night. With Bobby Kincaid.

What the hell universe is this?

I want to laugh. I want to cry. I'll probably just dance in the bathroom for a little bit to release my newest adrenaline surge.

In reality, I continue to sit at my desk like the boring corporate drone that I am, because I have a huge backlog of work to do for end of tax season, and I have to prepare budgets for the new year for all of our departments. I've been working on them for weeks, liaising with department heads, but some are holding back and won't cooperate. Because they're lazy jerks who think their time is more important than mine.

But despite my to-do pile standing taller than certain sexy fighters I've met lately, regardless of my good intentions, I've gotten next to nothing done today.

I can't stop thinking about Bobby, or our date tomorrow night. Between thoughts of what I should wear, having no clue because I don't know where we're going or what we're doing, and worrying about Jack's behavior at school and hoping he's being good at the gym today, I just can't focus.

I can't believe I agreed to him hanging at the gym today either, but practicality won out and I knew I wouldn't feel comfortable letting him stay home alone.

I thought Jack and I had come along so well lately — his behavior was perfect, his attitude such a pleasant change. He'd been working so hard with tutoring at home, and test results at school prove we were making progress. He was so appreciative of being allowed to train that I thought he'd never risk that by going back to his old ways.

I just don't know what came over him.

Why risk it all for a fight?

I have a meeting with Principal Reeves on Monday to discuss what happened, but until then, I only know what Jack's told me; nothing. Both thankful to not hear excuses, but wondering why he wouldn't try defend his actions, I'm simply left confused. And angry.

And sad that what I thought was progress obviously wasn't. I was tempted to not let him train last night, but didn't want to disappoint the guys at the gym by both of us not turning up to train. Plus, I genuinely think being there is good for him. However, I won't deny my own selfish reasons for wanting to be there too. I was terrible company, but Bobby's presence was still comforting.

On top of all that though, is my dad's pending estate. It's a damn mess and costing me a fortune in legal fees trying to finalize. Considering my dad had no money or assets and no insurance, who knew it would all be so difficult? This is why a will is so important, even for a person who didn't have 'stuff.' Having a minor child needing to be taken care of changes everything.

My aunts are making my life hell at the moment, not that Jack, or anyone else knows that, but frankly I'm clueless as to why they're doing it. There's nothing for them to gain except a surly teenager who eats nonstop and needs new clothes and shoes constantly.

I know they don't want him because they genuinely care for him, and I know they can't afford to maintain him.

Everyone knows my dad would've preferred Jack stay with me, and although my life would be so much easier if I gave up fighting them, I know for a fact it wouldn't be in Jack's best interests. I'd give it a few weeks before he got in trouble, following their lead into drugs and drinking and trouble. That's just who they are. They have zero aspirations for a better life and no interest in being contributing members of society.

Several of my cousins are currently, or have in the past, spent time in prison. Some for theft, some for assault, others for malicious damage, one for murder. Yep, that's my family. I'm a catch for any lucky man. Suitors, form a straight line.

I look at the clock on my computer for the hundredth time today, and note it's after five. Time to go home. I've been working longer hours lately trying to get through my work, but since I'm getting nowhere today, I may as well just go. I'll pick up Jack, hope he's not dug my hole any deeper today, and go home to stuff pizza in my face.

I've been working on cleaning up my diet lately, and it's helping, but pizza is, and always will be, an exception. It's like a religion for us, and I have no regrets. I'll just work harder tomorrow night to counteract it. Totally worth it.

I pack up my desk, tidy the mess of paperwork in front of me, and stack it all away where it goes. I grab my phone, noting no missed calls or messages — so I guess at least Jack hasn't been horrible — and stuff it in my bag. Keys in hand, I walk out the door and toward my car.

It's a quick drive to the gym from my office, and I realize a little late that my music was a bit loud and the guys probably all heard me coming from a mile away. I actually wish my work commute was further, since listening to music in my car is so relaxing for me.

I hop out and start walking in, not feeling as put together as I did this morning. My skirt is wrinkled from sitting all day, my hair is coming loose in places, and I've long ago tossed my jacket, too hot and uncomfortable to wear it for long. The silky blouse I'm wearing is one of my favorites. It's an ivory color, and the fabric is soft to touch. It tucks into my skirt, and the sleeves cinch at my wrists. The neckline goes a little low, not inappropriate for the office at all, but still, probably inappropriate for church — not that we ever go.

I walk in and find Jimmy and Jack sparring in the ring, and Bobby outside of it, coaching Jack, verbally correcting him.

This is not what I was expecting, at all. I thought he was here to work. I do note though that the display cabinet in reception is shiny and clean, and the contents organized better than I remember. I can smell pine in the air, which is certainly different than the sweat smell I remember from every other day. I instantly slow my steps when I catch sight of the 'wet floor' sign. The last thing I need right now is to fall on my ass in front of these guys. I look closely though and realize the floor is dry. I guess Jack forgot to pack away the sign from mopping earlier.

I stop and watch the guys for a few minutes. I hear a lot of "hands up, Jack", "combo!" and "teep, teep", not that I know what that last one means. I wonder how long they've been at this because he's actually doing really well, at least to my untrained eye. Eventually the buzzer sounds and they stop sparring, then they separate to their corners, panting and guzzling their water.

Bobby steps up to Jack's corner and leans on the ropes. "You're doing really well, but you need to keep those hands up. You'll get knocked flat on your ass if you don't. Your opponent will be watching you, waiting for a weakness. I know you're tall, but you're not invincible. They'll figure out that you drop your hands as soon as you kick, they'll set you up, and they'll knock you the fuck out."

I appreciate Bobby's words of wisdom, even if they contain a lot of profanity. Jack hangs on his every word and guzzles as much water as he can in his two-minute break. I giggle. *Rookie mistake.*

Three heads whip up as soon as the sound passes my lips, then Bobby smiles lazily and Jack tenses up, "shit."

He probably thinks he's in trouble for training instead of cleaning, but that's not my business; if Bobby wants him in the ring instead of on a mop, well, it's his gym and his punishment.

In true Jimmy fashion, he pulls out his mouth guard and smirks. "Hey there, Kitty Cat." He winks and Bobby rolls his eyes. I think I'd almost be disappointed if Jim ever stopped flirting with me.

"How long were you watching?" Bobby asks.

"A few minutes. Long enough to hear you repeat 'Teep, teep' but not long enough to actually know what that means."

He smiles. "Remind me tomorrow. We'll work on it. Did you see his combo?"

"Yeah, heaps of punches and then a kick? Yeah, saw that. It looked really cool."

"We've been working on it. Jack's a fast learner."

"Except the 'hands up' part?" I ask with a grin.

Jimmy laughs, and Bobby makes an "oh shit" face. "You heard that, huh?"

"Yup. You know, I've been working on limiting his swearing to the less offensive words. Trying to get him to stop saying 'fuck.'"

He winces. "Ah ... sorry about that."

"It's okay, it's a learning curve for all of us." I turn to Jack. "Are you almost ready to go? I'm starving."

"Actually, pizza's coming," Jack says.

I look to Bobby's smug face in question. He looks up at the clock, then back to me. "Yeah, pizza will be delivered soon. We're watching the Hernandez fight, which starts in about forty-five minutes."

I can't believe it's already fight night; I completely forgot about it. We never miss a fight, but the drama lately meant it slipped my mind. This is awkward, now that I realize their dinner is due any minute and we're still here.

"Alright Jack, well, we should hurry out of the way. Let the guys get on with their night."

"What? No. We're invited too. Tell her, Bobby."

"Yeah, I mean we're all watching the fight. Here. It's tradition. We have a projector screen we pull down, and we eat pizza. It's fun," he smiles charmingly, then frowns and steps closer. "You're not mad, are you? I know you normally have your own fight night tradition, but Jack told me you hadn't planned anything for tonight."

"Umm, no that's okay. We hadn't planned anything. I forgot it was even on tonight. Are you sure you don't want to just hang out with your brothers though? We can leave, I don't mind at all."

Jack groans. "Kit, please. I want to stay." His whiney voice is annoying as hell and it certainly doesn't sway me. I refuse to crash the gym party. I look to Bobby for his answer, but before he can, a sweaty arm rests on my shoulders and Jimmy leans in close to my ear. "Please stay, Kitty Cat. I want to spend time with you."

I can feel his goofy grin, then he smacks a juicy kiss down on my cheek just before I shake him off.

Jimmy laughs at my reaction, but Bobby looks like he might rip his brother's lips off. I hate to upset Bobby, but his reactions to Jimmy's flirting are really quite entertaining and probably the only reason Jimmy continues to do it.

"Stay, have dinner with my Kitty."

"Are you guys sure we're not intruding?"

Bobby shakes his head. "No, definitely not. We want you to stay."

Jimmy walks away from our group toward the locker room. He turns and walks backwards. "We ordered enough pizza for everyone. Plus, you're family, remember?"

I look back to Bobby's chocolate eyes, pleading and irresistible, and I nod softly. I guess we're staying for dinner and a fight. I look down my body, my skirt suit, my heels, my hair that feels too tight. I don't quite feel much in the 'relaxed pizza night' mood with what I'm wearing, but I have time to run home and get changed if I hurry.

I rifle through my handbag again looking for keys, and Bobby steps in closer, placing his large hand on my arm to stop my escape. "Please could you stay? I really think you should. We ordered loads of pizza, expecting extras. It'll be fun, I promise."

I look up to Bobby's disappointed face as I hold my keys between us. He seems genuinely disappointed at the thought that I won't stay, and that makes my stomach feel warm. It's a nice feeling.

I smile. "Yeah, we'll stay. I just want to run home and get changed. I feel a bit shit in my work clothes."

"Well ..." he leans in closer, his face lightening from disappointment to mischief, and his stubble brushes against my cheek as he whispers, "I think you look sexy. This top," he presses his finger on the 'V' on my neckline, "makes your tits look amazing. And those heels sure are nice to look at after a long day."

I'm surprised by his obvious flirting, but I'm definitely enjoying the return of the 'club' Bobby, rather than trainer or friend. Giant butterflies flap around in my stomach at the reminder that I have a date with this man in twenty-four hours. I'm excited and terrified at the same time. I bite my bottom lip and smile as his eyes drop to the movement. "I appreciate your appreciation."

I turn to Jack, who stands with Aiden across the room. "Jack. Come on. We'll go home and get changed, then we'll come back."

He shakes his head before I finish my sentence. "Nah. I'm just gonna get a shower here. I have spare clothes in my bag. I'm all good."

"Sooooo, Kit ..." Bobby leans in close again as Jack walks toward the locker rooms and out of sight. "Need a hand to get changed?"

I'm actually half tempted to say yes and take him home to work off some tension. I'm pretty damn sure he'd know just the way to help me. But, as usual, shyness and insecurities win out. I mean, what if I accept then find out he's only joking. I'd die of humiliation. "No, that's okay. I'll be quick."

Bobby walks me outside and we head toward my car.

With one hand on the door handle and my keys in the other, I turn and face him, and I startle to find his face so close to mine. He raises one hand and runs his fingers along my jawbone, and my heartbeat hammers in my chest. If he leaned forward just a fraction, he could probably feel it too. "Be fast, drive safe."

I can't speak. I'm overwhelmed at his nearness, and am silently begging him to kiss me. I know my head screams that this won't work, that my life's too complicated, that he is well and truly out of my league, but my heart and my hormones scream 'yes please!'

Both answering my prayers and smashing them to pieces, he leans in and places a closed mouth kiss on my lips. So soft and warm, and oh so comforting.

I want more. I want him to open my mouth with his, I want him to press me against this car, I want to wrap my legs around his hips and feel his large hands holding my ass. Instead, he only pulls away and rests his forehead against mine. "Hurry back," he whispers softly against my skin. He places a hand on my hip and pulls me away from the car and opens my door.

I hesitate, not wanting to move away from him, scared that when I return, things will be weird. With no choice, though, I turn and get in, but before I can close the door, he leans in and turns my chin toward him.

"You sure you don't want me to join you? I could wash your back." He smirks.

I'm dying to say yes. I'd love for him to wash my back. I'd love for him to be in my house, in my shower. He must read my hunger because then he quietly laughs, though it's humorless and bordering on desperation. "Shit, woman, you're killing me. Yes, no, yes, no. We can't right now, Kit. We absolutely don't have enough time for a quickie in the shower. I promise you, we need more time than that ..."

Part of me, most of me, considers dragging him home and missing the fight altogether.

"It's not all or none, babe, don't worry. We'll get to it. Soon," he promises then kisses me again. It hot, and this time comes with tongue, but before I can appreciate what he's giving me, he pulls away. "Drive safe, hurry back," he repeats, kissing me on the forehead and closing the door. I let out a huge breath as I look at myself in the rear-view mirror.

My pupils are huge and dark, my cheeks stained pink. Whew! Get yourself under control, girl. I switch my car on and look around to make sure all is clear to drive away, and as I look over my shoulder I screech when I realize Bobby's still standing there with his face near my window, and a huge grin spread from side to side. Fuck! He saw me flustered, checking myself in the mirror and now he's laughing at me. Shit.

He plants a juicy kiss on my window then walks away laughing.

I rub my hand over my eyes in an attempt to erase my dumbassery, then I turn my music up to blaring and race home. I'm such an idiot, but I'm an idiot with an informal pizza date with a sexy man tonight. I run to my room and flick my heels off, accidently pinging one so high it bounces off the ceiling fan.

Oops.

I unzip my skirt and rip my blouse over my head, then I stop in front of my full-length mirror and study my underwear.

For a moment, I seriously consider changing into a matching bra and panty set, but then I shake my head. No. He won't even see them–tonight at least. I rummage through the pile of 'not dirty enough to wash, but not clean enough to fold and put away' clothes, and select my favorite cut off shorts. I live in these things outside of work—they're so comfortable. I find a comfy sweater top and grab my white high tops as I flee my room. I run to the bathroom and flick on some extra mascara and pull my hair out of my barely-there bun. I comb my hair out to give it a bit of volume, then tie it up in a high pony. I run through my kitchen in search of some gum, then stop with a skid when I pass the fridge.

Shit! Should I bring something? Since the guys are supplying pizza, should I bring wine or soda? Oh, my god, oh my god, I don't know, and in this moment, I feel like the whole world rests on this decision. Calm down, Kit! I grab a six pack of alcoholic apple ciders and a six pack of diet cream soda cans. They'll either drink them or they won't. Whatev's. At least I won't arrive empty handed.

I blow out the front door with my hands full, and toss everything in the car. I stop in my driveway to put my shoes on and realize I forgot socks, shit! With a huff, I run inside and back out in record time, socks in hand, then head back to the gym. I look at the car clock and realize I've been gone for about fifteen minutes total, and feel proud of my hustle.

I stop for a moment and wonder if I was too quick, if I'm coming across as desperate? Fuck knows. But Jon is walking through the parking lot, arms full of pizza boxes and has spotted me anyway, so I can't escape to time my arrival better even if I wanted. Which I don't.

He stops walking to wait for me, and I try to hurry and grab my own offerings, hoping I'm not making him wait too long and that the pizza isn't burning his arms.

"Hey there, Kit. How's it going?"

"Hey Jon, I'm good. Thanks for inviting Jack and me tonight."

"Ah that's okay. It's a good thing the rest of us like you, because I'm pretty sure we had no choice anyway. Bobby wouldn't have it any other way."

I look up through the corner of my eye to find his smirk, and I feel the blush fill my cheeks again as we continue to walk.

"So…"

I look up at his shy voice. "So what?"

"Seen Casey lately?"

I smile. "Yeah I've seen her lately. I see her all the time. Like daily. She's my best friend."

"What's she doing tonight?"

"I'm not sure actually. Usually we do pizza and fight night at my house, like you guys do, but I totally forgot the Hernandez fight was on tonight, and we didn't make plans. She's probably at home, watching alone, in her cute Peter Pan pj's."

His head whips my way. "Does she really wear Peter Pan pyjamas?"

I laugh as we walk. "No, she doesn't. I was kidding. Maybe I should get her some for Christmas though. It's a cool idea."

"Definitely a cool idea," he says with a faraway look, and I try not to think about the fact he's imagining her in sexy Peter Pan garb right now. "So if she's not busy, maybe you should call her. Tell her to come watch the fight with us. She can bring dessert."

I'm pretty friggin sure he wants more than ice cream from her, but I'm okay with this. I really like Jon, and know she could do worse. She certainly has in the past! "Sure. I'll text her. Any preferences on ice cream flavors?"

I'm teasing, but he just looks at me with devilish eyes. Oh geez, these guys are trouble. I tell him I'll meet him inside in a minute, and I take my phone out after I pile all my crap on the ground next to me. He winks and walks away as I type.

M: Hey! Whatchya doing, right now?

It takes only a minute for her to answer, which tells me she is in fact chilling on her couch.

C: Hey!! Just sitting down, opening a beer. Watching TV. What about you?

M: We're at the Kincaid gym. Watching the Hernandez fight.

C: Bitch! I'm waiting for that fight to start too. I didn't want to mention it because I know you've been stressed and busy.

M: It's cool. You should have! I totally forgot. The guys do a pizza fight night thing like we do, but at the gym. They invited us. You should come!

C: Really? Now? Are you already there?

M: Yeah, Jack and I are here, and the guys. Pizza is here, and I brought some drinks. You should grab some ice cream and come over. Quick! Fight starts soon!

C: Argh! But I'm in my pj's! It'll take forever to change and get there.

M: Wear them! It'll blow Jon's mind.

C: Jon's there?!? Omg omg omg.

M: LOL, yeah, he's here. Seriously though, I'm wearing casual shorts and a messy pony. Just come, and hurry!

C: Okay okay, already running to my room. See you soon.

Pleased with my work, I bend to pick up my stuff, but stop when I realize it's not there. But I do see shoes. I quickly look up to see Bobby watching me and almost jump back and fall over. "Jesus, Bobby, you scared the crap outta me."

"Sorry babe." He looks down at my phone. "Who you talking to?"

I know I was smiling like an idiot while texting Casey, and if Bobby was watching for long, that might have looked strange. Acting coy though, I flick my hair over my shoulder, "Oh, no one. Just a friend of mine, from way back."

He narrows his eyes at me. He's not impressed. "Did you want some more privacy, to speak to your … friend? Or will you be joining us now?"

I bite my tongue to keep my laughter in. Jealous Bobby is adorable, with his bunching muscles and ticking jaw. "Actually, my friend will be here soon. Hope you don't mind I extended an invitation?"

If I live to see another day, I might realize that challenging a world champion fighter might not have been my smartest move. Not because I'm afraid of him, but because I could never compete with his competitive streak.

Bobby leans into me, pressing me against the wall of the gym. His hands are full of the drinks I brought, so he uses his chest to hold me in place. He face is within an inch of mine, and he speaks low and deep. "You should know by now, Kit, I'm very much … interested, in you. I've tried being gentle, easing you into it, so to speak. I can be more assertive though, in case you missed my intention." He gently bites my chin and my body breaks out into convulsions and mini orgasms. "But I'll have you know, I don't share. I'll never share. So if you aren't interested, tell me now, and I'll back off. No hard feelings, no awkwardness. I'll even keep training you and I'll keep my hands to myself, even if that means chopping them the fuck off. But if you want me too, tell me and we'll do something about it."

My heart pounds in my chest, and I know for a fact he can feel it against his own. "So, what is it? Do you want me too? Or will I walk away and let you wait for your friend?"

I can't speak for a long moment, my brain scrambled from his proximity and intensity. I want him to press against me harder; I want him to bite me some more. Fucking hell, I want him to run his finger through the moisture pooling in my panties.

"Kit?"

"Hmmm?" What was the question?

"Do you want me, too?" He pushes his hips against mine. I draw in a breath at the feel of his hardness pressing against me. I'd give anything to feel it, skin on skin.

"Hmm ..." I struggle to speak, and clear my throat to try again. "Uh huh. Yeah, I do ... want you ..." my voice is a low throaty moan that I've never heard before.

He leans forward and licks along the seam of my lips. I open my mouth to taste, but he pulls back. "So we're clear then? I want you, and you want me? No games, and no sharing. Right?"

I nod. "Right." Please just fucking kiss me now.

Thankfully, mercifully, with a satisfied smirk, he leans forward and kisses me, transporting me back to the parking lot on the night we met. His warm mouth envelops mine, tasting me, crushing me back against the wall near the gym's front entrance. I tighten my arms around his thick neck and I brush my fingers through his hair. It's so soft and grabbable.

His hands are full so he can't touch me, but I can touch him. Lowering my hands, I run them along his shoulders and down to his chest, thrilling at the solid muscles and the twitching movements I feel through his shirt. Bobby's teeth nip at my bottom lip, and I open to him, finally, finally, getting a taste of what I've been craving. He's so warm and sweet, like he ate strawberry candy and something with cinnamon recently. I wonder if he stopped at the bakers at some point today, and I push back at my irrational jealousy of a pastry.

Starving for more, I pull him tighter against me, pushing back against him, winding my arms around his neck again, and pulling him down to me. I'm tall, but in this moment, not tall enough. I wonder if I can hitch my legs up and let him hold me, all while his arms are full with drinks and stuff. Why is he even holding those when I want him to hold me? I *need* him to hold me.

I push my tongue into his mouth, tasting more, and he pushes back, meeting me stroke for stroke and his chest crushes mine, forcing me to take shallow breaths or die.

"Ahem …"

Somewhere in the back of my sex fogged brain, I hear someone clearing their throat. It takes me a moment before I remember where I am, and when reality comes crashing back to me I jump back, trying to escape and put distance between myself and the man I was dry humping in public. I slam myself into the wall behind me and winding myself.

"Shit babe," Casey jumps forward, though she laughs like a hyena. "Are you okay?"

I press my hand over my chest. "Asshole. What the hell are you doing, sneaking up on people?"

She smirks. "I'm here for pizza and sexy fighters. You knew I was coming."

"Well yeah, but I thought you'd be a while yet. I only texted you a minute ago."

"You texted me ages ago, and now I'm here. See!" She holds up a shopping bag that contains ice cream bars. Shit.

My eyes snap back to Bobby's to find him smirking. "This is who you were texting when I came out?"

"Umm… yeah." It almost sounds like a question, and now he's laughing at me too.

"Whatever, I'm going inside. I'm hungry." I try to push past, but Bobby stops me with a hand on my arm.

"Hold on a sec." He turns to look at Casey. "Hey Tink. Good to see ya. Now get lost."

The Casey I know would scour this parking lot for the thickest piece of timber she could find, and she'd smack him over the head for his dismissal, but *this* Casey, this new and weird Casey, simply smiles at him, grabs the drinks from his arms and walks away. "Have fun, kids."

Where has my best friend gone? Who did this to her?

Suddenly, Bobby's in my face again, this time his hands holding my hips so tightly I couldn't move even if wanted to. He lowers his lips to mine but only kisses me closed mouth. I sigh at the almost kiss, then he moves his nose to my neck, just below my hairline and just stands there, breathing me in for a moment.

I wonder if he can feel the wild beat of my pulse? I wonder if his is beating as hard as mine?

"Alright babe, let's go in," he says reluctantly, his hands still tight on my hips. "The fight has probably already started."

He's right. It probably has, plus the pizza has been here for twenty minutes or so, so it's likely all gone, or cold.

We walk in, shoulders bumping every few steps, but otherwise not touching. I search the room for Jack, realizing I've been gone for the better part of an hour, and want to make sure he's behaving himself. He's sitting inside the ring with everyone else. He has a pizza box in front of him, and I make a mental note to drop some cash at reception for his share before we leave.

Everyone's sitting, laying, sprawling on the canvas, facing toward a soft screen that's been hung from the ceiling. It's not a super sharp picture, but we can still see the written detail clearly enough.

The presenters are still discussing the fighters' stats, comparing reach, height, weight, and previous fight records. Hernandez is the favorite to win tonight. He has an undefeated UFC record: twelve fights, twelve wins to date. Although his opponent Noah Wheaten, looks almost as impressive. He has nine professional fights, eight wins by KO, one loss by TKO.

As we approach, I look around the ring from face to face, and I feel less guilty as I note Jimmy is sitting with his own pizza box as well. Next is Aiden, and then Jack. On the end is Jon, and then surprise, surprise, Casey is next to him, a shared pizza box between them.

There's empty space next to Casey, so I head toward them. Jimmy notices our approach and stands to spread the ropes for me, then as soon as I step through though, he winks at me then releases the rope and it whips back in place, barring Bobby's entry.

Geez, Jimmy's asking for trouble.

Bobby climbs in behind me. "Asshole."

I attempt to stifle my giggle before he gets mad at me, then I sit down next to Case and realize it's going to be a tight fit for us all. Bobby stands in front of me and comes to the same conclusion.

"Move your asses, guys. Move a few inches to your left." There's silence as everyone stares at him; unmoving. Eventually he sighs. "Please?"

"A few inches?" Jimmy laughs as we all shuffle. "That's all the space you need?"

Bobby rolls his eyes, then squeezes in and presses his back to the corner of the ring, sitting on an angle, his left leg bent and right leg out straight.

I lightly lean against his bent leg, and although he notices and shoots me a soft smile, no one else does.

Jack looks up at us and passes a pizza box. "Hey, saved you some pizza."

I open it to find three quarters of a loaded pizza, then I sit it down in front of Bobby's bent leg and we both dig in. I eat and listen to the chatter from our friends discussing their favorite for the fight. The announcers on the screen are introducing Hernandez as he walks down the tunnel toward the octagon, his opponent already inside.

Bobby leans forward and reaches for the drinks that Casey brought in for me, holding up a cider and a soda, silently asking which one. I nod toward the cider and he pops the cap off and passes it to me. He grabs one for himself and sits back to relax again.

Jimmy frowns at his brother's rudeness. "Where's mine?"

"You can go fuck yourself," Bobby replies, but without malice.

Jim scoffs and starts crawling toward the drinks, but Bobby stops him. "No seriously, these are Kit's. She brought them."

"Oh, no it's fine." I tell him, feeling shy all over again. "Help yourself, Jim. All of you can."

"Sweet." Jimmy smiles lopsidedly and grabs one. Jack's eyes light up. He takes my offer literally and leans forward, reaching for one too.

"Sit the fuck down," Bobby snaps at Jack, startling me since I was focused and getting ready to smack Jack down myself. "No underage drinking when you belong to this gym. Not ever. Not here, not anywhere else."

Jack looks up to him, then toward the other guys who all nod their heads to confirm Bobby's statement. He sits down heavy, then leans forward again and snatches a soda instead.

I don't know what the hell he's thinking. Did he honestly think I'd sit here and watch him drink? Am I such a failure in my new role that he still hasn't figured this out? I want to cry at what feels like a hopeless next few years, I want to hit him for not being smarter about his choices. I want to go back in time and make my dad better.

"Hey," Bobby whispers in my ear, and I jump in fright. "It's cool. Relax. Jack won't get into trouble when he's with any of us. We've got your back. We always will. So ..." he softly kisses my ear, then turns me to face him. He taps his bottle to mine. "Cheers."

I nod softly, then I lean into him and sip my drink.

We all sit together, sprawled all over the place and it reminds me of how my girlfriends and I would relax together at a sleepover.

Jimmy and Jack have moved toward each other, laughing and joking and goofing off. Having bounced back from his reprimand, Jack laughingly tells us how he would do a certain move differently, comparing how much better he is than the fighters on screen and declaring that he'll one day be world champion.

Aiden appears to be sitting back relaxed, but the intensity of his eyes tells me he's studying the fighters closely. Taking notes, I guess.

Jon and Casey are huddled together, their sides touching as they recline; they have their eyes on the screen, but they talk in whispers and smile a lot.

Everyone is utterly comfortable together — no awkward silences, no hosting or pretenses. Just hanging out. It's the first time in a long time that I've felt at peace, and it feels so much better because Jack's a part of it, enjoying himself without drinking, and I bask in the fact we can have honest fun together.

Bobby's still sitting in the corner on an angle, and as time passes and we relax more, he eases me further against his leg. He slings his left arm around my shoulder, pulling me closer until I'm resting entirely in the apex of his thighs with my back against his broad chest and his chin resting on the side of my forehead.

His left hand rhythmically rubs circle patterns on my bent leg, and every few minutes he'll lower his face and nuzzle my ear or neck or hair.

I could die a content woman right now.

Time seems to both stand still and zoom away from us. The fight lasts until the third minute in the third round, and was an even fight till that point, when suddenly Wheaton lands a high roundhouse kick and pops Hernandez on the chin, whipping his head around and dropping him to the canvas. Wheaton pounces onto Hernandez's back immediately and wraps his arm around his neck, then no more than twenty seconds later does Hernandez end up tapping, and suddenly we have a new champion.

Our group sit in stunned silence except for the random 'holy shit' and 'no fucking way,' the latter coming from Jack, and I roll my eyes. The fight was so consistent and not overly eventful, lulling us all into a sense of security that it wouldn't end any time soon. I guess that was Wheaton's plan all along, and he was successful in making Hernandez comfortable too, because when that roundhouse came around, it took us all by surprise.

Our group, along with the crowd on TV, were all yelling during the head lock, but when Hernandez's palm slapped the mat, we were all stunned. Silenced. I wasn't the only one who expected Hernandez to win today and I bet there will be a lot of money exchanging hands around the country from betting on the wrong guy.

I'm sad that the fight is over, because I don't want our little party to end. I wasn't prepared to leave Bobby's arms so suddenly, but as expected, like an ant's hill that was just disturbed, the other guys stand and talk a million miles a minute about the fight.

I start to move but Bobby's hand tightens on my shoulder, "Stay," he whispers. I attempt to hide my smile as I watch people disperse.

Jimmy and Jack walk toward the hanging bags while Jack asks to be shown the correct way to do a roundhouse kick. Casey and Jon walk toward the front door, talking quietly and shoulder bumping. Poor Aiden appears a little lost; he looks at us, then around the room. "I'll ah, just go over ..." Then points and walks toward the younger guys.

I giggle as he leaves, but then I melt into Bobby's chest again as he kisses my temple. I wouldn't complain if I had to stay in this position for the rest of my life. He seems pretty happy with the arrangement too, as he winds his other arm around me, cocooning me in his warmth and letting out a contented sigh that feathers across my forehead.

"I really like the feel of you in my arms right now," Bobby tells me in a low voice.

I sigh. "I really like the feel of being in your arms."

"Looks like the boys get along just fine." Bobby adds, nodding toward Jim and Jack, "No need for you to worry tomorrow night ... I mean, you could be out, say, all night, and he'd be fine."

I look up to find his big mischievous grin. "Yeah, I guess I could ...Who knows what we could get up to in all that time. Several games of mini golf, at the least."

I can feel Bobby's growing length pressing against my lower back, and suddenly we've gone from joking to urgently needing more privacy. Can a guy smell a woman's desire? Perhaps pheromones in the air? I'm pretty sure I'm producing enough that all the street dogs will come looking.

"I had fun tonight," I change the subject. "Thanks for inviting us."

He chuckles softly. "You're welcome. I'm glad you stayed. I was worried you'd already made fight night plans. Good timing on Jack's part to get grounded; he told me today you were free for the evening."

I know Bobby's just playing, trying to make me laugh, but all he succeeds in doing is reminding me about Jack's fighting. Suddenly, I'm not feeling so relaxed. "Shit. I forgot about that. How was the day? Was he good?"

"Yeah, he was good. Did everything he was told to do."

"Why was he sparring when I got here? I thought he was on cleaning duty and stuff?"

"Yeah, he was. He did heaps of cleaning, but I ran out of ideas, so just threw him in the ring. I haven't really gotten a chance to watch him yet, and I wanted to know how he goes. It must run in the family, he has talent too, just like you. I can see similarities in some of his kicks and strikes."

"Oh well, that's good … I guess."

How do I explain to Bobby that if Jack keeps pushing his luck, I couldn't possibly allow him to continue training. How could I actually follow through with my threat when I never want to stop coming here either?

"Kit?" He waits until our eyes meet again. "Don't be so hard on him, okay? I think when you talk to the school you'll find that he's not completely to blame."

My back snaps straight and I sit up quickly. "What are you talking about?"

He frowns at my quick disappearance from his lap. "It's just that, I spoke to him today. I wanted to set him straight on how we expect people who represent Rollin' to behave. And how he should treat you, since you're all he has."

I narrow my eyes at his overstepping.

"Just hear him out, okay? It's not as bad as it sounds. Well okay, he did get in a fight, which is bad, but his reasons were honorable."

"Honorable? What the f-- Jack is a teenage ass with a giant chip on his shoulder. How could he have possibly convinced you he did the right thing?"

Like the flip of a switch, I've gone from sloth-like relaxation to red hot pissed. The stress I've been under lately has worn me to nothing. I'm tired, I'm emotional, and thanks to this guy next to me, I'm hormonal. My voice is starting to rise, my emotions boiling over, and the guys littering the gym are starting to look our way.

"Hang on," Bobby says and jumps to his feet. He holds the ropes for me to climb through and follows me, then he takes my elbow and we walk down a hallway I've not been down before.

We stop in front of an office door and he gestures me inside first, and I walk in to find a desk and computer with a chair on either side. I look around and see pictures of Bobby and his brothers on the walls. Some pictures are old, the boys in their young teens, easily recognizable as the Kincaid brothers, plus Jon and Iz.

They weren't kidding — they've all known each other forever. I stop on a picture of Bobby and Jon wearing the cutest karate gi's ever. They look like they're about six years old. A baby Jimmy and a toddler aged Aiden posed in front of them. Another picture shows Bobby, aged ten or so, with a high kick suspended in the air. Another shows the four boys, early to pre-teen age, all sweaty faces and hair and grinning ear to ear.

So much love.

So much history between these guys, suddenly making me feel like the outsider that I am. That thought brings me back to the reason why we're in this room, and I'm embarrassed for bringing my drama to these good people. The anger I was feeling in the ring has now simply turned to exhaustion. Physically, as well as mental.

I'm not mad anymore, not at Bobby — I was never mad at Bobby — and I'm not mad at Jack anymore either. I'm just … tired.

"Listen Bobby." I turn from the wall of history and face him. I need to get this off my chest, then I intend to run away and cry for a little (long) while. "I want to say I'm sorry." His mouth was open, he was ready to argue with me, now he just snaps his mouth closed and frowns down at me. "I'm sorry for making a scene a few minutes ago. I embarrassed you, and I embarrassed myself, so I apologize for that. I also want to apologize for the drama with Jack. I got lazy and allowed you to deal with my problems by watching him today. It won't happen again. I'll take him home now and we'll distance ourselves. Your gym won't be connected with us in any way, so he won't be representing you … or *mis*representing you, if he gets in trouble in the future. I don't mean to sound ungrateful, because I'm not, I really appreciate everything you've done for us. I appreciate the friendship you and your brothers have given me and mine, as well as the training. I appreciate the one-on-one training you've given me, and somehow in a short time you've also turned into an ear to listen and shoulder to cry on.

"Quite beyond your pay grade, huh? Sorry about that too." I sigh as my heart stutters in my chest. "My life is just a little overwhelming right now, and I just don't have it in me to take on anything extra."

His eyes narrow and his jaw tightens. "Extra?"

"Extra…" I nod. "As in, you."

Jesus. Did I just break up with Bobby? Break up isn't the right word, since we hadn't even started anything yet, but I can't think of any other way to describe the pain coursing through my chest. Tomorrow night was supposed to be our first date, and I've ended it before it even started.

Bobby steps up close to me. He's pissed. Way pissed. "Are you done?" he snaps out. "So, you've decided, huh? You made the decision for us both? And for Jack too. You decide you're too busy for me? Like I'd be a burden?" He points at me as his jaw ticks angrily. "Did you ever stop to think I could help lessen your load? More hands make lighter work, Kit. Ever heard that?"

"But—"

"Nope, I let you speak, I heard you out. Now you'll shut up and hear me. I never said you embarrassed me, or yourself, earlier in the ring. I didn't say that, and I didn't imply it. That's on you. So what if you raised your voice? We do it all the fuckin' time around here," he shouts on the last words, and I look toward the door, worried someone will come to investigate.

"As for Jack being here today. That wasn't special treatment for him, or for you. Any fighter in this gym has to abide by a set of rules. If they break them, they pay the price. It wasn't babysitting, and it doesn't mean we're embarrassed by them. It means they broke a rule, and need to pay consequences. That's it. It'll probably happen a few more times over the years, because guess what? Teenagers are assholes. Don't let it get in the way of whatever we have here. Which, according to you, is *nothing*! Stupid me, I thought you liked me. I know I fucking like you. I want to know you. I want to take you on a date tomorrow night, possibly even touch your tits a bit, but it seems you think you get to make all the calls. Did you think I'd just sit like a good puppy and let you dump my ass before we even got started? I'm not ready to call it a day, Kit! So, you know what? I don't accept your apologies. Fuck that shit! And as an aside; that drama you think you're bringing here, with Jack fighting ... I strongly suggest you discuss that with him. He told me some stuff today that you need to know. Yeah, it's drama, it'll probably add drama to your plate, and I'm sorry for that. I'd shield you if I could, but I can't." He looks me straight in the eyes. "But you should know, he wasn't in the wrong. He faced down something potentially really difficult for him, and he stood up for the right thing even though giving in would've been easier. As for everything else you said, no, and fuck no! You will not distance yourself, not for the wrong reasons anyway. If you genuinely think this gym isn't working out for you, or you're just not interested, then go, break my heart, walk away. But if that's not true, then stop being a fucking martyr! You don't have to shoulder everything on your own."

I take a deep breath and let it out on a sigh. "Bobby. I'm sor – "

"So, I'll be expecting Jack back here tomorrow morning. Then I expect to see you for training tomorrow after work. After that, I'll come to your house to pick you up for our date. So you better be quick washing your pretty hair. I won't be late, and I refuse to waste a single minute of our evening together. Got it? *Good!*"

I bite my lip to stop the smile that fights to bloom. Big bad Bobby Kincaid just had a tantrum worthy of a three-year-old, and I don't know if I should be scared or just flat out impressed.

He stands on the opposite side of the room, facing away from me as his jaw clenches and his chest lifts and falls heavily. I bite my lip so hard it stings. But the tiniest of squeaks escapes my lips, then I dissolve into all out giggles. I'm dead. I can't even. *"Got it?"* I fall into a fit of laughter. *"Good!"*

Bobby turns back to look at me as I transition from laughter to hysteria, which makes me laugh even more. The stress of this past year has me bubbling over into crazy town. I've officially lost the plot, but then his own lips transform from scowl to smile and I hold my stomach from the pain my laughter causes. "Fuck it, Bobby. Don't fight it. Ride the high," I snort as tears escape from my eyes. The crazy snickering breaks him, and Bobby crosses over to the dark side and laughs too.

Fuck it, fuck it all.

"Look, I'll say it again," I tell him, hiccupping and trying to get myself under control, "I'm sorry, Bobby. But this time I'm just sorry for trying to blow you off. It wasn't personal. I don't mean to make excuses, but I have stuff, beyond Jack, which is beating me down right now. I'm tired and stressed and I took it out on you. You're right, everything you said was right. So yeah okay, we'll be back tomorrow. And maybe I'll let you touch my boobs sometime."

"Oh my god," Bobby cries out and laughs. "I can't believe I yelled that I wanted to touch your boobs. Who does that?" He dramatically throws his arms in the air. "I mean, I was thinking it, I'm always thinking it, but I shouldn't shout it at you!"

At a knock at the office door, we both turn and watch as Jimmy pokes his head in and Jack bobs around in an attempt to look over his shoulder. I continue to snicker, and I lean against Bobby's strong shoulder.

"What's going on? I heard Bobby having a tantrum."

Jimmy's description of Bobby's behavior has me snorting all over again. I try and stop it, I know it's not ladylike, but it just won't stop. All three guys watch my breakdown with smirks on their faces.

Casey squeezes by Jimmy and Jack easily, like water moving through rocks, and she walks right in and stops in front of me. "Well, I'm happy to hear that sound."

The smile on her face has me smiling even more, and I realize we haven't done much of this lately. I've probably worried her these last few months, gaining weight, always stressed and tired. Shit. I've been taking her support for granted. "Shit Case, I'm sorry!"

She frowns, bringing her hands up to my face, she thumbs a tear away. "What are you talking about? Sorry for what?"

"Sorry for being a miserable cow. Sorry for taking you for granted."

"Oh honey, don't cry. You've got nothing to be sorry for. We're sisters, and sisters always lift each other up." She swipes another tear, then a third. "You've always been there for me, and now it's my turn." Her green eyes turn soft as she frowns. "I came in here to join in the crazy laughter, not to make you cry! Jesus Kit, lemme hear you laugh."

"Maybe you should squeeze her boobs," Jimmy suggests hopefully. My eyes snap to his in shock. I forgot he was here. I forgot anyone was here except Casey. Oh my god, I just cried in front of everyone.

Jimmy's goofy grin turns down as Bobby steps out from behind me and moves toward him, but his terrified eyes have me laughing again. I can't believe he just talked about my boobs. "Oh god! Did you hear everything we said?"

He looks past Bobby and smiles at me. "Well yeah, he was yelling, which happens, but then I heard boobs, so came to look."

I look to a blushing Bobby, and my snorting begins all over again.

Tonight has turned out to be exactly what I needed. Laughter is the best medicine, and good friends feed my soul. I'm feeling lighter and happier than I have in months. I feel full of energy; not the usual sleepy dread I'm used to feeling lately.

Casey smiles and takes my hand in hers. "Ah, there she is."

~*~

The next morning, I'm hopping around my kitchen with one heel on, the other in my hand, and half a slice of toast in my mouth. We're not late yet, but by the time we get out the door and I drop Jack off at the gym, I will be.

I rush from the kitchen and stop at the bottom of the stairs. "Jack! Let's go!" Then I turn and run head first into his broad chest. "Shit!"

He smiles his dimply smile. "Stop yelling, I'm right here."

"Dammit, you scared the crap outta me. Have you eaten? Are you ready to go?"

He nods and sits on the bottom stairs to lace his shoes. "Yep, I'm good to go. I ate while you were in the shower."

"Okay, cool." I step into my second heel and run a hand over my dress. It's black and sleeveless, and in no way revealing; the neckline sits only an inch or so below my throat, and the hem an inch above my knees, but despite it being really quite tame and boring, it fits my body well and always makes me feel nice.

We're driving along the main street when Jack clears his throat awkwardly. "So, ah, did Bobby tell you I get to shadow them today, training instead of cleaning?"

I frown. "No, he didn't say. That's a strange punishment."

"Yeah, well, I guess I wanted to talk to you about that. Bobby thinks it's important I tell you, you know, so we're on the same page. A team and all that shit …"

I appreciate Bobby encouraging teamwork between Jack and me, but I'm actually kind of terrified to know the details of the fight. Bobby assures me Jack was in the right, but that it would still be stressful to hear. It would be especially unwise to try to bury my head in the sand, considering all the lawyer trouble, but damn, it's tempting. I don't want more. I'm already almost completely sunk. I sigh as we turn a corner, then steeling myself, I nod. "Tell me."

"So, yeah, I hit someone, and I initiated it, sort of. I hit Chris, as in dickeater's boyfriend."

Jesus. That's it. I'm done. I want to lay down and die. It couldn't be any worse. "Why, Jack? Why the hell would you do that? I thought you got along with them?"

"Yeah, well I did, I do, I used to."

"Why was he even there? I thought he dropped out years ago."

Jack shrugs. "He did. I don't know why he was there, except to talk to me."

I'm pissed that Chris had access to Jack long enough to even get into an argument. I'll be sure to address that on Monday. In the meantime, I work on my breathing. I can't die today. I can't die today. I can't -- I look up and nod. "Okay, keep going. What did he say that made you hit him?"

"Well, it's just that …" He winces then looks away.

"Jack?"

"Okay. Well, basically he said some things about you, some mean things, and kept banging on about how I should move in with them, or Aunt Lees or Aunt Renee. Basically, just that I should move out of your house …"

Those fucking assholes! Those fuckers are doing their best to screw me legally, but now they'll just corners and have him to make the decision for them. I fantasize for a minute how nice it'd feel to run them all down with my car. Unfortunately, if I do that, then I'll lose Jack anyway.

I sigh. I'll call my lawyer when I get to work… Or on second thought, I'll email. That way it's all in writing, and I can edit all the curse words out before I hit send.

Goddamit! It costs me money every single damn time my lawyers read and reply to emails.

"Anyway, I told Chris to leave the school grounds, but he wanted to make trouble and wouldn't go. In the end, because I wouldn't agree with him, he ah, he …" Jack closes his eyes as though it pains him to tell me. "He called you a … fat … club rat … whore." He refuses to meet my gaze. "That's when I hit him."

"Shit Jack, I'm sorry that happened." I slow the car down as I take deep breaths in and out. "I'm sorry you had to deal with that. Considering you don't actually like me a lot of the time, I appreciate you standing up for me …"

His eyes snap to mine in surprise. "I do like you, Kit. I know we've had a shitty time so far, but that's on me. I promise to be better. I get it now; no chick in her twenties wants a teenage kid, so I appreciate what you do for me, even when I'm a dick and forget to tell you."

"Oh, well," my heart beats heavily as my little brother heals just about every wound he's ever inflicted on me with one single sentence. I smile over at him. "I appreciate that, but listen, there's some stuff you need to know…" I pull into the gym parking lot and turn the car off, then resigned to being late, I turn to him. "Umm, so I probably should have told you this earlier. Lisa and Renee, for some reason, are having their lawyers fight mine. For custody, of you."

His eyes grow wide. "Why? It's not like I'm five and can be fought over. Pretty sure I'm old enough to choose myself."

"Yeah well, I'm not sure what their game is. I'm confused too. I don't know why they're fighting so hard, but they are. In the meantime, I'm still working on Dad's estate, trying to get it settled. Maybe after that, they'll piss off."

"Jesus." He scrubs his hands over his face in frustration. "I'm sorry for being an asshole. Especially …" He nods. "You know. I'm sorry I was so horrible."

"It's okay. I appreciate the apology though." I smile softly and look over at him. "Hopefully we can be better from now on."

He chuckles and unsnaps his seatbelt. "Ha yeah, we'll work on that." He opens his door, but I grab his arm before he jumps out.

"Wait. I got mad at you the other day without even hearing your side of the story. So, I'm sorry."

"This is getting weird, all this *I'm sorry, you're sorry* stuff, it's giving me the creeps." He climbs out of the car with a laugh. "I'll see you this afternoon."

I smile and nod. I can't even blame him for getting weird and running away. He got his stealthy avoidance skills from me. I drive out of the lot and head for work, and I arrive at my office officially thirty minutes late. I sit down quickly and write my email while all the details are clear.

And the rage.

I tell them what Jack told me, word for word, and ask them to look into it, then I add my signature and hit send. It felt somewhat cathartic getting that written down, like I released the anger with the words, and the act of sending it off made it my lawyers' problem for now.

My phone beeps near my arm, and I look down to a text from an unknown number. *What did I do wrong this time?*

Me: Who is this?

Unknown: -_-

M: Bobby? That face actually looks like you. Hold on, lemme save your number.

Bobby: Go ahead, keep pretending that you didn't already have it memorized.

M: Saved. Now what do you mean, what did you do wrong?

B: You didn't come in and say Hi this morning. I saw you drop Jack off, but I got nothing, not even a boob grab :'(

M: Cutesy faces; you're one of those *people, huh?*

B: ;P don't change the subject.

M: Yeah, so it's confirmed. Not sure we can continue… seeing each other. The text faces kinda make me angry.

B: :) I'm gonna use them more, just for you. In fact, I might google and learn more.

M: So what did you want?

M: ????????

M: Bobby?

B: Hold on. Still googling.

M: Bobby!

B: Sorry. Mostly I just wanted to say Hi. I was prepared to see you this morning, I even brushed my hair, and nothing. Where's the love?

M: Sorry. I was running late. Hi! Jack and I talked this morning...

B: Oh yeah? Cleared the air? Everyone ok?

M: Yes, to all of the above.

B: I'm glad. Since you're not mad at him anymore, it means I won't have to be mad at him either. I ran out of things for him to clean!

M: Nice try. He already told me that he gets to shadow you today. Wouldn't shut up about it.

B: Damn. I better find time today to have a bro's code chat.

M: Huh?

B: It's understandable that he doesn't know yet, since he only has a sister, but there are expectations now that he's one of us; #1 don't tell the womenfolk everything. :P

M: I wanna send you a text face right now. Picture this; narrowed eyes, flat mouth, exclamation point!

B: Oooooh, scary ; D

M: Ah well, if you're only here to be a pest, I have work to do.

B: :'(

M: Have a good day, Bobby.

B: Fine, if you must. Have a good day Kitty. I'll see you this afternoon. xx

M: Bye :)

B: .... *waiting*

M: ?

B: I sent you two kisses...

M: ....

B: ....

M: xx

B: :D x

I throw my phone down with a giant grin stretching across my face, then I look to my computer and realize I'm now an hour late. I have to get a lot of work done between now and five, because there's no way in hell I'm working late tonight.

My day flies by as I immerse myself in budgets and arguing with department heads, but I switch my computer off at five-thirty feeling accomplished and ready to tackle the next portion of my day.

Training.

I arrive at the gym with spare clothes and snacks for Jack, with about fifteen minutes to spare before class starts.

Tonight, I'll be joining Aiden's class - my first ever group session, and I'm more than a little nervous. So far Bobby's the only one who's seen me train, and I'm nervous about meeting new people.

I head through the entrance of the gym in search of Jack to deliver his things, and I find him silently standing with Bobby and Jimmy, as the Kincaids bend over the reception desk and discuss something they see on an iPad.

I creep closer as quietly as I can, but as soon as I'm within a few feet, Bobby stands abruptly and turns toward me with a smile stretching his face. "Hey Babe, we were waiting for you."

I frown. "You were? How'd you know I was here?"

He taps his temple with a silly smirk. "I know everything."

Jim laughs as he turns and leans back against the counter. "Hey Kitty. You look good. I've had a long hard day at work, wanna give me some sugar?" He makes a stupid kissy face and I laugh. Bobby's eyes narrow and he snaps, "Fuck off, Jim," at the same time Jack complains "gross."

The Kincaids both snap their faces toward Jack in disgust. "Not Gross!"

I just laugh at them and point toward the tablet on the desk. "What were you guys watching? Why were you waiting for me?"

Bobby looks at me warily, "Actually we wanted to discuss something with you."

I look around the group of guys as they watch me nervously. Jack looks flat out scared, and I worry that he somehow got in trouble today. "Okay, so talk …"

"Alright. Well, we were watching some amateur fights. Every quarter, we send students to compete in what we call a *development day*. It's basically competitive fighting, but for the beginners. It's full body protection: head gear, shin pads, gloves, mouth guard, the lot. The competitors are all beginners, none have had more than five fights. Once you've had five, win, lose, or draw, you get moved away from the development day tournaments and into proper competition."

"Okay …"

"Well," he smiles charmingly. "We wanna enter Jack."

"Jack? But -- huh …" My first instinct is to say 'hell no,' but then I stop at Jack's fallen face and I reconsider. "When is it?"

"In a little over three weeks," Jimmy answers seriously. That might be the first time I've ever heard him speak without joking or sexual innuendo. I giggle at the absurdity.

"What?"

"Nothing, never mind. Is three weeks enough time? He only just started here."

Bobby steps forward hopefully. "Remember it's just a beginner thing. It'll be the same as sparring here, just with a bit more excitement. He won't be competing against some pro, just another teenager with the same experience and same weight. He won't get hurt, I promise."

"Alright …" I look toward Jack, "do you *want* to compete?"

He smiles a full dimple popping smile. "Yeah! It would be so cool. The thing is, it costs twenty-five bucks to enter, and I need my own gear ..." His face falls almost like it's a lost cause already.

"But don't worry about that," Bobby adds. "We have a fundraising committee here at the gym. Students' moms get together and raise funds for these exact things. Tournament fees, travelling, that sorta stuff. So his entry fee is covered, and we can either lend him gloves and gear, or he can work for it to buy some from us, though we recommend the second, since he'll be wanting his own gear eventually."

"Okay well," I look from face to face, "if you guys think he's ready, and if you want to, Jack, then sure. Why not?"

Jack's eyes light up. "Really?"

"Yeah, sure. But don't worry about the money and stuff. We'll get you your own gear. We'll work out the details later."

"Really?" he asks again, and stares at me like I have a second head.

I laugh. "Do you *want* me to say no? Remember our talk this morning; we're working on being better, yeah? Plus, you stood up for me, and I feel kinda feel guilty for getting mad at you about it."

He stares at me a minute more, then a smile stretches from ear to ear. "Whoop!" He dashes through the gym toward the locker room, and I just laugh at him.

"Okay, sweet." Jim smiles. "I'm glad that's sorted." He quickly steps forward and slaps a wet kiss on my cheek, then bolts off in the direction Jack ran.

I laugh and use Jack's spare shirt to wipe my face, then I finally stop and take a minute to study Bobby as he stands thee scowling after his brother. He's wearing one of his sexy muscle tanks today and red and black shorts that go to his knees. His shirt teases me with bits and pieces of tattooed skin, that despite my best ogling efforts, I still haven't been able to study fully.

He stands in front of me, bare feet, like he is ninety-nine percent of the time when he's here. His hair is damp and curling at the ends, and the longer bits almost touch his jaw. God, he's pretty, with his eyes of melted chocolate, and devil's smirk. My heart thumps faster as I think of the date we're going on in a few short hours.

"You like what you see?"

I laugh, surprisingly less embarrassed this time at being caught. "Yeah. Were you all freaking out waiting to ask me?"

"Oh shit," he laughs. "Jack totally was. He thought for sure you'd say no. He was wetting his pants waiting for you to get here." Bobby steps closer and takes a loose section of my hair, twirling it around his fingers, and resting his hand against my collarbone.

My skin feels hot as hades and tingles at the contact. He ducks his head an inch lower to catch my eyes. "Not me though, you're the least scary person I know. Softer than a kitten."

My skin breaks out in goosebumps at his nearness, but I swallow heavily and clear my throat. "I can be scary."

He shakes his head as his breath bathes my face. "Nah."

Focus! "But he really wants to do it, right?"

"Yeah, he does." He smiles down at me and backs up half an inch to give me breathing space. "And what's more, I think he'll smash them. He's huge, and has natural talent. I mean, he'll still be a beginner, he won't have the best moves or combos, but I guarantee you he'll have enough to win. If he sticks it out, he'll be fucking amazing."

"I'm not entirely sure how I feel about that. It's one thing to send him to an amateur fun day, but another entirely to let him work up to adult fights."

"Well, once he gets a taste of competition, there'll be no stopping him. So you should prepare yourself for a lifetime of ringside seats and heart attacks."

I roll my eyes. "Oh goodie. I'm happy that he's really enjoying this though. Before we came here, he was bored, and when he's bored..." he gets into trouble.

"You can send him straight here after school if you want. He doesn't have to wait for you to finish work. We can use that time for him to earn his classes and stuff. A busy kid doesn't have time for trouble."

"Really?"

"Sure. Send him, he's not a burden to us, just another one of the guys.

I reach out and touch Bobby's arm, and his eyes snap to the movement as the muscles in his forearm bunch and twitch under my hand. "I appreciate that, Bobby. Just let me know if it does become a problem and I'll yank him. Also, since you mentioned it, I'll pay the entry fee and stuff. I'm not poor or anything -- "

"Nah, it's cool. Honest, we almost always tap the fundraising committee for comp fees. He'll have to pay for his own gear, but don't bother buying him anything except gloves and a mouth guard. Everything else is temporary stuff that he won't need in the long run, so he can just borrow ours."

"You're sure?"

"Definitely. He'll only use shin pads and head gear for the beginner fights. After that he won't need them. If he's consistent here, he'll have his development days done by next year, and won't need that stuff once he turns sixteen."

"Alright, thanks. I'll take him shopping for gloves this weekend. May as well get them sooner rather than later then, if I'm gonna buy them anyway."

"Sounds good. You should buy your own gloves too. You must be sick of using the communal set by now. They're permanently soaked in sweat and stink. Pretty gross. But then again, you could use mine if you want." He bites his lip and ducks his head lower. "I could picture you wearing *only* them. That'd be hot. I wouldn't mind covering you with my sweat." He laughs. "Actually, I think that's an evolution thing, like pissing on you."

I laugh at him. "I'll buy my gloves when I buy Jack's. No need to pee on people."

He tsks and shakes his head. "You're missing out."

"Whatever. I have to go to class now, so I'll see you later," I start walking away, but stop and turn back "Oh, before I forget, where are we going for dinner?"

"It's a surprise, why?"

"A surprise?" I laugh. "As in, you haven't planned anything yet, have you?"

"I have too!" He almost looks hurt that I'd accuse him of such a heinous crime. "Really, I have. Why do you ask?

"I just wanna know how hard I have to work out, you know, to offset the calories."

Bobby snorts. "You should give one hundred percent every time, Catherine. Doesn't matter about what you're eating later. Earn it every time."

I sigh. "Fine, thanks for your wisdom, Mr. Miagi. Catch ya later."

He walks toward me, then slaps my ass as he walks past. "Bye, Kitten. I'll see you soon."

12

Bobby

It's Date Night!

I had to take a group class tonight, which meant no personal session with Kit. Disappointment washed over me when Jon showed me the class schedule, but in the end I decided it might be best, you know, to build anticipation for our date.

I'm on my way to Kit's house now to pick her up, an hour after class ended, just as I promised. Perhaps threatened is a better word. I made a table reservation at Club 188 since it's the nicest club in town and the food is good. It's not as fancy as some of the restaurants we have, but the dress code is flexible and I figured it'd be more comfortable for us than a stuffy five-star place where we couldn't even sit beside each other.

I've swapped out my training shorts and tank for a shower and a fitted black shirt under an unbuttoned T-shirt, and my comfy black jeans with the 'trendy' fraying that they have these days. I'm wearing my black and white high tops, since they're comfortable as fuck, and I went with less is more in the hair styling department, just towel drying it and running a hand through. Done.

My favorite band plays through my stereo, pumping my excitement at what tonight may bring. I've been so fucking anxious for this day, anticipating *finally* having some alone time with Kit. I'm terrified at the depth of my feelings for her. She could smash me beyond recognition; the fact she almost bailed on me before even giving us a chance, broke me a little bit each time I had to plead my case.

If she'd just try, jump with me, I just know we could be amazing.

I blatantly lied to Kit's face today, and I'm not sure if I should be sorry, or embarrassed. I told her she doesn't scare me, which is the biggest load of shit to ever cross my lips. She's the *only* thing in this world that scares me.

Never has anyone had the kind of control over me that she has - or *could* have, if only she cared to pull my strings. She's not the type to purposely lead someone around, but if she did, I'd follow her anywhere. I've tried my hardest to make her comfortable, to lessen her nerves around me. I want her comfortable, I want her to lean on me, rely on me, to seek comfort and strength from me.

I'd give her anything—she only has to ask.

I pull up at her house behind Jimmy's Jeep and I roll my eyes at how at home he makes himself.

We agreed he'd meet me here and he'd hang out with Jack. I actually trust Jack to do the right thing. He's been a rebellious shit in the past, but I think deep down he's a good person, and with his teenage wisdom came the realization that although Kit's older, as the man of the house he's now responsible for her safety and happiness. Fuck if I don't respect the hell out him for that. He's fifteen and has lapses in judgment, but he's shaping up to be a good man, and I guarantee his and Kit's unique situation and Kit's guidance is directly responsible for the way he is now.

Though whether I trust him or not, if it makes Kit feel better that Jimmy 'supervises' tonight, and since I know neither Jimmy nor Jack mind the company, I made it happen. I'd do anything to make her happy.

I unfold myself from my car and walk up the front path, and I lift my hand to knock, but Jimmy opens the door before I get the chance.

"Hey, thanks for meeting me here." I try to walk through the doorway, but he steps in front of me, blocking my way and smirking.

What. Tha Fuck.

"Hey. How's it going?" he asks, oh so casual. "Nice hair."

I narrow my eyes at him. "Wanna get out of my way?"

"Fuck no. You're here to take my girl out on a date?"

"Your girl? The fuck you talking about?"

He winks at me before continuing; he fucking winks! "Yeah, you see, I'm in this house right now, and as the man of the house, you need to get past me to get to her. What's the magic word, Bobby?"

I can't do this. Not tonight. Any other time I'd probably find it funny, but not tonight — I've been waiting forever to get to this point. "Fuck off, Jim."

I push past him, popping him in the ribs on the way and forcing him to fold over double. The sound of his whooshing breath actually lightens my mood and I laugh.

"I'll always be your big brother, Jimmy. Don't fuck with me." I turn around to face him and I return his wink. "And don't get in-between me and *my* girl."

He laughs as I walk away, then I walk into the kitchen to find Jack popping a soda. Tink walks down the stairs, fluttering about the way she does with a giant smile. "Well, hey there, good lookin.'"

"Hey Tink. How's it going?"

To my surprise, she doesn't even flinch at her nickname this time. Maybe she's decided to accept it, and accept that it'll be around for as long as I am, which makes my smile grow. I plan to be around for a long time.

She's a brave little thing, walking right up and kissing me on the cheek–after she grabs my shirt and pulls me down. I'm well over a foot taller than her, the top of her head below my pecs. I'm surprised by her forwardness, but return her hug and smile down at her.

"It's good to see a friendly face, Tink."

"I'll always be a friendly face — as long as she smiles, I smile."

I don't know exactly what's happening between her and Jon, but he'd be lucky to have her. Just as she'd be lucky to have him. Fuck if I don't approve of that potential relationship.

"Casey!"

We all look toward the stairs at Kit calling voice, and my heart thumps heavily at being so near her.

Tink rolls her eyes and shouts back, "What?"

"Come up here, I need help with something."

"Can't. I'm greeting your sexy guest."

We hear a thud and some swearing. "Bobby's here? Shit." I can hear her stomping–hopping?–around, then some more muffled curses. "I'll be down in a sec …"

"That's okay." Tink smiles at me. "I'll keep him and his sexy brother company while we wait."

Jimmy leans against the counter with food he swiped from Kit's fridge, and he blows noisy kisses her way

"Casey!"

Tink jumps to action. "Coming. Cheezus Crust woman, don't get your panties in a twist!"

With a wicked smirk, she turns back to me and murmurs quietly, "Or maybe do. Then Bobby might help you untangle them. That'll make everyone happier."

She runs upstairs, leaving the three of us standing in silence. Jimmy eats completely at ease, while Jack and I pretend that this isn't awkward. He continues to look up at me, his face part angry, part scared, part nauseous.

I'm already strung out with nerves, I can't take anything else. "Alright, fess up Jack. What's on your mind?"

He swallows heavily. "Umm, well, I wanted to talk to you."

"So talk."

"Shit ... fuck ..." He rubs his hand across his face in frustration as Jimmy watches with a lifted brow. "Well okay, I know our situation's weird, mine and Kit's, that is, and I know you're technically my ... superior?" he tests the word out as he gathers his thoughts.

"Okay..."

"Well--" he stops and looks to Jim, then back to me again. He groans. "Okay. I just wanna know ... your intentions," he mumbles. He bolsters and looks me square in the eye. "I wanna know that you'll treat her well."

Jim, being Jim, lets out a whoop of laughter and slaps Jack on the shoulder. "He's asking if you're gonna bump and run, B."

I nod. Yeah, I got that much. "Alright Jim, fuck off."

"But -- "

"Beat it. Jack and have to talk."

"But I wanna listen in --" He scowls. "Fine, you're both being too damn sensitive. Don't talk too long, your periods might sync up." He leaves the kitchen on a whine, then he turns into the front entrance and stomps up the stairs. Trust him to make himself at home so casually.

Jack watches me as his face burns red, and though I'd like to run far away from this shit, I know it was seriously brave of him to question me.

"Just forget I said anything, okay?"

"Nah, we won't forget it. I respect your question, Jack. I respect the fact that you asked me." I take a couple steps away as I think, then back again and I stop. "I *intend* to get to know

your sister. I *intend* to pursue a friendship with her, and …
hopefully something more."

Jesus, this feels so much weirder than if it were a father
asking about his daughter's boyfriend. A dad thinks his little
girl's too good for anyone. A brother, a fifteen-year-old, thinks
his sister's gross and is weirded out by the prospect of anyone
taking an interest. "Anyway, my intentions are honorable. I'll
never intentionally hurt her. I'll treat her well. I want her to be
happy, and I hope I'm able to be that for her …" I stop and
look into his eyes. "You should know, I know that asking me
was probably pretty fucking scary, and although you're the
younger sibling, I admire your protectiveness. I respect that,
Jack. And I respect you."

He stares in silence for a few long moments, and I can
almost literally feel the awkwardness in the air between us.
He shifts his weight from one foot to the other, then finally, he
looks up and nods his head. "Good talk."

He bolts out of the room, and I laugh quietly. Someone
should acknowledge how fucking scary that was for me too. I
hope to never repeat the shit again.

I hear stomping around at the top of the stairs, and I
walk out with waves of nerves and giddiness washing
through my belly. Jimmy's feet are the first I see, then the
stupid grin still on his face. "I saw your girlfriend in her
panties."

I don't even get a chance to hit him before Casey
follows close behind and swats him on the back of the head.
"No, he didn't."

"Seriously I did. She's wearing a black lacy thing with
little kittens printed on."

Tink just rolls her eyes. "He's lying."

Once he gets to the bottom of the stairs, I walk forward and I slam my fist down on his shoulder. "Don't ever talk about Kit's panties again or I'll knock you the fuck out,"

Tink laughs as Jimmy massages the ball of his shoulder and cusses me out. He'll learn, eventually. He's had far too much fun as far as Kit's concerned, and I'm ready to start some beat downs. Every time we're all together, he either makes me look like a bitch, or he flirts and kisses her. If I can barely touch her, then he definitely can't.

My spine tingles with awareness, and I look up just as Kit reaches the landing on the stairs. I'm frozen to the spot. Call it cliché or whatever you want, but I'm frozen, speechless, staring at the utter beauty standing before me. My heart tumbles in my chest, and I think it terrifies me.

At least, it should.

I've gotten used to seeing her hair in fancy buns for work or messy ponies for training, but tonight it hangs loose, the way I saw it the night I met her. It reaches down to her elbows almost, her blonde hair in beautiful smooth curls bouncing against her back and shoulders as she descends. Her eyes look amazing; they've done something with makeup to make the blue stand out so much more. Her eyes, always so big and beautiful, are now highlighted and appear as innocent as Bambi's.

Shit, this girl is trouble.

I look down and study her dress; it's black with a high neckline and capped sleeves. It covers her chest completely, and cinches in at the waist before it flares at the hip. The kind of dress a little girl would spin circles in, just to see the skirts fly. The hem stops mid-thigh—mid-wonderful, toned, sexy, tanned thigh. My eyes follow the line of legs that go on forever, noting a few light bruises on her shins that are typical for a fight sport, and stop at sexy black heels that have some kind of black ribbon twisting around her ankles.

Suddenly, I'm uncomfortably trying to stop thinking of fucking her with those heels digging into my back or resting on my shoulders.

Fuck! Fuck, fuck, fuck. Grandmas. Puppies. Babies. Our old postman. Kittens. Fuck, not kittens!

I must have been quiet too long, because Kit clears her throat nervously. "Hey. Am I dressed wrong? I didn't know where we were going, so I wasn't sure -- "

"No, you look good-- " I squeak on the last word. I fucking squeak! "Great. You look great."

"It's not too much?"

She looks good. Long and lean. Sexy. "I promise, you look perfect ... You look amazing."

"Well, I think you look hot, Kitty Cat," Jimmy throws in, and I don't even hit him this time. I mean, it's the truth. She looks at him and smiles her kind, motherly smile that she uses on Jack, and I'm comforted to know she's securely put him in the kid brother zone. Sucks to be him.

I offer her my arm. "Let's go?"

I don't want to waste a single second of my night with her. I love my family, but I don't want to see them right now.

"Sure." Kit slides her arm into the crook of mine, her side brushing against mine, her breast lightly touching my arm, her perfume filling my senses, and I feel giddy at having her by my side tonight.

"Well, you whippersnappers, you have fun tonight. Be home before the porch lights come on."

I roll my eyes at Jimmy, and flip him the bird behind Kit's back, then I lead her to my Rav and wait for her to climb in to the raised cab as elegantly as her dress and shoes allow.

Closing the door, I run around to the driver's side, and I climb in and just sit for a moment. She meets my gaze with a soft dimply smile, and my heart hammers in my chest. She's smiling. She's happy to be here with me. The weight of the evening sits on my shoulders and the pressure is terrifying.

I know we've only known each other for a little while, but I feel as though I've been waiting my whole life for this girl. I've never felt the urge to date before, as in dinner, talking, spending time together. I was content to dance and drink, then take her home for some fun. And the girl at the time always seemed happy with that arrangement. But from the moment I laid my eyes on Kit, sad and sitting alone in a club, something inside me changed. I feel it in my gut—this is important, and I'll do anything to make her happy.

I'm not happy anymore unless she is. My goals don't seem to matter anymore, just her. My mom and brothers are still immensely important to me, but it's as if the entire order on the totem pole of my life dropped down a peg, specifically to make room for Kit at the top.

I grab her hand and bring it to my mouth, and I kiss the top softly. "You look beautiful tonight, just so you know."

She blushes, but smiles. "Thank you."

I lay her hand back in her lap, then a moment later, we're pulling out of her driveway and heading toward town. My music is still loud, so I reach out to turn it off.

"No. I like this song, leave it on."

I'm impressed. "You know this?"

"Sure. I love Fort Minor. They're great to work out to. They always made me run harder, faster ... further."

I look at her out the corner of my eye as we drive. "You used to run a lot?"

"Yeah ... I ran track when I was younger, then again in my late teens. It was therapeutic. It was nice alone time, and listening to angry rap pumped me up."

"Why don't you run anymore?"

After a long pause and a deep sigh, she replies, "November last year I fell and injured my knee. I don't really know why or what exactly happened. I was just running and it made this horrible snap noise and I fell. I mean, we thought I'd torn my ACL, but thankfully, it wasn't that bad. Dislocation, a bit of a sprain, stretched tendons, but really, best outcome. It could've been worse. But it hurt so much, so fucking much. I wore a brace for a couple months, and still wear it every now and again when it's sore. That same month, my dad was diagnosed with cancer, and I just haven't gotten back. I didn't have time when he was sick, and I have even less time now."

"Does it bother you when we train now? Your knee?" I clarify.

"Yeah, a little bit, especially when we do take downs."

"You didn't write it down in the medical section of your gym forms." I know that for a fact, because I read her forms a million times. I don't like that she omitted this information. I don't want her to injure herself more, as her trainer, and as someone who cares about her on a personal level.

"I dunno, I feel like it's not a very legitimate injury, you know. It was only a sprain …"

"If it hurts you, if it worries you, if it's in your history, you should've told us. Why don't you wear your brace at training?"

"Didn't want to draw attention to it, I guess."

I scowl at her. Typical martyr. "I want you to wear it from now on. No point in hurting yourself again and actually tearing the muscle … genius."

She smiles and salutes obnoxiously. "Sure thing, boss."

I shake my head as we pull up at the parking lot next to the club, then I climb out and run to her side, pulling her door open and instantly being met with her silky thighs.

She turns to climb out, but I stop her. I just want to look a little longer. She slides her body around, her legs facing the door, and I step in front of her, placing my hands on each thigh, open palmed.

She watches me as I slowly slide my hand from the hemline of her dress down to her knees, then I look up in question. Which knee is injured? Shyly, she puts her hand over mine covering her left knee, and after a moment of caressing it, I lean down and press my lips against her skin.

Hovering a moment longer, I hear her sigh and I look up to see love in her eyes.

Wait, love? No. Do I *want* her to love me? Do *I* love her? I couldn't possibly. I hardly know her, we've kissed only a couple times, haven't even made love yet. Fuck, there's that word again!

I don't know what to call it, but I do know that when she's happy, I'm happy. When she's near, I feel at peace. I'm comfortable leaving it at that for now, and happy to see where it takes us. The rest terrifies me.

I place a quick kiss on her lips, then taking her hand and helping her from the car, I throw my arm over her shoulder and pull her in tight and we walk inside.

It's pretty busy tonight, and I smile, realizing it's a good thing I know people in high places– Tink –who made sure we had a reservation for tonight, and thankfully, we're led to our table immediately.

To my immense satisfaction, we're seated in a booth in a dark corner at the back, the alcove with a narrowed opening, and giving us the most privacy possible in a public place.

Thank you, Tink.

I put my hand out to indicate for Kit to slide in first, and I thoroughly enjoy watching her attempts to scoot gracefully. I slide in next and throw my arm over her shoulder. We're finally here, so I'll be sitting as close as stalker laws allow.

A skinny hipster looking waiter walks up to our table, with tight black jeans and a trendy haircut. His lip and eyebrow piercings twinkle in the light as he smiles at Kit. "Welcome to Club 188. Can I get you something to drink?"

He stares at her for a long time, almost as though I'm not even here, and I tighten my hold on her. Fuck no, fuck face. She looks at me with a soft smirk, then back to our waiter. "Vodka and orange, please."

"And I'll have a beer."

I turn back to Kit and dismiss him, and she looks at me with flushed cheeks when he walks away. "That was weird."

"The waiter?"

"Yeah, he stared, like, into my soul," she laughs

I let out a deep breath as her giggle relieves the tension coiled in my chest. "Yeah, can't blame the guy though. Did you look in the mirror before you left your room?"

"Ha, funny guy, yeah I looked."

"So we're all on the same page, then," I smirk, then add, "You look amazing, Kit, and I intend to make sure everyone knows you're with me. Can't let these fuckers get any funny ideas about my girl."

She laughs, she doubts my words, but I'll make her believe. I'm determined and I won't stop trying.

The waiter returns with our drinks a few minutes later, and he literally doesn't even look at Kit this time. I watch him closely to make sure. Message received loud and clear.

He clears his throat awkwardly as he takes out a pen and notepad. "Are you ready to order?"

Kit hastily picks her menu up, then orders the very first thing she must see, and I order a steak and hand him the menus in dismissal. He walks away as she picks her drink up and sips, then puts it back down, carefully placing it on the napkin. She's nervous again.

"Okay …" I begin, drawing her gaze back to mine, "what other music do you like? Last time we spoke here, we discussed romance novels, so a simultaneous love for Fort Minor surprises me."

She smiles and plays with the condensation on her glass. "I don't know, I guess I don't slot into any one category. I never have. I like romance, I like rap. I like being lazy, I like running. I like sweet, I like savory. I guess that makes me fickle," she laughs. "I listen to Taylor Swift, but I also listen NWA. I love all sorts of music. There's a song for every mood, you know. It calms me."

"I get that. Music helps me too. Keeps me calm. Helps me relax. Or alternatively, hypes me up for a fight."

Her eyes snap wide, twinkling and mischievous. "Wait, do you have a song when entering the octagon?"

I laugh. "I do, actually." And she's already, unknowingly, nailed it.

"Let me guess."

I nod and relax into my seat. "Okay, go ahead."

"Is it Fight Song by Rachel Platten?" She bites her lip in an attempt to keep a straight face, but fails miserably when she snorts at my expression. "No? Okay, is it Christina Aguilera's Fighter?"

"No, you dork. The word 'fight' doesn't have to be in the title you know."

"Okay, I'm sorry." She's not sorry at all. "Is it 'Eye of the Tiger'?" Her face turns beet red from trying to hold herself together. The hand I was using before to trace circles on her thigh, I now use to squeeze her near her knee, and she's scrambles away laughing.

"Don't! I'm ticklish!" She slaps my hand away and wheezes with laughter. I file that new scrap of information away for another day – ticklish knee. Got it. I don't even care that she's making fun of me. I just love seeing those dimples.

"Sorry! I'm sorry, please, don't tickle me." She tries to catch her breath and continues to snicker. "Okay, I have no idea. You tell me, what's your song?"

"No, I don't think I will. You don't deserve to know."

"Oh, please?" She exaggeratedly flutters her eye lashes and laughs again. "Pretty, pretty please?" Fuck she's cute.

"Of course, sure, I'll do anything you want now."

She snorts at my sarcasm, then sobering herself, she asks seriously. "Please. Seriously tell me?"

I look at her through narrowed eyes for a moment, but it's futile. She can flutter her lashes, and I will, in fact, do anything she wants. "Okay fine. It's a Fort Minor song."

Her eyes twinkle, "I know now. This is easy!"

"You think so, smarty pants?"

"Yeah. It's Remember the Name?"

When I say nothing, she cheers. "Nailed it!" and laughs. "How does it go? Something like *Twenty-five percent awesome. Twenty-five percent skill. Fifteen percent ego. Thirty-five percent I'm sexy, and a hundred percent Jimmy's my bro.*"

She's cracking herself up, and fuck if she isn't funny; I happen to find wit a very sexy personality trait.

I nod. "You totally nailed it. Those are the exact lyrics. I can't believe you know them by heart." I poke her in the ribs, and she yelps and squirms away as she wipes tears from her eyes. Yeah, I could definitely get used to keeping her around.

"Okay, well, you know all my deep shit." She gets comfortable under my arm again and look up at me. "Tell me some of yours?"

I pause with a frown. What to tell her?

"Boxers or briefs?" she supplies with a serious face, but then laughs again. "No seriously, tell me about your mom?"

I nod thoughtfully. "Okay, I can do that … I wear both. Briefs for training. Boxers the rest of the time." She laughs again and I smile. "Though I wear nothing while I sleep. I'm wearing boxers right now." I don't even try to hide my grin when her face turns warm and her eyes drop to my crotch. I wait till she can meet my gaze again, and I lean in, "What do you wear to bed?"

Her eyes grow wide with scandal. "I can't tell you that!"

Aww, she's shy, and so, so cute.

I nod softly. "So you sleep naked then? That's hot. Just give me a second." I sit back and rest my head against the wall and I close my eyes.

"What are you doing?" she whispers after a long minute.

"Shhh, I'm imagining you naked."

"Don't do that! Jesus Bobby!"

I laugh and divert her smacking hands. "Okay, okay. I'll stop. Just lemme ask you one question?"

She watches me for a moment, hesitant, but finally nods. I have to know.

"Do you own a single pair of underwear that has kittens on it?"

My question doesn't embarrass her like I expected it would. She just laughs at me and shakes her head. "Jimmy told you that? He said he would. He's such a troublemaker."

"Yeah, he really is. He's an asshole." I smile. "Okay, let's get serious. My mom's name is Nel. Well, her name is Chantelle, but people call her Nel or Nelly. Not us though, and not Jon. Or Iz. We call her Mom, or risk her wrath. She turned fifty not long ago. We had a stupid big fancy dress party. It was a lot of fun actually. Ahhm, she's shorter than us guys, but not actually a short person. Probably not much shorter than you. She's really amazing. She raised three boys– plus extras, more often than not—by herself. My dad died when I was young, and she never remarried."

"I'm sorry about your dad."

"Yeah, thanks. I guess you can relate, huh. He died in a car accident when I was thirteen; so it's been a long time. Mom was pretty wrecked at the time, of course, but she didn't drop the ball. She was a stay-at-home parent, and my dad worked and supported the family, but when he died, she had to go back to work. She actually opened a dress shop with her friend. Teenage boys eat a lot I guess, and it got expensive fast. I guess you know all about how much teenage boys eat too." She nods at me. I have no doubt Jack's appetite has bumped her grocery bill like crazy.

Our meals arrive - with a different waiter - and he sets our plates down and leaves. Kit scoots over a couple inches to give us both room, and we pick up our utensils and start eating. She ordered some creamy pasta dish that smells really good, and hoping she'll share, I watch her eat.

She pauses with the second fork load on the way to her mouth, and looks at me. "What?"

I nod at the fork. "Is that good?"

She smirks and looks at my untouched steak. "Yup, it's delicious. How's yours?"

"I saw yours and I changed my mind on what I want ..."

She raises her brow in challenge. "Okay ...?"

"Gonna share?"

She scoffs. "Didn't your mama ever teach you that's rude?"

"She taught me lots of things. Doesn't make your pasta smell any less awesome, doesn't change my heart's desire."

"Your heart's desire?" she snorts. "Really? Way to lay it on thick. Jesus, Bobby." She laughs and pushes her plate toward me, and hands over her loaded fork.

Feeling a little guilty, like, just a tiny smidge, I offer the loaded fork back and offer to feed her myself. She watches me for a moment as her cheeks stain pink, but then she opens her mouth and takes the pasta. I watch her lips stretch around the fork and close around the pasta. I watch her tongue caress the fork, taking the sauce with it, then licking her lips, and suddenly my jeans don't fit right anymore.

She has no clue how sexy she is, or that she just put on a porn-worthy show that'll fuel the next several years of shower sessions. She doesn't notice the eyes that follow her when she walks across a room. She just doesn't get it.

In an attempt to not embarrass myself, I quickly load up the fork for myself. It's fucking delicious, and I totally regret the steak right now. However, my mama did in fact teach me not to be rude, so I slide her plate across the table after only one heaped forkful, and start on my own dinner.

It's pretty amazing actually, but still, my petulant self wants to share hers. "Anyway, my mom. She's really cool. I don't say that in a dependent mama's boy way. We're all grown men, contributing members of society and all that shit." I look up to catch her smiling and shaking her head. "But she's a tough cookie, raised us all with an unshaking foundation. She let us train and fight; which can't be easy for a mom. I guess you'll experience all that with Jack soon. She's an independent woman, happy with her life and business. But we feel bad that she lives in the big house all alone now, so we go over a lot to visit, eat, yard maintenance, that sort of stuff. You'd like her, really you would."

She watches me with a kind smile, then slides her plate toward me, and with a big grin I load up the fork and eat, then pass it back. "Tell me about your mom?"

Her face instantly turns sad and I hate myself for bringing it up. I'm an idiot.

"Forget I asked. I'm sorry I brought it up--"

Kit shakes her head. "My mom. Well, her name is Annmarie. Was Annmarie. She died when I was a kid. Jack was only two."

"That's so young, I'm sorry that happened."

"Shit ..." She sighs and looks down at her hands. I don't know how to naturally steer this conversation back to happier topics. I hate that I've upset her.

"I'm sorry, Kit. I'm sorry I brought it up. We can talk about something else -- "

"No, it's okay. You misunderstand my hesitation. It's just that ... I have more deep stuff that you don't know. It's not something that upsets my life now. But it's my history, I guess. I just don't want to make our date depressing."

"I want to hear anything you want to tell me," I tell her, truthfully. "It won't matter if the topic is a little down, we can always recover, if you share your pasta." I grin in an attempt to lighten the mood. She smiles and slides her plate across the table, so I take the fork and load it up, but offer it back to her. She takes it, then I eat some myself, and slide the plate back to her. She looks at it for a moment, clearly considering her words.

"Okay, well, it's not what you think. I'm not ... sad because my mom died. I know how horrible that sounds, but it is what it is."

Well shit. That's not where I thought this would go.

"So, my mom ... wasn't like Nelly. She didn't like me. At all ..."

How could a mom just not like her kid?

"Although no one ever said it out loud, I'll go ahead and assume I was an unplanned pregnancy. Before me, she was my dad's whole focus, and then she had a baby girl, and she became jealous. I'm not saying she was abusive, that's a pretty heavy word, you know, but she was quick to punish, and she was harsh at it. She was fast to lose her temper, and she hurt me a lot. Nothing too bad, nothing permanent, nothing to call authorities over, but it hurt all the same, and her lack of affection for me was obvious."

"Where was your dad?"

"He was around, but he worked long hours. We weren't rich, so he had to work every minute he could. He knew we didn't … get along, but he didn't know she beat me."

"You didn't tell him?"

"Well, it's all I knew, I guess. How was I to know it wasn't normal? Until I was older anyway. Then Jack was born; she wanted him, you know?" She looks up at me. "She wanted her baby boy, just not me. She left me alone for the most part then. Still quick to punish me, if Jack cried she'd assume it was because I shoved him or something." She laughs. "Sometimes it was true."

"So how'd she die?"

"She got pregnant a third time, with a boy, and they both died from complications during labor. Something about her blood pressure. I'm not entirely sure, but it happened, and suddenly my life wasn't as miserable anymore. I rarely think of her. Sometimes, but not often. Jack doesn't remember her at all. We all just … went on with our lives. I'm not entirely sure my parents were in love with each other. I think I was an accident and there's no way my dad would leave me, so he stayed. I don't actually know why she stayed, spite maybe?

"So yeah, that's my story. Here, have some pasta," she abruptly pushes her plate toward me with a forced grin. I nod. I'll let her have her distraction and I won't make it weird.

At least she told me.

Our plates are almost empty now, our posture slackening from full bellies, and I throw my arm over her shoulder again, snugging her into my side and nuzzling her hair. My favorite spot. "Do you want some dessert?"

I kiss her ear, and she practically purrs. "Not yet. I just wanna sit for a bit. Despite your hard chest, you're really very comfortable to cuddle with." She pushes in closer, and I smile.

"Okay, tell me about your dad? If you want to, I don't want to upset you."

"No, it's okay, I mean, I'm devastated he's gone, but the memories I have of him, they're all so happy. He was my best friend," she looks at me with a smile, then turns back again and snuggles in. "I was such a daddy's girl. Everywhere he went, I went. Literally, every time he had to work weekends, I went with him. For years. I'd hang around, they had a TV and basket of toys in the staff room, and I'd sit on a shitty red and blue futon and play while he had to work. Eventually, I became the staff coffee maker. Not that I was forced to, I wanted to, it made me happy to help people, so I would do rounds and make coffee for everyone.

"He had this old muscle car. It was a beauty, and when he'd spend his free time fixing it up, I'd be in the garage with him. I'm not exaggerating — wherever he went, I went. He wanted me to be girly, wearing silly fru fru dresses all the time, so here I was, puffy dress on, and dirty hands." Kit laughs softly at her memories, and I easily picture everything she's describing.

"I was such a good girl, I never gave him trouble when I was a kid. Then when I was fifteen, I met a boy," she looks up at me with a sassy grin. "And we all know what typically happens next. I turned into an asshole. I feel pretty horrible about it now, but at the time, I thought I knew everything. I turned sixteen, and lost my virginity to this guy, worst experience ever, by the way, and my dad went bonkers!" she giggles softly. "Seriously, he was a pussy cat, but you take his daughter's virginity and suddenly he turns into The Hulk. My sixteenth year was kinda shitty, and it was my fault. I moved a thousand miles away with this guy and broke my dad's heart, then I turned seventeen and realized, after a year together, that the guy was actually a piece of shit, so I left him and I was back to being a good girl again.

"I guess I got that rebellion out of my system in one short year. I never heard from the guy again, and Dad and I were close again; not that we grew apart during that year. My dad, he can be very unselfish, and although he absolutely hated that guy and hated me leaving, once he realized my mind was made up, he swallowed his pride and resumed being my best friend, silently waiting to catch me, which …" she nods, "he did. And he never once said 'I told you so.' I'll always be thankful he was my safety net. Ever since I was fifteen or so and had a cell phone, we spoke daily, even when I moved out. Even after I moved back, he'd be at work and I'd call to chat. I moved out again when I was nineteen because I bought the house I currently live in. He was so proud of me, so unbelievably proud of me," she says, suddenly sad again.

"You see, he was a hard worker, but he never really got ahead in life, never owned his own house, never won against the rat race. So when I bought my house, at nineteen no less, he was so fucking proud. I asked him and Jack to move in with me, to stop renting, but he was happy where he was. Our daily phone calls and visits increased, we'd talk about anything. He was knocking on my door at six most mornings to have a coffee and chat. At some stage, he stopped being my dad, and became my friend, my confidant."

She takes a deep breath and looks back up at me. "Anyway … one day last November, he called me on my work phone, which was odd. Normally he'd call my cell, and when I answered he was crying, saying he had cancer. He called it leukemia at the time, but we later found out it was lymphoma. Same same, but different." She shrugs her shoulders. "He started treatment pretty quick. I was by his side for most of the appointments, work was very understanding, but he got so sick, so fast. Lymphoma is supposed to be a fairly treatable cancer, but I guess it wasn't meant to be.

"He died in April this year, five months after he was diagnosed. He was only forty-seven years old. He celebrated his forty-seventh birthday while in hospital."

Fuck if she doesn't almost have me weeping for her. I squeeze her tight, unsure if I'm giving her comfort, or taking it for myself. She's silent for a minute, burrowing her head into my chest, but eventually speaks again, "Anyway, I loved him, so damn much. I miss him more than I can even say right now. I really fucking want him back. But even though I love him and miss him, I'm also so angry with him."

She looks into my eyes then. "He was a single dad with a single kid at home for a long time, and I think to compensate for his own hard life, he let Jack run wild. He created a spoiled brat with an attitude. I know my dad never intended him to get so naughty, but by the time he figured it out, he was already sick and just so tired. That's about the time Jack started drinking and partying, and he was brought home by the police a couple times. Then my dad died, and I was left holding the pieces, and trying to keep a brat teenager out of trouble. Add on to all of that, he left a bit of a mess behind with his estate and whatnot, and it's all been just a bit heavy for me lately."

I let her rest against my side for another long minute as I stroke her hair and will my chest to stop freaking out. It's okay. It'll be okay. "Hey, Kit?" I whisper against her hair and wait for her gaze to meet mine again. "If it means anything to you, I think you're doing an amazing job. You were handed a really shitty deal, but Jack's turning out just fine. Because of you."

Of all the things to make her cry tonight, that's what did it. Her eyes water, then spill over, and she ducks her head to my chest again. I let her hide for a moment, to give her someone to lean on for a change, but after a few minutes I place my thumb under her chin and bring her gaze back up to mine.

"You're amazing, and strong, and so brave. You're a hard worker, and so humble. You're beautiful, the most beautiful woman I've ever met and … well. I'm in love with you, Kit."

I expect to feel panicked at my revelation. I know my words surprised us both. But the panic just doesn't come.

Instead I feel content. I've never spoken truer words in my life.

"Bobby ..." she shakes her head softly as big fat tears drip from her lashes. "I never expected you. I never expected to like you, or for you to like me back. But ..." She looks down at her lap for a few seconds, then looks back up with a fiery resolve in her eyes. "But, I love you too. I've been scared, so scared of you, but only because I know you could hurt me. I love you Bobby, so much. And that scares the shit out of me."

I place my hand on the back of her head and I drag her forward until our lips meet. This is what it feels like to kiss someone you love. To be with someone you love. I pull back and thumb away a tear from her cheek. "Do you want to leave?"

"Yeah," she laughs softly and flutters her lashes. Not jokingly this time, but seductively. "I do. I really want to go to your house right now."

"Fuck. Let's go."

I want to touch her right here, right now. I want her in this booth, right now. She leans forward and kisses me again, pushing her tongue against mine and meeting me stroke for stroke. She runs her hand slowly across my zipper, and my hips jerk forward. "Fuck, fuck, fuck Kit." This is really happening. "Let's go. Now." I stand up and rearrange myself, then toss some cash down for dinner.

I grab her hand as soon as she's free of the table and drag her toward the exit, walking straight across the dance floor and cutting through couples to get there.

We race outside, and I drag her to my car, hitting the key fob to unlock the Rav, and practically ripping the door off its hinges to get her inside as fast as possible.

Giggling, she puts one leg up to climb in, but I grab her hips and lift her the rest of the way. She laughs throatily, then pulls me by the collar of my shirt until our lips meet again and her arms wrap around my neck.

I don't want to move, I don't want to break this contact, but I so desperately want to feel her, *all* of her, and I need to get her home for that. I force myself to step away and hurry to my side of the car, throwing myself in and slamming the door.

I look toward her and freeze. Her finger rests on her chest and her eyes scream mischief. Without speaking, she watches me watch her, and she slides her finger slowly down her chest, tracing the swell of her breast, then down the valley between …

Down she goes, across to her ribs, down, and then across her abs to rest where her belly button lies under the fabric of her dress. She stops there and waits for my gaze to meet hers, then licking her lips, my dick twitches.

She looks at her hand again, forcing my gaze to follow hers, and she lowers her hand further, pressing in at her crotch and making herself gasp.

That single nearly has me coming in my pants.

Fuuuuck.

She runs her hand along the inside of her thigh until she reaches the end of her dress, then lifting the fabric, she slides her hand underneath. She begins to work back up but I slam my hand over hers to stop her. I can't take any more. "You fucking minx, are you trying to kill me?"

She runs her tongue along her teeth, then smirks. "Would you prefer to do it yourself?"

"Fuck yes, I would. But not in my car. Behave yourself!" I switch the ignition on and slam my foot down on the peddle, and she just straightens her dress and smiles at me.

My Rav is a stick shift, so in order to drive, I had to take my hand off hers. She uses the opportunity to place her hand on my own leg, squeezing near my knee and making my heart knock in my chest, then slowly she begins to move her hand higher. My heart stops completely. She's really trying to kill me.

I want to stop her. I want her to keep going.

She reaches my zipper and runs her nail across it, and I feel every. Single. Bump. She reduces me to a whimpering mess, and I'm terrified that I'll blow my load like a virgin high schooler. She daringly lowers her hand and cups my balls. I'm done. I can't take anymore. "God, please stop, Kit. I'm about to embarrass myself."

She squeezes me again with a sassy smirk, forcing my eyes closed and my teeth to clench together. I can't do this. I can't take anymore. I'm about to crash this damn car, and then I'll never get to be inside her.

She takes pity on me. She knows I'm about to break, and she lets me go with a cheeky fucking grin. Thankfully, we're turning into my street now, and I fly into my driveway. Ripping the hand brake up, and without giving her time to touch me again, I throw my door open and run to hers, tearing it open, and physically lifting her out.

I slam her against the car, wrapping her legs around my hips and fusing my lips to hers. My hands cup her bare ass cheeks beneath the fabric of her dress, as some lacy cheeky type underwear tease the tips of my fingers. I'd literally die a happy man if she'd just show me those underwear right now. Our mouths remain connected, and my hips grind forward against her core, and we both whimper at the contact.

So close. So fucking close.

Still kissing, I lift her away from the car and carry her toward my front door. It's tempting, but I won't be giving my neighbors a show tonight. I've waited too long for this, I won't be sharing a damn thing.

With strong arms, she boosts herself up, as her tongue plays with mine. She tastes sweet like the finest desserts. We're all tongues and teeth as I move, and I have to work hard to not trip over my own feet. We get to my front door and I push her against it, using my hips to hold her weight while I frantically search my pockets for the keys. Pockets, pockets, so many fucking pockets. I can't find them, and I have no idea where they could be.

She stops kissing me, and her panting breath bathes my face, "What's the matter?"

"I can't find my fucking keys." My voice comes out cracked and panicked. If I took a step back for half a second I'd remember I had them only a minute ago, so they can't be far away. Kit starts laughing and untangles her legs from around me. I don't want to let her go, but she gives me no choice. "They're still in your car," she says with a giggle.

"How do y -- " I stop, and the noise from my car stereo filters through the night air. Motherf —

I point at her. "Don't you fucking move!"

She's laughing at me, bent at the waist and snickering like a fool. I lift her chin and kiss her hard, biting her lip, and eliciting another moan as she wraps her arms around my neck. I step back and her arms drop heavily. "I'm begging you, Kit, please don't move."

I run to my car and back again faster than humanly possible, then I unlock my front door and throw my keys to the floor. I turn around and pick her up again, then shuffling inside, I kick the door closed then slam her against it. I need to feel her. I need to taste her.

She pushes back against me, and the warmth of her pussy permeates through my jeans, swelling my dick painfully and making me groan. She lowers her head, biting my neck while I use my hips again to hold her weight, and I let my hands venture up to her tits, squeezing them, molding them, testing their weight.

The neckline of her dress is too high to pull down without ripping, so I reach behind, running my hands along her back in search of a zipper, then when I find it I yank it down.

Her bare breasts pop free, and hungrily, I swoop down and take one peaked nipple into my mouth. She cries out and squeezes her legs around me. I raise my hand to lightly pinch her other nipple, and they bead and peak. She's biting my neck and grinding her core against me, her teeth no doubt leaving bruises, and I thrill at the thought of her marking me. Of me marking her.

I switch nipples, taking the neglected one in my mouth, and I lower my other hand and run it along the sweet smooth skin of her thigh.

I slide my hand between us, searching for her warmth and when I find it, I grind my palm against her lace covered clit. She jumps in my arms, then she pushes herself back against my palm with a moan.

I love how responsive she is. I never imagined she'd be this hot, this eager, wanting it as much as I do.

Fuck, I want to be in her now.

Using my fingers, I peel her underwear aside, then I look to her eyes for permission. She nods frantically, then slams her mouth on mine again, growling as I slide two fingers inside. She's so fucking tight, tighter than I expected.

Her juices run down my wrist, and my dick swells with the need to feel her. To taste her. To fill her. I pump my hand and curl my fingers inside her, and she clamps down around them. She lifts her head to cry out, but I slam my mouth over hers again, capturing her screams and almost coming just from watching her.

I can't wait any longer so I pull my hand from her panties, spin us around and walk toward my bedroom. I navigate the stairs, never so glad in my life for the profession I've chosen, and the body — and muscle — it's given me.

I carry her with ease, finding the landing and turning toward my room at the end of the hallway. I push her against the wall just beside my door, latching my mouth to her nipple again, suckling, making it peak, and grinding my dick against her wet core.

Her hands are in my hair, holding my head against her chest, her grip on the pleasurable side of painful. My hips slam against hers without conscious permission. Lifting my head again, I carry her inside, dropping us both on my king size bed.

Finally, I have her beneath me.

I reach up to pull her dress the rest of the way down, exposing her abs and a shiny metal piercing, then those lacy underwear, finally sliding the dress down her legs and over her shoes and throwing it to the floor. I look back at her and stop to take in her whole body.

She's so perfect. So fucking perfect.

I look at her panties and follow the line of the lace across her lower abdomen, then I stop dead at a tiny tattoo peeking from beneath. My eyes snap to hers and I swallow hard.

My hands shake as I slowly reach out and slide her underwear lower. I'm dying to know what was so important that she inked it on her body. Only two inches tall, an inch wide, it appears to be a mascot of some sort. I stroke it with my finger and look up into her eyes.

"It's my old team mascot. For track."

I nod, kiss it, then continue running my hands up her stomach. I stop to flick my tongue over a silver belly piercing, then tapping my teeth on the dangling jewel. She's just a hive of secret treasures. Tattoos. Belly bars.

My hands continue their explorations over to her ribs. Her skin's so smooth, like touching warm silk. I lower my head and kiss just above her navel again, kissing my way across to her right ribs, running my tongue along them, making goose flesh rise and making her shiver.

Smiling, I continue kissing her softly, moving over to her left ribs, then repeat and lick her again. This time though, I catch some swirling line work of another tattoo and bend my head to get a better look.

This is almost like unwrapping a present on Christmas morning, but better. Every inch I uncover, I find treasures—sexy, beautiful treasures.

Lifting her gently to expose her ribs better, I discover some kind of bird stretching from her bra line right down to her hip, with a big swirly tail, and wings stretching toward her back.

Fuck if this doesn't turn me on.

I never expected my sweet, shy Kit to have ink, but it might be the sexiest thing I've ever seen in my life.

I lower her to the bed again, pushing her shoulders to the mattress, and continue kissing my way up her torso, worshipping her body the way a man should.

I suckle the tip of her left nipple and she thrusts her hips up in search of friction. Soon, baby. When I'm satisfied with the left, I switch to the right to tease and enjoy the unique taste of her fragrant skin. Her hips piston wildly in search, and she lets out sounds of frustration when she doesn't get what she wants.

"Hold on baby, just wait."

I'm just as desperate as she is. My boxers are moist with dripping pre-cum, but I make us both wait longer. She reaches out to pull my shirt up, her movements clumsy with desperation, so I help her. I rest my weight on one arm and use the other to pull my shirt over my head.

She stops and stares at my chest, biting her lip and studying me from one shoulder to the other. I realize she's never seen my tattoos either, beyond those that are exposed on my arms. It's only fair I keep still and let her look, then after a long tense moment, she lifts herself and latches her own mouth onto my nipple.

"Oh Fuck!" My hips jerk forward violently. "Fuck, do that again, baby."

She does, and she uses her hand to pinch my other nipple. My dick grinds forward and my breath whooshes from my lungs.

Time to speed things up.

I roughly thread my fingers into her silky hair and pull her back, then latching my mouth to hers, I suckle her tongue and bite her lip. We're both rough hands and biting teeth, our hunger for each other perfectly matched.

She reaches her hands between us, undoing my belt and pushing my jeans down my hips. Before I can push them all the way down, her hand's inside my boxers, fingers wrapped around my dick and she's squeezing.

"Oh god!" I cry out as she moves her hand up and down and massages my shaft. I can't take any more. I just can't. I've reached that line between sanity and death, so I jerk my hips away, then place my fingers on the stitching of her panties and rip them away.

"Oh, god" she giggles as I throw the destroyed fabric to the floor. "That was so ridiculously hot."

I chuckle desperately, then using her distraction, I quickly shove my jeans and boxers off the rest of the way, kicking my shoes off when they tangle in my jeans.

Laying my weight back on her, we both sigh at the skin to skin contact. My dick rests on the apex of her thighs, the slickness between her legs reminding us both what's about to happen.

I stop moving and I look into her eyes. I need proper permission. I'd die if she regretted this tomorrow. "Are you ready for me?"

She nods quickly, and my heart hammers heavily in my chest. Thank god. I keep my eyes on hers as I line myself up, then I push in an inch. Her eyes snap closed as she lets out a groan of pure delight and hunger. Given the green light, I slam in the rest of the way and she cries out in surprise.

"Shit. I'm sorry, I didn't mean to hu—"

"No, no, don't stop Bobby, please don't stop," she begs. Her eyes come back to mine seriously and she nods. "Please keep going."

Jesus. She feels so fucking good. So tight. So warm.

Grateful I didn't hurt her, and relieved I don't have to stop, I start moving, slow at first, giving her time to adjust to me. When she relaxes her face and she wraps her legs around my hips again, her heels dig into my ass, just like I fantasized they would, and my dick jumps inside her.

Fuck she feels good, like warm wet velvet, and so fucking tight. I thrust deep into her, pushing in as far as I can go, and she uses her legs as leverage and meets me every time.

I won't last long, and knowing it, I put my hand between us and start rubbing circles on her clit. Her hips start buckling wildly, and she rears up and bites my shoulder. Fuck she's sexy. I can feel her walls closing around me, letting me know she's close, but the tightness is bringing me dangerously close too.

She teeters, seemingly frustrated and unable to step off the edge. "Come on, give it to me, baby."

She clenches at my words, then her walls relax again. She likes it when I talk to her. She wants me to talk. Alright. I slam deep inside her, "Come Kit. Now." I pinch her clit. "Do it, fucking now."

She screams and her walls clamp down on me, her orgasm bringing me down with her. "Fuck! Oh, fuck," I moan into her hair. "I love you, Kit."

After a minute to catch my breath, I lift my weight and roll over, bringing Kit with me, laying her on top of me with her head on my chest and my dick still seated inside her.

We're both panting, still trying to catch our breath and we just lay for a while, content to touch in the silence.

"Bobby?" she whispers and lifts her head to look at me.

I kiss her swollen lips. "Yeah baby?"

"I love you too."

I lean up again and kiss her, nibbling at her lip, then licking the sting away. She presses her tongue against mine, and my dick suddenly fills and twitches inside her. At the same time, she moans and grinds down on me, making us both sigh and start moving together.

Fuck, I can't get enough of her. I feel like I didn't just come only minutes ago; I'm completely ready and anxious to go again. She pushes my shoulder down, making me lay down flat, and she raises her torso, sitting up straight, riding my cock, and fuck if it isn't the most beautiful thing I've ever seen in my life.

I reach up and grab her breasts, molding them between my hands, pinching her nipples. I want to taste them again, but don't dare move and lose the sight of her riding me.

She grinds down, her hands stretching past me and resting on the headboard for leverage. I lower my hands and hold her hips, taking some of her weight to help raise and lower her, and slamming my hips up every time she lowers herself. She cries out every time we join, and our eyes meet.

She starts making those frustrated noises again, unable to reach her peak with penetration only.

"Hold on, baby. Raise up."

I gently push her up and off me, and using the best hip escape training ever taught me, I slide out from beneath and move into position behind her in less than a second. She's still in the same position: on her knees, her hands holding the headboard, her ass presented for me, but now I'm behind.

I grab her hips and I slam myself straight back inside.

She cries out in pleasure. "Oh Bobby, you feel so good."

I stop moving, frozen in place at the sight before me. Her hair fell to the side with our momentum, and now I'm faced with a tattoo that goes from the top of her spine, and stretches right down to her ass. I didn't see this one before.

"Oh god," I groan, closing my eyes and breathing deeply to stop myself from coming. "Give me a second," I whisper, then open my eyes and look at the ink covering her. Down her spine is a tree trunk, the branches spanning her shoulder blades, the small pink flowers the only color in the otherwise black tattoo.

The blossoms are placed strategically on the limbs, and dark winged birds scattered here and there. The birds match the one on her ribs, but smaller, the larger birds' wings blending into the tree, so that the two tats join seamlessly. My dick twitches again, and feeling it, she grinds herself back against me, and we both moan.

I take hold of her hips again and start pumping into her. "Hold on to the bed, Kit, hold on tight, baby."

She continues to slam her hips backwards. "Harder Bobby."

No. That's not what she needs. Instead, I push her head down so her arms fall from the headboard and hug my pillow, and changing the angle her body's on, I pump again and she screams out in pleasure.

"Oh, you feel so good, baby. So fucking good," I growl as her pussy clenches around me. "Give it to me, squeeze my dick."

I continue slamming myself into her, and with one hand, I grab her hair, pulling her head back, making her spine arch deeply. We both whimper at the new angle, and I know I'm running out of time. I let go of her hair and reach around to find her clit. I start running circles around it, not directly touching the nub though, not yet.

"Oh god, oh god, oh god," she whimpers, bringing me closer and closer.

"Come on my dick, baby. Come now." I pinch her clit again, and she cries out her release and clamps down around me, forcing my own orgasm to smash down over me.

We collapse onto the bed, sweat slicked and exhausted. I'm conscious enough to hold the majority of my weight off of her, but I'm so fucking relaxed as our skin touches and slides together.

I straddle her for a moment, nuzzling her hair, licking her neck, dragging my tongue down her spine, and I enjoy watching her otherwise prostrate body curl and her skin prickle as my tongue tickles her back. I brush her hair aside and peek at her face, thrilled to see her dimples, and I lean down a give her a quick kiss before I finally collapse and throw all my weight down beside her.

13

Kit

I'll be doing what, now?

We lie on our sides facing each other, breathing each other's air, comfortable in the silence while we catch our breath. I'm hyperaware of my entire body, as my skin tingles and puckers as Bobby trails his fingers, soft as feathers, along my arm.

I'm reeling; not only from the best sex I've ever had in my life, but also from, well, *mostly* from Bobby's declaration of love. I never expected him to love me back.

I knew I loved him. I've known since he locked me in his sight at the club. I felt my stomach turn and my heart tumble. I knew he had power over me that I never wanted to surrender to anyone.

To have that kind of power to make me so happy, but the potential to crush me; giving that away didn't sit well with me. I didn't want it. I fought it. But it seems it was never something for me to give, but something to be taken, and Bobby… he took it.

He didn't have my permission, but that doesn't seem to matter anymore, because I love him, and he loves me, and I physically ache at the thought of him not being around.

When he told me he loved me too, my earlier uncertainties; my complications, my self-doubt, any thoughts I had about my body physically lacking—all of it—no longer mattered to me, because I believed him. My heart believed his.

Bobby's a man of honor, not one to throw words like that carelessly around, and I believe his words with every fiber of my being.

I thought it would be scary, loving someone, having them love me back, but the scariest part was in the not knowing. Now that I know, I feel as if something clicked into place, and we just … fit.

"What are you thinking?"

My gaze snaps to his chocolate eyes, as he sits up and rests on his elbow with his face in his hand. He smiles softly and drops a kiss on my shoulder.

"Hmm, I was thinking about you," I mumble out, thoroughly relaxed, and he raises his eyebrows in question. "I was thinking that maybe we should go out for pasta more often." I clarify.

He smiles wolfishly. "We can go out for pasta every day for the rest of my life, as far as I'm concerned." He bounces his brows and licks his lip, "Soooo…"

I don't even know why, but I blush. "Yeah?"

He continues watching me for a moment, his eyes slowly moving across my face, almost like a physical caress. "Who knew there was this whole other side to you, huh?" His face transforms into a grin, and I blush deeper. "My own femme fatale. Who knew shy Kit would almost make me blow my load just by watching you … Fuck, your little show in my car, you could kill me. You have the power to end me, do you know that?"

Leaning down again, running his tongue along my lip, he takes a moment then backs away again. "Or that you'd have tattoos. Amazing tattoos!"

I giggle lightly. "Yeah, they're kinda my secret. Cool secret, though, right?"

He nods softly as his eyes dance. "So cool. Which was your first?"

I look down my body. "The one on my hip. It hurt a lot at the time, but then before I even got home, I was already planning my next one: the bird on my side. I'm addicted." I push his shoulder so he lies on his back, then I get to my knees and rise above him. "May I?" I ask, running my finger along his collarbone, finally getting a close up view of his tattoos.

"Sure," he says easily, and I yelp as he grabs my hips, lifting me over to straddle him.

I lean down first to kiss his lips, then sit up again, finally basking in the unrestricted view I've been wanting since the first moment I saw him.

His pectoral muscles are clearly defined and have a tattooed clock resting over his heart, the hands sitting at a little past three o'clock. The face of the clock appears to be a mandala design, with chains dangling from the bottom, making the whole design look as though it's also a dream catcher.

Tribal art stretches toward his left shoulder, working its way down, various flowers and other designs filling in a three-quarter sleeve. He also has some script scattered about, some in English, some appearing to be Latin, woven in seamlessly with the rest of his art. I lean down and kiss the inside of his elbow, then work my way up and place a soft kiss in the center of his dream catcher.

He inhales deeply, and my eyes are drawn back to his. With tender eyes, he leans up and drops a soft kiss on my lips. "I love you, baby."

I thrill in the confidence to be able to easily reply, "I love you too." I peck him on the lips again, quickly snatching my head back when he tries to catch my lip between his teeth, and I laugh. I push his shoulder back down, then continue my examination, exploring across to his right side now, noting some numbers on his right pec; they appear to be dates, and I look up at him in question.

"Important dates in my life," he answers, then points at one. "The first day I stepped into a fight gym." Then moves his finger to another. "The first day I graded." Then another. "The day I got my black belt." Another. "The day I won my first title." This time looking at me, arrogant smile firmly in place. "The second time I won the title … The day we bought the gym." Then he moves his finger to a blank spot beside it and looks at me. "The day I bedded Kit Maree Reilly."

I slap his shoulder and laugh. "Shut up!"

He laughs and pulls me against his hard chest. "Don't be shy, babe. This is a big day. It's definitely worthy of ink."

"Stop it," I say, my face burning. To change the subject, I move my finger along his chest, deliberately drawing his attention to tattoos further down. I stop at script on his bicep. *"Pick the round. Knock 'em out."* I look up at him curiously.

"It's a simplified version of something Muhammad Ali said."

Nodding, I continue tracing the tendons in his arm, coming across a silhouette of what appears to be Peter Pan, and my eyes snap to his in surprise.

"I got that for my dad; he never really got to grow up."

I nod, then looking back to the clock on his chest, I get it now. My eyes start to itch and I quickly look away in an attempt to hide it. But he notices, of course he does, and grabs my chin, drawing my eyes back to his again. "What's the matter, baby? Don't be sad." He leans forward to place a gentle kiss on my lips.

I knuckle away a single tear and clear my throat. "Remind me to show you my notebook next time we're at my house. I want to show you something."

He stares into my eyes for a long moment, then silently, he nods gently. "Okay." Then he smiles wolfishly at me. "Are you done looking yet? I might have some ink on my ass. Wanna look?"

I laugh and lift onto my knees. We both know I want to check him out. "Sure."

He spins beneath me, then I'm treated to an artwork of perfection, both the ink and bodily varieties. His back is so wide, so powerful. The muscles so well-defined, his spine a deep valley between his lats, leading down to two deep dimples above the curve of his ass. He has more artwork on his back—none on his ass though, I note with a giggle—that stretch over both of his shoulder blades. The left shoulder blade has some kind of Japanese symbols and a circle with a different symbol inside. His right shoulder has an anime girl, long straight hair to her waist, fluttering around behind her as though she's standing in the wind.

She's wearing a sports bra and long skirt, her hands in fighting wraps, with more wraps on her ankles. She's standing in the fight stance that Bobby yells at me a hundred times per class, and she looks so badass, like she's about to dominate anyone who dare cross her.

I wish I were as badass as she.

He must feel my finger stroking along her body, because I hear his muffled voice, his face pressed into the pillow. Then he turns his head to look at me. "That's you."

My eyebrows knit in confusion.

"What do you mean? This tattoo clearly predates us ever meeting."

"True, but do you not see it? Do you not see that she's a warrior? That she's stronger than any man that ever lived. She represents to me, the pinnacle of strong and brave. To be a woman, and so badass, especially in, traditionally, a man's sport. To me, that's the epitome of brave. To me … that's you."

Is it possible to love this man any more?

My heart pounds almost painfully at how sweet he is. I lean down, doing my best with the awkward angle, and kiss the stuffing out of him. "I love you, Bobby."

He smiles his sexy smirk, then he taps my thigh to get up. "Are you hungry?"

"No, not really."

"Good. Are you tired?"

I kind of am, but I couldn't sleep now, even if I tried. The glow I feel from the inside out; he put it there, and I can't seem to get enough of him. "Nope, full of beans."

"Excellent. Want a shower?" he says with a big smile, but then suddenly his face falls, his color gone ghostly white. "Oh god, oh shit. Oh no!"

"What? What's the matter?"

"Condom! I forgot to use a fucking condom. I'm sorry, Kit! I'm so sorry. I swear to god I've never forgotten before. I'm clean, you have my word. I've never done that before, it's just, with you, I can barely think straight ..."

"Whoa, calm down. It's okay ..."

"No, it's not! I didn't even give you a choice. I just wasn't thinking. What if you – "

"Bobby! Cool it. I'm on the pill. And I'm clean too. We're okay."

"Are you mad? I'm so sorry."

"No, I'm not mad. I was there too, remember? I knew what I was doing."

"You're on the pill?"

"I promise I am. I promise. I won't accidentally get pregnant and trick you into a ..."

"Jesus Kit, I know that." He lets out a deep breath. "I'm not worried about that. I was worried that you might be upset."

"I'm not. We're okay … I promise."

Bobby still looks worried for a minute, but then he visibly, conscientiously, relaxes his face then nods. Smiling at me, he leans forward to place a kiss on my lips.

"So, about that shower …" I remind him.

He laughs. "Good idea …" He grabs my hand and drags me from the bed. "There's something I've been wanting to do in there since I first met you."

~*~

I open my eyes and squint into the harsh sunlight. Looking around, moving my eyes only, I search for a clock or my phone, something to give me my bearings again. I know I'm not at home in my own bed, that's easily obvious, since I can still smell him. His bed linens smell deliciously of him, and my back's still warm from him being my big spoon. I know he's awake too because I can feel him running his finger softly along my rib cage, over the birds' wings.

It feels so nice.

His nose is resting on the back of my neck, randomly placing soft kisses or nuzzling the nape of my hair.

"Mornin."

I shiver at the deep baritone of his '*I just woke up after a long night of good sex*' voice. And good sex, it was.

"Mmm, good morning," I reply, stretching my whole body as joints pop and I groan at how deliciously sore I am.

I turn over to face him, unable to resist looking at him any longer. I want to see him in the daylight, I want to confirm that last night really happened, and most importantly, I want to confirm that he loves me too.

He doesn't disappoint. My first sight, after I settle myself comfortably on my other side, is his sexy grin, his beautiful, straight pearly white teeth, his melted chocolate eyes, dancing with glee.

"Hmm, you're prettier than I remember," he says, laying a quick kiss on my lips. "Or maybe it's just different now, since I've seen you naked. Since I've made love to you. Since I love you." My heart trips in my chest as he leans down and kisses me again. How could he know that I need this reassurance this morning? How is it he knows exactly what I need? I sigh, letting myself fall deeper into his kiss, enjoying the intimacy he gives me, enjoying the knowledge that is all real.

"Want some breakfast? We're having pancakes." Bobby wiggles his eyebrows in excitement. My stomach rumbles noisily, as if on cue, making him laugh and turn to get out of bed.

"Wait, what time is it?" I know I should get home soon.

"It's early. Almost seven," he says after he looks at his watch, then looks back at me and slaps me on the ass. "It's breakfast time. Get up, baby."

He grabs some shorts off the floor and runs out the door laughing, knowing that if I could reach him, I'd hit him back.

I sit up in his bed and look around his room. This is the first chance I've had to look around, and I can't resist peeking into his life.

Straight across from the bed are windows that take up the whole wall, with the dark curtains currently closed. The wall to my left is completely built in closets, leaving only space for the door that Bobby ran out of. The wall to my right has a mounted flat screen TV and framed pictures; so many pictures spread out and taking up most of the wall, all similar to those in his office—Bobby and his brothers, Bobby and Jon, the guys as young teens and a middle-aged woman I assume is Nelly. A younger man who looks so handsome and familiar, he could only be the Kincaid dad.

There are also random posters of Bruce Lee, Georges St-Pierre, Mahammad Ali, and some other fighters I don't recognize. Scattered between all those are pictures of comic book characters—Hawkeye, Iron Man, Thor, The Hulk, and Black Widow are some I recognize immediately.

Yep, the man I love has comic book characters on his bedroom wall. I laugh to myself. This collage of people, fictional and real, are who inspire him, who make him happy, and so, they make me happy too.

I get out of bed and walk toward his bathroom, needing to pee and clean up. I approach the sink, looking at myself in the mirror, shocked at who I see looking back. That's me, I know that, but I look different, even to myself.

My hair is a mess, but it's a sexy mess. The curls looking so soft and smooth. My cheeks are flushed, but not in an embarrassing way, just the perfect way to add color to my face, making me glow. My eyes seem happier, the blue green I got from my dad seem to twinkle. I enjoy the new leaner shape my face and body are taking, and due to working out at the gym, I've lost about ten pounds so far.

When I walked in here, I expected to look like a mess, but I just look … happy. I feel happy, and I feel sexy.

I take care of business and wash my hands, then head back to his room, searching for my underwear and a shirt to wear. I find the black tee he was wearing last night and put it on, then find my panties under his bed and remember he tore them off me last night. Heat pools in my belly at the memory, and I reconsider my breakfast choice.

I grab a pair of his boxers instead, sliding the silk up my legs, then rummage in his drawers looking for socks to wear. It's my thing; I can't not wear socks first thing in the morning, even in summer. I feel like my freshly woken feet just aren't tough enough to go barefoot. Not until I've at least had my first cup of coffee.

As dressed and presentable as I can possibly be, I wander out to the hall in search of the kitchen. We didn't take time for formal tours last night, but I can smell coffee and pancakes so I just follow my nose.

I enter the kitchen to find Bobby with his shirtless back to me, flipping pancakes at the stove. I just stop to watch for a minute. The flex and movement of his broad back hypnotizes me, the warrior princess on his shoulder blade ripples when he moves.

With zero hesitation, as though he sensed me there, he turns and strides toward me with a big smile. Without stopping, he picks me up easily and wraps my legs around his hips, and he kisses me as he slowly walks toward the counter.

He sits me down and stands between my legs, nuzzling my hair, kissing my neck, running his hands along my thighs.

It's as though he craves me and can't get enough, and I feel the same about him. I take the opportunity to run my hands along his powerful shoulders, follow the veins down his biceps, remembering the power he possesses, my heart thumping at memories of the night before.

"Mmm you taste good," I mumble as the taste of maple syrup transfers from his tongue to mine.

He gently bites my earlobe. "I could say the same about you… Some coffee?"

"Yes please. Cream and one sweetener."

He pecks me on the lips again then moves away to the coffee pot. "I gotta say, there's something about seeing you wearing my underwear first thing in the morning."

"You don't mind, do you?"

"On the contrary, babe. It's hot." He looks at me over his shoulder and smirks. "But those socks; well that's something else. Can't say seeing you in my socks does anything for me."

"Shut up. I can't go barefoot before coffee. It's like, my poor sensitive feet hurt from the tiles."

"Your poor sensitive feet?" He laughs and walks back to me with my coffee. "Those are fighter's feet. We'll toughen you up soon enough."

"I don't want them to be toughened. I like my socks, thank you very much."

He laughs and drops a sweet kiss on my forehead. "I'm so glad you're here, Kit. I feel like I've waited forever to finally be with you."

I sigh and look up at him. "Sorry, I've kind of given you a hard time since I've known you, huh?"

"That's okay. I like your sassy self … Just don't give up on us, okay? We're a team. I'm on your team now, so don't shut me out if things get tough, alright?"

I nod my head, overwhelmed at this man's ability to love so much, and ask so little in return.

He places his finger under my chin and forces my gaze up. "Promise me, Kit."

I nod again. "Okay, I promise. I won't shut you out."

"You'll ask me for help if you need it?"

This is a tough one, since I've gone most of my life not asking for anyone's help. I'm an independent woman, and it grates to not be able to do something on my own.

"Kit?"

I nod again "Yeah, I promise … We're a team."

"Good. Come on then, Sexy Socks, come to the table. Breakfast is ready." Bobby walks back to the counter, grabbing the coffee pot and a large stack of pancakes and leads the way.

I look over to find the table already set, plates and cutlery set out, juice and glasses waiting for us, and my stomach rumbles again. Yum.

I sit down and Bobby immediately flips a pancake onto my plate. I drown it in syrup and dig in.

"Mmm, so good."

Bobby's eyes snap to mine, his face coloring slightly, and without knowing why, I blush. His eyes are just so intense, hungry. I pick my coffee up, hoping to distract myself, and sigh at the first sip. So good.

"You're a good cook, Bobby. These are delicious."

He looks back down to his plate and starts cutting. "Don't get too excited. The pancakes came from a bottle, I just add milk. And the coffee, well yeah, I've gotten decent at that, it's a necessity in my life."

"It's okay, I get it. Coffee is life, it's my first stop in the morning." Well. After the sock drawer.

"What are you up to today?" he asks, licking syrup off his pinkie finger.

"I have work to do." I roll my eyes at the reminder. So much work to do. "I bring my laptop home to do stuff I didn't finish at the office."

"That sounds lame."

I laugh. "It is lame. But it has to be done. End of financial year keeps me super busy. I'm not sure what Jack's doing today. He'll probably end up at your gym, actually. He said something about hanging out with Michael, then Michael's staying at our house tonight. Do you have to work today?"

"Yeah, I have to be there in a bit for a kid's class. After breakfast, I'll drop you home and Jimmy and I will go straight to the gym." His eyes scan across my face thoughtfully. "Too bad you have to work, I'd rather hang out with you."

"Yeah, I'm not really in the mood to work. At least it should only be a couple hours, not all day. Then I've got to go to the store; we're making pizza for dinner."

"Making?" His brows crinkle quizzically. "Like homemade?"

"Yeah, like, I need flour and yeast and stuff."

"That's so cool. You just got hotter."

I laugh. "Uh, thanks, I guess." I flick a piece of pancake at him that he somehow manages to catch in his mouth. I freeze, staring at him, unable to process what just happened.

He snorts at my facial expression and cuts up the last of his own food. "Eat your breakfast, Kit. You do not want to start a food fight with me. You can't win."

He gets up and walks to the dishwasher, putting his mug and plate away.

Mmm, he just got hotter. Cooks breakfast, and puts his dishes away; it's practically porn for women.

"Kit?"

My eyes whip up to his when he snaps his fingers in my face. "Stop staring at my ass. Or do, whatever. But wake up," he says, still chuckling. "Let's go."

He takes my hand and drags me to my feet. "Where are we going?"

Walking toward the stairs, Bobby looks back at me with hungry desire in his eyes. "To the shower."

Yes please.

Bobby turns the taps on, the room quickly filling with steam, and steps back toward me, placing his hands on my hips and drawing me closer. Our hips touch, and moisture gathers between my legs when I feel his solid length resting against my lower stomach. I lean forward, hands on his chest, and place my lips on his. I want nothing more than to taste him, to enjoy our last moments of privacy before we have to go back to real life.

He slides his clothes off my body, treating me like fine china, afraid to break me, then walks me slowly backwards into the shower. The warm water pulsing down on my back is heaven, relieving sore muscles both from a long night of pleasure, and from long weeks of training.

He backs away from me and pumps liquid soap into his hand, then methodically washes me: shoulders, chest, ribs, stomach. Then lowering himself to his knees, he washes my thighs, my legs and feet. He then stands up and pumps more soap and turns me, cleaning my shoulder blades, my lower back, seemingly taking his time here, and I assume he's busy studying my tattoos again. Bobby lowers himself and washes my buttocks, the backs of my legs and ankles.

By this point, I am a panting mess, wishing he'd get to the point this second, but he just continues to rinse the soap from my body. When he's done, he leans in and kisses the back of my thigh, then my butt cheek. I hold my breath in anticipation.

He taps my leg. "Turn around," he says with a husky voice. I turn and he places his open palms on my thighs, then before I even know it, he has his face buried between my legs. His tongue flicks over my clit, and I expel all the breath I forgot I was holding.

My hands instantly fly to his hair, to hold him in place, to beg him not to stop. I grind my pelvis into his face, making me groan, making him growl, the vibration enhancing my pleasure. I begin riding his face, wanting more friction, and he puts his hand between my legs, inserting a finger and making me cry out on a sob.

"That feels so good. Don't stop, Bobby. Please, don't stop."

He doesn't verbally answer me. He just continues and adds a second finger, and my walls contract around him. He continues to use his mouth, every now and again suckling on my clit, bringing me right to the edge, only to stop at the last moment and letting my climax leave me again.

My hips thrust against his face without conscious effort, when suddenly I feel him curl his fingers inside me and his teeth bite down on my clit, and my orgasm screams through me like a freight train.

As soon as he feels my walls clamp down, he takes his fingers away and stands. I let out a sob at the injustice, but before I can vocalize my thoughts, he has me pinned against the wall, my legs wrapped around him, his dick thrust deep inside me, his sudden girth making my orgasm crash down on me again.

My vagina clamps down on him and I'm sobbing as my climax robs me of breath, my teeth clamping down on his shoulder.

He hisses out a breath, his face almost pained. "Oh god, you're so tight, baby, so tight, you feel so good."

He hasn't moved his hips yet, although I can see it pains him not to. He just impales me and lets me ride out my pleasure using him.

I lay my head on his shoulder, trying to catch my breath. We're both panting hard, and I can feel him throbbing inside me, sparking pleasure anew. I lift my head and kiss him, my tongue exploring his mouth, my hands tugging his hair.

I can taste myself on his lips, and I expected that to gross me out, but really, I can't feel anything right now except love for this man, and raging passion. I continue kissing him as I use my legs as a lever and start moving my hips.

Instantly, the movement sparks pleasure deep inside me, and he tenses. Groaning, he takes over, holding my ass and pushing into me, my back pressed against the shower wall. He dips his head, taking one of my nipples in his mouth, gently biting and sucking, the sensation shooting new shock waves straight to my core. I am hyper-sensitive, still reeling from my orgasm moments ago, so it doesn't take long to bring me to peak again.

"Not yet, babe, hold on," he pants, biting my neck, his hands likely leaving bruises on my ass, but the pain feels so good. I clamp around him, unable to stop the movement—I'm so close to going.

"Not yet, not yet. Wait for me baby," he growls, pushing into me, the pleasure so intense. I thread my hands in his hair, pulling it, sometimes gently, sometimes rough. My face is buried in his neck, sucking, biting, nuzzling. Bobby continues pumping into me, the force knocking me into the tile over and over. His large hands feel so good on my ass, his dick stretching me, suspending me on the edge.

"Now. Come on my dick, babe. Come now!" he groans, and as though my body knows who it's master is, it does exactly what he asks. "Oh god," he pants, over and over again. "Oh god, Kit," he says, still slowly moving inside me.

A few minutes later we slide to the floor, still connected, still breathing hard, both utterly spent.

"You're amazing," he whispers, kissing my ear. "You feel so good. Like you were made just for me."

~*~

After getting dried and trying to hide my embarrassment at getting dressed in front of him minus panties, we're finally driving back to my house. We sit without talking, and we listen to the music playing through his stereo. When he isn't shifting gears, he holds my hand, or he holds my thigh, or he kisses my knuckles.

I enjoy the intimacy, but now that we're headed back to real life, I worry what will happen when we get there. Will he be distant? Will he be too shy to tell people what we are? Will I be? I hate the uncertainties that sneak up on me now that we aren't locked away in the privacy of his home.

"Will Jimmy be mad he had to stay all night?"

Relieving some of my tension, Bobby snorts, "No, but he *will* tease you mercilessly. Be prepared."

Shit, he's right, this is going to be so awkward.

"Babe, its fine. He won't say a word, I'll talk to him ..." he kisses my knuckles again.

"No that's okay. Jimmy doesn't worry me. But are you okay with him teasing? I mean, you may not want people to know … that we spent the night together."

I'm so lame.

His head whips my way, with anger in his eyes. "The fuck I don't. The world already knew I wanted you. You were the last one to get on board." His jaw clenches angrily. "You promised, Kit. You promised we'd be a team. We're together, and we're a team. No take backs."

Hurt burns in his eyes, and I realize in my lame attempt to help him, I've hurt him. "You're right, I'm sorry. I didn't mean it like that. I just meant …" I groan and run my fingers through my hair. "Look, I'm finding it hard to reconcile the fact a guy like you would be interested in someone like me. But—" I hurry on when he narrows his eyes, "but, I'm sorry. I love you, and you love me. So we're good. I promise we're good."

He grabs my hand, pausing with it in front of his lips. "My only wish would be that you could see yourself the way I see you. You are honestly the most beautiful woman I've ever known, Kit. I wish you could see that… Don't sabotage us, okay? We can be amazing together. Don't cheat us both out of something so good. Just enjoy it with me, yeah?" He's right. He's absolutely right. I smile and nod, and he lets out a deep breath. "Thank god, I was ready to take you back to my lair and fuck you into submission." He bites my hand, and I screech out a laugh when his teeth tickle my skin.

Soon, we turn into my street and I begin to panic at the sight of Jimmy's Jeep parked out the front. I mean, of course it should be there, but still. I'm kinda of terrified.

But it gets worse. So much worse. Casey's hatch is there too, as is a third strange truck. Seems Bobby recognizes it though because he laughs.

"Shit. Looks like we get to run the gauntlet straight out of the gate."

"Oh God. Whose truck is that?"

"It's Jon's. Guess he came looking for Jimmy and me … Then again, maybe he came looking for Tink." He looks at me out the corner of his eyes. "It's okay, he won't give you trouble, I promise. Jimmy's always the only one of us you need to worry about teasing."

Little does Bobby know I secretly enjoy Jimmy. Most of the time. But maybe not today.

Bobby parks the car and pulls out the keys. "Are you ready?"

I feel a little ridiculous, since this is my house. If anybody inside wants to tease me, I'll kick their ass. Well, that's not true. But still, that's the attitude I'll go in with.

"Ready," I answer and lean across and kiss him with a little more heat than Saturday morning in public calls for. I try to pull back but he laces his hands in my still damp hair and pulls me in for more.

"Mmm, that's better. There's my warrior princess. Go inside with that attitude." He nips my lip again, smiling, then hops out of the car.

I join him at the front of the Rav, and he automatically throws his arm over my shoulder, erasing any worry I may have had over touching versus keeping distance. We're going in guns blazing, I guess.

We climb the front steps and I unlock the front door, then we step into a silent house. Considering there are so many people here, the silence scares the hell out of me.

We walk through to the kitchen to find Jack, Jimmy, and Case sitting at the table, and Jon standing at the stove. I can smell pancakes in the air here too, but everything feels awkward. Everyone is just staring at us. Except Jack; he won't look up from his plate at all. No one speaks for a full minute, but then Jimmy squeaks and lets out a howling laugh.

"Kit's doing the walk of shame!"

No one says anything for a long moment, probably wondering if I'm going to cry or something, but what kind of best friend would Casey be if she didn't help throw me under the bus?

"Bobby?" she stands from her chair and walks up to him, bringing her hand up to touch his skin. "Are those bite marks on your neck?"

My face burns as I study Bobby's neck, but with more howling and snorting, I realize I've been hustled. There are absolutely no marks on his neck, none that can be seen by these assholes, anyway.

But by this point I'm laughing too, which gives everyone else permission to. Except Jack; he looks slightly ill and rolls his eyes.

"Whatever." I wave them off. "Shut up, assholes." I tap Bobby's stomach then walk to my coffee pot. If I'm going to put up with these ass's, then I'm going to need more coffee.

"Listen to the sass in this one!" Jimmy complains. "Mom would never speak to us that way."

"Well that's just not true," Bobby argues with a laugh. "She has, she does often."

"Whenever I imagined getting a baby sister, she never spoke to us that way. She made cupcakes and was a precious little princess."

I turn from the coffee pot and narrow my eyes. "You sound like you've put a lot of thought into this, Jimmy. Did you not have friends when you were a kid? Lots of spare time?"

"The sass! So much sass. Whatevs princess." He walks by me and slaps my ass with a stinging crack. "Go put some underwear on."

My face burns brighter. He wins. He wins hands down, and when all else is lost, what does any self-respecting smart ass do when they have nothing else? I flip him the bird and I practically sprint to the stairs as the sounds of laughter trail behind me.

Just as I reach the landing of my staircase though, I hear a muffled thump.

"Ugh. The fuck, B?" And more laughter.

I snicker and walk into my room.

I lost, but he still got hit. I call that a draw, and I'm okay with that.

Since I already showered at Bobby's house, I search my closet for underwear and casual clothes. I find a pair of comfy cut-offs and a tank and I strip off my dress and throw my fresh clothes on. Feeling much less conspicuous now, I find socks then head down the hall to my bathroom to freshen up.

I brush my teeth and braid my hair, then I swipe some mascara on and declare myself done.

On the way out, I pick up a couple towels off the floor and throw them in the hamper with an eye roll. Walking down the stairs, I pick up discarded socks, another towel, two pairs of shoes, and a shirt. Boys are pigs.

I can hear everyone chatting in my kitchen, and I stop a moment to listen to the sound of happiness. It's been a while since I heard this in my house, and I realize that I want it back.

The stresses of the last few months has dulled my spark, and I decide I won't let it control me any longer. I walk the last few stairs and turn into the kitchen, spotting my friends and my family surrounding my table, pigging out on empty calories.

Bobby notices me first and walks toward me, smacking Jimmy on the back of the head on the way. I don't get a chance to see anyone else because he's already there in my space, his hands cupping my face, his forehead resting on mine.

"You look beautiful, babe."

"Hmm thanks."

"I missed you."

I snicker. Who knew this giant fighter would be so comfortable talking this way. I love that he's so comfortable expressing his feelings. I lean forward and kiss him again, uncaring who's watching. I open my mouth and lick his lips, tasting syrup on his breath again.

Eventually, he looks down at my loaded arms and raises a brow in question. I face everyone else and hold each article up one at a time.

I hold up a pair of socks. "Whose are these?"

"Mine," Jack answers, so I throw them at him.

I hold up the towels. "These?"

"Mine …" Jack answers again, so I ball them and throw them at his head.

"These?" I hold up a pair of shoes, but don't need an answer because Jacks face says it all. I throw them, and luckily for him, I aim lower than his head.

"Alright, who owns this?" I hold up the shirt, and this time Jimmy clears his throat.

"Ah, that's mine … So are the shoes," he finishes lamely. Bobby laughs at his brother's shameful face, and since I'm not one for favoritism in my house, I throw his shoes toward his legs, and while he's distracted with those I peg the balled-up shirt at his head. "Pick up your shit, guys. This Princess ain't your maid."

Bobby laughs and kisses me again, then taps my ass and leads me to a spare chair at the table, sitting between Casey and the empty chair he just vacated. He goes to the coffeepot that I didn't end up finishing earlier, then brings me back a steaming mug. I taste it, enjoying the aroma, pleased that he made it exactly how I like it.

Casey leans toward me, knocking her shoulder into mine discreetly, and I look toward her to find her grinning bigger than I've seen in a while. Again, I'm reminded what a good friend she is and that I have to work at repaying her for being so awesome. She bites her lip softly and whispers, "Did you have a nice night?"

My lips curve, and I simply nod.

She nods too, then quickly drops a kiss on my shoulder. "Good. You deserve it."

She sits back comfortably and sips her coffee, then with another shoulder bump, she silently lifts both hands, holding them in front of her and putting distance between them, non-verbally asking about Bobby's size, and I choke on my coffee.

She laughs but then slaps my back to make sure I don't die. What was a discreet moment now has all eyes on me. "Casey!" I sputter, still trying to clear my airways.

Bobby leans into me. "You okay, babe?"

I just nod and wipe my mouth, deciding I absolutely will not answer her. "Yep, I'm fine." Then I look to my left again, "Casey, why are you even here? Did you spend the night?" I look to Jon and narrow my eyes. Did he spend the night too?

He puts his hands up in surrender. "Calm down, mama bear. I just got here. I swear."

I look back to Casey.

"I got here half an hour ago. I was looking for you. Mostly I wanted pancakes. I don't work this weekend, so I was looking for girl time. Looks to me though, that it's not *girl* time you're interested in."

She tosses a sassy wink at Bobby, and he smiles. "Anyway, Kolby's staying tonight, yeah?"

Jimmy glares at us. "Who's Kolby?"

Aw. Jimmy can be jealous too. That's cute. "He's ... my *special* friend," I tease.

He narrows his eyes, then he looks toward Bobby, then back at me.

Casey nods her head casually. "Yeah, well, I figured I'd come over and *hang out* too."

"Hold up! Neither of you get *special friends* now that you're … *seeing* my brothers," he says, definitely serious. "B? You can't be okay with this?"

Bobby knows that we're actually talking about Jack's friend Michael, so plays along. "Eh, it's okay. Kit knows who to come home to." He kisses me on the temple, turning Jack's insiders smile into a green-faced frown.

As if on cue, the doorbell rings, but before I get a chance to stand, Jimmy's eyes narrow and he bolts to the door. I shrug and help myself to more coffee, then a minute later, we hear, "ah, motherfuckers," and I laugh.

Jim and Michael walk into the kitchen. Michael, comfortably at home, grabs a plate and pancakes for himself and eats while standing at the sink, while Jimmy flops back down into his chair.

"You bastards. Why are you always teasing me?"

I just look up at him with a raised brow.

He shrugs. "So what's happening tonight? Pizza? I'll bring dessert."

"Actually, that's not a bad idea," Casey agrees. "I'll bring drinks." She stands and rinses her empty dishes, then loads them in the dishwasher.

"Sweet," Jack answers, then walking past Michael, he taps him on the shoulder. "Come on man. I'm just gonna put on my shoes and we can go."

Jack walks out of the kitchen, and Michael follows only two steps behind him. I look at the table to Jack's dirty and abandoned dishes. Then the counter, and Michael's newly empty plate. "Jack. Michael!" The Kincaid guys jump at my shouted words, but Casey just smirks.

The younger boys run back into the kitchen, muttering apologies as they hastily pack their dishes away, then they run out again and stomp up the stairs.

"Shit Bobby." Jon laughs. "She's scary."

Bobby looks at me and smiles. "Yep. She's pretty amazing ..."

A few minutes later, Jack comes back to the kitchen with his shoes in his hands. "Alright. We're ready to go. Can you give us a lift or will we ride our bikes?"

"It's okay," Bobby answers before I do. "We'll drive you."

"Really?"

"Yeah, we're going to the gym now too. Load up," he says, then he stands as well. The younger guys head out the door quickly and Bobby grabs my hand, walking me to the living room and leaving Jon and Casey alone in the kitchen.

"Thanks for a really great night," I whisper, as my heart races again, "I had a good time."

He steps toward me and rests his hand on my cheek. He leans down and kisses me, his juicy lips teasing mine apart. "Mmm, you're welcome, babe. For all of it. I'll see you again this afternoon. I'll drop the boys back here."

"Are you sure it's not a bother? I can pick them up."

"I promise, I'm happy to. I want to see you again. Plus, I'm coming over for pizza night, remember?"

I can't even say I'm sad that Jimmy muscled his way in to our evening. In fact, I'm thrilled. "Okay, well," I kiss him again, slowly, deeply. "I'll see you after."

"I love you. Have a good morning."

I sigh happily. "I love you too, Bobby."

He drops his hand from my face and steps back, taking my hand and walking toward the front door. Casey is already standing there, looking into my yard, laughing at something someone — probably Jimmy — is doing. Bobby taps me on the bum on the way out the door, then pats Casey's head, which is significantly lower than his, in a patronizing way, and I'm surprised she doesn't snap his arm off.

For some strange reason, she tolerates him in a way she tolerates no one else. Before Bobby, she'd never allow anyone to make fun of her, but it's almost like she enjoys it the way I enjoy Jimmy.

I look out in time to see Jon driving off and Jimmy starting his car. Michael and Jack are waiting in the Rav, but before Bobby gets to it he turns around, blocking their view with his back.

"Oh hey, Tink," he calls out. He puts his hands in front of himself, opening them wider and wider, stopping at about fifteen inches apart, and she snorts.

"Ha! He's dreaming." Jimmy yells from his car, then puts one hand up, thumb and finger half an inch apart. "I've seen it!"

Bobby just flips him the bird, but laughs and climbs into his car.

~*~

Monday morning, I walk downstairs, buttoning my blouse and mentally planning my day. Normally I'd start work about eight am, but today we have the meeting with the school at nine, so I'll just go straight there, then to work after. I'll work through lunch to make up for time away, and maybe do some more at home later tonight if I have to.

I'm dreading this meeting, hating to ruin the good buzz from such a wonderful weekend spent together with our friends. After the guys left for the gym Saturday morning, Casey and I fell on the couch in a fit of giggles like we were thirteen all over again.

She told me she and Jon aren't actually a thing and though she admits they're both interested, both are also hesitant to commit. Casey, I know, is a free spirit. She's not promiscuous, but I'd definitely call her flighty. I do know she'd struggle committing her time and energy to any one person. Likewise, Jon also worries and doesn't want to risk hurting the best friend of his best friend's girlfriend. Phew, that's a mouthful.

She did tell me they've made out, and they talk, a lot, but haven't taken it further than that.

I worry that she doesn't see what I do.

I watch the way he watches her, the way his body unconsciously turns in her direction when she's near, how he protects her, guarding her front or her flank if she needs the backup. I hope they work out what they both want, and I hope that's each other, because I know they could be good for each other.

She hung around for an hour or so Saturday morning, and we nearly blew ours heads off with a caffeine overdose, but then she had to leave, promising to be back for pizza night. That afternoon, I ran to the store for dinner ingredients, then caught up on work and paid bills that I'd been procrastinating on.

Dinner that night was lovely; my kitchen was overflowing again, the sound of laughter non-stop. Michael brought over a newly released DVD for everyone to watch, so after the pizza was all gone and the dishwasher was loaded, we flopped all over my living room and we watched together.

Bobby lazed on his back, his head resting against the couch, and pulled me down to rest my head on his chest. He spent the next two hours running his hand through my hair while I traced circles on his torso. Every now and then I'd brush my fingers over his shirt covered nipple, mostly on purpose, and he'd have to rearrange himself.

I took a sick satisfaction in my ability to torment him. The bolder I got, the tighter his hold on my shoulder and hair would get, and I was desperately tempted to give him a full house tour — concentrating on my bedroom.

Jon and Casey sat together on the couch, seemingly platonic, but still, they appeared to enjoy themselves. I won't snoop, and I won't pressure them. They'll handle themselves.

Aiden was at the gym when the guys arrived, and came back with them. He hung out with Jimmy, who joked and bullshitted most of the movie with Jack and Michael.

Although much older than them, Jimmy's immaturity aids in the friendship with the younger boys. It bridges the gap, so to speak. Jack and Michael, on the other hand, idolize him and wouldn't leave him alone even if he wanted space.

On Sunday, I had to catch up on housework, but I was dragging ass since Michael and Jack were noisy most of the night playing PlayStation. Thankfully, they were also dragging, so I exacted revenge by putting them to work.

Bobby arrived at my house when the boys were outside; Jack on the mower and Michael trimming the edges, and I was in the kitchen making iced lemonade for when they finished.

He looked good, wearing his usual workout shorts and a muscle tank, allowing me to stare at his shoulders and tattoos some more. I can't seem to get enough.

We only had a few minutes alone before the boys would come in, and he didn't waste a second, silently grabbing me by the hips and boosting me onto the counter. I felt his erection resting against my thighs, and my mouth watered at the thought of what we could be doing right now if we were completely alone.

He leaned in, taking my mouth like a starving man. His hands still underneath my ass squeezed and kneaded, molding it to the shape of whatever his hands desire. His tongue warred with mine, and I met him, equals in want. I pressed my chest against his, the swollen flesh of my breasts craving any friction he might be able to provide, and I ground myself against him, unable to stop the movement.

He groaned into my mouth and pulled back, pressing his forehead to mine as his heavy breath bathed my face. "Jesus babe, I want you so much. I missed you last night."

"Hey. I missed you too."

"You look very pretty today," he added with another kiss.

"I have dirty hair and no makeup, I look kinda crap actually. But thank you," I said with a smile.

"Nope, you look beautiful, like always. So fucking beautiful," he whispered, kissing me again.

He couldn't stick around for long, since he and his brothers had plans to help at his mom's house. He asked me to come with, but I had a lot of work to do myself, plus, you know, meeting his mom. Scary as hell. That's a hard no from me.

Now it's Monday morning, and Jack and I have a little over an hour till we have to be at the school.

I walk into my kitchen, slipping my heels on as I go, and head to the coffee pot, needing my second caffeine hit of the day — the first was inhaled while in the shower. I sit down at my table with the coffee and some toast when Jack walks in.

He stops when he spots me. He's worried, but I guess I can't blame him. Nobody wants to meet with the principal.

"It'll be okay, Jack. I'll take care of it."

"Am I going to be in more trouble after this? From you?"

"Why would you be? Is there anything I don't know yet?"

"No, but still. Mr. Reeves isn't happy with me."

"Well that's okay. I'm not very happy with Mr. Reeves. Don't worry about it. Eat some breakfast, we'll be leaving soon."

He continues to look at me for a minute more, but eventually turns to pour his cereal. An hour later we're shown into the principal's office by a plump older receptionist.

"Jus' take a seat, Mr. Reeves will be with you shortly. Can I offer ya a coffee? Or water?"

I intend to politely decline, but don't get the chance, because Reeves walks in and snaps at the poor older woman. "That won't be necessary. Go back to your desk, Mary."

He walks straight to his desk as she flees the office, and he sits down, taking the power position and looking down his nose at us. Alright, so that's how this is going to go.

"Ms. Reilly. Let's cut to the chase. I'm a very busy man and don't have time to waste talking to someone masquerading as a parent as she allows her charge to run wild."

"Wait, hold up a sec—"

"No. We all know why Jack was suspended. Frankly, I feel like a few days wasn't enough, considering his transgressions, violent as they were, but since it was a first offense - *on school grounds* - I had to follow protocol. But know he's on, I suppose we can call it probation, and the very next time he's caught acting out, he'll be expelled from this school."

"Expelled? What—?"

"Listen to me, young lady," he interrupts again, speaking to me as though I was a four-year-old having a tantrum. "I know about your father, you have my sympathies, you truly do, but we both know how this is going to end. I know that you graduated here, and I always had such high hopes for you; you exceeded any expectations I had for someone of your … lineage. But the fact remains, you're a young woman who must house and clothe an unruly teenaged delinquent." He speaks about Jack as though he isn't even in the room, and my blood boils. "My best hope for you is he doesn't disrupt your life for long, and when he decides school is no longer for him, that he moves on and hasn't caused you or your promising career too much trouble."

"When he moves on? He's not yet sixteen years old. When do you expect him to *move on*?"

"Oh, I imagine it won't be long. He's without parental guidance now, he's getting into fights at school, and I'm lead to believe you actually encourage this barbarous behavior and *pay* for him to fight. I must say, Ms. Reilly, that lapse in judgement certainly surprised me. I know of your extended family, and their … criminal activities, so I don't suppose it'll be long before Jack *moves on* with them. In the meantime, I encourage you to focus on making sure your employer considers you a valued employee. I'd think that concludes this meeting, so if you'll just follow me …"

Asshole Reeves actually stands, his hand extended in case we forgot where the door was. I look toward Jack who looks like a puppy that's been repeatedly kicked, and I've had enough.

I remain seated, staying silent for a minute longer, forcing Principal Reeves look back down at me in question.

"Well, now that you've said your piece, I have a few things to say myself."

I bolster all of my bravado, struggling to separate this asshole from the man who taught me years ago, the disciplinarian of my teenage years.

He's right in a way. I guess he did have a soft spot for me when I was younger, because I remember him as a decent human being; fair, encouraging, if not a bit snobbish. But now I see how he treats those he considers a lost cause, and he's dead wrong if he thinks I'll tolerate him writing Jack off like that. "Mr. Reeves, I have a few questions for you."

Reeves looks bored and impatient, staring me down, waiting for me to give up the act and scuttle away. But I can't. Jack's too important for me to run away with my tail between my legs. After a long, tense moment, he finally nods his head, indicating I continue.

He doesn't sit down again though, so I stand. I'll meet this man, toe to toe. I will not shrink down from him.

"How is it, Mr. Reeves, that Jack got into a physical altercation, on school grounds in school hours, with someone—much older than him, I should add—who does not in fact attend this school? How did Chris have access to a minor, a student, when said student was in your care?" Point one for me, because I didn't choke on my words, and I sound professional as hell.

"I don't know, *Ms.* Reilly." He emphasizes the 'Ms,' as though it were a dirty word. "Chris is actually a cousin of yours, is he not? So perhaps this is family business, and Jack should keep it away from our school."

"Incorrect. Chris is not a cousin of ours. He's nothing to us. But let's backtrack for a sec … So, because you don't approve of Jack, or my family, you fail to protect him. He was harassed, he was taunted and provoked on school grounds and during school hours, yet you label him as the bad guy and suspend him."

"This is not up for discussion, Catherine. Jack engaged in a violent altercation and was dealt with appropriately. Next time he messes up, he'll be suspended again, for longer. Next time he fights, he'll be expelled. His grades have been steadily declining for the last two years anyhow, we all knew this was coming."

"His grades?" I snap. No fucking way! We've worked hard on those damn grades. "*Exactly*, how is he performing, in each class? I want to know exact grades and where you think he's lacking." I know for a fact his grades have made a turn around, his test scores have been amazing.

"Well, I can't tell you exactly right this minute, I don't have access to … and I'm busy …"

"Please, call your secretary back in here. I know she has access to that information, and I want to see them. Right now."

He sighs, clearly put out by the direction this conversation has turned. But honestly, I'm past the point of giving a damn. He will not label Jack a piece of shit just because he's related to pieces of shit.

Reeves picks up his desk phone, quickly mumbling instructions, then when he hangs up, he sits down, putting his fingers on the bridge of his nose, as though entertaining us is giving him a headache. We probably are. Want to know how many fucks I have to give?

We wait for Mary to join us, no one speaks, the air thick with tension. I feel my phone vibrate in my bag. Uncaring if I look insolent in front of this arrogant man, I look at it to find Bobby's name, and I try to hide my smile.

I quickly look to Jack first and note with relief he no longer looks defeated, but now hopeful, as though my championing him really surprises him. I hate that he worried I wouldn't. As long as he's in the right, as long as he works to be a good person, I'll always have his back.

He smiles at my phone, as though he knows who texted me.

Bobby: How's it going?

I don't know how to answer without going into long explanations, or getting angry again, and I run out of time, because Mary bustles in, so I simply reply with an angry face, hoping to make him proud with my dreaded emoji use.

I shove my phone back into my purse, already feeling it vibrate again, but I ignore it as Mary shows Reeves a stack of papers. I sit and wait, smug in my confidence.

They speak to each other in hushed tones, every now and again Reeve's looking up at Jack or me. After a few moments, the secretary bustles back out again, long skirts swaying, her floral perfume wafting past me, and she lays her hand on my shoulder in a quick pat as she passes.

Reeve's throws the stack on his desk and pinches his nose again, making a whistling noise as he breathes out.

"Right, well it seems his grades, while still below average, are increasing, so I say we just leave this here. Jack, you can go to class now," he says, arrogance personified, as though he can insult us then brush it under the rug when he's proven wrong. Jack looks to me for direction and I just shake my head.

"No, stay another minute. Mr. Reeve's, please share Jack's academic reports. As his guardian, I'd like to know. So we're aware of his … shortcomings, and know what to work on." My smile is sweeter than sugar, as I taunt the arrogant man.

He looks back up at me again, and I feel like he's imagining wringing my neck. I sit up straighter, exposing more neck just to tease him, and I raise my brows in question.

Please, do go on, asshole.

"I don't appreciate your attitude Ms. Reilly. I'm the principal here …"

"Yes, but *I* am no longer a student here, and *you* are no longer *my* principal. I'm a grown woman, and legal guardian of one of your students. I'll demand the same respect you give any of the middle-aged parents you brown nose for fundraising money, and I'll accept no less than fair treatment of Jack when he's a student here, treating him no different simply because he was born on the wrong side of the tracks. So please, *sir*, Jack's reports?"

He blows a noisy breath through his nose then picks up the papers again. "Fine!" he snaps. He throws one sheet down. "World History. Was a D," he emphasizes the 'was' grade and

I lift my brow, urging him to continue, "is currently a B." He throws another down. "Economics, was also a D, now a B." Then another. "English, now a B minus. Geography, currently an A. Mathematics," he looks at the papers again, then at me, "was a D … now an A. Now if that'll be all, I have a meeting I must attend."

That's fine by me. I've made my point. Below average, my ass. I stand and offer my hand and he stares at it for a full minute before finally taking it.

"Thank you for your time. If I could just remind you to ensure non-students stay off school grounds, and please try harder to keep Jack safe, rather than blame him for an adult screw up, then I'd be very appreciative. Have a nice day, Mr. Reeves."

I keep my smile sugary sweet, and my hand squeezing his. *Fuck you, asshole.*

As Jack and I walk down the hallway he smiles as though he just won the lottery. "That was awesome, Kit! Seriously cool." He fist bumps me and I laugh.

"That's okay. It was my pleasure taking the asshole down a peg. Make sure you let me know if you get any unfair treatment because of this, okay? Be good, don't fight, pay attention in class. But if you get unfair treatment, extra detention, things like that, you let me know."

"Will do," he says, smile still firmly in place.

"Alright, go to class. I'll see you at the gym later. You go straight there from school, okay? The guys will be expecting you."

"K. See ya!" He practically skips down the hall. I hope I've done the right thing. I wouldn't normally speak out to a superior in front of Jack; not to undermine their authority, but he needed to be put in his place. I won't allow that man to push a kid out of school simply because he doesn't like him.

This affects Reeves for another year or two, but it affects Jack for the rest of his life. Jack will finish school if it's the last thing I do, and he'll certainly make something of himself. I refuse to let him become a bum.

I walk through the large double doors and head toward my car, pulling my phone out of my bag as I walk. The screen shows five messages from Bobby, and I smile at it like a lunatic.

B: *How'd it go?*

B: *You okay?*

B: *Reeves is a dick!*

B: *Just saying.*

B: *Love you. Want me to deliver a knuckle sandwich?*

I giggle at him. Who the hell says knuckle sandwich anymore?

Me: *I don't think we can see each other anymore. :P*

B: *Oh lordt, what now? Tell me so I can yell at you, then I'll grab your ass.*

I laugh at his reply, glad that he knows I'm joking.

M: *It's just that… knuckle sandwich…? You kinda dulled your hotness by saying that. And without your looks, there's just nothing left to keep me interested.*

B: So sassy! Come here and I'll give YOU a knuckle sandwich.

M: Oh puhlease! You don't scare me. I have a good trainer! I know how to hit back.

B: Yeah, tell me about your trainer… he kind of awesome? Good looking?

M: Yeah, he is! A bit younger than me, but I could make an exception for Jimmy

B: Jimmy?!? So sassy!! :(

M: Sorry baby. Love you xx

B: Can't charm me now. I would cry, but that wouldn't be hot. Instead, I might go kick Jimmy's ass. That always makes me feel better.

M: Have fun kids! Don't break your mama's china. I have to go to work now anyway.

B: Wait, you still didn't tell me how it went at school.

M: Ugh, yeah, it was a clusterfuck. But I got the last word in, so all's right in my world.

B: That's my girl. Love you. See you this afternoon - you owe me some tongue.

M: I got you. Bye.

~*~

I arrive at the gym at six p.m. and find Jack sparring in the ring with his friend Calum. Both boys have gloves and headgear on, and both are circling, trading shots every now and again. Jimmy is coaching them both from the corner, shouting instruction, encouragement or insults when needed.

It's so strange to see the two wildly different personalities that is Jimmy. Outside of training, he's crazy and immature and funny as hell.

In this gym, though, when on the clock, he's the perfect professional, knowledgeable in his sport, the ultimate authority.

I watch them for a few minutes, noting that Jack's improving fast. He appears to be dominating this round, deflecting everything Calum throws while getting his own shots in easily. I thought watching him fight would make me feel differently, scared for him, but frankly, I'm just proud.

He's found a safe, sanctioned physical outlet and is becoming a force to be reckoned with, and his attitude and demeanor improves dramatically the longer he's exposed to these guys and the discipline the sport demands. No, I've not made a mistake bringing him here. The Kincaids are good men, and I'll be proud for Jack to idolize them.

I get nervous thinking about this development day fight he's entered, though Jack doesn't seem worried at all. Quite the contrary, he seems so excited for it he might wet his pants.

I jump when I feel a stinging slap on my ass then a soothing hand rubbing it away, and I smile.

"That's for trying to dump me today," Bobby whispers into my hair. He does this so often, I think it's his favorite way to pass time. Note to self: buy pretty smelling shampoo.

I spin in his arms, resting my hands around his neck and threading my fingers in his hair. I suddenly realize I spend a lot of my time playing with his hair too.

"Lucky you, you get PT with me tonight. I have some stuff I want you to work on, and since Aiden and Jon are taking classes, you're the lucky recipient of my undivided attention." He peppers kisses on my face as he speaks.

"Mmm, I could be okay with that."

"*Could* be?"

"Yeah well, are you going to push me a trillion times harder because you only have me to focus on? Or, are you going to go easy on me because you love me, and we'll spend a lot of the time making out?"

"While I like the sound of the second option, and I do in fact love you, we'll be working hard. Sorry babe. Making out with me won't help you win. So, we train."

"Win? A … competitive fight? Umm no, I'm not winning anything. I'm not particularly interested in getting my ass kicked in front of an audience."

"You won't get your ass kicked. I promise you that. We have a month to work on defense and then you'll get your first taste of fighting victory." He smiles as though he's got everything figured out. "Don't stress though. I'd never send you to a fight that I wasn't one hundred percent convinced you could win."

"A month? What's in a month?" I ask. I seem to have missed an entire conversation somewhere, because I have no idea what the EFF he is talking about.

"Your first fight. Are you even listening to me?"

"I can't fight!"

"Babe. Yes, you can! You need to trust me. If you're not ready in time, I'll pull you out. But I promise, you will be."

"But, but …"

"Come on. Give me a kiss then put your gloves on," he says patting my ass. Patronizing jerk.

After running a million laps of the room, two million squat jumps and sixteen hours of planking—I swear I'm not exaggerating—we work on defense.

"Alright, check babe," he says then kicks me in the thigh. "I said check. Lift your leg, check it," he says, kicking my leg again before I get a chance to 'check it.'

"Stop kicking me!" I snap at him. Doesn't he know I can't *check*, because my legs are weighed down by cement and fatigue?

"I won't kick you if you lift your leg and check it. This is important, babe. Check it or risk a dead leg."

"I hate you," I whine, all petulance, making him smile. "Okay, go again." I make sure I'm ready this time. He kicks out with a relatively soft roundhouse to my front leg and this time I lift in time.

His shin connects with mine and the bones smack together painfully. "Fuck! That hurts more than the dead leg."

"It won't for long. This is why we condition. Your first fight will have shin pads anyway. But in this gym, in training, we condition. Again!"

And so we keep going, achieving about a seventy percent success rate of checking in time. My shins sting with every kick, and my legs feel like they weigh a ton.

"Alright, now I want you to defend your head. Like this …" he says, showing me where to hold my arms, then he walks toward the corner of the room and comes back with a foam pool noodle. "Okay, hands up, baby, strong arms. If you're sloppy, you'll just knock yourself out."

Bobby starts hitting the sides of my head with the noodle, simulating side hooks, and throwing in a leg check every now and again just to annoy me. Checking the noodle is a much more pleasant experience than checking Bobby's stupid legs.

After a while — feels like a week later — we hear the double doors opening and the remaining Kincaid's, Jon and Jack walk in. And Izzy too, sporting a giant smile. I haven't had a lot of opportunity to chat with her, but she's always friendly when I do see her.

"The noodle? You're hitting her with the noodle?" Jimmy complains. "Bobby's gone soft!"

I don't want Bobby to get any ideas to hit me with a baseball bat though, so I speak up. "What are you all doing here? Get lost."

"No way, princess. Especially not now we know Bobby's going soft on you. Did he tell you the good news?"

I look around and note most of the people standing around are smiling too, Izzy and Jacks just as big as Jimmy's. And Bobby's. Fuckers! Traitors! The lot of them.

"Good news? The fact that you get to watch me get my ass kicked in public is good news? You're all jerks."

Jimmy laughs again. "You won't get your ass kicked. We promise."

"That's why I'm here." Izzy adds. "You'll be doing PT with me a couple times a week from now until the fight, so you can get the feel of actual sparring. I won't be pulling punches like the guys would ... or using noodles," she says, looking at the object as though it insults her.

"Great! So you get to kick my ass first, then send my already broken body into the ring to get kicked again. Joy!"

"Kit, stop!" Bobby snaps at me. "No one will be kicking your ass, especially not your opponent. But you need to fix that attitude. You won't win if you keep telling yourself you can't."

Ugh! "Fine! I'm sorry," I concede.

Jack laughs. "How do those words taste, Kit? Did they burn coming up?"

Can I ground him for that alone? Or is that misusing authority?

Bobby leans in and kisses me on the temple, speaking softly, "You'll be fine babe, I promise. I will never, ever, let anyone hurt you." Then louder, "we're done for tonight anyway. Good job. You worked hard." Bobby smacks me on the ass again then takes my hand, and we walk toward the others so we can go home.

14

Bobby

Development Day #1

Jimmy spent a lot of time with Jack the last few weeks prepping him for his fight, and today's finally the day. I've been keeping an eye on his progress, as well as Kit's, and I'm absolutely thrilled with how they're doing.

I've no doubt they will both do well, and personally, I feel like a proud parent waiting for Jack to be called to the ring.

Watching Kit train does strange things to me. Her body is developing such strong sexy muscle, her long legs are what dreams are made of. Literally.

Her attitude though, is the sexiest change of all.

Along with her new skills and added muscle mass, her confidence has taken a huge boost. She now believes she can fight, and fight well, and that confidence translates to fucking sexy.

She and I spend the majority of our downtime together, and Jack considers me a constant fixture in their home. She hasn't slept at my house since that first time because she doesn't feel comfortable leaving Jack home alone, but I've stayed over at their house a few times.

Those nights are the best; being able to turn to her at any time of the night, to be able to touch her, to smell her, to wake her up slowly by pleasuring her. She's amazing, and I've gone from a guy not wanting to commit to any one person ever, to knowing exactly who I'll marry. She's it for me, and I don't regret it one bit.

The nights we don't sleep in the same bed, we text or call. She's the last person I speak with before sleep, and the first when I wake up.

I know she's still busy at work, and I know she's still working with her lawyers, trying to finalize her dad's estate, although they advise her it'll still be a while. They did tell us her aunts have backed off with their lawyers, and Jack says he hasn't had any more issues with the asshole Chris, so basically, life has been smooth sailing.

Now that it's August, I'll start to increase my own training hours and back off teaching class sessions in preparation for my fight in December. The other guys will alternate between training me and picking up the classes I have to pass on — the same arrangement we have when any of us have a fight coming up. As December gets closer, I'll commit more and more hours per day.

My training shouldn't really impact my time with Kit, since the majority of my training time is when she's at her office. I'll still see her in the evenings when she trains, although I won't be the one training her. But that's okay, we'll be fine. If I'm lucky, I'll get extra nights in her bed, even if only to be near her.

Now we're in the locker rooms at the fight center, and Jack and Jimmy are skipping rope about ten feet away from me, as Jimmy murmurs tips and Jack listens intently.

Poor Jack, he's been totally pumped for this, but today he looks a little ill, though I have no doubt he'll be fine. He's a fucking machine in the ring, and I know once he gets hit for the first time, he'll snap to action, and he'll dominate.

A few minutes later an official comes into the room, his clipboard in front of his nose and he speaks without looking up. "Three-minute call for Reilly."

"Alright Jack, put the rope away and come over here."

He's so nervous now; his hands are shaking, his movements jerky. His face has gone from slightly green tinged to imminent puking green.

"Okay, you need to calm down," I tell him as I pass his water. "Have a sip, slow your breathing. Don't stress. Your opponent is just as fresh as you, and just as nervous. The difference is, he isn't as good as you. No one has worked as hard as you, so you have nothing to worry about. Keep your strategy simple. Go for legs, go for the body, and then when you see the opening, take his head. Legs, body, legs, body, legs, body, head! Got it? Remember, you don't have to knock him out to win. Disable his legs and he's out. Don't waste your energy on head shots unless you know they'll pay off."

"Come on," Jimmy says, as he passes Jack's gloves, "we have to get your gear on. You have about a minute and a half left."

Kit ended up buying them both new gloves when I suggested it, and Jacks are already showing wear — a testament to his hard work. He'll treasure these gloves for the rest of his life. The first gloves he ever owned. The first gloves he ever competed with. The wear and tear is coveted.

To own mark free gloves means he never even tried.

Geared up, we walk side by side out the doors and down the hallway leading to the main room. Usually this place operates as a regular gym, but today they've cleared everything out except the ring and brought in chairs for the spectators. There'll be twelve fights today, and since Jack is both male and a heavyweight, he's number ten on the drawcard, only preceding the more experienced male heavyweights.

I spot Kit as soon as we enter the main room. It's as though she has some inner magnet, my personal compass pointing me in her direction. Always.

Apart from her own personal shade of nervous green, she looks amazing today, like she always does. I'm so fucking happy she's feeling more confident in herself now, but I just don't understand how she was always so self-deprecating, how she couldn't see what I saw.

Not that I mind reminding her daily; as her man, that's a job I'll relish doing.

Today she's wearing her hair half up, half down. In her usual high-tops and cut-off shorts, but instead of any old tank, today she's wearing one of our gym shirts. It does things to my dick to see my label on her.

On any fight day, we always show support for our fighter and the gym we come from by wearing shirts with the gym logo printed on it. I kinda feel like she's wearing my name plastered all over her, and it makes me feel all caveman and possessive.

Sitting in the third row of chairs with Aiden, Jon, and Tink, she's sitting on the end, next to Aiden, and I figure she chose that spot because he'll talk her through Jack's fight and her own nerves. I assured her he'd be fine and she should just try to enjoy the experience, but I know she won't.

Add on the fact she's fighting next weekend; I know today's experience is just making her more nervous. Her eyes latch onto mine and I smile, trying to let her know everything's fine. Hesitantly she smiles back then looks at Jack but he doesn't notice, too caught up in his own nerves.

The announcers finish calling the last fight, declaring the winner and holding his hand in the air to the applause of the crowd.

"Alright Jack. Just breathe, okay, just breathe. Trust your body, trust your muscle memory to get you through this. I only want you to concentrate on breathing. If you don't, you'll gas and then it's all over. Breathe, and fight smart. We're not looking for fastest or strongest. Smart is what will get you through."

I hit him in the chest then walk him to his corner and hold the ropes open for him. He climbs in and Jimmy and I stay on the outside. "Jack!" I call for him to bend over so I can put his mouth guard in. "Just breathe. I promise you'll do great. Trust me, little brother, I promise!"

He looks in my eyes for a moment longer then nods his head, his eyes transforming from terrified to steely resolve. Atta boy.

The ref calls the boys to the center of the ring and grabs a glove in each hand. "I want you to defend yourselves at all times. You know the rules, make it a clean fight, boys. Tap gloves. Go back to your corners."

They bump fists and Jack heads back in our direction. He doesn't appear nervous anymore. He looks ready. His adrenaline has him on track now and I fully expect a good fight. I quickly glance toward Kit to find her biting her nails, probably down to the skin. I want to give her a hug and tell her to relax, but the bell indicates the beginning of Jack's fight, so I swing my gaze back to the ring.

Both boys gingerly step toward each other, unsure who should hit first, unsure how much it's going to hurt.

"Jab, Jack!" Jimmy yells from beside me. "Jab, leg, leg!"

I know from experience when fighting that some fighters will hear everything. Time slows down and they're able to think and plan. Other fighters get tunnel vision and hear nothing, doing their best to throw whatever they can in an attempt to win. Both approaches have advantages but I want my fighters to be able to concentrate and think, to not feel overwhelmed in the moment.

I'm fucking ecstatic when Jack jabs, hitting his opponent square in the jaw, then follows it with a kick to the outside thigh, so fast the other guy had no hope of checking it. His opponent buckles at the leg momentarily and then they circle each other.

I make mental notes on things we can work on next time in training – things like the fact Jack could have kept attacking the leg instead of backing off and circling.

They move in again, the other guy trying but missing any head shots, all the while getting pummeled in the ribs as Jack spots the opening easily.

"Good Jack! Keep it up. Teep, get your distance, strike!"

The fight can last up to three rounds of three minutes each. The first round ends with the bell and Jack comes back to our corner, winded but completely untouched.

"You're doing so good Jack! How do you feel?" I take his mouth guard and squirt water into his mouth.

"It's great! It doesn't hurt at all!" His adrenaline has him shouting, and Jim and I laugh. He might feel it tomorrow when he comes down from the excitement.

"Okay, you're doing great." I squirt more water into his mouth. "I want you to concentrate on his legs in this round. Take 'em out. Finish the fight. Don't back off unless you have to. Don't give him time to catch his breath. Got it?"

He nods quickly, then the boys are called back for round two, so I quickly shove his mouth guard in and step back.

I look to Kit, hoping to give her a thumbs-up and reassure her, but when I find her in the crowd, she's glaring at us, and my brows pinch. What the hell did I do wrong?

Jack's doing amazing. I don't understand her expression or her anger. I mouth the words, 'are you okay?' and she rearranges her features and gives me a small smile; worst liar ever. Aiden and Jon look fucking pissed too. What the hell is going on? I want to run to her, I want to demand answers, but the bell snaps me back to Jack and I watch as he approaches his opponent again.

Kit's safe. My brothers have her back, so I force my attention back to the fight. I made a promise to Jack, I told him I'd have his back.

Jack follows my instructions perfectly and takes the legs again and again. Each time hitting the exact same spot, making the other guy buckle more each time. Every few kicks he'll throw a few punches, drawing his opponent's attention away from the leg, and then he'll take the leg again.

Jack is a fucking powerhouse, and I know he's already won by points alone. He changes it up and starts kicking to the ribs, bringing the guy's arms down to protect them. Legs. Ribs. Ribs. Legs. Ribs. Ribs. Then suddenly, he spins, throwing a roundhouse kick and hitting his opponent square in the jaw, knocking him the fuck out!

Jimmy and I are yelling our voices hoarse, jumping on each other and cheering as the ref holds Jack's hand in the air and the medic checks over the other guy. As soon as his hand is lifted, Jimmy and I jump into the ring, tackling Jack in our excitement.

Jack's face is just pure joy — and a little unbelieving. I'm so proud of this little fucker!

"Winner by K.O. Jack Reilly!" the referee announces, and our ragtag group of friends in the crowd all jump to their feet and cheer. All signs of the earlier trouble is completely removed from their faces.

Kit's my family now, and therefore, Jack is too. If they're my family, then they're my brothers' family too, and the guys all show their pride in their new brother's success.

The ref indicates we need to leave the ring, so I open the ropes and let Jack climb out, then Jimmy and I follow. We take him back to the locker rooms to remove his gear and let him shower, then we'll join the others once we've debriefed with Jack.

Whenever one of us fights, whether it's a development day, or the world title, we debrief immediately after. We discuss how it went — win or lose — what we could do better next time, how we feel about it, if we're hurt. It helps us process what's just happened, and helps bring us back to earth a little bit and slows the adrenaline rush.

Twenty minutes later, we emerge from the gym warehouse, laughing and high on victory and ready to celebrate with our friends, when yelling from the parking lot has our heads snapping up. We know those voices, and the three of us round the corner at a sprint to see Aiden — a trained fighter, yes, but never the first to anger or act rashly — hitting a man and dropping him to the ground.

I bolt the rest of the way, desperate to reach them, even more desperate to find Kit. Thankfully, she's being held behind Jon, and the guy on the ground is Timms, our former student.

He hasn't been back to our gym since that day he confronted Kit and was shooed away. To be honest, I haven't even thought of him again since that day.

"Fuck you all," he spits past his bleeding lip. "You think you're some kind of special. Just a bunch of cocksuckers and their slut groupies."

I stand over him, blocking his view of the group, blocking his view of Kit. "What the hell's going on here?"

"Nothing! Get the fuck out of my way, faggot." He stands and pushes past me, walking toward the others.

"Hey, Kitty Cat," he says, essentially to Jon, since Kit is stuffed behind him. At the mention of her name, my whole body tenses. I'm ready to wreck a motherfucker. She doesn't look like a damsel in distress though. She looks ready and willing to fight him herself. "Come see me when you want to suck a real dick. I'd be willing to slum to show you a real man."

Jimmy jumps and grabs me as a roar rips through my chest and I move forward. "Get the fuck out of here," he snaps at Timms. "Next time, I won't stop him." Jimmy locks down on my arms and Aiden pushes me back as I fight them.

Kit moves out from behind Jon and is in front of me with her hands on my chest in a heartbeat. "Calm down, Bobby. It's fine."

"The fuck it is. What the hell happened?" I shout at her. She flinches against me, and guilt washes through my body. My anger isn't directed at her, but my adrenaline has me ready to run Timms the fuck over.

"Bobby. Cool it," she snaps at me, then she looks at my captors. "Let him go."

They look at her, then at me, then toward the car pulling out of the lot as Timms spins his wheels on the way. They release me and I slump forward until Kit wraps her arms around me. I'm not sure if she's hugging me or restraining me, but she presses her face into my chest, kissing it and softly shushing me.

The feel of her against me is like aloe on a burn, relaxing me, and I wrap my arms around her and kiss her hair.

"Okay, I'm alright." I'm not alright. I want a round in the ring with him. I want to beat Timms unconscious, then I want to show Kit, show her the stronger man, show her I can keep her safe.

Jack hovers around us she breathes against my chest. He's checking her over, making sure she's okay. It would blow Kit's mind if she knew just how protective he is of her.

After a few quiet minutes, I look to Aiden for answers. "What happened?"

He's hopped up on adrenaline too, his movements jerky as he brushes his hands through his short hair. "Timms was … interested in dating Kit. She said no thanks. He wouldn't take no for an answer."

My eyes narrow and my hands squeeze Kit against me. "Define *wouldn't take no for an answer!*"

"He spoke to her inside, during the fight. Dunno what he expected, considering she was sitting with us. Guess he never considered she wouldn't be interested."

"Okay, she said no." I look back to her. "You said no."

She nods, and her angry eyes turn emotional, filling with tears that threaten to spill.

"Babe? Talk to me."

She hugs me close again, her arms coming suspiciously tight around my waist, and I feel like I'm being restrained again.

"He, umm… I came outside, after the fight, to take a quick work call. I knew you'd all come out in a few minutes, so I stood in plain view of the doors. He saw me and came to ask again. I said no, he said some mean things about you, so I swore at him a bit …"

She trails off and my stomach flips with nerves. "Finish it babe, please." My heart pounds painfully as anxiety washes through me. What happened? What *could* have happened?

"He crowded me … against the wall. He didn't touch me!" she rushes out, as my body vibrates with violence. "He just crowded me a bit, talking shit about how I'm a … cock tease and slut and stuff. That's when the others came out and Aiden hit him, then you were here right after that."

I move her back away from me, holding her at arm's length and I scan her from head to toe. I'm sick to my stomach; I was so close, but not close enough when she needed me. "You're okay? You promise you're not hurt?"

"I promise."

"Do you want to file a report, press charges, anything like that?"

She shakes her head quickly. "No, he didn't touch me. Aiden will probably get in more trouble, because he did hit him. I promise I'm fine. Can we just forget it?"

I look into her eyes for another long minute, but she's begging me to let it go, so reluctantly, I nod and bring her back into my chest and I whisper, "I'm sorry I wasn't here. I love you, Kit."

She sighs and her muscles relax against me. "I love you too."

She pulls away and heads to Aiden, then surprising the hell out of him, she wraps her arms around him too. "Thank you for your help."

He's hesitant at first, awkwardly patting her shoulder, but he smiles when she pulls away to face him. "It's cool, Kitten. I got your back."

"Alright, shows over," she says, walking to Jack and hugging him too. He's been standing quietly, his body vibrating from the adrenaline of his fight, then the added adrenaline of seeing his sister in trouble. But when she hugs him, he visibly relaxes as his world snaps back to balance. He makes faces, he pretends he doesn't like her attention, but he's full of shit.

She pulls away from him with a giant grin. "Now we celebrate Jack's awesome knock out. This is your party, so you choose dinner. Where do you want to go? What do you want to eat?"

I smile in anticipation, because I know the answer before he even speaks.

"I want pizza at home, and I want everyone to come over to watch the fights on TV."

"Okay, it's a deal. You'll all come over, yeah?" She turns and looks at everyone else. Tink nods an enthusiastic yes, then Jon nods when she nods, which makes me chuckle.

Dude's either got to get with her, or stop acting so whipped.

"Yeah, I'll be there," Jimmy smiles, then he turns around our group. "Where's Iz anyway? She said she'd be here."

Izzy is several years younger than us, born when Jon was seven, and by the time she could walk and talk, she was following him everywhere he went. Which meant she followed us all everywhere we went. Since she's so much younger, she was always considered our baby sister; though technically, Jimmy's only barely a couple years older.

She has a rough time meeting guys, since she has four older brothers and a whole gym of overprotective friends watching over her. We're not saying she can't date, we're just saying the guys she's been interested in in the past have been dicks.

"She texted me earlier," Jon says. "She came and watched Jack's fight but had to leave straight away. Quote, 'I have plans tonight.'"

We all make a face at her 'plans.' We don't like when she does that.

"Okay," Jim turns away from our group and spins his keys between his fingers. "I'm going home to get changed. I'll meet you all at the house in a little bit." He stops and hits Jack on the shoulder. "Awesome fucking fight, Jack! I'm proud of you."

Jack, Kit, and I drove to the fights together this morning, so they follow me back to my car and we get in. I hate that we're not quite as excited as we should be, considering Jack not only just won, but he obliterated the competition.

Kit settles herself in the passenger seat, and I reach across to hold her hand, taking comfort in the fact she's right here, soft and warm, and safe.

So, for the sake of celebrating Jack's win, I decide to shrug that fucking asshole Timms off and enjoy my love and celebrate Jack.

I'll deal with Timms another time.

Turning around, I look at Jack and wait while he focuses on buckling his seat belt. When he's done, he looks up and freezes.

"Alright Jack. And Kit," I say, looking at her too. "I'm sorry about that shit with Timms, but it's done now." I kiss her knuckles and wait for her smile. "So he's out of our minds. I want you to know how fucking proud I am of you, Jack. I'm not sure you understand how good you did today. You didn't just win. You didn't just win by decision. You knocked him out. With an amazing roundhouse, at that. I know you were both nervous, but I had absolutely zero doubt in my mind you'd be fine. So, now we celebrate. Tonight's your night, Jack, nothing else matters. Enjoy it. It's the first of many post fight celebrations in your future. Let's go home."

That night, we celebrate with pizza and pay-per-view fights. Jon, Tink, Jim, and Aiden come over to hang out, and even Izzy dropped by around nine, surprising us.

We weren't complaining though; nine p.m. means she didn't like him. Good news for us.

We sit around watching the fight channel, enjoying talking over the strategies and discussing Jack's fight from today. He's on cloud nine, the smile impossible to wipe from his face and his happiness is infectious.

The party hit another level when Izzy arrived and made herself at home, hooking into cold pizza, and teasing the guys. Jon and Tink stick close like usual, and we all roll our eyes when they pretend to keep their distance.

I'm touching Kit in some way the entire evening, whether she's sitting against me, cuddled up against me, holding my hand, or when standing side by side, I keep my hands on her back or over her shoulders. I can't get enough of her, and find myself wishing everyone would get lost so I could take her to bed.

I notice her drink is empty, as is mine, so I stand to go to the kitchen for a refill, but stop and turn when I feel a tug on my pants.

"Wait for me," she says, unfolding her long legs to stand. I take her hands to help her up, but I don't step back to give her space. She bumps into me and her soft chest rests against mine.

She knows what I'm doing, and she smiles back, all flirty sass. I love when she's feeling playful like this, my dick standing at half-mast just thinking about it.

I keep a hold on her hand and we head to the kitchen, then I open the fridge and help myself. "What do you want to drink, babe?"

"I'll just have a soda, thanks. I don't feel like beer at the moment."

I pull a can of cream soda out and pop the tab open, then grab myself a beer and open that. In no apparent rush to join the others, she sits her beautiful ass on the counter, so I walk to her and stand between her legs.

I sit my beer down next to her and run my hands along her silky thighs, and with my gaze drawn down to my hands, she leans forward and places a soft kiss to my forehead. I close my eyes, feeling all emotional and shit at how comforting her kiss is.

"I love you, Bobby."

"I love you too, babe." I lean forward and drop a kiss on her lips. "You having a fun night?"

"Yeah. I love hanging out as a big group. You?"

I smile softly. "Yeah, I just love hanging out with you. Full stop."

"Hey Bobby?"

"Hmm?" I nibble at her neck.

"Do you want to stay over tonight?"

"Mmhmm." I nibble on her collarbone. "Yes please."

"Do you want to stay over … every night? That is, do you want to live here?"

Her hesitant question snaps me out of my lust filled daze and my head whips back. "I uh, really? Um …"

"Oh, my god! Shit!" Her hands cover her face as her cheeks burn red. "I'm sorry. Never mind! Please, just forg—"

"Whoa up, hold on, babe."

"No. I'm sorry. Please don't answer. Forget I mentioned it."

"Can you stop? Let me speak. Okay?"

"Nooo," she groans. "You hesitated, and now you feel pressured."

I lean forward and kiss her deeply to shut her up, then once she stops fighting me, I pull back and stare into her eyes. "Can I speak now?"

She looks terrified, her cheeks still burning red, but she nods softly. "Okay."

I laugh and kiss her nose. "You need to relax, baby. You misread my hesitance. I was surprised only that you're ready for that, since it's always been you running scared from me." I smile to convey lightness to my words. "And now you want me here all the time?"

"Yeah, well, I guess now I love you. And, well, I trust you. So I won't run anymore."

I laugh at her words. She almost sounds mad that she loves me, that it's a hardship for her. I've never been so happy to annoy someone. "You promise not to run?"

She looks into my eyes, and I see the truth there. "I promise."

I smile and trace her jaw with my thumb. "Then yes, I'd love to live here with you. That would make me really fucking happy actually."

"You sure? Are you feeling put on the spot? You can take time to think about it, if you want."

"Baby, I don't need time. I want to live with you. I've wanted to, but didn't want to scare you off. I want nothing more than to share your bed every night."

She bites her lip nervously. "I only suggested here, because of Jack, you know. Do you mind that you're the one to move? You could probably even touch my boobs every day, if you were so inclined ..."

I laugh and thrust my fist into the air. "YES! Deal!"

She giggles and slaps her hands over my mouth to shush me.

Jimmy walks into the kitchen with a goofy grin and a handful of chips crushes in his mouth. "What's so exciting?"

"Look what you did now," Kit laughs as the rest of our friends wander in. I gently bite the hand still covering my mouth, and she yelps and snatches it back.

I turn back to the group, then my eyes meet Jacks. "Move your toothbrush over, bro. I'm moving in."

~*~

A couple hours later, I practically shove everyone out the front door, well and truly ready for some alone time with Kit, then I take her hand and head for the stairs. "Night, Jack!"

He's old enough to know where we're going, and he's old enough to not need to be tucked into bed, so, we're done for the night as far as he's concerned.

As soon as we reach the staircase landing I yank her to a stop, surprising her but cutting off any questions by taking her mouth with mine. She catches on immediately, her tongue darting out to play. The way her body reacts to my every touch, since the very first time we met — it's like she was made just for me. She's a fucking miracle. She's *my* miracle.

I'll always work hard to please her, just to convince her to keep me. I'm so unbelievably happy that she asked me to live here, and I understand that it would've been hard for her to ask. I've wanted to, for a long time, but I needed her to be the one to take the step. I needed to know it's what she really wanted.

We continue kissing as I back her into her room, into *our room*. The backs of her legs hit the bed and I bend down and grab her thighs, then I lift her and lay her down so her legs dangle over the mattress. I pull her top up to expose her belly and I start nibbling, enjoying the taste that's uniquely hers. I inch my way up, licking her naval and then kissing each individual rib. I find her sweet, bra-covered breasts and find her nipples, gently biting through the bra cup as she arches her back and pushes herself further into my mouth.

I pull the cups down, leaving them settled under her breasts forcing them to sit above the cup and I stay here a while; suckling, licking, biting, drawing her beautiful nipples to stand tall, concentrating on one with my mouth, the other getting attention from my hand, pinching and pulling her taut.

She's almost levitating off the bed, her back arched almost impossibly. She wants more. But I make her wait.

"Bobby ..." she groans in frustration.

I continue playing with her nipples. "Hmmm?"

"Touch me. Please, touch me."

I lift my head to look at her. "I am touching you, babe."

"No. Touch me ..."

"Where baby? Where do you want me to touch you? Say the words."

"Touch my ... touch my pussy, Bobby, please touch my pussy."

My dick throbs at her beautifully filthy words. Instead of using my hands though, I move down her body, licking and nipping along the way, then sitting on my haunches at the end of the bed, I move quickly, pulling her shorts and panties down and opening her legs wide enough to accommodate my broad shoulders.

Before she gets a chance to protest, I lick her, my flat tongue moving from bottom to top and her whole body spasms.

"You taste so good, baby. So fucking good." I have to concentrate hard on not coming in my pants.

She bucks out of control, so I lay my hand on her hips to still her jerking. Using only my mouth, I continue to lick front to back, enjoying the way she purrs when I near her ass, then her bucking when I move back to the front to suckle on her clit.

She's close, so I insert two fingers and pump them and drag my fingers along the inside wall. She's almost sobbing, and I'd give anything to have the freedom to make noise now. I want to hear her scream for me. Instead she turns her face into the pillow to muffle the sounds of her pleasure.

She's on the very edge of coming, so I quickly pull my fingers out and push my pants down, then still standing, I slam into her. She instantly detonates around my cock, grabbing the pillow and screaming into it. I concentrate hard on holding back, wanting to give her one more and wanting to finish with her.

I let her ride out her pleasure and when she stills, I lean forward and pull the pillow away from her face. When her blue eyes stop on mine, I smirk arrogantly. "You okay in there, babe?"

"Mmmm, so good," she purrs as the aftershocks ripple through her and her pussy continues to squeeze me. Leaning down, I kiss her deeply, letting her taste her own desire on my tongue.

"That was so good. Thanks babe." She taps my shoulder with a cheeky grin on her face. "Could you let me up? I need to go clean up."

"You're done then?"

She nods and bites her lip to stop her smile.

"The fuck you are." I slam into her again, reminding her we still have more, so much more. Instantly, her smug smile is replaced with molten eyes and a slack mouth and her walls squeeze me in an iron grip.

I continue pushing into her, pulling her hips off the bed and resting her legs over my forearms so her weight rests on her shoulders and the top of her back. I'm standing and able to slam into her, using all of my strength to go as deep as her body allows.

She's breathing in fast little pants, her walls a constant grip, her legs squeezing me. I enjoy watching as her tits bounce each time I thrust into her.

She's so fucking beautiful, but I want to be closer. Leaning down, I put my hands behind her back and lift her up, I spin and sit on the bed, making sure not to break our connection.

"Ride me," I demand, then I press my teeth down over her nipple until she cries out. She places her hands on my shoulders and lifts her weight, then dropping, she slams down on me.

We both moan as she continues to move, and she drops her head to my neck, biting the muscle there, the pain sending sensation straight to my groin.

"Oh, I'm so close, Bobby."

I grab her by the hips and hold her up, then I slam her down and fuck her from the bottom. "Wait for me, baby. Wait for me."

"Bobby …?"

I continue, trying to hold off for another minute, wanting to prolong this amazing feeling.

"Bobby!" she growls angrily. Giving in, I pinch her clit and she bucks like a wild horse. She bites down on my shoulder in an attempt to contain her sounds of her pleasure.

"Go now," I allow. "Come with me." I push up deep inside her one last time and I let myself go as my face burrows into her hair.

We sit like that for a while, chests pressed together, both panting and trying to catch our breath as her pussy continues to ripple around me.

Twenty minutes later after a quick shower together, I lie us both down in her bed, *our bed*, I remind myself again, and we snuggle in the way we do in the center of the bed; with our legs tangled, her head on my chest, our hands linked on my stomach.

"Go to sleep," I whisper. "Dream of me, baby."

I nuzzle her hair as I mentally plan my day tomorrow. I have a lot to do and I'll need to text my brothers for help with it all.

15

Kit

What was I thinking?

This week flew by so much faster than I wanted it to. I've trained every day except yesterday — it was my *'rest day'* — and now, today's the day.

What day, you may ask?

The day I publicly step into a boxing ring and pray I don't humiliate myself. Bobby assures me I won't, as does Izzy and the rest of the guys. Jack's been giving me advice all week, thinking himself a pro from way back since his win last weekend. I just tell him thanks and privately roll my eyes; albeit none the less proud of his achievement.

It's been quite the celebratory atmosphere all week, with Jack's win and Bobby moving in, everyone just seems so … happy. I wasn't sure what Jack would think, but he assures me he thinks it's awesome that 'THE *Bobby Kincaid, UFC Champion'* gets to live with us, and apparently, his popularity at school has never been better.

Bobby, Jack, and the guys moved his stuff over to my house last Sunday.

It was so much fun having them all over for a large part of the day, the noise and happiness making me lighter with every passing minute. Jimmy never seemed to run out of material at Bobby's expense; locked down, whipped, under lock and key, ball and chain, and a billion other overused yet no less funny, clichés. Bobby laughed it off though, there was nothing that could bring him down. It's been amazing waking up to him every day since, and I want this happiness to last forever.

When I asked him that night in my kitchen, I was terrified when he hesitated, my whole body sizzling with humiliation. I was ready to dump and run, to never show my face in public again, but he assures me his hesitation was surprise and nothing more, and since he's never given me reason to doubt his word before, I've decided to trust him and enjoy having the love of my life in the same home as me.

Every day since, we've enjoyed waking up together, having breakfast together, training together, and then coming home to eat together. Thankfully, the gym is closed by eight every night, so even if he has classes to run, or my own training nights, we're both home at a good hour to eat and relax. Sometimes it's just Bobby, Jack, and me. Other times it's a full house. I love those nights as much as I love the quiet nights.

I slept pretty awful last night, the nerves of today getting the best of me despite Bobby's best efforts to exhaust and relax me. and now I find myself outside the gym where I'm to fight today, in an attempt to get some fresh air. I'm genuinely concerned I might lose my breakfast all over someone if I stay inside watching the fights any longer.

According to the draw, I have about thirty minutes until I'm due in the ring. I thought it would be beneficial for me to stay and watch the other fights. I mean, who doesn't get pumped when watching *Rocky*? But I was dead wrong. Every second I spent watching made me feel more nauseous. So instead, I escaped outside to try and relax. My heart is thumping against my chest and I'm thinking of texting Bobby — who's inside — to come outside with me. He offered to come out when I did but I declined, wanting time alone, but I realize being alone and inside my own head is just making it worse.

Taking out my phone, I open the text app and find his name at the top of the list, smiling that he's almost always the last person I spoke to.

Me: Babe? I send the text, thankful I don't have to wait more than thirty seconds for a reply.

B: Want me to come outside, baby?

M: Yes please. I'm out by the car.

B: On my way.

"Kit."

I was smiling at my phone, already feeling Bobby's calming effects when my head snaps up at the familiar voice, and my heartrate spikes faster than it has today.

"Chris?" My cousin's boyfriend stands in front of me with an ugly scowl as he looks me up and down in challenge. "What are you doing here?"

I look toward the gym, but don't see Bobby yet. I hope he hurries. I hope he doesn't. I know whatever this is, whatever Chris wants, it won't be good and I don't want Bobby involved in anything to do with him.

"Just came to tell you, you need to stop your lawyers. Now. Back them the fuck off the estate."

"Chris, what--"

"There's money in there that'll be going to Renee and Jack, not you. Jack will be coming with us, so the money will come too."

He's lost his damn mind. "There's no money, Chris, there's only debt."

I'm genuinely dumbfounded why they think my dad would have money stashed away, when I know he lived week to week. I also know, without a doubt, if there *was* money, he'd make sure it came to his kids. Sure, he loved his sisters, but his kids always, always came first.

"No, there's money that he told Renee about," Chris argues. "Before he died. He told her he'd send her the paperwork but he never got around to it."

I shake my head. "There's no money, Chris. And even if there was, there's no way whoever's in charge of that stuff would give it to his sisters when he has biological children living. But all that aside, what has any of this got to do with you? You're my cousin's *sometimes* boyfriend. How could you possibly have any interest in this?"

My eyes snap to Bobby's as he rounds the building, then instantly he transforms from smile to narrow glare. His stride increases triple time, and Chris steps back quickly.

"Well, maybe we'll have to make sure he has no *living* biological children anymore," Chris says softly, as he takes another step back. "Or maybe your rich boyfriend will shell out a few dollars to keep his live-in pussy around." He smirks, then turns quickly and runs to his beat-up dirt bike and speeds out of the lot just as Bobby reaches me.

"Babe?" He slings his arm over my shoulder and pulls me in tight against his body. Did Chris really just threaten me, or was he just being a dick? A dick with poorly chosen words. And how does he know Bobby and I live together?

Bobby squeezes me again. "Babe? You're shaking. Who the fuck was that?"

Adrenaline rushes through my whole body, leaving me shaking and a little light headed. I turn toward Bobby as his jaw flexes with anger and his arms squeeze me almost painfully.

"That ... was Chris."

"Chris?" Bobby's eyes search my face in confusion. "The guy Jack got in a fight with?"

I nod.

"What did he say? Why are you shaking?"

I genuinely have no idea what to tell him right now. I don't want to tell him Chris scared me. That would only piss Bobby off, and I don't want any trouble. "He, ah, he *suggested* I drop my lawyers. Apparently, there's some money in my dad's estate that they want."

"What the fuck? If there's money, they won't be getting it!"

"That's just it, Bobby. There's none. Apparently, my dad told them there was, but I just know there isn't. And if there was, he'd ensure his kids could easily access it. There's no way, absolutely no way in hell he'd leave me holding the bill for a funeral if he had the money for it. Or for Jack's living expenses. That's just not who my dad is."

His eyes turn unbearably sad. "You paid for the funeral yourself? You lost your dad, had to take your brother in, *and* had to finance it all? By yourself?"

"Bobby, focus." I don't need him focusing on my finances. I'm not broke, but in direct comparison to him, I feel pathetic.

"I am focused, babe! I know how much funerals cost. It almost ruined my mom when she had to bury my dad. So there's nothing? Absolutely no money being left to you? Nothing but bills?"

"No Bobby. There's nothing, nothing but bills and a teenager. Does that make you think poorly of me?"

"Think poorly of you? No baby, never. The very opposite. I was already in awe of everything you're dealing with, but to take on complete financial burden as well. You're the strongest woman I know." His hands come up to my chin gently. "But, are you okay?"

"Yeah, I'm fine, I've mourned, and I'm too busy not be okay."

"No honey. You've not mourned and moved on. Not yet. But that's not what I meant. I meant are you okay — financially. Can I help you?"

Fury fills my every limb as I snap my chin from his hold. Humiliation burns me all over. Bobby thinks I need his money. "No, I don't need your fucking money! Is that what you think this is?" I gesture with my hand between us. "You think I'm dating you for your money?" I'm practically screaming at him. I'm such a bitch.

"What? No! That's not what I said."

"Maybe I sought you out from the beginning, put on the innocent act, played hard to get, all with the intention of recouping my dad's funeral expenses?"

"Babe, stop! That's not what I --"

"No Bobby, you're probably right, I'm poor as fuck, as we all know. Maybe if I suck your cock, you'll write me a check like some common whore." I hate myself. I hate every single venomous word that passes through my lips.

"Kit. Stop that now!" He steps in and shakes me so hard, my teeth rattle around together. "You've had your say, so now you'll shut the fuck up before you hate yourself any more." Pulling me against his chest roughly, he wraps his arms around me - To keep me from running away. Or possibly from hitting him. "You're angry right now, and that's okay. And I know you're not actually angry at me. I'm just the lucky fucking target right now. You *know* none of that's true. You *know* I love you, and I know you love me. We made promises, remember? No more running. I didn't mean to offend you, I only meant to lighten your burden. I love you, baby. We're a team."

His words are all truth, I know that, and I'm deeply ashamed for the things I said. I can't stop the flood of tears spilling over, so I just step in and cling to him, soaking his shirt, sobbing into his chest, finally letting go some of the pent-up rage and anguish the last year has left me with.

I've not taken any time at all to cry for my dad. Not since the day he was buried. I've bottled everything up and soldiered on. I had no choice. I had no one to hold me up when I was unable to do it myself.

I'm crying for the injustice of having to rally and support a teenager who didn't want help. He's come around now, but there was a long time where I was metaphorically bashing my head against a brick wall. I was angry, but now I just feel the unfairness of it all settle heavy on my shoulders.

Bobby continues to hold me tight, holding my chest together when my heart just wants to break out and step in front of an oncoming bus.

He nuzzles my hair, shushing me and rubbing my back, telling me he loves me over and over again. I'm embarrassed that I can't seem to find control over my body right now, my emotions hijacking it and wringing me out. I'm unsure how long we stand there, or how much of a scene I've made. I'm embarrassed that I'll have to face that any moment as well, but for *this* second, I refuse to face reality. I just want Bobby to hold me up, I want to take this chance to lean, if only for a minute.

After a while, my tears slow down and my sobs turn to sniffles. My body relaxes, no longer hostage to out of control emotion, and taking cue from my body language, Bobby moves his head back and lifts my chin to look him in the eye.

"Are you okay, baby?"

My tears stream again at his kindness.

"No baby, don't cry."

"I can't help it. They won't stop." I hiccup into his chest again, even as I bring my hand up roughly to swipe tears away. "I'm okay though. I'm okay. I sorry, Bobby." I sniffle and try to regain my composure. "I didn't mean what I said."

"I know honey. It's okay. You can use me for a punching bag any time." He lowers his face to meet my gaze. "Maybe sucking my cock will make me feel better?"

"Oh god!" I laugh and cry at the same time. "You and I have serious issues with what we say to each other when we're mad."

"Ha yeah, I scream at you about touching your boobs. You scream at me about sucking me off. I'm so fucking happy to realize I win in both of those scenarios." He waggles his brows jokingly, breaking the last of any tension between us, then he uses the heel of his hands to wipe away my tears. "Are you okay now, baby?"

I nod. "I'm okay. Thanks for being there, Bobby."

"I'll always be here. Always," he promises. He looks at his watch and his face crinkles with worry. "Do you want to go home?"

I look at my phone and realize I have less than ten minutes before I'm due to fight. I'd completely forgotten about it. I groan, unsure if I should just go hide under a rock somewhere.

"We can leave, honey. It would be totally alright. I'll pull you from the draw and we'll try again another time."

Thankfully, I'm already dressed and have wraps on my hands, needing only to get my gloves and head gear on to be ready. I take another minute to breathe, then with a large exhale, I'm decided. "It's okay, let's go in."

He pulls on my hand as I start leading him back toward the gym entrance. "You want to fight? Are you sure?"

"Yeah, what better time than this? I'm not nervous at all, I just let out a shit ton of emotion. And I'm kind of angry, so I can use that." I laugh when his brows furrow. That's right, he's warned me about fighting when angry. *It'll make you sloppy. It'll make you hurt yourself.*

"I'm fine Bobby. Physical exertion is exactly what I need right now."

I turn back to look at him waggling his eyebrows again, and I hit him in the stomach for his dirty mind.

He pulls me up short, holding onto my hands and forcing me to look into his eyes. "Wait, baby. Are you sure?"

I let out a deep breath and nod my head. "Yeah, I'm sure. We've worked hard for it. Plus, it's just another beginner chick. I won't get hurt. What's the worst that could happen?"

He watches me for another moment, then leans forward and kisses me. He pulls back and rests his forehead against mine. "Bravest fucking woman ever. And I get to keep her forever… Alright, well if you really wanna do this, we have to go then." He pulls me along at a fast jog. Before I get time to reconsider, I'm sitting on a padded bench in a locker room, Casey's pulling my hair into a braid to make the head gear a more comfortable fit, and Bobby's putting my gloves on.

We're the only people in here, and I'm thankful for the quiet. Casey knows something's wrong, but she doesn't ask.

I'm the world's ugliest crier; my eyes and face puff up and go red, and take a long ass time to return to normal. My opponent will probably think I've been in the locker room terrified to face her.

A man knocks and pokes his head in the room, "Three minutes for Reilly."

Any idiot could understand exactly what that means, and my heart beat picks up speed, slamming against my chest as adrenaline rushes through my veins. Surprisingly, adrenaline is all I can feel, not nerves. Chris' visit helped put things into perspective for me. I've got bigger problems in my life—a possible loss inside a sanctioned competition is way low on the list of shit to worry about.

"Babe? Are you listening to me?"

My eyes snap up to Bobby's. "Huh?"

"Honey. You sure you're sure?"

"Yeah, babe. I promise. I'm good to go." I hop off the bench. "Actually, I'm excited."

"Whoa. You still have a minute and a half. I'll walk you out when it's time. I need you to concentrate when you're in the ring, okay? Izzy's out there waiting for us. You'll have us both in your corner the whole time. Just concentrate and try to hear us, we'll help you. Keep your hands up. The whole fucking time baby, hands up. Oh god," he grabs his chest. "I think I'm going to have a heart attack. You can still stop this, baby. We can go home. Let's go home."

The poor guy looks like he's genuinely having chest pains. I never stopped to think how watching me fight will affect him. I don't think he thought about it either.

His concern has me giggling though. I've never heard him so desperate before. "Bobby, stop!" I put my gloved hands on his chest. "Babe, stop. I'll be fine. We've already been through this, what's the worst that could happen, right? Come on, I can hear them announcing the last winner. It's my turn now, walk me out." I kiss him quickly on the lips as he stares desperately.

Eventually, he hesitantly nods his head, and we turn and walk side by side as we move through the hallway. I look to him out the corner of my eye, and I start singing softly, *"Ten percent luck, twenty percent skill…"*

Bobby's steps falter and he looks at me. His eyes are wide, surprised, scandalized even, and his worried face is replaced by a dirty smirk.

When I'm done the whole chorus, he stops our progression by grabbing my arm, pulling me up and slamming his mouth on mine. It's a quick dry kiss, not at all lacking power though.

"You think you're a funny fucker, don't you?" he asks when he pulls back. "I love you so much." He smacks another kiss on my lips.

Casey was walking behind us and clears her throat, reminding us we have somewhere to be. We continue walking again and emerge into a big room similar to the one Jack fought in. In the center is a ring, then surrounding it are temporary chairs taking up the rest of the space. I look around for my friends, finding them in the front row, right by my corner.

They're all there, faces beaming, excitement rolling off them. Jack's is the only face that drops when he sees mine.

Oh, that's right. Puffy eyes. Snotty nose.

I nod my head to let him know I'm okay, then I turn when Casey taps me on my shoulder and hugs me. "Good luck, Kit. You got this! That whore in the other corner is a scrawny ugly bitch who needs an ass whoopin."

We laugh, because we both know she doesn't mean a single word of what she said. I take a quick peek at my opponent and note she's neither scrawny, nor ugly, and I turn back and shake my head. "Thanks, Tink. I love you."

Her head whips back angrily, and I realize my mistake too late. My gloved hands fly to cover my mouth, trying to stop the laughter from bubbling up.

"Seems to me, *you* need an ass whoopin!" she snaps playfully. "Excuse me while I go sit on the other side and cheer *her* on. Whore!"

My laughing is interrupted by Bobby tapping my shoulder again. He tips his chin toward the ring, so we start moving, and as we approach, Izzy steps to me, pushing my mouth guard in, then holds the ropes so I can climb in.

"Okay!" she yells over the crowd. "Hands up. Do what Jack did: legs, body, legs, body, legs, body, head. Especially use your legs; your reach will keep her out of range. You're better than your opponent. Remember, no one's worked as hard as you have. This is yours, go get her."

I nod my head at her instruction then look to Bobby. He's watching me closely. I'm certain he won't blink at all until this thing is over. I kiss my glove then 'blow' it his way, and he smiles and his shoulders relax fractionally.

Okay, I'm as ready as I'm going to be. *Legs, use your legs, use your legs, use your legs.*

I look at my opponent again, wondering if she's a raging bitch, if she's going to lay me out any minute, or if she's as scared of this as I am. She doesn't give anything away though, so I take her cue and school my face, showing no emotion at all.

She and I are dressed similarly, both in shorts with a thick high waist and flare to just below our knees. They're made of a soft silky material, and I will admit, they're comfortable as hell, if not a little ugly. We both have a sports bra thing that shows an inch or two of midsection, but cover our chests completely. Both of us are wearing head gear, hers red, mine black, and we're both barefoot.

I'm wearing my new gloves; they match Bobby's, but mine are white and pink, where his are black and red, and they make me feel a little badass when I wear them.

The ref steps to the middle of the ring and calls us to the center. My heartbeat triples, and I quickly glance back to Bobby, needing him for just a second. He's watching me, his body primed and ready to jump in and swoop me away at any second. His concern is really very comforting; it's been a long time since someone's worried about me.

"Alright ladies, we already discussed the rules." I swear the ref seems bored already. "Defend yourselves at all times. Listen to my instructions at all times. Make it a clean fight. Touch gloves then go back to your corners."

We look at each other, and the lack of malice in her eyes makes me feel better. But when we slam gloves against each other's in a 'tap', my stomach threatens to explode. This is really happening.

Izzy pats me on the leg when I reach my corner. "Legs, Kit. Use your reach. Go hard, keep your ears open." Then she pats my leg again.

I turn around to face the center and wait for the bell to sound. Standing here in this in between time is strange. Time stretches on, but at the same time, everything is moving in fast forward.

After what feels like forever but also no time at all, I hear the *ding ding* of the bell, and I feel - literally feel - the adrenaline flood my body. Fuel pours from my heart and fills my chest, spreading down through my arms into my hands and fingers. My stomach turns hot, like I swallowed a hot water bottle, the heat spreading down through my legs and into my feet.

I feel like I weigh nothing and can move at the speed of light. Like my muscles are made of molten lava and pack the strength of an army of grown men.

We step toward each other, circling and we tap gloves again. My hands lift to cover my head the way Bobby so mulishly taught me, and I vow to not drop them.

Testing my reach, I step in and jab, not intending to hurt, just getting my bearings. I find if I place my hips correctly and extend the way I've been taught, I can reach her with my left while still covering my head, and she cannot reach me, falling short by a couple inches.

This knowledge empowers me so I step in and jab again, this time intending to fight. I jab, jab, and then throw a right hook.

My jabs hit home but my hook fails, completely missing her when she ducks her head.

While I recover my stance, she uses my distraction to hit me back. My whole body knows the strike is coming before it actually arrives, my body tensing of its own accord, my muscles flexing and waiting to absorb the strike. I overcompensate my head cover because Bobby screams at me to keep my hands up, which leaves my body exposed, and she digs in a rip to my ribs - left, left, right - forcing my breath out in a big whoosh.

"Kit! Cover up!" Bobby shouts at me, but I smile, because I just got hit in my first ever competitive fight, and there's power and relief in knowing, it didn't hurt!

I hadn't realized I was still scared; I thought I was ready, but now I know I was still hesitant, scared to be hit. Now I approach her, knowing, believing myself when I ask *what's the worst that could happen?* I'm smiling like a friggin idiot now.

I strike out, jab, jab, and then lower left kick, hitting her at exactly the spot above her knee joint where thigh muscles meet, intending to deaden her leg. Her face registers instant pain, her leg buckles and her hands drop, then shaking her head, she stands tall and lifts her hands again. We continue this way for the whole first round – jab, rip, jab, leg kick, one two, one two hook.

Again, time seems to be completely warped, the three minutes feeling like they went for an hour, but also over in seconds. Eventually the bell rings and we're sent to our corners.

I stumble back to mine and slump into my stool. I don't feel weightless anymore. I feel like I weigh ten tons.

Not even a second passes before Bobby's in my face, his smile stretching from one ear to the other. Izzy's head practically squishes against his so I see them both at the same time. He takes my mouth guard out and squirts some water.

"You're doing so good, baby! So fucking good. Keep hammering her leg, she's almost finished."

"Kit, you're a fucking natural!" Izzy says, excitement vibrating through her. "How do you feel?"

"I feel good. A bit tired." I giggle, high on adrenaline. "It doesn't hurt, though. I really thought it would," I admit.

Bobby laughs and pats my knee. "Okay honey. Keep it up. You've got two rounds to go, but feel free to end it sooner."

"Keep hammering her leg," Izzy repeats, grabbing my mouth guard from Bobby and shoving it back in for me. I stand again and my stool and water bottle are removed ready for round two.

Ding ding.

We step toward each other again, and although she appears to have a slight limp, she's come back with more determination; her corner people must give a really good pep talk.

To try keep her at a distance, I raise my leg for a front kick, the mythical *teep* that I asked Bobby about that time, but instead of colliding with her stomach like I intended, she kicks out too, her front kick connecting with the bottom of my bent leg, pushing my backwards and making me fall on my ass.

I fall hard with a *thwump*, winding myself.

I can literally hear the gasps from my friends, and Bobby having a heart attack. I'm not hurt at all, just pushed over - which happens a hundred times in training. Calm down people!

The ref steps in between us to give me a chance to stand again, and I do, resuming my fighting stance and lifting my hands. The ref steps back and indicates we start again, and for some dumbass reason, I step in with a front kick, again, and she kicks my leg, again, making me land on my ass, again.

Thwump!

Well fuck! The ref jumps in between us, as though he's genuinely scared my opponent will attack me while I'm on the ground. She doesn't. She's in this for the sport too, not for bloodshed.

Bobby's swearing at me now, as though I've personally offended him by getting knocked down a second time. I guess I probably have.

He doesn't worry me, though. I'm having the time of my life, I'm unhurt, I haven't lost yet, and I'm ready to get up again. I can't wipe the smile off my face. I probably look fucking crazy.

The ref starts us again, but I'm not stupid enough to make the same mistake — a third time. Twice is enough for this dumbass to stop and re-evaluate. My opponent assumes I'll do the same again though, because she pre-emptively kicks out, but this time I step to the side, letting her miss me completely and she lands heavy on her front leg, her balance out. Working with her momentum, I throw a jab, a straight right, and then a knee, and I enjoy the satisfying contact that she practically walked into.

It was nothing spectacular, no fancy knock outs or anything, but it felt good, and it got the crowd on their feet. Luckily, we're both wearing head gear, so she's not actually hurt.

She takes a moment to balance herself then starts toward me again, pissed that she let that last one in. She starts throwing flurries at me, missing almost every single time, or connecting but sliding off because her aim is out. Now I get why Bobby says fighting angry doesn't help. It makes you sloppy. She's just gassing herself, using all her energy while I watch and dodge.

I start pounding on her sore leg again. Every time she leaves it open, I bring my right leg down heavy on the exact same spot. I may not be as tired as she, but I'm still tired, and my legs feel like I'm wearing concrete shoes.

Jab, jab, right, leg. Jab, leg. Jab, right, hook, leg. Each time I hit her leg, she stumbles more and the crowd cheers louder. I continue going, taking a few hits myself since I'm so focused on hitting her and my guard is down.

Knowing the round is due to finish any second now, I try and try again, throwing all my weight behind my leg kicks, and each time she stumbles but she keeps going.

I throw a final left, left, right, knee, step back, lower leg kick, the final kick connecting at the same moment the buzzer sounds. She stumbles down onto a knee, but because the bell has rung, her people are already moving her back to her corner, meaning, I have to face a third round.

I turn to my corner and find Bobby already in the ring waiting for me. Fuck I love that man! His smile is magnificent, his chest puffed with pride, and my stomach jumps at the sight of him.

I sit down heavily and Izzy takes my mouth guard out, which results in spit dribbling onto my chin. I giggle, and Izzy smiles and shakes her head. "You're having a good time, huh?"

"I *was* having fun. Now I'm just tired!"

Bobby chuckles. "You're doing so good baby. You've already won. Keep up what you're doing, don't slow down, don't get knocked out and it's yours. You'll get her on points. You don't *have* to knock her out. Keep hammering that leg! You're a fucking machine, baby. I'm so proud of you."

The officials let us know we have ten seconds left before round three, so Bobby quickly leans in and smacks a kiss on my face—making the spectators whistle and laugh—then Izzy puts my mouth guard back in.

Bobby rises in front of me and pulls me to stand, but as I do the crowd goes nuts. We look around in confusion, but I get knocked solidly into Bobby when Izzy jumps on me and cheers. "You won, Kit!" she shouts.

My head continues to whip around in confusion, but next thing I know, Bobby lifts me in the air, cheering like everyone else, and smacking kisses all over my face.

"Winner by T.K.O." The referee shouts into the crowd. "From Rollin' On Gym, Catherine Reilly." He moves around Bobby and takes my hand, lifting it in the air as the people surrounding the ring continue cheering.

I look around for my opponent. I'm so confused. She's still in her corner, her people surrounding her, but on the floor at the ref's feet is a white towel.

I won? She threw in the towel?

Throwing in the towel is an actual *thing*?

Holy shit, I won? I turn back to Bobby for answers, and when I'm greeted with his giant smile, I jump up and down.

I won!

Like a jack rabbit on a pogo stick, I jump up and down and hug the ref. He just laughs and pats my arm as he attempts to disentangle himself from my hold. Next thing I know, Bobby has me in his arms again, my legs wrapped around his waist as Izzy hugs us from behind.

All of my friends are at the ropes on the outside, their hands stretching up and I wildly throw gloved high fives to anyone who wants one.

After a few minutes of the referee laughingly pushing us out of the ring, Bobby lets me down and opens the ropes, then he escorts me back to the locker room. As we walk I get shoulder pats, fist bumps, and congratulations by a bunch of people I've never met before, and I won't lie, it feels pretty fucking good.

I shower quickly, wanting to rush out to Bobby and my friends, feeling on top of the world and wondering how much it would cost to hire one of those planes that write messages in the sky.

"I won!" would look nice on a fine day like today.

I quickly wash and towel dry my hair, finger combing it, then swiping on some mascara and consider myself done. I run around collecting all my shit, my gloves and shorts and Bobby's head gear and shove it all in my gym bag. I roll my towel into a ball and shove that in too then shove my feet into my Chucks and sprint out the door.

I don't get more than two steps though before I crash straight into a group, *my* group, and Jimmy lifts me into the air, hugging me so tight I can barely breathe. I'm laughing so much I can't catch my breath anyway. Jimmy smacks a big wet kiss on my cheek and pats my ass. "Well done princess. That was HOT! I'm so fucking proud of you right now."

"Put my girl down, now, asshole." Bobby physically takes me from his brother like I'm the size and weight of a toddler. He slides me down his body, my toes touching the floor at the same time his lips touch mine.

"Gag!" Jack whines.

"I'm so fucking proud of you," Bobby murmurs. "So proud. Are you sore?"

Sore? I'm on top of the world, not an ache to be found. I shake my head in answer. He smacks another kiss on my lips then turns us toward the others and tucks me into his side.

I look at them all and bathe in their excitement and praise. Aiden steps forward and holds out his hand for a fist bump. "Good job, hon. You smashed it!"

Casey hugs me, hip bumping Bobby aside and making us all laugh again. "You looked amazing up there! I never doubted you for a second. You had her beat from the second you stepped into the ring."

"Really?"

"Totally! You weren't worried at all, just casually strolling in and chillin' with your man. And let's not forget *who* your man is. World champion. She probably thinks you train together 24/7 and would kill her dead. She was definitely shitting herself!"

Her description makes us all laugh again. I never think of Bobby as a famous fighter. To me, he's *just* Bobby. I do notice when he gets stopped at events like this and asked for a quick selfie or autograph, but since we spend the majority of our time at home or at his gym—where he's *just* Bobby to them too—I don't see it often.

We all begin to walk along the hall, ready to go home and relax. As I pass Jack, he hits me in the shoulder, his version of congratulations, then he falls into step and follows behind us. Izzy and Casey walk out side by side; I'm so happy they seem to be getting along really well.

I can't believe I was scared of Iz that first time I saw her. I mean, she's formidable when fighting, and she's a hard ass trainer that I enjoy hating, but outside of that, she's amazing. She's funny and smart. Witty as hell, and has the attitude to perfectly match the other guys. I guess that comes from growing up with them all.

We decided earlier that win or lose, we would all go back to our house and hang out. Not that I mentioned it out loud, but my plan B, had I lost, I would have certainly gone straight to bed and hidden under the covers. Thankfully that won't be necessary, and I'm excited for a night of pizza and good friends.

We exit the double doors and start toward the parking lot. Bobby still has his arm tucked around me, holding me in tight, not risking losing me to Casey's surprisingly strong grip again. Or to Jimmy's wandering hands.

Jon and Casey follow Aiden to his truck and they hop in, then Aiden calls out to Jack, asking him to ride with them.

Jack looks at me then runs toward them.

"Sissy, you need a ride?" Jon asks Iz.

"She can ride with me," Jimmy answers for her as he heads toward his Jeep. She looks at her brother then starts walking toward Jimmy, sliding into his raised car and throwing her bag onto the backseat, clearly comfortable with the Kincaids.

That leaves Bobby and me to ride alone in the Rav, and I love that they all thought to give us some privacy. He takes my gym bag and holds the door open for me, hamming up the chivalry and kissing me on the temple, then ruins the gentlemanly behavior when he slaps me on the ass.

He tosses my bag in the back seat and runs to the driver's side, hopping in and looking at me. His smile is amazing, his eyes dancing. He turns the car on. "Where to, champ?"

"Can we just go for a drive? Nowhere in particular, just cruise?" I know exactly where I want to go, but I don't tell him yet.

"Sure thing, babe. It's your party," he says, turning back toward the front and switching the stereo on.

I'm not even kidding; Fort Minor comes on. We look at each other in shock then burst out laughing.

Soon, we're cruising around town, slowly driving down one street then the next. Up and down we go, enjoying music and talking about nothing in particular. My favorite times ever with him are spent like this, enjoying each other, music and easy conversation.

We discuss my fight, exciting me all over again by reliving the adrenaline-charged time I spent in the ring.

I'm biding my time until we hit the roads closer to the edge of town. I fully intend to give this man the blow job of his life, just as soon as it's safe enough that we won't be spotted.

The excitement from today, the drama, the adrenaline, and the love and support I received from Bobby has had me on edge since my shower in the lockers, and my panties are soaked in anticipation of what I'm about to do.

Once Bobby exits the town proper I turn toward him, unable to hide my smile and he looks at me quickly, smiling back. "What?"

"Nothing," I say, but lower my seatbelt, the lap belt still done up, but the shoulder section now sitting under my arm. I lean toward him and kiss his cheek softy, then begin nibbling his ear. His smile at the kiss turns to a moan when I start nibbling, making his hands tighten on the wheel.

He's still driving, but with no cars to be seen anywhere, I lean further toward him, running my hand down his chest and making him groan as I skim over his belt buckle, then my hands run down his thighs, the feel of the solid muscle making my core tingle.

Working my way back up, I stop at his belt and start undoing it.

"Babe?" Bobby asks, his voice weak, the car slowing down.

"Don't stop the car. Keep going."

"Oh, god." he groans, but the car starts moving faster again. I undo the button of his jeans and slowly, torturously, drag the zipper down.

"Lift," I instruct, tapping his thigh, needing his help to lower his pants. We get them down enough to comfortably pull him out, and we both groan when my bare hands touch his hard length, both of us relishing in the skin contact.

I look at him for a minute, then he hisses when I pull the skin back, exposing the head and I watch as liquid beads at the tip. It begins to roll toward the side, but not wanting it to escape, I swoop in and lap it up. The car jerks and a growl rips from his chest at the contact. I can count on one hand the amount of times I've ever done this, but what I lack in experience, I make up in enthusiasm.

Holding him with a firm hand, I place my mouth over him, tightening my lips around the head and suck gently, lapping at him with my tongue. At his growl and muttered profanities, I work my mouth and hand up and down, fitting as much of him as I can in my mouth and stopping only when he whimpers.

The car speeds up again and I keep working him while he takes fast corners. Less than a minute later we screech to a stop, Bobby rips the hand brake on, then throws his head back against the seat rest as he swears at God.

Taking this as positive feedback, I continue my ministrations, meanwhile, I rub my thighs together, needing to satisfy some of my own need, never recalling ever being so turned on in my life.

Bobby's whole body is tense and I know he's trying to hold himself back, but failing every now and then when his hips jerk upward, thrusting himself further into my mouth.

I work on suppressing my gag reflex and move my throat muscles each time he thrusts, making him groan so deep I can feel the vibration.

It doesn't take more than a couple minutes before his hip thrusting is out of his own control, he's basically fucking my mouth, and on a loud curse, he lifts my head and pushes my shoulders back, then hurriedly unsnaps my seat belt and drags me into his lap.

In less than three seconds, he has my shorts undone and pulled down just enough and his seat pushed back, before he lifts me again and impales me. We both let out strangled cries as we join at the center.

We just sit there a minute, catching our breath and enjoying our connection as our hands and eyes softly roam each other. I begin to move my hips, using the door frame and his shoulder as hand holds. I ride him, ducking my head low to not bump it on the ceiling. His hands are on my hips, lifting me and slamming me down again, both of us lost in sensation. I lean down to kiss him, our tongues at war, and I enjoy touching him with every part of my body.

"Fuck, Kit!" he growls, unable to keep himself under control anymore. He moves his hand down and starts circling my clit, and I buck over him, riding him wildly while he leans in to nibble on my bra covered breasts.

"Bobby. I'm going to go. Ohhh Bobby…" I whimper, then cry out when he pinches my clit and bites my nipple, his hips jerking into me with all the power his thighs possess. My orgasm rips through my body at the same time Bobby's does.

His hands crush me against him as his hips jerk again and again, then he stops and buries his face against my chest. "Ah, baby!"

My fingers move through his hair as my chest lifts and falls heavily. We both work to catch our breath in the small space of the closed in car.

"Could you be any more fucking awesome?" he asks breathlessly. "I get a blowjob, even though you are the one to be celebrated today. I love you so much, baby."

"Mmm, I love you too. That was fun, huh?"

He laughs and feathers kisses along my forehead. "Fun? Yeah it was fun."

Suddenly remembering where we are, I shoot up and look around us. We're on a deserted dirt road with plenty of trees, but not much else around. Understanding my concern, Bobby shakes his head. "Don't worry, babe, no one around. I'd never let anyone see you like that."

Comforted, I lay my head down again, breathing him in and enjoying the comfort, though disappointed we still have our shirts on and wishing we could lay skin to skin.

Tapping my butt though, he says, "But we should get going. There's bound to be people coming along eventually. There are farmhouses along this road, few and far between, but still, some people live around here."

Nodding my head, I lean in and kiss him again, my tongue darting in to stroke his. I can feel him swell within me and he groans. "You're killing me, babe." He physically lifts me off him, and I drop into my seat and fix my shorts as I watch him pull his own up. "Speaking of," he says, looking over at me as he readjusts his seat and turns the car on, "I'm never letting you fight again. I almost died a hundred times today. I aged at least thirty years watching her step up to you. I don't think I could handle watching you again."

He's smiling, but he's not lying either.

Looking back at the road, he pulls out and does a U-turn, and we head back to town.

I fix my seat belt, and I lean against the door to look at him. I fix my hair as he drives. "I'm sorry babe, but that was fun. There's no way in hell I won't do it again. Besides, this whole fighting thing was your idea!"

"I know, and now I take it back. I think it's a terrible idea. No more gym time for you."

I roll my eyes. "Now you know how your poor mother probably feels watching you guys fight."

He chuckles softly as we enter the town proper. "That's true. She hates it! Especially when Jimmy fights. I'm pretty sure he still resembles a fat little baby in her mind." He scoffs. "She isn't far off. He's still a fat baby."

He pauses for a long moment, as nerves suddenly appear in the space between us like a living thing. "Um... While we're on the topic." He looks over at me and he taps his fingers on the steering wheel nervously. "I'd like to introduce you to my mom. Do you think that would be okay?"

"What if she doesn't like me?"

Bobby leans across and takes my hand in his immediately, squeezing it and resting our joined hands on his thigh. "She will, baby. She already does. Jimmy doesn't shut up about you when he's over there." Bobby and I both laugh, though mine sounds closer to hysteria than his. "If I didn't know better, I'd think he had the hots for you. Thankfully I do know better, and he only brags to Mom because he knows she won't leave me alone till I bring you over."

Personally, I'm fairly sure I know who Jimmy *does* in fact have the hots for, and I know when he finally acts on it, everyone else will be surprised as hell. Meanwhile, I have my own dilemma to deal with.

I squeeze Bobby's thigh. "Should I be scared of your mom? Nervous? Should I just run away now and never return? Is she cool, or a mama bear who'll aim for my jugular as soon as you go to the bathroom?"

"No, baby. She's really awesome. I promise, she'll love you. She already does."

"She does?"

"Oh yeah. She knows a happy kid when she sees one, and I've never been happier than I am now." He lifts my hands and kisses my knuckles. "You have to trust me on this. So… do you think that would be okay? Will you meet my Mom?"

I'm actually quite terrified. I haven't had a mom of my own for a very long time, and our relationship was pretty awful. Max's mom was fine — a pretentious social climber — but pleasant enough. Funny though, I was never scared to meet her.

"Okay. But I'm scared," I admit truthfully. "Don't leave me, okay?"

"I promise, baby. I won't move from your side until you're ready."

16

Bobby

Nelly Kincaid

"Where is everyone?" I yell as I walk in the front door, kicking my shoes off and hanging my black ball cap on the hooks behind the door. Jack and Kit should be around somewhere; Kit said they'd stay home all day because they had stuff to do around the house.

We're due for dinner at my mom's in a little over an hour, and I know Kit's been freaking out about it all week. I had to run classes today at the gym, but I was careful not to mention anything to the guys, lest they turn up and make Kit any more nervous than she already is.

"We're in the kitchen," she calls back, so I head in that direction. I walk in to find them both at the table, school books spread all over and Jack bent over his notebook.

I found out after I moved in that the nights they don't train, Kit is actually tutoring Jack. They were careful to not let me see, since Jack was embarrassed that he spent his down time studying, but when you live with people, you can't keep those secrets for long. It gave me a new appreciation for them both.

For Jack, for working hard to better himself, for making up for a couple years of laziness at school while their dad dropped the ball.

And for Kit, who's so fucking selfless, I'm terrified of tarnishing her. She's always working so hard to make Jack's life better, even when he didn't want or appreciate it.

After I found out about their tutoring, I asked about his grades, learning that he's gone from C's and D's to A's and B's. Kit was proud as punch to share this information, but Jack shyly kept his head buried in his books, only popping up to mention the lashing that Kit gave that asshole Reeves.

Funnily enough, that was when she buried her head.

She's just as much the mama bear that she fears my mom is. Fuck if that doesn't have me imagining the kids we could raise together—yet another thought that's never crossed my mind before meeting her.

I'm even more stoked that the thought doesn't scare me. Frankly, it makes me want to take her to bed and fill her belly with my babies now, to get the show on the road.

I walk across the room and kiss Kit on the top of her head. "Hey babe. How's it going in here?"

"Shit." Jack grumbles, flicking his pen against the table. "It's going shit."

"Don't swear, Jack. He has a quiz on Monday," Kit explains. "He'll be fine. He's just tired. I was about to suggest we pack away for today anyway." She stands and cracks her back, then collecting her dirty dishes, she walks to the dishwasher and tosses them in.

Jack throws his pens into his bag and snaps the books closed. He tosses them in his bad with a filthy scowl, as though they've personally offended him.

"Everyone remember dinner tonight?" I ask them, noting neither are dressed yet and worrying we'd be late.

My personal experience in the past with women does not include them dressing and being ready to leave the house in anything less than two hours. I look down at my watch, noting Kit has about forty-five minutes before we have to leave.

Not that I'd be angry at her for taking longer.

Fuck, she can do anything she wants and I could never get mad at her.

She turns away from the sink and walks toward me, tucking her arms around me and lying her head on my chest. Her light perfume fills my lungs, the smell of home.

I'm a dead man.

If she ever decided she was done with me, I'd be broken beyond repair. Good as dead.

"Yeah, we remember. I'm heading upstairs now to shower and I'll be out soon. What should I wear tonight? What will you wear?"

"I was just going to wear this," I lie, looking down at my sweaty shirt and gym shorts. I've worn this to my mom's a million times before, but the night I introduce her to my girl, I'll shower for the occasion.

"You are not?" she asks, a question not a statement, and I chuckle.

"No." I drop a quick kiss on her lips. "I'll be wearing jeans and a shirt. Nothing fancy."

"Okay," she says quietly, thinking, "alright, I'll work it out. I'll go shower now." She steps back, running her hand along my pecs and arm as she walks by. I know she's quite fond of them, and it'd be a lie if I said I didn't do extra reps, just for her.

"She's really freaking out, you know that?" Jack says from behind me. I'd forgotten he was there, and he caught me ogling his sister. Oops.

I turn around and lean against the counter and I face him. He looks almost as worried as Kit does. "She's okay though, yeah?"

"She'll be okay. But she's nervous. She'll be fine as long as your mom's cool." My brow lifts at his clear warning. Jack's still got those brass balls he had when he walked into my gym that first time, but I'm finding it hard to hate on him for it, since it's Kit he's standing up for.

He pauses a moment, as if debating whether or not to say something else. "I don't know what you know, but she didn't get a good deal with our mom. And if she has told you, whatever she told you is probably super watered down. So yeah, she's nervous your mom won't like her, or that she won't even know how to act around her."

I nod my head in understanding, not surprised that Jack assumes Kit downplayed her story. I'm inclined to agree with him.

My mom already knows about Kit's parental situation. There was no way in hell I'd leave the first meeting between the two most important women in my life open to those potential landmines. I'll do everything I can to ensure they get along perfectly. I need them to.

I'd die if I had to choose between them.

Clapping Jack on the shoulder, I tell him thanks for the heads up, then head upstairs to shower and change. I walk into our room to find Kit in front of the mirror in the master bathroom. With a towel wrapped around her, I watch as she applies some makeup to her eyes.

She smiles at my approach, then continues with what she was doing. I watch while she transforms them from innocent and wide, to smoky and sexy doe eyes. Next, she adds some powder to her face, then lip color — that I want to suck straight back off just to taste it — then starts blow drying her hair.

Finger combing it, I watch as she thoroughly works from scalp to end, over and over again, the heat of the dryer blowing the sweet perfume of her hair around the small room.

Peeling myself away, I jump into the shower quickly, leaving the water barely warmer than cold and enjoy the smooth sluice over my skin. I quickly soap up and wash my hair, the thought of an almost naked Kit only feet from me resulting in a throbbing dick and making me desperately consider dragging my girl in here with me.

Grudgingly, I acknowledge she wouldn't appreciate me messing up her hair and makeup, and knowing we have to leave in about twenty minutes, I leave her be.

"Hey babe?" she calls out, and I realize she's turned the hair dryer off.

"Yeah?"

I watch her hip swaying approach through the frosted glass of the shower. She lays her glossed up lips on the glass, and leaves a big pink smudge as she pulls away. "I love you, Bobby."

I snatch open the door and grab her arm, pulling her back to me. I kiss her deeply, tasting that gloss just like I wanted to. "I love you too, baby. So much."

I let her go again before I frizz her hair. She walks back to the mirror to fix her gloss, then heads to the room, rummaging in the closet for something to wear.

By the time I finish and walk to the room, she's putting earrings in, fully dressed except shoes, and it baffles me how she can be so low maintenance. She can be showered, done up, and dressed in twenty minutes, even though she hadn't even planned her outfit prior. She looks beautiful in a black vest top and lacy white tank under, then flaring black shorts that go to mid-thigh. Her hair is done in a high messy bun, and she has a gold cuff on her right wrist and a gold watch on the left. She's flung some strappy black pumps onto our bed and I pick one up, one finger on the toe, and one on the pointed heel.

These things scream sex, and suddenly I remember I'm still in a towel and genuinely concerned it might fall off.

This reminds me that she's dressed, but I am not. Now who's slow and high maintenance?

Throwing her shoe down, I head to the closet and pull out some clean boxers and jeans. I drop my towel to start dressing when I notice her sitting on the bed watching me. She twirls a loose strand of her without a care in the world.

I step into my boxers and pull them up. "You good, there?"

"Mmhmm, I'm dandy. Do that again. Slowly …"

I laugh. "You like what you see, baby?" I walk to her, jeans still in my hand, my dick standing and pointing me toward her, as though it knows exactly where it belongs.

She leans forward and hugs me around the hips, laying her head on my stomach. She nods. "I definitely do."

I carefully thread my hands into the hair at her nape, massaging her neck and listening to her purr. "You look very pretty tonight, baby. Like usual."

"Thank you. I look okay to meet your Mom?"

"You do, definitely." I pull back and squat down to look her in the eyes. "I know you're nervous, but please don't be. I swear on everything, she's cool. She'll love you. You've already met and won over my brothers, she'll be the same. I promise."

Her eyes are almost desperate, her hands shaking though she tries to hide it. She bites her lip, but eventually squares her shoulders. "Okay. We better get moving so we're not late. Who else is going?"

"Just you, me, and Jack. Just a quiet one so you can meet her and get to know each other. No pressure."

~*~

Twenty minutes later, we knock and let ourselves into my mom's house. I hold Kit's hand as we walk into the living room to find everyone, *everyone*, is here. Jimmy's acting out some stupid shit to the laughter of the group, Aiden's standing with one arm around Mom, and Jon is sitting next to Tink, close but not touching, and I roll my eyes.

Kit tenses at my side and I panic. It took everything I had to get her here tonight, and now it's going to be ruined. Having everyone here is just too much – too much noise, too much pressure.

But then Jimmy falls on his ass after he attempts a spinning heel kick in the middle of the living room, and my mom shoves him over before he breaks her TV.

Kit laughs when Jim lands on the floor, and the tension shaking her body evaporates into thin air. Everyone looks up at Kit's laughter, and Jimmy pastes on a ridiculous goofy smile.

"Well hey there, Kitty Kat," he says, getting up and walking to us. I genuinely think she enjoys his banter; he seems to relax her. He pushes me away and puts his arm around her shoulders, making everyone laugh again, and walks her toward my mom.

"Mama," he says, exaggerating the baby pout as he makes a big production out of squeezing her against his side, "this is Kit. She and I are … serious."

I move forward and shove him off her. "Let her go, dumbass."

Mom snaps at me about my swearing at the same time Kit elbows Jim, making him cough out a laugh.

Mom's eyes snap to Kit's elbow, then toward me, as a smile breaks out on her face. Anyone who'll set us in our place is a winner by my mom's standards.

I replace Jim's arm with mine, noting Kit's newly shaking body, then I look into my mom's eyes and I take a deep breath. "Mom, this is Kit Reilly. Kit, this is my mom, Nelly Kincaid."

They look at each other a moment longer as the entire room's occupants hold their breath, then Kit puts her hand out to shake my mom's. "It's a pleasure to meet you, Mrs. Kincaid. I really like all of your sons ..." she adds awkwardly, "so, good job."

Mom just looks at Kit a moment longer, then gently pushing her hand out of the way, she moves in and hugs her instead. "The pleasure is all mine, honey. Please call me Nelly. I'm so happy to meet you at last. I've heard a lot about you." She pulls back, though she keeps Kit's arms in her hands to keep her close. "You sure are pretty. Your eyes are amazing."

Kit blushes at mom's words, though she gently pulls away and moves back into my side. "Thank you, Mrs. Ki -- Nelly. That's kind of you to say." Kit turns, and indicates behind us. "Umm, this is my brother, Jack."

He steps forward, looking as nervous as Kit did. "It's nice to meet you, Mrs. Kincaid."

"Oh, call me Nelly, please. It's a pleasure to meet you." Mom moves forward and hugs him too. "James won't shut up about either of you. I hear congratulations are in order, for you both. Must be something in the Reilly blood to produce two winners straight out of the gates, huh?"

Jack blushes as Jim laughs and my mom gushes.

"I'm not sure how I feel about more fighters in the family though. You've just added two more people for me to worry about," Mom adds.

I roll my eyes. "It's okay, Mom, Kit won't be fighting again anyway."

Jack scoffs and Jim calls 'bullshit,' and my mom laughs as Kit tells me I'm absolutely wrong.

"Ah, so now you know how I feel. You worry for her, don't you, honey?" Mom winks at me in that smartass way she hides from newcomers like Kit and Jack, then she turns away from me and speaks to Kit, "Alright, well, you know everyone else here, so why don't you take a seat with your lovely friend Casey, who I've also just met tonight, and Bobby and I will get some drinks."

Mom leads Kit to the couch next to Tink, then grabbing my arm, she steers me to the kitchen. Walking to the fridge, she grabs a few beers and a bottle of white wine, sitting them on the counter, then grabs a bottle opener from the cutlery drawer. I take it from her and start popping the caps off while Mom heads to the glass cabinet, still without speaking. Her silence makes me nervous.

"Do you like her Mom?" This is one of the most important questions I will ever ask her, and her silence has my gut churning sick. "First impressions?"

She looks back at me, a wine glass in each hand, and studies me for a minute. "Yeah baby, I like her. She's very beautiful, and she seems lovely. And she certainly knows how to handle you boys," she laughs. "The stuff about her parents is so tragic, but she's handled it with grace. The fact she's taken Jack in and doesn't make a big deal about it, well, she's special. Yeah, I like her."

Walking toward me, she sits the glasses on the counter, then she hugs me, reminding me how comforting and amazing my mama is.

Her head sits an inch or two lower than Kit's does when resting on my chest, her hug making me feel like a little boy again, safe and comfortable in his mother's arms, rather than a grown man, more than a foot taller than she.

I drop a soft kiss on the crown of her head as she squeezes me. "Thanks Mom, that means a lot to me."

She pulls back after a moment and pats my chest. "Okay, now tell me about Casey? Are she and Jon an item?"

I laugh and squeeze her one last time. My mom knows everything. "Well, yes and no. He likes her, she likes him, neither will admit to it. So, we're all just gonna wait them out for now. It'll happen eventually. But she's really cool. Her and Kit have been best friends since they were kids, both have wicked senses of humor. Casey — we call her Tink, so get onto that — Tink's feisty, but she's cool. She'll fit right in, as soon as Jon takes his head out of his ass."

I roll my eyes when mom smacks me for swearing again, but she laughs too. "Okay well, we better hurry back or they'll know we're talking about them." She pours three glasses of wine, then she smiles up at me. "I imagine Kit made you promise not to leave her side tonight."

"Oh yeah, but that only counted when you were in the room." I laugh, but quickly sober up again. "She's terrified of you, Mom. I mean, it's not personal. She'll love you. But she's terrified of you not liking her."

"Oh, well …" Mom says as sadness washes over her face. "I'll make sure she knows I love her. How could I not? She loves you, doesn't she? Come on, baby," she says, picking up the glasses and nodding toward the bottles I opened, "let me go and get to know our new family."

Simple as that, Kit, Jack, and Tink, are now family.

We spend a great evening together, sitting around the table, drinking, eating, and laughing. My mom cooked an amazing Irish stew with a side of fresh bread with some garlicky rosemary stuff on it. I doubt neither my Kincaids, nor Kit's Reillys have stepped foot in Ireland in at least two or three generations, but still, the food is amazing.

I still don't know how the guys knew about tonight, but I'm actually quite happy they're here; Jimmy helped keep the tone light and relaxed, and Tink kept the attention from being exclusively on Kit.

"You should have seen his face, Mom," Jimmy laughs, referring to my near-death experience watching Kit fight. "He was literally holding his chest, crying every time she got hit. She was a beast, no way she needed help, but he was ready to jump in and carry her away."

"James! Why do you think that's funny?" my mom scolds him. "You, of all people should know how he feels."

Jimmy's mouth snaps shut and his face flushes white, and despite my rabid curiosity, Mom turns to Kit. "Did you enjoy yourself?"

Kit's smile is breathtaking. "Yes, I did. I was pretty terrified, to be honest, but after she hit me the first time, and it didn't hurt, well, it was an amazing feeling."

Mon smirks knowingly. "Did hurt the next day?"

"Yeah," Kit laughs, "yeah, I was sore the next day. Lots of bruising along my forearms and shins. They're mostly all gone now though."

"That just means you blocked well," Mom says. "Good job, it's better than bruises on your head."

Kit laughs and leans into me. "Definitely better than on my head."

"What would your dad think about you fighting? Do you mind that I bring him up?" Mom rushes on, noting the new tension fill the table. None from Kit, or even Jack for that matter—just from us guys that worry Mom hit a sore note.

"Oh no, I don't mind bringing him up. His memory makes me smile," she says, doing just that. "I'm not sure what he'd think. He was never one of those dads who treated me like I couldn't do something just because I was a girl. Quite the opposite, actually. I was taught things *because* I was a girl and needed to know how to look after myself. I was changing tires and cleaning spark plugs by the time I was ten, I think. No, I think he'd be stoked. He'd have been terrified, probably holding Bobby's hand and crying foul every time I got hit, but he would've supported me. And he would've been my biggest and loudest cheerleader."

The way she speaks of him proves how close they were, how he must've been a great man. I wish more than anything that I could have met him, to seek his approval to date, and someday, marry her.

"He sounds like a good man," Mom says.

"He was. He was amazing."

"He was always so immature though," Jack adds with a laugh. "Remember how he'd buy us toys, like remote controlled cars or whatever, but *he'd* use them. We knew they were really for him."

"Remember when he bought those little peewee motorbikes?" Tink adds. "A grown man trying to ride a bike made for five year olds …"

"Or that time he strapped an old hood to the back of his car, then he'd speed around the lake on the mud and we'd ride on the back. Remember when Tim's finger broke?" Jack asks, wheezing with laughter. "Tim was an old school friend of Kit's, back when you were, what, fifteen? Tink was there that day too," he adds, looking up at her.

I love that her nickname is so easily used now, even by people who've known her as Casey their whole lives.

"Tim and Tink came sliding with us that day, and he broke his finger when he caught it under the hood," he explains. "Tim's mom was a little … strict, so she didn't know what we were doing, and Dad dropped him off with strict instructions not to tell her."

"He wasn't the most responsible adult," Kit adds with a giggle. "That particular day, he misjudged the turn and the car ended up in the lake. Only a couple feet in the water, but still, enough that the floors of the car got wet. Then he tried to vacuum the water out," she says with a snort. "He broke the vacuum too. He did some seriously stupid stuff."

"I'm sorry we couldn't know him," Mom tells her.

Kit nods. "Yeah, me too. He would have loved you all. Well except Bobby," she laughs as she looks at me. "He would've hated you on principle."

That thought should probably worry me, but it doesn't. I know I would've won him over. I love his daughter, and he would've seen that eventually. There's no one in this world who'll love her more, or take care of her as well as I will. That's all every father wants for his daughter, right?

Yes, I'm certain he'd approve.

"Jon, where's Izzy tonight?" Mom asks.

His face instantly turns sour at the reminder. "She's on a date."

The girls at the table all smile at this news; the guys not so much. Even Jack's face scrunches in disapproval.

Jim's eyes narrow on Jon. "She's on a date? With who?"

"Dunno. Some asshole, probably."

"Jonathan!" Mom scolds him.

"Sorry. I mean to say, I don't know who she's with. She didn't tell me. Someone she met at school, I think. She's been staying with me, so I'll see her later."

I'm not surprised she's been staying with Jon; their home life has never been the best. Their dad is an abusive drunk and their mom has always worked two or more jobs to maintain their bad habits. Jon and Iz spent the majority of their childhood at our house, coming here after school every day and during the summers just so they could eat something more substantial than crackers.

If nothing else, I'm glad we're all older now, and we can provide Iz with a safe space to sleep and work. She has a natural talent in the octagon that's unsurprising, considering the way she and Jon grew up.

"Well, that's nice," Mom smiles and picks up her glass of wine. "I hope she has a nice evening. She deserves it."

Jon simply grunts, as does every other man at the table.

Mom sits her wine down and wipes the fancy fabric napkin across her mouth. She doesn't get these napkins out for us on regular nights. Come to think of it, the shiny knives and forks aren't for everyday use either. "Kit, honey, would you mind helping me with dessert?"

Kit's formerly relaxed body tenses against me as her eyes grow wide like a skittish animal. I franticly try to think of a way to get her out of it, but she shakily stands before I come up with anything. "Sure Nelly, I'd be happy to help."

I try to catch her gaze, I try to apologize with my eyes, but she smiles at me in the fakest and shakiest grin I've ever seen on her face, then she drops a kiss on the top of my head before she follows Mom to the kitchen.

She'll be okay. She *has* to be okay. My mom would never say anything to hurt her, and Kit could handle anything that was thrown at her anyway. It'll be fine.

Jesus Christ, my mom has my whole future in her kitchen right now.

It takes them more than five minutes before they come back, the minutes seeming to drag for me, but no one else seems to notice. Jack's having a great time listening to Jimmy's fight stories, Jon's busy talking quietly to Tink, and Aiden's pulled his phone out to text.

While I sit and wait, unsurprisingly, my thoughts are focused solely on Kit. I recall her breakdown after that fucking asshole Chris confronted her. It's the first time since I've known her that she's let down her walls so completely and taken a moment for her own grief.

The way she sobbed into my chest, the way her body shook uncontrollably; it hurt me, so fucking deep in my heart. I have every intention of finding out just what the fuck's going on with those assholes. I need to know why they think they can harass her, and if there is money, there's not a chance in hell those assholes will get it. I don't care if it's one dollar or a hundred million, it'll go to Kit and Jack if it's the last thing I do.

Now that she's with me though, Kit will never struggle for money again. She doesn't even realize my net worth, or that I have about eighty million in the bank. I'm a simple man—I live simply, and I'm happy to do so. I leave my title winnings plus any gym income to sit in the bank, earning interest and waiting for a rainy day. I still drive my old Rav with the door trim peeling, and before moving, I lived in a regular house that I paid only $200,000 in cash.

If Kit decides she wants more, she has only to ask, but I know that's not who she is. I grew up with a very humble childhood. My mom worked hard to feed and clothe us after Dad died, and although we never went hungry, I know she struggled. For her to also feed Iz and Jon too shows my mom's heart, and we're all determined to repay her some way.

Sensing Kit nearby, I look over to watch them exit the kitchen together. I didn't even realize how fucking tense I was till my chest loosened at the sight of her laughing. Kit sits down next to me again, and I greedily suck in her perfume, relaxing at her proximity and placing my hand on her thigh. I lean toward her and kiss her temple. "I missed you, babe,"

My heart feels lighter, my chest less tight, and my stomach more relaxed just by having her near. I don't even know exactly at what point I became so dependent on her presence in my life, but if she disappeared from it now, I'd be destroyed.

I place my arm around her shoulder, pulling her into my side, and we settle back in to enjoy some chocolate mud cake.

After saying our goodbyes and spending an eternity while Mom smothered us in hugs and kisses at her front door, we escape around 9:30 p.m. Loading ourselves back into the Rav, Kit, Jack, and I drive straight home.

I sit on the end of our bed and watch Kit undress and take her jewelry off, carefully placing it in the top drawer in her closet. As I watch, I realize I've not bought my girl any jewelry yet. Making a mental note, I plan to fix that as soon as possible. I know she doesn't need it, but I do. I want to see her wearing something that I gave her, to hope that every time she looks at it, she might think of me.

She walks around in her bra and panties as she prepares for bed, ridiculously alluring in her comfort around me now. Although nothing particularly fancy, just a matching set of black with lacy spots, my dick stirs at the sight in front of me.

I watch her putter around the room. She's totally unaware that I'm watching and I know without a doubt she's the sexiest woman I've ever laid eyes on.

"Hey, babe?"

She turns to me with a small smile as she pulls her earrings out. "Hmm?"

"Was tonight okay? Did my mom give you a hard time in the kitchen?"

"Oh no, not at all. She was so lovely. Not nearly as scary as I expected," she says, walking toward me and stopping between my legs, her naval in line with my eyes, so I lean forward and kiss it softly.

"Thank you for coming." I lay a second kiss on her belly. "I'm so happy you met her and that you like each other."

"Thank you for inviting me," she says, then pauses. "Your mom told me some stuff ... some of your secrets."

I worry for a second, curious to know what secrets I have and what Mom told her, but her smile tells me that whatever it is, I'm not in trouble.

"Bobby, your mom told me you bought that house for her." Pulling back, she looks me in the eyes, but I find hers aren't accusing, just curious.

"Well, not just me," I hedge. "All four of us did. A year after we opened the gym we all put money in to buy it for her. It's our way of saying thanks, you know, for being an awesome mom. For working so hard for so long."

She smirks. "I can't imagine your mom accepted it gracefully."

I laugh at Kit's uncanny ability to hit the nail on the head. "No, she got pretty mad at us actually, for 'wasting our money.' Something about being an independent woman and not needing her kids to support her. She had a tantrum pretty similar to the one you had when I mentioned money the other week."

"Ah, I knew I liked her," Kit laughs. "It's a shame though. I would've liked to see your childhood room, you know, poke through everything, snoop at all your notebooks and Valentine cards."

"Well, I'm pretty sure that's all still around, packed away somewhere at the new house. No Valentine's cards though — you're the only one for me baby." I nuzzle her belly and she giggles.

"Oh, so no girls came before me? That's interesting ... If I'd known, I would've appreciated your virginity a bit more."

"I was embarrassed to tell you, babe. But don't worry, you didn't hurt me."

"I'm glad," she laughs, lowering herself to sit on my lap, her legs straddling my hips and resting on the bed. Leaning in, she places kisses all over my face — on my forehead, my eyelids, my nose, and my lips.

On the last one, I stick my tongue out, surprising her, forcing what was a chaste kiss to turn into something hotter. Our mouths open and her arms squeeze tighter around my neck. She grinds her core down onto my already hard dick, and we both whimper at the contact.

I grab her by the ass, and I flip us over so she's laying on her back. I start kissing down her belly, working toward the spot that I know tastes of pure sweet heaven.

17

Bobby

To give a gift

A few Sunday mornings later, I walk into the kitchen, but stop short when I find Kit dancing and shimmying her hips, listening to music through her earphones while she starts the coffee machine and unloads the dishwasher.

Jack stayed at his friend's house last night, so I'm glad we have the house to ourselves for now. Only an idiot would interrupt this show, and I'm in no way an idiot, so I stand still and watch my girl shake her sinful hips.

Since it's a Sunday today and neither of us have to work, she's wearing her regular cut-offs and a tank. My mind is already flipping through a mental catalog of what tops she owns, wondering what todays says. I fucking love the silly tanks she wears, and the anticipation of finding out today's is almost as exciting as watching her dance.

This is our last free day before I officially start training for my December fight. I have about eight weeks to go, so starting tomorrow, I'll drop a few group classes and start concentrating on my own conditioning and training. The guy I will be fighting, Thomlassen, is a Brazilian Jiu Jitsu black belt, so I need to really work on my ground game. I know a lot, but it's not my specialty like it is Thomlassen's. Or Aiden's. Luckily, I have Aido to work with, and we'll be spending a lot of our time together in preparation.

Jimmy and Jon will also work with me, but not as much. They'll pick up a majority of the classes Aido and I have to drop. It's our system, and it works. It's worked for my previous three title fights, and Jim's fights too.

I'm bummed that I won't get to train with Kit or Jack for a few months, but other than that, my training won't really affect our time together. I'm determined to take today for just the two of us; I want to spoil my girl, and I want to love her.

I continue to watch her as she dances uninhibited, her long tan legs moving, her hips swaying, and I listen to her humming a tune, though I don't recognize the song right away.

I walk to her and place my hands on her hips as she bends over to the dishwasher, and she jumps but instantly relaxes into my hands, sassily pushing her ass back against my dick.

She stands, leaning against me and lies her head back against my shoulder, giving me a glimpse of her sneaky dimples. Leaning in, I use my teeth to pull the headphone out and drop it against her shoulder, then I go back in to nibble around her earring.

"Mmm, that feels good," she purrs. I love when she purrs.

"What are you listening to?"

I've asked this question a hundred times before. She wasn't kidding when she told me she loves music and listens to it non-stop. This is not the first time I've watched her dance when she thought no one was around, and her answers vary so much, never failing to surprise me.

She has answered with the Goo Goo Dolls one day, to The Eagles the next. Nelly, Run DMC, Katy Perry, Miley Cyrus, Elton John, Irish rock, and Justin Bieber are just some that have gotten a mention. Then there was this one time she was listening to the soundtrack from the Beauty and the Beast Disney movie. Her tastes in music are wild, and she makes no apology for it.

"Lila Royale," she says, pushing her neck toward me as I nibble lower. "Shake it up."

"Mmm so that explains the hips."

"You were watching me?"

"Mmhmm. Feel free to dance for me anytime, baby. Sexiest fucking thing I ever saw."

She doesn't answer me, just nods her head slowly, swaying softly against me as I work my way up and down her neck and shoulders.

"Why are you already up? I missed you in bed."

"I couldn't sleep. I was going to bring you some coffee." She nods at the empty mugs she'd left sitting beside the dripping pot.

"Thank you, babe. You don't have to do that."

"I know. I wanted to. I enjoy making you happy."

My heart pounds at her confession. I just couldn't love this woman any more than I do.

I can feel the long jewelry box burning a hole in the back pocket of my jeans. It took me a couple weeks to find the gift I wanted to give her, scouring stores whenever I could discreetly get away with it, when yesterday, Jim and I spotted it in a window display. I knew immediately it was what I was looking for, so I bought it with the background noise of Jim busting my balls about being whipped.

"You make me happy all the time, babe," I tell her, running my hands along her ribs and my lips along her shoulder. "Listen… I got you something."

I hate that she instantly tenses. I haven't forgotten the way she reacted that day of her fight, nor have I forgotten she's a proud woman. I just want to get her a gift. I want her to accept it and love it.

I reach into my pocket and pull the box out, and while I remain standing pressed to her back, I hold it in front of us. She doesn't move for a few long seconds; she just stares at the navy-blue box with gold trim. Eventually, she takes it in shaky hands.

Without opening it, she spins in front of me and lies her head on my chest, holding me with surprising strength.

"Thank you, Bobby."

A full minute passes, and I have to ask. "That's it?"

"What do you mean?"

"Are you not going to yell at me? Are you mad?"

She smiles. "Do you want me to be mad?"

"Well, no. I want you to accept my gift and love it. I just thought maybe you wouldn't make it easy on me. Well, open it, then."

Pulling back from me, she studies the box in her hand for another minute, then lifting the lid, she gasps when she spots the gold bracelet inside. "Bobby..." She strokes the intricate pattern of the weaving gold, then she looks up at me shyly. "Is this an everyday bracelet, or a formal events bracelet?"

I cock my head to the side at her odd question. "What do you mean? You can wear it whenever you want."

"I just mean, I'm scared of wearing it and losing it. I'd be devastated if it were a vending machine bracelet and I lost it, but if it was super expensive and only intended for fancy events, well, that would make it so much worse."

"Don't worry, babe, it's for everyday wear. That's exactly what I want you to do, wear it every day, and think of me."

I take the chain from the box and secure it to her wrist. She stares at it for a while, twisting her arm this way and that, watching it slither and twinkle. "Thank you, Bobby. It's beautiful. Truly," she says, leaning in and kissing me. "I'm sorry you were scared of my reaction. I love you."

I laugh at her apology and kiss her back. "I love you too. So, what do you wanna do today?"

She continues to twist her arm to study the bracelet. "What are our options?"

"Well, we could have sex ..." I waggle my eyebrows at her when she laughs, "or watch a movie. We could go out to lunch, or order dinner in. More sex is always an option. Perhaps play Monopoly? What time's Jack due home?"

"Later. He's due back much, much later. So, all of the above?"

18

Kit

Speak of the devil

November, 2014.

Four weeks till Bobby's fight

Sitting at my desk on a Tuesday morning, I sip my hot coffee as I wait for my computer to start and my email to load. I've set up automatic reports to run overnight and need them first thing each morning to balance company finances, which needs to be done before I start my day.

I watch my bracelet twinkle in the sunlight as the sun shines through my office window, enjoying the way the little diamonds glint and grab my attention so often during the day. I never take it off, except to train. This bracelet has become a part of me, and just as Bobby hoped, I think of him every time I see it, which is often.

Bobby's been living with us now for about four months, and it's been wonderful. I wasn't at all sure of how it would go, to have two—well three, if you counted Jack—stubborn asses living under one roof; there was sure to be fireworks, but it's been wonderful from the start.

To be able to wake up next to him, to have him at the breakfast table, to relax with him in the evening in front of the TV, and to be able to go to bed with him every night; it feels good. Really, really good.

I've never felt for anyone what I feel for him, and I realize I was never in love with Max at all. I'm not even sure why I was with him, and I'm not surprised now that our break up was so easy.

I didn't love him and he didn't love me. I practically saw him cheat on me at my own father's funeral and I didn't feel anything. But to think of Bobby cheating, or of breaking up with him, makes me feel a literal ache in the pit of my stomach.

No, Bobby and I have something different. Something much better. He's my forever, and I'm not even scared to admit it. I know, deep in my heart, he's my forever and that he'd never do anything to hurt me. His actions, his words, the way he looks at me, it all tells me all I need to know. I'm more important to him then even he is to himself. It's as though his happiness depends on mine. And in one of those wonderful life cycles, his happiness is the most important thing to me, so here we are, trying so fucking hard to make each other happy, and we're both succeeding.

I look up at the sound of my email indicating it's done loading, and quickly scroll through, stopping on one from my lawyers with the subject line: *Deceased Reilly Estate – Urgent.*

Opening it, I quickly skim the couple short paragraphs, seeing that they wish for me to call them to discuss, so I pick up my phone and do that.

The receptionist answers and I ask to speak to one of the lawyers handling my case and get put back on hold. I only have to wait a minute though as she picks up. "Hello Kit, this is Aleesia speaking."

"Hey Aleesia. I just got your email. Break it down for me?"

"Sure," she says as the sound of ruffling papers comes across the line. "Okay, so, we've consolidated all of your father's finances. He'd had a few bank accounts open that he'd forgotten about. Nothing much in them, but we consolidated anyway, so we can close accounts and finalize everything. We've also found insurance papers, all of which are expired and or invalid, because he hadn't paid anything into them for years. However, we found one that, although he hasn't paid into, it was still open and active simply because he'd had money in there. So," she says, tapping keys, "in that account, he had $1,043.76 — which you'll receive a check for — and because that was there, the insurance portion was still active, and in very small print there's actually a death or total paralysis section, meaning you're entitled to $50,000, bringing your total to $51,043.76."

"Oh, okay." I'm shocked that there was in fact a few dollars laying around.

"I highly doubt your dad even knew this was there. This was an account set up by an old employer more than eleven years ago, and hasn't been paid into for quite a few years. The average person probably wouldn't have known to look for it, but this is our job and we know where and how to look. Now, in regards to your last email, about your family and money you weren't sure existed, well I did some digging. Turns out, your father opened an insurance policy in …" she ruffles more papers, "December last year. The policy ensures a payout of $750,000 to his nominated beneficiary in the event of his death. The paperwork was filled out and sent in by mail. Get this, the 'witness' signature belongs to a Mrs. Renee Finlee."

My eyes narrow at Aleesia's words. Renee. That snake bitch.

"The beneficiary, *also* a Mrs. Renee Finlee … The account was paid by a direct debit from your dad's bank account, but payments lapsed when he stopped working and his balance was no longer enough to cover the fees. Here's what I think happened. Your dad was diagnosed in November, 'he' opens a life insurance policy in December. However, we have no proof at all that he ever spoke to the company in person, and I suggest he had no idea at all it existed. I think we'll be pursuing Mrs. Finlee very soon with a case for fraudulence. She missed a few pertinent details, though. One, whether she's the elected beneficiary or not, as long as he has living minor children, no matter what the policy says, that minor will receive it, and no one else."

Well that makes sense as to why they wanted Jack to live with them.

"Also, the fine print stated *'accidental death only, not to be paid out for suicide or pre-existing illness.'* Since your dad was diagnosed before the policy was begun, the cause of his death is considered pre-existing. Clearly, Mrs. Finlee is terrible with details.

"So after all is said and done, I regret to inform you, you won't be receiving the $750,000 payout, because the policy had lapsed, due to non payment, but even if it had been paid, it's still considered fraudulent. Either way, they were never going to pay that one out, but you *will* receive a check for $51,043.76, minus taxes and our legal fees, which I'll send you a statement of account sometime this week. According to state law, because your dad had no legal will, and because you're an adult, you won't receive a cent, but Jack, being the sole minor child, will receive it all. It'll sit in a trust account, managed by you, until he's twenty-one years old. Am I making sense so far?"

"Yeah, $50,000. Trust account. Fraud."

"Correct. You needn't worry about the stuff with your aunt. She won't be receiving any money, and the insurance company will be advised and they'll investigate. She'll likely be charged with attempting to fraudulently receive monetary gain, if they decide to pursue it. Which they will.

"As for everything else, after we cut you a check for Jack, the estate will be finalized and you won't have to talk to me ever again. I'll contact you in a few days to make an appointment for you to come in. We'll need you to sign some papers, and we'll go over your role as trust account manager. Basically, you can use the money for Jack's essentials: school clothes, books, you can charge him rent at a fair price, things like that. You can also invest the money if that's what you choose to do. I'm sorry that you receive nothing; I know you've paid for everything so far, but at least now you can charge him rent and take it from the trust. Just a way to make things a little easier on you. At our meeting, you'll sign the estate paperwork, declaring it closed once you receive the check, and then that'll be the end of that. Does that sound okay? Do you have any questions, Kit?"

My mind is spinning. "No, I can't think of any at the moment."

"Okay well, if you do, email me or write them down and we'll discuss them at our meeting. I'll let you go for now, Kit. Thanks for calling me."

"Yeah, cool. Thanks. Talk to you later."

I place the phone back in its cradle and I look around my office, completely at a loss. I get what happened, theoretically, but I'm stunned. That phone call was… surreal.

19

Kit

Girls night out…?

December 6, 2014

Less than three weeks till Bobby's fight.

It's Friday afternoon and I'm eager to pack my desk away and start the weekend. I have to go to training after work, then Casey and I are going out to 188 for belated birthday drinks—it was my birthday yesterday. It'll just be the two of us, which is exciting since we don't get to do that as often as we used to, but we're a little bummed Izzy can't come; she's not yet twenty-one.

We've all grown really close the last few months and we consider her one of us, despite the age gap.

Bobby also won't be joining us tonight; he'll train late with Aiden, then go home to sleep, but told us to have a blast and to call him to come pick us up when we're done.

His fight is on Christmas Eve, eighteen days away, and he only trains, eats, or sleeps these days. No partying or drinking until after the fight.

Not even pizza allowed. What a miserable life!

Bobby has been training super hard in the lead up to this, his efforts doubling the last few weeks. He's been leaving home about six thirty in the morning, and getting home about six thirty at night, six days a week. He's dropped all group classes and PT sessions, and has been working with each of his brothers, averaging eight hours a day working on his own technique, strength, and conditioning.

Once he gets home, he eats enough to feed an army then flops onto the couch, pulling my legs onto his lap, then promptly falls asleep. I feel terrible that he's working so hard, but everyone assures me he's right on track and everything is going great.

Plus, the physical results from so much training … well, my mouth waters at the sight of him. I mean, he was always beautiful, his tan skin wrapped around perfectly defined muscle. I was always a slave to him.

But now, he's packed on at least another thirty pounds of pure muscle and he looks like a perfectly cast statue of masculinity and virility.

I try and leave him alone to rest, but sometimes the temptation is a bit much — not that he's complained.

For my birthday yesterday, I was surprised to wake to a giant bouquet of flowers on my bedside table and breakfast in bed. After we made out and ate strawberries and made a mess of the sheets, I went to the kitchen to find two wrapped gifts on the table; one from Bobby and one from Jack, and Jack sitting there, patiently waiting for me to open it.

As we walked in and I sat down, Jack jumped up to pour me a coffee from the already full pot, placing it in front of me with a quick kiss on the crown of my head and a whispered "happy birthday."

Jack's changed so much in the last year, transforming from the bad attitude source of stress in my life, to my friend and over protective 'big' little brother. He has some kind of hero worship thing going on with Bobby, and frankly, I love it. I love it all.

The day that I spoke to my lawyers, I called a 'family' meeting and the three of us sat down at the table, and I told them what I found out hours before. Jack flipped his shit about me *giving* him $50,000, and he thinks we should split it evenly.

And Bobby flipped his shit about the insurance fraud and the fact I don't get to recoup any expenses, which just fueled Jack on in his rampage.

That was a big night and we all yelled at each other a lot. In the end, none of us really came to a decision. I just decided in my mind that the money will stay in trust and Jack can have it for college or for a down payment on a house in a few years. I've already been to college, and I already have a house, so really, fair's fair.

Ever since then, Jack has tried extra hard to be kind to me. His way of showing thanks, I guess, and his behavior has not gone unnoticed.

His grades have steadily risen, his training has improved tenfold, his attitude is pure honey, and his protective streak and kindness toward me are unheard of.

It's his birthday early in the new year, and he'll be sixteen, so I intend to think of a special gift for him.

"Kit? Are you going to open it?" Jack asks, pulling me out of my musings. I look down to both wrapped parcels in front of me. My smile is huge as I start to tug the ribbon off the gift labeled from Jack. I mean, really, who doesn't like presents?

It's heavy and about the size of a shoe box and I carefully peel back the paper to find a white box. Opening the white box, I discover a jewelry box. It's silver and has floral pattern work and claw feet. A swing latch holds it closed.

"Thank you, Jack! It's beautiful," I tell him, turning to hug him, but he stops me.

"Wait. Have a look inside." His dimpled smile gives away his excitement, so I turn back and carefully undo the latch and lift the lid to peek inside.

The interior is made of green velvet, with sections for rings and earrings, and pockets for bit and bobs. In one of the earring sections is a delicate pair of diamond studs, and in the 'bit and bobs' section is the Swarovski box they must have come in.

"Thank you, Jack," I tell him again, genuinely touched by the thought he put into this.

I imagine the other man standing with us knew about this and possibly bankrolled it too. God, I love these guys.

"Okay, open mine now," Bobby says, looking as excited as Jack did. He pushes the second, much smaller package in front of me and with shaking hands, I open it to find a cardboard envelope. I peel it open and look inside to find tickets.

"Oh, my god, oh my god, oh my god!!" I'm so fucking excited and I don't even know what exactly the tickets are for yet. I do know they're music though, because I recognize the ticketing company brand. I pull them out, so gentle, treating them as though they are two-hundred year old documents, touching only the corners. "OH, MY GOD!" I squeal when read Lila Royale's name, with full backstage access.

The date of the tickets is for February thirteenth and there are two.

"You get to choose who you want to take," he explains and drops a kiss on my brow. "Me or Tink. It's up to you baby. Or, I can get as many tickets as you want, if you want us all to come."

The rest of the day, although I had to work, was filled with so much love and happiness. Bobby had a chocolate bouquet delivered to my office, Casey and Izzy brought lunch and we picnicked in the gardens, then Aiden, Jon, and Jimmy made a huge production out of bringing over cake and balloons that we all shared in the evening.

Now it's Friday and I'm psyched to go out with Casey for a bit.

I've lost all the weight I set out to lose when I started training, and my old clothes are fitting better than they ever did. I'm excited to be able to wear something from my old wardrobe tonight, to get to feel like I have no responsibilities for a few hours. To feel young and free, the way I did before Dad was sick.

I look at the time on my computer, noting it's 4:33 p.m. and roll my eyes. When you have somewhere you'd much rather be, Friday afternoons drag. Usually I work a little longer on training days and drive straight to the gym, instead of going home then crossing back again an hour later to get to training. But today I'm just feeling antsy and want to go. I don't really have enough time to get anything worthwhile done, and if I start a big job it'll keep me going hours longer than I can stay. So I decide to just pack away and head out. I'll go straight to the gym and visit with Iz or something.

I switch off my monitor and grab my bag, waving goodbye to my colleagues as I head out the door. It's so cold out now; we're only a few weeks out from Christmas, and the sun is already a fair way down in the sky, the clouds grey and ugly and no doubt will be full dark and dumping snow within an hour or so. I rush to my car and quickly switch it on and start the heat. I sit and breathe into my hands for a full minute trying to warm up again, then put my car into drive and start onto the road.

Bobby tells me each morning what he's working on that day, so I know he's busy with Aiden today while they work on his ground technique. I won't disturb them when I arrive — no matter how tempting it is to see his face. Driving slowly down Main Street, I pass the store and make a mental note to pick up some groceries I know we need, and I tap my hands on the steering wheel, listening to the Glee channel on Pandora. Deciding I have time now instead, I quickly pull in and walk around the store, grabbing toilet paper and bread and a few other bits and pieces. I wander down the aisle with magazines and such, browsing a few covers and catching up on Hollywood gossip. I even gasp and giggle when I see a men's health magazine with one of my favorite Kincaid men posing on the front. His hair is wet and hanging in his chocolate eyes, his shoulders pumped and bulging, his hands high in fight stance. My heart hammers and my belly swirls with nervous energy. I'm not even fighting in a few weeks, but I feel like I am. I feel nervous for him, but a good nervous. Excited. Adrenaline fueled.

I throw the magazine in my cart on top of my other groceries and I smile. I think I'll frame this one.

I'm startled from my daydream and jump when my cart gets bumped into the shelves with a solid whack. I look over and almost jump again when I realize the cart owner is none other than my cousin Rita.

Shiiiit.

I wonder if Aunt Renee, her mom, has been approached yet by the lawyers? I wonder how much of this Rita knows about?

"Hey, nark bitch."

Well shit, she knows everything then.

"Hey Rita, sorry I can't stay, I'm late for an appointment." I attempt to turn my cart, but she grabs my arm, surprisingly strong for such a skinny girl. In fact, she seems much skinnier than I ever remember, her flesh pulling in around the bones.

"We know that you snitched on my mom. What the fuck do you think you're doing, sending the cops to our house for?" Her eyes are dark and narrowed as she glares at me. My heartbeat picks up and sweat breaks out and trickles down my spine. She's my younger, smaller cousin, and I've never been afraid of her before, but she's beyond fucking angry right now. I wouldn't be surprised if she tried to slit my throat with a magazine. I hope she doesn't use Bobby's.

"Look, I have to go. If you want information, you'll have to speak to your mom, or the lawyers. See ya." I quickly dodge past her, and rush toward the registers.

"Don't get too comfortable in bed with that rich boyfriend of yours. We're gonna fuck you up, then I'm gonna fuck him." She shoulder bumps me as she walks by, then she walks to the sidewalk and watches me unload my groceries onto the conveyor belt. Eventually, she takes her phone out and puts it to her ear.

The hair on the back of my neck prickles and my stomach feels like I swallowed hot oil. I take my own phone out and dial Bobby, knowing there's basically zero chance he would answer, but feeling shaken and needing him for a second. I was right though — he didn't answer, but the sound of his voice on voicemail helps. A teeny tiny little bit.

I pay for my groceries and slowly walk to my car, watching in every direction, feeling like Rita is still here and watching me, though I can't see her anywhere. I throw the bags in the back and take a quick last look, but I see no one, so I hop in and slowly drive toward the gym.

I was going to take the groceries home first, but I feel like I need to be around other people. I don't want to walk into an empty house right now, especially since its dark out and the snow clouds have opened up.

My cousin has officially given me the creeps and I need my family — my fight family, that is.

I drive cautiously, careful not to slip in the snow, and arrive at the gym almost ten minutes later. I pull up and switch my car off, and I take a slow look around the lot. Bobby's Rav and Jimmy's Jeep are here, as is Jon's and Aiden's trucks, and a bunch of other regulars' cars. Jack would have ridden here from school, and Izzy usually catches the bus, since she's still saving for a car.

Still feeling uneasy from earlier, I take my phone out and text Izzy, assuming she's on front desk duty.

M: *Hey, you at the gym?*

I: *Yeah babe. Where are you?*

M: *Outside. Can you come out?*

I: *Are you scared of the dark? Is the clown out there? Lol. On my way.* She pastes some crazy faces and fruit emoticons that imply I'm a dick, and she actually drags a chuckle out of me and loosens my chest a little bit.

I sit in my car, watching the front door and I smile when she comes out not a full minute later, wearing her teeny tiny workout gear and a big stupid furry hat you might see in Russia during a hard winter. She waves and I open my door. Just seeing her makes me feel better.

I step out and sling my bag over my shoulder when something, a movement in shadow makes me look to Iz's right. I don't even get time to react or warn her before she's hit from behind, a large dark shadow coming down heavy on the back of her skull and she drops to the ground like a sack of potatoes.

I'm frozen solid, in shock, unable to move or process what happened, when suddenly an arm wraps around my throat, pressing in on my windpipe and making me panic.

Rear naked choke, baby, we've practiced this. You know what to do. I can hear Bobby's voice in my head, and immediately my muscle memory kicks in. I stomp on my captor's shin then lift my hands, pushing his loose elbow up and pulling my head through the gap. Making sure to not let his arm go, I extend, spinning so he's now in front of me and I shove down hard until his shoulder pops.

He shouts out in pain, but before I can celebrate or escape, I feel pressure on the back of my own head. My body feels like it weighs 300 pounds as I fall, and then sharp pain sears through me as my skull bounces against the concrete ground.

20

Bobby

How would it feel
to kill another man?

"Okay, try it again," Aiden instructs, watching as I run Jimmy against a padded wall, drilling me on take downs.

"Again!" he yells, tweaking the smallest moves, making sure I get it right, perfection, before we keep working it. I fight the way I train, so if my technique is wrong in my own gym, it'll be wrong, and worse, under pressure and in the octagon.

I don't know what the time is, but it's dark outside the windows, and I'm pretty fucking hungry. We've been going on this for hours, and we were working on stand-up earlier. Jimmy and I are trying to work each other into locks and submissions, but often slip off each other, both of us sweating like crazy, despite the weather outside.

"Alright." Aiden stops us. "Bobby, you need to work on your sprawl. If Thomlassen gets his arms around you, you need to drop your weight. Spread your legs and just drop. If you can do that, then you can spin and take his back. If you don't, he'll have you on the floor and that's where he rules. Like this," he says, and indicates for Jimmy to come forward. They work it over and over again, slowing it down and showing me every tiny movement, then speeding it up and doing it in real time. I stand and watch, walking around them to eyeball every single angle.

I catalog exactly where Aido's feet are, what angle they're on, which part of his foot is touching the floor, how far from the floor his knees are, where his hands are, whether they're locked together; committing every detail to memory.

"Okay your turn. Jimmy, you try take him down. Bobby, you sprawl."

A little while later Aiden steps up to pull us apart. "Okay, that's enough. I wanna work on a couple more things then we'll call it a day."

Jimmy and I let go of our positions and flop onto the mats, sweating and panting for breath. "Bout' fucking time," Jimmy complains and takes the water bottle Aiden hands each of us.

"Bobby, you need to work on your leg placement when you sprawl. If you go too far forward, he'll be able to take your leg and use it and lock you down."

I nod as I sip my water. I lay my icy bottle against my brow, feeling drained and little nauseous now, and attempt to cool down a little.

Our heads snap up at the sound of a commotion in the main gym area. Aiden, Jim, and I look at each other, then realizing that three quarters of the gym management team are all in this room, and since Jon should be running a class right now, we realize we should go check it out. Leisurely, we groan and stand and walk toward the doors, but at the sounds of panicked voices, we sprint down the hall.

My heart pounds and my stomach rolls. Even though I don't know what's wrong yet, I know it's something big. I know it to my very core.

Jim and I reach the door at the same time, and Jimmy lets out a roar and bolts to Izzy's unconscious body as she lies limp in the arms of one of our regular members.

"Izzy? Izzy? What the fuck's going on?" He snatches her from him and lays her on the floor. She's unconscious. And blue! She's fucking blue.

"Call an ambulance, now!" I shout to the milling crowd. "And blankets. Someone get the first aid kit and get her some blankets." I drop to my knees on her other side as Jim's hands skim across her small body. I put my hand out to feel her throat, hoping to god I find a pulse, but Jimmy slaps my hand away. "Don't fucking touch her."

"Jim, let me touch her. We need to feel for a pulse."

"I'll do it," he says, already moving his hand as he speaks. The whole room holds their breath as we wait for him, but my stomach loosens when his breath comes out in a whoosh. "She's okay, she has a pulse," he sobs. "Blankets? Where are the blankets? She's so cold."

"What the hell's going on in here?" Jon shouts as he storms into the front room, then his eyes flare wide and he skids down beside us. "Sissy? Get the fuck off her." He pushes Jim. "Sissy? Wake up, baby. Why's she unconscious?"

"She's breathing," I tell him. "Ambulance is coming, blankets are coming."

"What happened?" He runs his shaking hands along her skin. "She's so cold."

"I dunno. Steve just raised the alarm. He was carrying her in. That's all we know."

Jon looks toward Steve, a client of ours for years, with murder in his eyes. Steve's a big guy—fucking huge, actually. He works hard, he has a promising fighting future, but he's a pussycat, with two kittens and a wife at home. He didn't hurt her.

"Jon, no. He just carried her in. He didn't hurt her."

Sirens can be heard coming closer, all of us breathing a little easier, knowing help is on the way. Jon continues studying Iz, brushing her hair off her face, touching her as though to reassure himself she's alive. Blankets were brought to us and the three of us rip them open, laying them over her as fast as we can.

No one else dares touch her. Even though this whole gym is a family, they know it's us guys and Izzy who are true family. And Jack and Kit.

My stomach drops again. "Where's Kit and Jack?"

"I'm here," Jack says, edging closer to us, seeking permission to intrude our circle. "Kit's with Tink tonight."

"Oh yeah, Tink. I forgot." He's right, she's with Tink tonight. That's what she told me this morning, but still …

Paramedics rush through the door, being led by another of our clients who must've been waiting out the front for them, and they shove us all out of the way. "Hop out of the way guys …"

~*~

Aiden, Jack and I sit on hard as fuck plastic chairs in the hospital emergency waiting room, while Jimmy and Jon prowl, vibrating like caged and pissed off lions. We're all wearing nothing more than our training shorts and tanks. No shoes, no wallets, no nothing.

Izzy hasn't been conscious at all since she was found, and we've been waiting in here for the last two hours, with absolutely no fucking answers. I've wanted to call Kit a dozen times, but my phone is at the gym, as is the other guys'.

"What's taking so long?" Jon demands as Jimmy sits down beside me, dropping his weight suddenly, as though he has no strength left. He drops his head in his hands and hums something I can't hear clearly.

"I don't know Jon." I concentrate on breathing in and out as emotions slam into me from every direction. I'm worried for Iz, I'm worried for Jon, I worry about Jimmy, even though his extreme stress is confusing to me. I want to talk to Kit. I feel like part of me is missing right now, and I have no way of contacting her. I hate to interrupt her birthday celebrations, but I know she'd want to know about Iz anyway.

I consider getting up to grab coffee and head to a payphone when a man in scrubs walks into the room, shrinking back when we all surround him and demand answers.

"Whoa!" His hands come up between us. "My name's Dr. Kelly, and I'm looking after Ms. Hart tonight. Which one of you are her next of kin?"

Jon steps forward. "She's my sister. Is she okay?"

"Ms. Hart is awake now. She has a concussion, and a mighty big bump on the back of her head."

"She … what? A concussion? Did she fall?"

"I don't know, Mr. Hart. I was coming to you for answers. But no, I don't think she fell. At least not without help. Her injuries are consistent with a strike to the head. And for that reason, the police have been notified and will be by to speak to her, and the rest of you, soon."

"Someone hit her?" Jimmy snaps as his eyes go wild with worry.

Kelly's eyes narrow. "Who are you?"

I step between them. "This is Jimmy, and I'm Bobby and this is Aiden. Kincaid. And that's Jack. We own the gym together, with Jon. Izzy is an employee and client of ours. And our sister. We're family. All of us," I tell him, feeling more and more sick that Kit isn't by my side. I need to see her, to touch her. I don't even care about disturbing her night anymore. I need to see her.

"*You're* Bobby Kincaid?" he asks suspiciously. I nod my head as my stomach jumps. "Okay, well, if you'll come with me in a moment, Ms. Hart is asking for you. But first, like I said, she's awa—"

"Me? She's asking for me?"

"Yes, but first I want to talk to you all, so I won't have to repeat myself."

"Why would she ask for me?" I mean, I love her, she's family, but there's no reason why she'd ask for me first.

"The sooner you stop interrupting me, the sooner I can update you all and you can see her. Ms. Hart has a large contusion on the lower portion of her skull, only an inch or so above her spine. I suspect she was hit there with a closed fist. The area isn't consistent with being hit with an object—like a bat or something. I think it was a large, closed fist. She's really very lucky, as there have been deaths from this exact type of attack. There appear to be no defensive marks, no struggle. I suspect she was hit from behind and rendered unconscious immediately. She has scraping on her chin, forearms and hands from the fall. She has early signs of hypothermia, though I'm confident there'll be no permanent damage. I think she must've been unconscious and exposed to the elements for less than fifteen minutes. She's still feeling quite cold, but that's shock. We'll keep her here overnight at least, to monitor her concussion, but other than that she'll be fine. She's in the ICU at the moment, but is being moved to a room as we speak. Mr. Kincaid, if you'll follow me, she's requested you first, then the rest of you may see her."

"We're all coming," Jim demands.

Kelly stops walking and looks back at us with a raised brow. He's not scared of the five fighters in front of him. He's probably seen this a million times before; angry families. Eventually he sighs, but nods, "Alright fine, let's go. Since Ms. Hart has been moved to a regular room, you can all come."

We follow him through a maze of corridors, moving faster because of his access key cards, not having to wait for doors to be opened for us. Finally we arrive in a large ward and Kelly stops to speak to a nurse for a moment, then looks back at us. Sighing again, he walks back to our group.

"Nurse Robens tells me Ms. Hart is asleep again. She's okay, just a regular sleep," he rushes on when we all start talking at once. "Ms. Hart has been given some pain relief for what is likely a whopper headache, and she's just tired from tonight's events. We'll be monitoring her closely, so don't worry. I expect a full recovery."

"Can we still go in?" Jon asks.

"Yeah, you can go in. Don't try and wake her; she needs her rest. Be considerate of her pain, be quiet, but yes, you can go see her. When she wakes, be sure to buzz the nurse so she can have her vitals checked. Otherwise, Nurse Robens will be in often anyway to check."

We all leave him, done with him, and walk toward the nurse Kelly indicated. She takes a couple steps back as she looks up at us. "All of you?" she asks, her voice clipped and full of slang. "Y'all sure are tall. Y'all are related to that itty-bitty thing in there?"

"Yeah, she's our sister. Please show us to her room," Jim demands on a low growl, obviously struggling to not rip this place apart.

She purses her lips in defiance and squares her shoulders. "Sure, follow me, then."

We only walk another thirty feet or so before she stops at room 1314 and opens the door quietly. She peeks her head in first. The room is dark, the only noise is the heart rate monitor. We all follow her in, and my stomach rolls at seeing Iz's tiny body in that huge bed, the machines surrounding her, overwhelming her. She's not actually hooked up to anything important; she's not needing any fluids or help to breathe. Just the monitor. She has an IV tube in the veins by her elbow, but it's not connected to anything, just taped back to her arm and a quick bandage covering it.

"Take a seat," the nurse whispers to us, "let her rest. Call me if you need anything."

Jonno walks straight to Iz's side, taking her hand in his as he bends and rests his forehead against their joined hands. I look away to give him privacy. I won't ever mention that I saw his shoulders bouncing as he cried.

Jimmy walks to her other side and pulls up a chair to sit. He doesn't take his eyes from her face, he simply watches her and touches the longer strands of her hair that hang toward the edge of the pillow.

Jack hasn't moved more than a foot from me since the gym, as though he needs me for direction and comfort, since Kit isn't here to do it. My stomach tugs again as I think of her. The longer I'm away from her, the more I feel sick, my stomach feeling like I swallowed something disgusting and oily. I lean against the wall and slide down until I'm sitting on the floor, and Jack mirrors my movements. I put my hand on his head for a second, silently letting him know I've got him. I don't though. I don't even have myself.

Aiden just floats around us all, totally out of his element, unsure how to help; his organized self is at a loss since there's nothing for him to do.

We sit mostly in silence for a long time, mutterings and questions being quietly asked every now and again. Mostly revolving around why. And who?

A little later, a knock at the door has us all looking up as two uniformed officers walk in. They swagger in with hands on hips and scowls on their faces. I don't bother standing for them. I already don't like them.

"Officers," Jon says quietly, trying not to disturb Iz.

"Son," the first one replies, patronizing as fuck, though he couldn't be more than a decade older than us. He's maybe forty years old, and has a severely receding hairline. He's about as tall as us, but has a visible spare tire around his waist and old acne scars marking his face. "I'm Officer Brennan, this is Officer Evans. We're in charge of …" He looks at his notepad, as though he can't remember her name. As if she's not important to him. "Ms. Isabelle Hart's case. Who are you?"

"I'm Jonathan Hart, Iz is my baby sister. These guys are Bobby, Aiden, and James Kincaid, my business partners and friends, and this is Jack Reilly, also a friend."

Brennan's eyes stop on me when Jon says my name, and they narrow as he stares me down. "Nice to meetcha boys. My partner and I have already been by your gym. After speaking to hospital admin, we understand that is where Ms. Hart was attacked and subsequently found. We've collected witness statements from those who were present when she was carried in. And we spoke to the gentleman who found her. We'd like to speak to all of you, and to her, when she wakes. At the moment, we're treating this case as suspicious. We have questions for you as a group, and then I'd like to take each of you aside to speak separately."

"Are we suspects?" Aiden asks, finally able to direct his attention to something.

"Well I'm not sure, Mr. ... Kincaid. Did you attack Ms. Hart? *Should* you be a suspect?"

"Of course I didn't attack her. Every single one of us were inside the gym, training or teaching at the time Izzy was carried inside."

"So, you all have alibis. It's always so tidy when that happens..." He writes notes in his book.

"We have a gym full of men who can verify that!" Aiden snaps at him.

Brennan looks up and sucks his lip arrogantly. "Please, calm yourself, boy."

My blood boils and I'm tempted to punch this fucker in the back of the head.

"Does Ms. Hart have a boyfriend? An ex-boyfriend?" He pauses and looks at each of us. "One of you, perhaps?"

I jump up to intercept both Jon and Jimmy from beating the snot out of this fuckstick. "We did not hurt her," I tell him as I push everyone apart. "Not a single one of us in this room would ever hurt her. If you're not gonna investigate this properly, then I'll go over your head and I'll have someone else assigned to this case."

"Oh, yeah?" he says with a lifted brow. "You threatening me, boy? That sounds like guilt if I ever heard it."

"No, sir ..." I grind out, "not threatening, just asking that you get to the bottom of this as soon as possible."

"Well then, I 'ppreciate your apology," he drawls.

What the fuck is this guys deal? How many times did his mother drop him?

"Bobby?" I hear a croak and my head snaps toward Izzy as Jim and Jon rush back to her.

Jon takes her hand. "Sissy, are you okay?"

She shakes her head and looks at me. "Bobby."

"Yeah, honey?" I walk to the side Jon is on, and Jimmy mashes his hand against the nurse call button. "Who did this to you, Iz?"

"Kit," she croaks as tears fall.

I almost spew everywhere. That's not right. Izzy's confused. She's wrong. "Kit did this? Honey, that doesn't make sense."

She shakes her head as Jack jumps up from the floor at the sound of his sister's name. "No. Kit. Go find Kit. They took her."

I was right all along. I need to see Kit right now, I knew something was wrong. I ignored my instincts, thinking the sick feeling was for Iz, but now I know, my stomach knows, Kit's hurt. "Who took her? What are you talking about?"

"Someone hit me," she says, attempting to touch the back of her head, but Jimmy grabs her hand again. "Someone hit me, and then they took her. She was scared. She called me from the car, because she was scared … I came outside," she trails off, and my heart is trying to break out of my chest, my whole body hurting.

"Who the fuck took her?" Jack demands loudly, not backing off even when Jimmy nails him with death eyes for yelling at Iz.

"I don't know," Izzy cries, "I didn't see. It was dark and I … I didn't see."

I feel like my skin is too tight, like I need to break out: out of my skin, out of this room. I need to find Kit, now.

I'm going to kill a motherfucker, just as soon as I find her, as soon as she's safe, I will kill someone.

"Wait for me!" Jack shouts.

21

Kit

I feel like I'm in a cheap mafia sitcom

"Call again!" Rita screeches at Chris, as she prowls back and forth past me.

"You're gonna make me look desperate, leaving all those missed calls on his phone," I taunt, just to piss them off. I've been in this stupid fucking room, tied to a stupid fucking heater for a while now.

I'm not sure how long, but an hour or two at least. I'm sitting on the floor with my arms secured behind my back, attached to a column heater that's attached to the wall.

I'm feeling very Jack Dawson right now. Where are all the axes at?

My hands are numb. My feet are numb. My ass is numb. And I have a big fucking headache. I'm not scared of these idiots, not anymore. I'm just pissed off. Though I seem to have the best seat in the house, because the heater is on and toasty warm.

They've taken my phone and keep calling Bobby, and I shake my head with embarrassment every time they mention ransom. Ransom. Like this is the movies and I'm the president's daughter.

"He won't answer," Chris whines and paces the room. I get a sick thrill as I watch him cradle his arm. Looks like Chris is the one who tried to choke me out.

"So, call him again! He'll answer, he'll come looking for her soon."

"I don't know why you're bothering," I argue. "I told you, he's not answering because we broke up. He won't come looking for me, and he won't pay you a cent.

Lie, lie, lie. Bobby would give them money in a heartbeat if I told him to. But I won't. Not in a million years. Thankfully his non-answering reinforces my break up story. I assume he hasn't answered because he's with Iz and the guys. I hope he is.

Last I saw, she was unconscious in the snow.

I take a moment to take stock of my own body, now that Chris is busy lapping the room on sentry duty, and Rita has stormed out.

I wonder where she's gone, and I wonder where my aunt is, if she's involved? And who else is involved? If Chris was behind me, who hit Iz?

Chris doesn't scare me, not at all. He looks like he regrets everything to do with my crazy ass cousin. Rita though, seems to have officially lost her mind.

Parts of my body are numb from sitting on this crappy concrete floor. My head aches like it never has before. My body folded like an accordion, my arms jerked and tied behind me. My left shoulder feels like it's on fire; it's been twisted around on an awkward angle, seemingly dislocated. I vow to make them pay. For us both.

I look around the room to try to figure out where I am. It's mostly empty except the heater, a crappy metal table, and a single chair littered with ash trays and rubbish. There's a small fridge in one corner, the outside almost exclusively rusted orange, and a sink next to it, overflowing with dishes and crap. The floor has no carpet or finish, just cold dirty concrete.

Is it unreasonable for me to be worried about rats and cockroaches right now? This place is disgusting.

There's one window. It's still dark outside, and no outside light is filtering in. I can't see any lights from passing cars, nor can I hear any. There's a door to my right that Rita passes in and out of, but I don't know if it leads outside or to other rooms. I don't know if there are other people here. I don't know anything.

In an attempt to relieve pain in my numbing legs, I shuffle my weight, but stop when hot angry pain radiates from my shoulder and spreads in all directions. My mouth waters and my stomach rolls and I nearly vomit from the waves of agony.

I want to put my head between my knees to breathe, but can't even move that far. I don't know what happened to my shoulder, but I'm glad it must have happened when I was unconscious. The waves of pain now must be nothing on the initial injury.

I sit and breathe for a few minutes longer, concentrating on every sound I hear, hoping for some clue on what the hell's going on, and after a while, when I think Chris' nervous pacing might send me over the edge into crazytown, Rita storms back into the room. "Call again!" She turns to me and kneels down close, "You better fucking hope he answers this time, or I'll hurt you."

Chris takes out my phone and redials, and we all wait quietly, so quiet, I can hear the ring tone from across the room. I don't know if I actually want Bobby to answer this time or not. I don't want him involved, but I also don't want her to hurt me. And I genuinely think she will. Something is making her nervous and she's starting to get twitchy.

The call rings out and sweat trickles down my spine when she looks at me again. I refuse to let her know I'm scared though, so I fall back on my trusty old friends — sass, sarcasm, and denial. "I told you. We broke up. There's a reason he's not taking my calls."

"Stop lying to me!"

"I'm not lying, Rita! What do you think this is? Hollywood? Should I call you Bonnie? You're an entitled whore who's watched one too many movies. You can't just *ransom* people, especially when the person you're attempting to sell me to doesn't even like me! Whose plan was this? You're both dumber than a bag of fucking rocks." I'm yelling now, my anger and pain needing a release. I just want to go home and see Bobby. And I need to see Iz. And the guys. And Tink.

"Last chance for you, bitch," she spits at me, then looks away. "Call again, Chris. If he doesn't answer, we end it and walk away. Maybe his fine ass really did dump her. She's no good to us then, is she?"

My heart pounds at the finality in her tone, my stomach sinking at what she promises will come after this. We all listen again, waiting for the dial tone to begin …

Ring, ring.

Ring, ring.

… And then end.

He didn't answer.

She looks at me and sighs, her face fallen as though genuinely disappointed in me. She watches me for a minute or two, then she turns to the makeshift kitchen and fumbles around in the sink. My lip curls as she digs around in the filthy dishes with her bare hands, but then she turns back around with a long knife — the blade long and narrow and almost the length of my forearm. I almost vomit as heat fills my stomach. My heart tries to desert me, every man for its self-style, when I realize what she intends to do.

She walks slowly toward me, reminding me of a big cat stalking a tiny mouse; a mouse that has its arm tied to a heater. I'm the fucking mouse.

"Okay, listen up," she says, her voice equal parts smug and taunting, and scared and jittery.

"Where's Aunt Renee?" I interrupt, not really wanting to listen to anything she has to say. Her steps falter at my question, but she decides to answer anyway. That's kind of scary in itself. Usually that means they're almost done with their victim, right? Shit, shit, shit. shit. I should have watched more CSI, studied more on these situations.

"Mom's at home, watching her shows."

"She has nothing to do with this?"

"That's what I just said, dummy. Though, I mean, she started it. She had this grand plan to get your old man to open a policy, but that didn't really pay out, did it? She's a dumbass just like you."

"You know, she'll still go to prison for that, right?" I actually have no clue at all if that's true, but I'm running out of material, and the fire in my shoulder is burning hotter every second. My five-year plan right now is to just keep her talking. I honestly cannot think of anything else to do.

"Yeah, probably, dunno." She shrugs. "Not my problem."

"Whose plan was taking me then? What did you actually think would happen?"

"Well, we planned on your boyfriend buying you back. We know he's rich as fuck and has a few dollars to spare."

"How do you know he's rich? I don't even know he's rich."

"Ever heard of Google, you dummy? He's worth millions, like a hundred million."

"Really? That's … strange," I say, honestly not able to process that he has that kind of money.

"He owns that gym, he owns his house, he fights professionally, duh! Then when Milla sold him that ring, we figured he must've been serious about you …"

"Milla? What ring?" I swallow down the bile as stars begin floating in my vision.

"Milla from school. She used to live down the street from me when we were kids. She works over at Davidson Jewelers now. She told me how hunky Bobby Kincaid and his brothers came into the store and bought a big ass rock. Maybe it wasn't for you? Nah, but she said Jack was there too, she remembers him. So, if it wasn't for you, then that would have been an awkward drive home." She cackles weirdly. "She told me he spent a packet, not on credit, and it was for a diamond. Not some Valentine's bauble. Maybe he changed his mind? Wouldn't surprise me, you're just bland Kit Reilly, after all."

She's still laughing, and she's just pissing me off. It's one thing for me to doubt myself, but for her to talk that crap, I want to smash her face in. My shoulder lets out another jolt of pain at the smallest movement, reminding me that I'm kind of stuck and can't do anything anyway, and my frustration and anger builds.

She smiles down at me as she pops gum obnoxiously. "So since you're about as useful as a balls on a dildo, and I can't actually just let you go, you know, because you'll call the cops and shit, we'll just get started."

"Whoa, get started on what?" I suck in a breath as my quick movement sends agonizing pain through my shoulder. I'm starting to think something more serious is going on with it, or maybe shock is wearing off and numbness isn't helping anymore.

"Well, first I'm gonna cut you, because you've always been a stuck-up bitch, and frankly, I just don't like you. Then we'll ... dispose of you."

"You ... What? This isn't a movie! This is real life. You can't just hurt me or ... dispose of me."

"Sure I can. You wouldn't be the first," she laughs again, and I suddenly realize I'm no longer dealing with my younger cousin, but a certified fucking crazy.

She leans over me, and I try to think of a way out, but I'm feeling overwhelmed at this whole fucking situation. I'm disgusted at myself; I've been working out and training to fight, and I haven't done a thing to get away from this damn heater.

White hot pain races through my arm, and I look down to find she's sunk that filthy fucking knife into my bad shoulder. I cry out in pain, then cry again when the movement jerks my arm. I look around wildly, like an animal with its foot stuck in a trap, and realize we're in the room alone. Chris has left me. She pulls back and slashes out with the knife again, slicing me straight down through my bicep, opening my arm like a warm loaf of bread.

The blood gushes hot and thick, and spots dance in my eyes at the combination of pain and blood loss. Rita stands from her crouched position in front of me, then swinging her leg wildly, she kicks me repeatedly in the stomach and ribs. She's talking nonsensically, rumbling about how I'm a bitch, how this is my own fault, how she was forced into it, how she just needs cash, and how it's my fault Bobby wouldn't pay for me.

My ribs crack painfully and my stomach feels hollow, as though she's kicking straight through to my spine. Panting for breath, she stops and looks at me for a long moment. Her eyes vacant, her pupils large but unseeing. She leans over me again and I twitch, scared for what she'll do next.

She cuts my ropes, slicing my hand and wrist in the process, and without the ropes to hold me up, I slump to the floor, unable to support my own weight. My eyes almost blank except for white and red as the pain tears through me, my arm feeling completely detached from my body.

Thankfully, mercifully, I'm starting to feel numb again, and I welcome it. I lie my head on the cool concrete floor, suddenly seeking cold rather than the heat from my former captor behind me. Rita seems annoyed at my lack of fighting and starts kicking me again.

Amazingly, I don't feel it anymore.

I know where she's kicking me — my stomach, my legs, my chest — but it doesn't hurt anymore. I wonder if this is what dying feels like? I struggle to catch my breath every time she kicks my stomach, every time she forces all the air from my lungs. I slump to my stomach, exposing my back to her and she starts stomping on me, my ribs just shifting around inside as though disconnected completely, my kidneys feeling inflamed, bruised.

I continue to lie there, finding a small satisfaction that she isn't getting the crying and begging she was hoping for. My eyes are closed so I can't see her anymore, but I can hear her screaming at me. Next thing I feel is her boot hitting the side of my face, and darkness overtaking me again.

22

Bobby

What do I do?

Twenty-seven missed calls.

Kit called me twenty-seven fucking times.

She needed me, and I wasn't there for her. I keep redialing her number, but the call goes straight to voicemail. The first call was hours ago, then a break, then twenty-six calls in the space of an hour. The last call was forty-five minutes ago, and now, nothing.

Jack and I raced from the hospital to the gym, arriving in under five minutes, but I still missed her calls; the last one coming through while I was still at the hospital talking to those fucking jokes that call themselves police officers.

I don't know where she is, I don't know who has her, I don't know if she's hurt, and I have no way of finding her.

I'm on the edge, teetering between wanting to tear this town apart to find her, and bawling my eyes out. I don't know what to do, and I don't know where to start.

Jack storms around the empty gym; all our members long gone home. "Who has a problem with her?" he screams. "Who would take her?"

He's asking me, but I don't know the answers.

He storms straight toward me, stopping with his face barely an inch from mine. "You were supposed to protect her, you piece of shit! You promised me! You promised," he screams, his voice breaking at the end. I can't blame him; I know what I promised. I swore to him I'd marry her, that I'd look after her for the rest of our lives. I made that promise, intending to keep it forever; I haven't even begun and I've already failed.

We both spin at the sound of thundering footsteps charging through the door, both of us taking a defensive stance ready to face whatever is coming. Aiden and Jon run into the room, stopping on a dime when they spot us, looking at our fists and faces as though they're loaded guns.

Aiden's hands come up quickly. "It's just us."

"Why aren't you with Iz?"

"Jim stayed with her," Jon answers. "We're here to help. What do we know?"

"We know fuck all!" Jack yells again in frustration.

"Have you checked her car? It's still outside," Jon says, and I realize in my blind panic I never noticed it. We all run outside and when I reach it, I realize I never saw it earlier because the street lights above are broken. That can't be a coincidence.

"Her keys are on the floor," Jack says, reaching past me to the keys somewhat hidden by the seat and floor mat.

"There are groceries in the back seat," Aiden adds, his hands cupped around his eyes as he peers through the window.

I frown as I peek in past him. "Jonah's? She went to Jonah's Store first then?"

We search Kit's car, top to bottom for any other clues. We also find her laptop in the backseat, but it is password locked, so I can't get in. Stepping back from the driver side door, snow and something else crunches beneath my shoes.

Looking down, my heart thumps painfully when I find her crushed bracelet. Picking it up, I notice the clasp has snapped, the soft gold crushed flat in spots. I look at the ground surrounding us and realize under a light dusting of fresh snow, there are drag marks and a few drops of what appears to be blood.

"Fuck! FUCK!" I yell, needing some release, needing something so I can think straight again before my brain and chest explode. The guys all look up at me. I'm not ready to speak yet, so I just hold her bracelet up.

"Fuck!" Jack repeats angrily.

"There are drag marks in the snow," I tell them, choking on the bile that threatens to come up, "and blood. WHERE THE FUCK IS SHE?"

"Okay, let's go to Jonah's," Aiden says. "Someone might have seen her then we'll take it from there." Aiden's always been our calm thinker. Unshakable under pressure. His calmness right now though comes across as uncaring, cold, and I want to fuck him up for not being more terrified.

Like I am.

I feel like I can't piece whole thoughts together right now, like my brain is having some kind of malfunctioning seizure or something. My skull feels too small, my brain wanting more space and is about to burst out of my eyes and ears.

"Bobby!" Jon calls out, snapping me from my daze as they run toward his car. I sprint forward and jump into the back seat next to Jack, and Jon peals out of the lot. The five-minute drive helps me realign my thoughts until they're tunneled, my sole purpose to find Kit and make her safe.

"Should we call the police?" I ask. Common sense is starting to filter in.

"They know," Aiden answers. "That dickwad at the hospital asked what was up, and we told him what we know. He suggested we file a report, tomorrow, twenty-four hours after she is *allegedly* missing."

"Fucking asshole. Deserves to be fired. And deserves to have the piss flogged out of him!"

"Yeah, probably. But that's a problem for another day. They won't help tonight, so we find her ourselves."

We pull up at Jonah's store and I jump out and race inside before Jon even has the keys out of the ignition. The other guys run to keep up with me and we all skid to a stop just inside the entry. I look around, hoping to see some I know, someone who knows Kit. I can't see old man Jonah anywhere, but his daughter, Belle, is tidying the magazine rack so I head straight for her.

"Belle," I call, startling her. She turns toward our group, stepping back a little as we descend on her.

She hesitates, but we've all known each other a long time; she has nothing to worry about, regardless of the murder in our eyes.

"Hey Bobby, where's Jimmy tonight?"

"He's busy. Listen, have you seen Kit tonight? She came in earlier."

Belle twirls her long hair around her nail as she looks at each of us. "Yeah, I saw her. A few hours ago. Are you two fighting, Bobby? She seemed upset, 'specially when she was talking to another chick. Jesus, you didn't cheat on her, did you?"

"No Belle, we're not fighting. But listen, who was she talking to? Did you hear anything? Did she say anything to you?"

"No, she didn't say anything to me. I didn't serve her, she was in Jenny's line. But I could tell she was upset, because this other chick, she had venom in her eyes. I'll tell ya Bobby, I can't blame Kit one bit for running out of here after they spoke."

"Kit was upset?"

"Oh yeah! The bitchy one rammed Kit's cart and everything, then she went outside. I kept an eye out, see, but she just stood on the sidewalk and spoke on the phone. That was it. The bitchy one didn't buy anything; her cart was empty the whole time."

"What did she look like? The other one. Young or old?" I so confused. This whole mess can't just be some catfight between girls.

"She was younger. Really young. Like, I'm not even sure if she can legally drink. She was sort of short, shorter than Kit anyhow, but that's not hard. She's lovely and tall, huh? I'd kill for those legs."

"Belle. Focus. What else did she look like?"

Belle's brows pull in tight as she attempts to rub two brain cells together. "Umm, like I said, short, kind of. She had long brown hair, but it was tied up high in a ponytail. She was wearing jeans two sizes too small for her; not that she was overweight or anything, she looked good, but I guess she likes showing off what she has. And boots. She was wearing really nice boots that go to her knees."

"Anything else? Can you think of anything else to describe her?"

"Nope, just what I said."

"I think … I think she's talking about Rita," Jack says quietly, as though he hadn't actually finished the thought in his head yet. "Our cousin, Rita."

"Yes! That was her name! How'd you know?"

Belle's chipper voice has me wanting to punch a fucking wall. "You knew her name? Why didn't you say so?"

"Well, I dunno. You didn't ask for her name. Plus, I don't actually know, I just heard Kit call her something that sounded like that. Like Ria, or Reena, something like that …" She steps back from the fury in my eyes and gulps. I don't stick around for more of her space head bullshit, I have a name now, so I dash out the front doors without another word.

As soon as Jack's in the car I turn to him. "Where do we go? Where will we find Rita?" Think fast. Think fast!

"I don't know. To her mom's house I guess. Head across town."

Jon starts the car and speeds back into the street. If the timeline in my head is right, Kit's been missing, and hurt, for going on four hours now. Four hours too fucking long. A few minutes later, we come roaring into a rundown street with shitty houses and overgrown weedy yards.

"Number forty-three." Jack points toward a house with a built-in veranda. Several couches are scattered around, and a half dozen beat up cars litter the front lawn—none of them looking roadworthy.

As soon as we pull in, I jump out of the truck and storm toward the front door. I'm thumping the door with a closed fist and much more force than necessary when the others catch up to me; Jack always my second. I keep bashing the door, increasingly frustrated that no one is answering and no one seems to be around.

I wait another minute, giving them only that long before I just let myself in.

"Jack, is there anywhere else they could be? Any houses, trailers, cabins? Anywhere you'd hang out as kids?"

"No, I don't know. I don't think so. Last I heard, Chris was staying here with them. His folks kicked him out ages ago. I don't know where else they could be."

"Alright. I'm going inside. You stay out here with Jon." I'm freaking out, but I'm still conscious of the fact he's only fifteen years old. No matter how grown he thinks he is, this is still his family. I don't know what to expect inside this shit hole, but whatever it is, Jack doesn't need to see it.

"No! I want to come inside with you."

"No, stay here, help Jon keep watch. If anyone comes running," — not that I expect anyone will — "you need to stop them. They may know where your sister is. Aiden, you're with me."

I turn back to the door and silently count to five, preparing myself that Kit could be on the other side. I'm terrified that I'll find her. I'm terrified I won't.

Three.

Four.

Five.

I raise my foot and kick the door in, smashing the handle to pieces and splintering the wood. I walk in quickly, trying to look in every direction at once, as well as watch Aiden too. I'm not willing to risk him on top of everything else happening.

I look around the filthy room and find a middle-aged lady unconscious on the couch, presumably Aunt Renee? I stop walking when I notice the needles and other drug paraphernalia littering the floor and small table in front of her.

In an armchair across from her, a younger guy — maybe my age — lies in the same unconscious state. Both appear to be alive; I can see their chests rising consistently, but I'm unwilling to go closer.

"Aiden, you wait here, yeah? I just wanna do a quick walk through. I don't think anyone else is here though."

Without waiting for his answer, I walk toward the kitchen, stepping over and around filth that covers the floor. I try not to touch anything, but I'm thorough, looking behind every closed door, checking every single space that Kit could possibly be.

I walk through three bedrooms in total, plus a bathroom and a backyard. The whole place is fucking disgusting and my skin crawls with the filth surrounding me.

I wind my way back to the front of the house, making Jon and Jack jump but they relax when they realize it's me. Jack's face falls when he notices that I'm alone.

I know, kid, I fucking know.

"Aiden! Come out here," I yell toward the house. He's out the door like a shot. Clearly as eager as I to get out of that dump. "I want you to call the police," I tell Jon, "there are a couple of unconscious junkies in there. Kit's not here though."

Where are you, baby?

23

Kit

Tinkerbelle. Peter Pan...
Snow White?

I open my eyes and look around. The world appears to be turned on its side, and I realize I am lying down, still on a cold concrete floor. I'm lying on my bad shoulder, which is mercifully numb now; my congealing blood providing the only warmth I can feel.

The heater must be off, as are all the lights, and I'm alone in this cold dark room. I can't see or hear anyone nearby, but I just know, somehow, that I'm completely alone. The space just feels ... empty. There's no life here. Does that mean I'm already dead? Or dying? I'm not sure.

I don't know how much time has passed, but it's still dark outside. I attempt to sit up but my shoulder instantly decides it's a good time to not be numb anymore, the white-hot pain ripping through me and finally succeeding in making me throw up.

Most of it is dry retching, since I haven't eaten in … I don't even know how long. The retching is jolting me and making my pain radiate further, meaner. Staying as still as possible, breathing through the throbbing, I wait for the pain in my ribs and shoulder to pass, begging for that numbness to return. I'd give anything to find the numbness again.

After a time, with minimal movement, the pain recedes a little, allowing me to hide behind a veil of ignorance and nausea. I feel dizzy and lightheaded, and I wonder briefly how much blood I've lost.

I look around again, knowing I need to figure out how to get out of here. Bobby can't possibly know where I am, and although I know he'd be looking for me, he can't find me without clues. Hell, I don't even know where I am!

I prepare myself to stand, knowing that I have no option. If I stay, I'll probably die from cold. Or blood loss. Whichever comes first. Slowly, I place my good arm in front of me on the floor and leverage myself up, trying my best to not move too fast, not wanting to jostle my arm or fall on my face from dizziness.

Despite being careful, I yelp, almost blacking out as black spots float in my vision from the pain shooting through my whole body. I can feel loose bones rattling around inside, scraping against each other. Broken ribs.

Breathing through my mouth, I stop and start, stop and start, working through the pain, slowly finding my feet. Eventually, I find myself standing upright, although I need to hold the wall because I'm swaying dangerously to the sides.

Not wanting to alert anyone to my presence — just in case there is actually someone around — I stay as quiet as I possibly can. I'm still wearing my work clothes, and I can see from the moonlight through the single window, my blouse is torn to shreds, especially along my left side and injured arm. My stomach and bra are exposed, and a patchwork of angry bruising between the ribbons of ripped fabric bloom angrily. My jacket is missing completely; I have no idea where it's gone.

I tuck my arm into my body as tight as I possibly can and I take a step forward. Stumbling forward, I realize in my disoriented state I only have one heel on. Like thick oil through a clogged sieve, my brain slowly wonders where the other fell off. Gone. It's gone. My knee length skirt is restrictive, so quietly, I kick the second heel off and pull my skirt higher to allow better movement.

Right hand on the wall, I shuffle forward, stockinged feet silently creeping forward, toward the single door leading to god knows where.

Hell? Or freedom?

I do my best to move quietly, but my ears feel like they're full of water, so I'm unsure how successful I am. I reach the door and test the handle, it's locked but the actual handle is flimsy and rattles around.

I stand there for another few minutes, listening and catching my breath, trying not to breathe too deeply because that makes my rib bones dig in more. Deciding there's nothing else to be done, whether there's anyone on the other side of this door or not, I can't stay in here indefinitely.

With no other choice, I step back and prepare myself to ram the door. My stomach rolls already, preemptively, knowing the pain I'll be feeling imminently, but I bolster my reserve. If I stay, I die.

Silently counting from three, I tuck my arm in, holding it with my right hand. Lining myself up, I prepare to ram the door with my good shoulder.

Three.

Two.

One.

I block everything out: all feeling, all worry, all thoughts of pain, and I run into the door and land with a solid thump. Letting out an involuntary cry, the pain has me vomiting all over the filthy floor beyond. The tearing at my stomach from the vomiting wracks fiery pain through me, coming full circle and making me retch some more.

It takes everything in me to stay on my feet; strangely, the filthy floor a huge motivator to not allow myself to lie down. I'm fairly confident I'm here alone, since the noise I've made is well and truly enough to alert the dead, and no one has come to investigate yet.

Mercifully, the flimsy lock didn't hold and I've entered what appears to be a living room with broken bay windows and piles of broken furniture and rubbish strewn everywhere. Standing still a moment longer, attempting to get my pain under control, I look through the windows to find I'm surrounded by a blanket of snow, trees, and darkness.

Breathing through my mouth again, I shuffle toward the door, almost crying in relief to find it has no lock at all; the handle snapped off and the door moving slightly with the wind. My teeth chatter from the cold so much my jaw physically aches, my ears drumming with a deep ache, reminding me how little I'm wearing.

I slowly shuffle outside, the snow soaking through my stockings immediately, my toes aching in the cold as I cross the yard.

Suddenly, involuntarily, I spin around, crying out in pain at the fast movement. I know this house. Inside, in the dark, with the filth and broken furniture, I didn't realize, but from the outside I can easily tell.

This was my dad's old house.

People — presumably Rita and Chris — must have been squatting here since he died and they've trashed the place.

My dad rented this house and when he died, I ended the lease and stopped paying the rent. I'm not sure what management are doing, but it's not managing this house.

I start giggling at the absurdity that the management team can't manage, thinking briefly that I may be a little manic and a lot lightheaded.

Pulling myself together, now that I know where I am, I have my bearings and know that the main road is only about thirty yards straight through these trees, and the nearest neighbor is the same distance but to my left.

Deciding I should walk to the neighbors to get help, I start trudging through the snow, tripping every now and again and sucking in a painful sharp breath each time. The world around me is completely silent, as though everything is tucked away from the cold and I can't help but feel bitter.

I'm so unbelievably tired and so, so cold. I should be at home, in bed with Bobby right now. He'd never willingly let me hurt or be cold. I just want to go home and snuggle with him. Maybe literally tie him to me so we never have to be apart again. Somehow, despite all my hard work this year, I was too weak to stop that bitch from hurting me, but no one could get through Bobby.

Or maybe he is home sleeping peacefully, not caring one bit that I'm hurt? No, no that's not true. He loves me, I know he does. I bet he's cranky right now, tearing people apart looking for answers.

I hope he sleeps though. He has that fight in a few weeks. And he has training tomorrow; I don't want to be a bother.

Plus, it's cold out; I don't want him to get cold.

I hope Jack's home in bed too. It's way past curfew now and he'll be in big trouble if he's still out. And Bobby will be in trouble for not making sure he's in bed. Which reminds me, I better organize Christmas presents soon. The snow reminds me of Christmas and my to-do list. It is crazy long.

My mind flits from thought to thought, unable to see one through to the end. I vacillate from anger to nostalgia, from bitterness to loneliness.

Some part of my brain knows that I'm going a little crazy right now, that I'm hurt and scared and cold and dizzy. I feel like I've been walking for about an hour, but that can't be right, the neighbors are only a minute walk away, tops.

I look up to see their house, completely dark, and still fifteen yards or so away. I let out a petulant sigh and keep walking, my mind tricking me into believing I still have fifteen miles to go.

I'm scared to look at my feet right now, scared that my toes will be black and frozen, some maybe even missing.

No, that's not right. I haven't been out that long. But my feet are numb, you know that so frozen feeling where they're so cold they actually feel warm. That's all I can feel. Not the broken twigs or rocks cutting into them.

I arrive at the side of the neighbor's house and hold onto the porch railing, shuffling toward the steps and front door. I trip on the first step, misreading the height and falling onto my ribs, and I scream out in pain.

I forgot. The numbness was protecting me, but then I forgot about my injuries and now I've tripped, the collision making me retch but nothing comes out. My stomach is officially empty. I'd kill for some water right now; my mouth and throat feel as though I've swallowed razor blades.

"Hello?!" I cry out, standing again, shuffling forward and banging on the door. "Hello? Mrs… fuckwhatsyourname? Is anyone home?" I cry and lean on the front door, but the utter silence inside tells me the house is empty.

Sliding down and feeling weaker than a newborn baby, I sit on the front step and try to catch my breath. My arm and shoulder still ooze blood and my vision turns spotty as I watch it flow.

Should I do something about that? I don't know. I think they told us about this in high school. Fucked if I remember what to do though. I wish I was Snow White right now — the little woodland creatures would fix me up in a jiffy.

Up you get, Kit! Pep talk, pep talk! Get psyched. If I fall asleep here, I might never wake up. I climb my hands up the railing, pulling myself to standing and wobbling my way down the three front steps. My wobbling reminds me of the few times I've gotten shit faced drunk with Tink.

I snort as I remember her nickname. God, Bobby's so funny. God, I miss him. Tinkerbelle. I snort and laugh again. Thinking of Tink reminds me of Peter Pan. Fuck! Now I miss my dad. I miss him so much. My snorting turns to sobbing. I wish my daddy was here right now. He'd help me. He'd make everything better. He always used to.

Sighing again, I start toward the road, hoping some dumbass — other than me — is also awake and outside right now. *"Hi ho, hi ho,"* I sing to myself, giggling at my own creativity. I should write that down. Nope, wait. I think someone else has already done that one.

I walk along the edging on the neighbors' drive way, which is lined with thick trees, hoping the cover will stop the stupid snow dropping on my face and frizzing my hair. I hate having long curly hair sometimes.

Maybe I should cut it short like Casey?

No, I think Bobby likes it like this. Yeah, he does, he plays with it often.

Further ahead, I think I see lights, but they come and go quickly. That's so strange. I try and move faster, maybe I can catch the light.

No, wait, is it *that* light?

Maybe I shouldn't go there. Bobby and Jack would be *so* mad at me.

There's a part of my brain, hidden deep below the hysteria, the shock, and the pain that knows I'm rambling and silly right now. It knows God doesn't send an actual light to come get me. Does he? Fuck, I don't know. I don't think so.

But I do know that I need to get out of this cold soon, or else I will die.

With renewed energy, I push on. There's only about ten yards to go till the tree line clears and then I might find help. I can see another light coming, so I follow that direction and walk a little faster, hoping to catch it.

"Fuck! Where is she? You search that way. Go!"

My stomach rolls again, fear and nausea and cold fingers of pain run through me. I can hear Rita somewhere close behind, but I don't know where she is. I forgot about her. I assumed she was gone, I thought I was all alone out here. I can't believe I wasted time when I should've been focusing, getting the fuck out of here.

In a blind panic, I run. My ribs and arm no longer slowing me down. Nothing will slow me down. I refuse to stay here and let her hurt me anymore.

Five yards to go until the clearing, and I'm crying. Bawling my eyes out, partially blinding myself. But I keep moving.

Two yards to go, I'm shuffling as fast as I can, working my way toward the light and noise from up ahead.

One yard to go. I let out a sob. I'm so close. Please, somebody help me.

I break through the trees, promptly tripping straight onto the gravel road. My hands and knees are further torn up by the impact. I look up in time to see the light, right in front of me, blinding me.

Then darkness again. At least I get to sleep now.

24

Bobby

Come back to me, Baby

Two a.m. and Kit's been gone for at least eight hours.

We've spoken to the police, insisting they do more, so now they're 'investigating,' but really, all they're doing is sucking each other's dicks and playing on their phones.

Jack wavers from anger and lashing out one minute to breaking down and crying the next. The crying moments kill me, each tear ripping strips from me, body and soul.

I'm failing him by not being able to fix this, and I've failed Kit by not preventing it in the first place.

We're no closer to knowing where she is, and Rita and Chris have disappeared. Renee is no help, and although she's in the hospital under police watch, she's either unconscious, or she's not talking.

Jimmy's still with Iz, but he's texting and updating often. Each time he asks our status, I feel more and more dead at the lack of answers I have for him.

Jon, Aiden, Jack, and I are back at our house. Kit's house. I'm unsure where else to go. Unsure where to look or what to do.

Jon and Aiden are sitting at the kitchen table, silently drinking coffee. I've lost count how many pots have been brewed tonight.

Jack wanders the house, as though in a trance. He's a little boy missing his mama. And I have no idea how to help him.

And me? I'm gripping desperately to my sanity, trying to ignore the booming tick of the clock hanging on the wall. I'd rip the batteries out and smash it, but it's Kit's clock, and I can't bring myself to touch it.

I walked upstairs earlier to our room but left as soon as I could grab fresh clothes and shoes; unable to stand in her room, looking at her things, smelling her clothes any longer.

I never went looking for love, I never wanted it, and now I know exactly why. The agony I feel at not knowing where she is, if she's hurt … it physically hurts me, so much more than any hit I could ever take in the octagon.

I just want her to come home …

I continue walking laps in the carpet, walking between the kitchen and the living room, trying to somehow relieve the pressure in my chest, when, suddenly, the sound of the phone ringing on the wall echoes through the house, the noise amplified in contrast to the silence that is two a.m.

All heads whip up at the sound, and I rush to it, almost pulling it from the wall in my urgency.

"Hello?" I want to know, but at the same time, I'm scared to face the potential truth about who could be calling.

"Hello, this is Nurse Robens, from the Stanley Mater Hospital."

I deflate at the familiar voice. "Nurse Robens, hi. Is this about Iz? Is she okay?"

"No sir, well yes, she's fine. But this is not about her. I'm looking for Jack Reilly. Is this Jack?"

My heart hammers painfully. "No, this is Bobby. You're looking for Jack?" I wave at Aiden, and he runs from the room shouting Jack's name.

"Oh, Bobby, hi. Yeah, I'm looking for Jack. If you could just pass him the phone that would be ..."

"Why do you need him? What's going on?"

But I know. In my heart I know.

Jack comes running into the room, Aiden less than a foot behind.

"Please just put Mr. Reilly on the phone, Bobby. Quickly, please."

"Okay, he's here, hold on," I say, but instead of passing him the phone I put it on speaker.

"Hello?" he says hesitantly. He's not stupid. "This is Jack. Have you found Kit?"

"Jack, hi, this is Nurse Robens. I'm calling because you're listed as next of kin for a Ms. Catherine Reilly ..."

We all stare at each other, willing her to finish. What will she tell us? Is Kit okay? I want this lady to hurry the fuck up and put me out of my misery.

But at the same time, I don't want to know. I'm terrified of living a life without Kit in it.

"… Honey, Kit was transported here about thirty minutes ago. She's in surgery as we speak. We need you to come immediately."

"We're on the way," he says, running toward the front door without even hanging up. Jack and I are at the car before the other two even come through the door.

"Let's go!" I demand. I don't know what to expect when we get there, but I won't waste another second not being with her.

Spinning the wheels and sliding in the snow, we arrive at the hospital in just a few minutes, skidding to a stop in the emergency department driveway. Jumping out, the four of us race through the doors, but security steps in our way to stop us.

Motherfucker better move, or I'll lay him out.

"You can't park there, son."

I don't say anything; I just drop my keys and keep running, hearing Aiden stay back and explain that he'll move it for me. Stopping at the front desk, I scare the crap out of the poor lady sitting there. "Catherine Reilly? We're here to see her."

She looks at her computer for a minute then looks back at me. "Are you family, sir? We can only give information to relatives."

"Yes!" Jack interrupts. "I'm her brother and next of kin. You guys contacted me. And he's her fiancé."

Whatever gets me through those doors.

"Okay then. Please follow me and I'll take you to a waiting room. A doctor will be in shortly to see you."

"Can you tell us what's going on?" Jack asks. "Is she okay?"

"I'm sorry, Mr. Reilly, I can't tell you." She stops walking and looks at Jon. "Sir? You'll have to wait he—"

"No, he's our other brother. And there's one more parking the car. Please send him through when he arrives, his name is Aiden," Jack says, impressing me with his fluent bullshitting.

Well, maybe not fluent, because the look on her face says she doesn't believe him one bit. But she lets us through anyway.

For the second time tonight, we're being led through a maze of hallways in search of someone we love and hoping to god she'll be okay. This is different though. Of course it is. I love Iz and I worry for her. But it's different. If Kit doesn't survive, then … neither do I.

We're on a different floor than where Iz is being kept. I don't know if that's good or bad. Don't they classify each floor in a hospital for different things? Like, the more serious cases are closer to ground floor, then as you heal you're moved upstairs to a regular room. We're on the first floor right now, signs on the wall indicating operating room after operating room.

I don't know which room she's in, and I don't know what they're doing to her. Why does she need to be operated on? How much pain is she in? Why was she even hurt in the first fucking place?

"In here, please," our escort says, leading us into a room filled with plastic chairs and nothing else. "I don't know how long you'll have to wait. A doctor will be with you eventually, but I'm not sure when. I'm sorry I don't know more."

"Can we speak to someone? Please." Jack begs. His whole body is shaking, and he's about ready to lose his shit. "We need some sort of update."

"I don't know, Mr. Reilly. Ms. Reilly arrived about an hour ago. She was sent to surgery immediately. Her doctor is likely still many hours away from finishing."

"Can we speak to a nurse or something? Someone who's in there with her?"

She sighs, probably overworked and as tired as we are. She stares at Jack for another long moment, then sighing again, she nods her head. "I'll go into the OR now. I'll ask for an update and I'll be back soon. Don't expect too much though. They've just begun and probably don't know the full extent of her injuries."

With no other option, we nod our heads and she turns and leaves us, the three of us finding chairs and sitting in silence, resigned to waiting for an update.

Ten minutes drag by then my head snaps up as I hear running in the hallway. I stand, my heart hammering, but sit down again when Aiden comes sprinting in. One look at our faces and he's caught up. We know nothing.

He sits next to me, not asking any questions, knowing we can't answer them.

Another agonizing five minutes drags by and Jimmy walks in. I look up and frown, but Aiden answers my unspoken thoughts. "I texted him."

"How's Izzy?" Jon asks him.

"She's sleeping. Nurses have been around a few times; they said she's going to be fine. What's going on here?"

"Kit's in surgery. That's all we know," I choke out.

"Who hurt her, Bobby? Who hurt Iz?"

"Don't know. I think it was Kit's cousin."

"Why?"

"Don't know …"

"Where is she now?"

"Don't know."

Jimmy just nods at my inadequate answers, then joins us in our silent vigil.

I feel so tired, like I can never fully catch up on my sleep again. I've had my fair share of all-nighters when out with my brothers, but this is just different. I feel defeated. My whole body aches; not a training ache, but like my essence, my soul, has been stomped on a few hundred times.

We wait.

And we wait.

And we wait.

I stare at the cracked linoleum on the floor, counting the lines and squares. I stare at the cracks in the cement rendered walls, following the lines as they spider in all directions. I look at the ceiling and the stains left behind by some ancient leak.

I look up sharply and stand when the nurse from earlier steps back in.

"Did you see Kit?" Jack rushes out, desperately searching for a connection to his sister, his only living relative.

Fuck!

I don't want to think it, my heart rejects the direction of my thoughts. But what if? What if she doesn't make it? Jack will be all alone in this world. At fifteen fucking years old.

No, he won't. He's my brother now, as much as Jim or Aiden or Jon is. He's not alone — he'll never be alone again. And none of that matters anyway, because she can't not make it. It's universally impossible, as though the world will implode if she isn't in it.

The nurse searches our faces, realizing our numbers are multiplying, but she doesn't comment on it. "Yes, I saw Kit. Dr. Bormann is her surgeon tonight, and he's one of our best. She's in good hands, I promise you. Her injuries, that we know of so far, include seven broken ribs, a punctured lung, deep gashes in her arm, her shoulder, and her wrists, and several cuts on her face and head that will need sutures. When Ms. Reilly was hit by the car, it broke her —"

"She was hit by a car?" Jack interrupts her, rage contorting his face.

"Yes, she was. The collision broke her left arm in three places, plus her shoulder is shattered and will need reconstruction."

"Who the fuck hit her?"

"An older couple; they're in this hospital right now too. Our hospital administration is in contact with authorities and we're fully informed on everything that has happened tonight. I want to assure you, the driver has nothing to do with Kit's earlier disappearance and they've been one hundred percent cooperative with the police and us. They called an ambulance as soon as it happened and stayed with her the whole time.

"Now, Ms. Reilly also has significant swelling in her brain and we're working on keeping it under control, but if she continues to swell, we may be forced to relieve some of the pressure surgically. Kit will be left in a medically induced coma for a few days, at least, to allow her time to heal."

"Will she be okay?" Jack asks, thankfully asking all the questions I can't force past the lumps in my throat. I feel like a selfish pig, a coward, as he cries, clearly hurting, but braver than me to be able to ask the questions.

The nurse is silent for a minute, the tension in my body compounding, weighing me down every silent second. Why won't she answer?

"Mr. Reilly—Jack … I'm sorry, I don't know. I'm not a doctor, I'm not authorized to make those statements. I just don't know. Her injuries are extensive, her blood loss severe, the swelling around her brain is dangerous … I just … I don't know. She'll be in surgery for hours yet, and the more they investigate, the more injuries they're finding. She's been through a metaphorical blender tonight and her body is struggling, but we're doing the best we can. I'm sorry."

And with that, she walks out, leaving a group of shattered men in her wake with nothing else to do but sit and worry.

Time ticks by, the only marker being Jim's coming and going. He stays with us for an hour, then spends an hour with Iz, back and forth, back and forth. When Jim is with us, Jon goes to Iz.

Every now and again we hear people in the hallway, but no one comes in to speak to us. Jack left three times to go to the toilet or to get coffee— Kit's done an amazing job of addicting a fifteen-year-old to caffeine.

Aiden didn't leave once.

Neither did I.

By the seventh rotation for Iz's guards, a very tired looking doctor comes into our room. "Jack Reilly?"

"Yeah?" his voice is thick from exhaustion and emotion.

"I'm Dr. Bormann. I've been working on Catherine this morning. I—"

"Kit. Her name's Kit." Jack interrupts the doctor. "She prefers being called Kit."

"Okay, alright. So Kit has pulled through surgery and she's looking … okay. Her vitals are strong, and despite the serious nature of her injuries, she appears to have a strong will to live." His lips pull up with a small smile. It's almost as though he and Kit formed a relationship while she was in there, even though she was unconscious. He's nailed her stubbornness and fighting spirit. I'm not sure if I feel jealous or thankful for such an intuitive and caring surgeon.

"When she arrived, her heart rate was very slow, very faint, and she was unable to regain consciousness. She'd lost almost half of her bodily volume of blood—which we've had to replace, to be able to safely operate. The cuts on her arm and shoulder were prior to the car accident and is how she lost most of the blood. I believe her damaged shoulder was also prior to the collision, as was the majority of her broken ribs. She's bruised extensively. I think she was beaten severely, kicked repeatedly, and one of the broken ribs punctured her lung. I honestly don't know how she survived that much," he says proudly. Yes, they definitely formed a relationship in that OR.

"If we piece together what authorities are telling us, she escaped with those injuries and ran onto the road, where unfortunately she was hit front on by a car. The collision caused severe head injuries and is the reason for the swelling. We still have the option to operate again and remove a portion of her skull to allow room for the swelling, but I don't want to do that yet. I'd rather give her time and see if she can do it herself."

"Can we see her?" Jacks asks.

"You can, soon. She's being moved to a private room now, and you can go in when they're set up. Maybe another forty-five minutes? Only two of you at a time, and only a short visit." He lets out a big sigh before he continues. "I need you to prepare yourselves, guys. Kit's been through a huge ordeal. She's bandaged top to toe. She's swollen all over, and she's hooked up to a lot of machines. It'll be hard to see her like that, so prepare. I can't give you any promises. About anything. I don't know how long she'll sleep. I don't know how the swelling around her brain will react or how long it will take to come down. I don't even know for sure if she will wake. Now we watch and wait. Those scary machines, they're important and will monitor her around the clock. We'll take her in for more scans in about twenty-four hours, and again twenty-four hours after that, to see what's happening inside. I'll be back in a few hours and I'll come see her, to see how she's going. I'll send someone to collect you shortly to show you to her room. Okay?"

We all nod and sit back down as he walks out. Sixty very slow, very long minutes later, a nurse knocks and pokes her head in. "Jack Reilly? If you'll follow me please?"

He stands and walks toward her, and Aiden hits my leg. "Bobby. Go."

His quick words snap me out of my hesitance. The doctor said she could have two visitors, so I'm going wherever she goes. I jump up and chase after them, catching up at the elevators and I squeeze in before the doors close. Jack and the nurse look at me but say nothing., though Jack looks relieved. He probably thought he'd have to go in alone.

We only go up one floor, then are led to a room halfway down the hall, just across from the nurse's station. Priority placing is both good and bad. I hate that my baby needs to be so closely monitored in the first place. The nurse stops at the door, not going in with us, holding it open and letting us pass.

I find myself in a dark room. The only sound is the rhythmic beeping and breathing from the machines, attached to a very fragile looking Kit.

25

Kit

A one-sided conversation

Beep, beep, beep, beep, beep.

I mark time by listening to the beeps. They were annoying as hell for a while there, but now they almost feel meditative. Not that I've ever meditated, but this is what I imagine it would feel like.

I guess it's still night time, because everything is dark. Darker than even night time should be. So strange. I can't even see moonlight. It's like my eyes are closed. Wait. Are they closed? I don't know.

How is she?

Huh? The mumbles float through my consciousness, but it's like I'm underwater. I can't focus, I can't place the voice. It must be Jack and Bobby in the kitchen. Those two hang out as much as Bobby and I now.

No change.

Oh, that was Bobby. Definitely. I'd know him anywhere. It's probably time for me to get up. I'd kill for a hug from him right now. I miss him so much—I feel like I haven't seen him in ages. But I'm so tired. Maybe I could snooze for a few minutes more then I'll get up and get dressed.

Yeah, that's what I'll do. It's the weekend anyway, so I have time. Tink and I must've been out super late last night if I'm dragging so much this morning. Yeah, I'll just sleep a little longer.

~*~

Music flitters in the air. So soft. So sweet. I want to smile. My brain's telling me to turn over, but I'm too tired. That's okay, I'll hit the snooze button again.

~*~

Beep, beep, beep, beep, beep.

Honey, why don't you go home and have a shower, maybe have a nap? I can sit here. I won't leave, I promise.

No Mom, I'm not going anywhere.

You need to rest, baby. You can't sleep in a chair forever. It's been a week, you must be exhausted.

I can't leave, Mama. What if she wakes? What if she never wakes?

I fall asleep again to the sound of weeping. And a mother's love as she hums a soothing tone.

~*~

Music continues to play in the air. I like it. I'm so comfortable chilling in bed listening to music. This is what weekends are for. If only that beeping would stop. Did someone leave the freezer open or something?

~*~

Wake up, baby. Please wake up soon. I miss you so much.

I'm so confused.

~*~

Hey there, Kitty Kat. I'd really appreciate it if you could wake up for me soon, princess. We all miss you.

What if I kiss you? We don't have to tell Bobby. I know you've thought about it since the day we met. Hahaha no? But this might be my only chance. We only have a few minutes before he gets back from the toilet. I'm pretty sure he's obsessed with you. It's weird!

Jimmy thinks he's so funny. Crazy guy.

~*~

Hey Kit. How you doing, babe? I bet you've got a headache huh? I have some gossip for you. You just have to open your eyes. I won't tell you till you wake up.

Izzy's words filter through my mind. I feel like I'm forgetting something. I just don't remember what.

~*~

No, I'm not gonna fight. It's too late anyway.

Yeah, alright, I'll speak to the organizers.

Thanks Aiden. I owe you, man.

Nah, that's okay. I'm gonna go home for a bit, okay? Mom said she'll come by later. I'll take Jack with me.

Thanks. That reminds me, we need to get him back to school soon. I've dropped the ball. Kit's gonna be so mad at me.

He can start back soon. Let him have a few more days.

Yeah … alright. See ya.

~*~

Kit. You need to wake up now. I need your help, baby. Come on.

~*~

Merry Christmas, Kit. So, listen. You're starting to piss me off now. If you don't wake up soon, I might hit you over the head again. Knock some sense into you.

They're making me go back to school on Monday. I won't go unless you wake up and make me. I'll get in trouble, might even get in a fight or something. Ha! Maybe I'll punch Reeves in the face. Do you want that? Huh? I'll do it, he's a dick anyway. Unless you wake up and tell me not to.

Seriously though, I kind of need you here. This is our first Christmas since Dad, and you've ditched me ...

~*~

Bormann. Why won't she wake up? It's been too long.

Bobby, I'm sorry, but I have no more answers for you. We've done everything we can. Scans show all the swelling has gone down. We're not sedating her. This is just her mind and body demanding rest. She's been through a very traumatic experience and this is our own way of protecting ourselves. She'll wake when she's ready. I can assure you, it's very promising that she responds, that she squeezes your hand when you hold it. She's in there. Studies even tell us she can probably hear you now. Keep talking to her, son.

I open my eyes, slowly, as though they've been taped shut, and it takes me a while to focus. The room is dark but I can see two silhouettes at the end of my bed.

One is definitely Bobby.

But this is definitely *not* my bedroom.

I want to reach out to him but my arms feel so heavy. He's facing away so he can't see me.

I'm still so tired. My eyes are droopy and feel so heavy, they feel so warm, as though they are burning. I'll just nap a little longer, then I'll yell at him for being weird.

Then I'll kiss him, because I miss him.

~*~

Kit! You promised. You promised you wouldn't run from me anymore. Please baby, if you wake up, I'll do anything, anything you want. Please, baby. Please.

~*~

Yeah, I'm Bobby Kincaid. And you are…?

I'm Lieutenant Stephens, this is my partner, Officer Bowers. We're investigating the attack on Ms. Reilly.

Someone attacked me?

Call her Kit. She'd prefer that.

Okay. How is she? How's Kit?

She's … the same. The doctors say she's in there and she'll wake when she's ready. What do you know?

Well, we're actually here to tell you that we've arrested several suspects in relation. Bail hearing was yesterday and they were refused. They'll be held, separately, until trial.

Who? Who was arrested?

A … Rita Finlee and Christopher McArden, attempted murder, kidnapping, assault and battery, plus a few drugs related charges. A Mrs. Renee Finlee for drugs related charges and attempted fraud. A Mr. Timms, for assault and battery, accessory to kidnap, accessory to attempted murder.

Oh god. Those names have my heart tripping and speeding up. Why does my cousin's name panic me?

Timms? John Timms?

You know him?

Yeah, he was a client at my gym. He hasn't been back in a while. Last I spoke to him, I … fuck.

Last you spoke to him, what?

I dressed him down … for flirting with Kit. Oh, my god, he had something to do with this? Was this all my fault?

Yes, he was a part of this. No, it wasn't your fault. We'll allege he was the person who attacked Ms. Hart, and then he assisted Ms. Finlee and Mr. McArden in attacking and kidnapping Kit.

My heart feels like it's going to burst through my chest any second now. The more they talk, the more I remember. Oh god. I was hurt. My arm. I try to move it but the pinch of pain stops me. It feels like it weighs a ton.

We'll also allege all three, plus the older Mrs. Finlee did this as revenge, needless revenge, as they claim Kit's at fault for getting caught trying to fraudulently gain money from an insurance claim.

They intended to use this money to repay for drug trouble they got into late last year. They owed some bad people a lot of money and saw Mr. Reilly's death as payday. Although Kit was not the reason they were caught, they still saw to blame her.

How does Timms connect?

We believe Mr. McArden contacted Mr. Timms when they learned of his alienation from your gym. They found someone ripe with a fresh grudge and gained an ally. When we arrested the first two, they threw Timms under the bus faster than I could ask the questions. They've all been charged, and since Isabelle's case connects with ours, we have taken over and relieved the previous investigators of their duties

"Is Izzy okay?"

26

Bobby

Am I dreaming?

"Is Izzy okay?"

For a second, I'm stunned, unsure if I'm dreaming or not. My head whips in Kit's direction faster than muscles should be able to move, but it's real, because she's looking right at me. The bags under her eyes are dark despite the fact she's been asleep for the better part of a month. But she's awake.

She's terrified. But she's awake.

"Kit!" I run the few feet separating us and take her good hand in one of mine while crushing the emergency call button with the other. "Baby. You're awake? How are you feeling? Are you hurting? Don't move, the doctor will come and help you. Please don't move, baby. Oh god, you're awake." I cry into the fabric of her hospital gown, my face resting on her stomach, but careful not to hurt her ribs.

I've never cried a day in my life beyond being a toddler, or the day my dad died. Nowadays, I'm a fucking crying mess. This is what she does to me.

"Bobby? What happened?" Her voice comes out on a croak, dry and gravelly and painful. Fuck! I don't know if she's allowed water.

I continue beating on the call button, please won't somebody hurry. "We're okay, baby. You had a rough time and got hurt. But you're okay now, you're safe." I brush hair from her face as a tear drips from the end of my nose. "I promise. I'm so sorry, baby. So fucking sorry. I should have protected you, but I fucked up so bad. You did it yourself, you got yourself out of danger. I'm so sorry."

I can't stop fucking crying. Or apologizing. And I feel like an even bigger cad now, because her hand comes over my head and weakly runs through my hair.

She is comforting *me*.

Pull yourself together you fucking pussy. Support her!

The nurse rushes into the room. "Bobby, move aside, honey." She leans in close to get a look at Kit. "Hi! My name is Terese. I'm your nurse for today. Welcome to our fine establishment." Her voice is loud and cheery, and Kit stares at her in confusion. "I'm so happy to officially meet you. Bobby here, bless that boy's heart, wouldn't stop talking about your eyes, and I wanted to see them for myself. He sure was right, such a beautiful blue, and so big. Could you just follow this light, sweetpea? Good girl," she shines a pen light and moves it around Kit's face. "How do you feel? Are you in pain?"

"I …" Kit starts, then coughs painfully. "Can I have water? Thirsty."

"Yeah honey, you can have water. Bobby?"

I'm already there, cup and straw ready to go. I press the straw between her cracked lips. "Here baby. Drink slow."

She sips for a minute then pulls back. Her eyes, round and terrified plead with me to help her. "What happened to me?"

I look at the nurse, unsure what I should say, but she just nods her head and gives me the go ahead. I sit on the edge of the seat beside her bed — my own makeshift bed for the last so many nights. I haven't slept at home once while Kit's been here. I tried a couple times but I couldn't sleep without her. I take the hand on her good arm, rubbing my thumb along her wrist while I think of what to say without terrifying her. "Baby. It's December 29th. You've been asleep for a little over three weeks."

Her eyes flare wide, tears coming to the surface and spilling over immediately. Well, that didn't work.

"Where's Jack?" she looks like she's almost trying to get out of the bed, ready to chase him down herself.

I hold her down before she flies out of the bed and hurts herself. "Calm down baby, please. Jack's fine! He's here, he's in the cafeteria with Jim. He's been with me, or Jim … or Jon or Aiden this whole time. He hasn't been alone once, I promise baby. He even stayed with my mom a night or two. They're practically best friends."

"He's okay? He said …" She trails off, her eyebrows pulling together, as though thinking and remembering is hard work for her. It probably is.

"What did he say?"

"He said he didn't want to go to school. And something about fighting …"

"When did he say that?"

"I … I don't know. When I was asleep, I guess."

"You could hear us?"

"Yeah. Sometimes. Music. You played music for me?"

I smile and swipe my hand across my eyes. I'm so glad she heard the music. I'd hoped it would comfort her, especially in the moments I wasn't here. "Yeah babe, I brought your iPod in and left it on shuffle. But don't worry. Jack didn't get into any trouble. It's winter break now. He's been off school since… well… since you got hurt. He'll start back after New Year's."

Kit nods her head slowly, carefully as though doing so hurts. I wonder if it does. "Was Nelly here?"

I take her hand again, and Therese moves to the other side to check the cast on Kit's arm. "Yeah, Mom was here. A lot. Everyone was here. Jimmy tried to talk you into dumping me. Aido and Jon sat with you a lot. Aiden even read you some smut chick books – he wants to know who won the fight in that story. He'll be mad he has no legit reason to finish the book now." I shrug and when her lip wobbles, I laugh and drop a kiss on her hand. "I got to meet your friend George; he came by, he's a cool guy. Jack was here every day and was forced to leave each night, one of us had to take him home to sleep. Izzy was forced to leave a lot after she was released."

"She's okay?"

"Yeah, she's perfect. She stayed in hospital for a couple days, had a concussion and a big headache, but otherwise was fine. She's all better now."

Kit nods slowly. "Good. That's good."

"Are you hurting, babe?"

She just looks at me a minute, as though taking stock and trying to give me an accurate answer. "Umm, I guess. My head hurts, and I feel sluggish like I've had the flu. My arm hurts," her brows furrow, then she looks toward it like she'd forgotten where it was. Her eyes widen when she spots the cast, and I'm not sure if she's shocked by the cast itself or by the writing covering it completely.

Jim and Jack especially had a lot of fun drawing all over it. Immature fools. I don't know for sure who wrote it, but someone— Jack!—drew a phallic symbol followed by 'tation'.

… He drew a dick on her arm. More than once.

"My stomach hurts too," she adds. "And it's hard to breath deep. And my butt hurts from lying down. Can I get up?"

Terese shakes her head and lays her palm on Kit's good shoulder. "No honey, you can't get up yet. Just lay a while longer. We need to get your doctor in here first and then we'll talk. Don't be a hero. I promise we'll let you go soon enough, though I wish your strapping men would stick around. They've definitely made my work day better."

She flits around the room for another few minutes, clicking buttons and reading slips of paper. She taps Kit's foot on the way past and assures us the doctor will be by shortly.

The police had been standing to the side this whole time, watching but not interrupting. They nod to me then let themselves out, and I understand — they'll be back later.

"Bobby?"

My eyes snap back to hers as my hand comes up to move her hair aside again. "Yeah baby?"

"I missed you." Unshed tears flood her eyes again. "Did I really sleep for three weeks? I thought last night was Friday night, I thought I must've gone out and gotten drunk with Case. I thought I was hungover."

I lean in and kiss her softly, on her brow, her nose, her lips, nuzzling her neck for a minute. "I missed you too baby, so fucking much. You scared me to death. I thought you were with Tink, safe and sound. I'm sorry baby, so fucking sorry."

"It's okay, Bobby. I'm okay."

"No, it's not. I knew something was wrong. I felt it in my gut. But I ignored it, thinking it was Iz, and training, and even just tiredness and hunger. But I knew, I knew from the moment you were scared. If I'd paid attention I could have found you before you were hurt."

"It's okay, Bobby. I'm okay."

"You did it all by yourself, baby. You got yourself out, and I'm so proud of you. I love you so much."

"I love you too." Her voice drags with fatigue, but I don't know if she's allowed to sleep yet. Will it be a regular sleep? Or will she stay asleep for weeks? I don't know what to do. Fuck, I don't know, but I don't want her to go away again, not now that she's back.

"Can you stay awake for me, baby? Until the doctor comes?"

"I'm not tired." Yawn. "Can I see Jack?"

"I don't want to leave you. Please stay awake for me, baby."

"Call him? Tell him to come here. I need to see him, please? I promise I'll stay awake." Yawn.

Her eyes are drooping again, and my heart rate is speeding. I'm terrified that she'll slip away again.

"Okay honey. I'll call him now." I'm hoping the distraction will keep her awake. I take my phone out and find Jack's name, then I hit the call button and wait for the dial tone. We look over to a pile of crap littering one of the visitors' chairs as it begins to ring, then my head snaps up when Kit giggles. That sound is music to my poor neglected ears. I've waited so long to hear it again, spent so many nights worrying that I may never. I'm only giving her a few more days to get better, then I'm marrying this girl. No fucking way am I not claiming her as my own.

I just can't. I almost lost her, and then I needed to work through Jack, as her next of kin, to get information about her and permission to stay in her hospital room. As her husband, I'll never be that helpless again.

I dial Jim's number, then lean forward and kiss my girl while I wait for him to answer.

"Hello?"

I continue to kiss her. Jim can wait a sec.

"Bobby? What's up?"

Kit slips her tongue in my mouth and I groan, so thankful to taste her again.

"BOBBY! I can hear you breathing!"

Kit pulls back and giggles at Jim's shouting.

"KIT? Is that Kit? Can I hear Kit giggling?" This just makes her giggle more. "Holy shit! Kitty Kat? You're awake? JACK! Let's go!"

"I remember him, from when I was asleep," she whispers when the line goes dead.

"Yeah?" I kiss her lips again. "He was here a lot. I think he's attached to you."

"Yeah. He said something about waking my lazy ass up so I can cook him some breakfast." She chuckles at the memory. I wasn't here for that one, but it doesn't surprise me. "He also wanted to kiss me. I remember. He was saying something about Sleeping Beauty and how you tried to wake me but clearly he should give it a go because he's the better man, but we had to hurry because you'll be back soon."

I laugh and swipe a tear from beneath my eye. "He's such an asshole."

"Yeah, he made me laugh a lot. Well maybe not out loud, because that would look weird to see me laugh while sleeping, but in my head, I laughed a lot."

"I'm glad you had a restful sleep," I say with mock anger. "It was boring as hell for the rest of us. There's only so long we can watch you sleep before it gets weird."

"Yeah, I also remember, I thought I was at home in bed and I could hear voices, I thought you'd brought people to our house. I was mad at you for being a weirdo and letting people into our room." Her words are turning thick and her slurring increases. "I was going to wake up to yell at you."

"Sorry babe. You did have a lot of visitors listening to you snore, I couldn't control them."

"I did not snore! I don't snore."

She's so cute. "Okay well, no, you didn't snore — in the hospital. But you do snore, sometimes, at home."

"Not true!"

I drop another kiss on her lips with a chuckle. "Whatever you say." She does snore, sometimes.

Thundering steps can be heard running down the hallway, but we don't have to wonder for long, because Jim and Jack start fighting at the door, shoving each other out of the way, jockeying to be the first through.

I help Kit sit a little higher and she holds her side in pain, and at the sound of her light gasp, the guys stop dead. They're a tangled mess of limbs — two very large, very broad-shouldered men stuck in a doorway and they freeze, looking at Kit as though she's the Holy Grail, the ultima Thule, an oasis in a desert.

And well, they're not wrong, because as far as I'm concerned, she is.

Jack's smile spreads across his whole face and tears pool in his eyes. "Kit?" He walks into the room and stops at the side of her bed. He stands there, scared to move, scared to touch her, and I'm reminded that he's still a kid, still so young, when his tears spill over and he begins to sob.

He lays his head down against her chest, his shoulders bouncing as he cries and cries and purges his body of the worry he's carried for most of a month.

Kit removes her good hand from mine and places it on his head, the way she did for me, and she runs her fingers through his hair. "It's okay, Jack. I'm okay."

She's so fucking amazing. She's the one who's been through a near death ordeal, and she's the one who's accumulated a small army of men who'd cry and kill for her, yet she's the one comforting us while we break down.

I look toward Jimmy and watch as he smiles and struggles to hold himself together. It does something to a guy when he watches his brother cry. It gets us deep and it hurts bad.

I know Kit will want to see everyone else, and everyone else will kill me if I don't tell them right away, so I take out my phone and shoot off a group text.

To: Aiden; Jon; Mom; Tink; Izzy;

She's awake!

Epilogue
Kit

Six Weeks Later

It's Valentine's Day tomorrow, but better than that, it's Lila Royale concert day today. Bobby reminded me a couple weeks ago about the tickets he got me for my birthday, and I've been so excited for today to arrive.

I decided in the end to save him some cash and take only him as my plus one. He did initially offer to buy more tickets so our whole group could go, and I know Case is pissed that she can't go, especially since we got meet and greet backstage passes — oh my god, I'm meeting Lila Royale tonight! — but still, I couldn't ask that of him, so it's just the two of us.

Plus, it was his birthday last month and it was a pretty quiet, gloomy affair. I was still sore and tired and we were all still working through the events of December.

Bobby wanted us to forget his birthday altogether, but after a few phone calls with his mom and help from Jack, I scraped together dinner and a cake and everyone gathered at our house for the evening. I'm hoping today can be a belated birthday celebration for us both.

Jack also turned sixteen last month, and the day didn't go by forgotten. Similar to Bobby's birthday, we pulled together a cake and pizza, and had a quite night at our house. Bobby and I gave him small gifts, but we actually planned on getting him a car. I haven't taken him to the DMV to get his license yet — we have an appointment next month — but when we do, that's when we'll surprise him with his real gift.

Physically, I'm feeling pretty good nowadays. My arm is out of the cast, my stitches all gone, my ribs and lung mostly healed. My shoulder is still pretty messed up; I ended up needing a reconstruction, and although now I've lost the slings and cast, it's still pretty tender. It'll be a while before I get to train again — and that's only if Bobby ever lets down guard duty to allow me to put gloves on again.

I'm not sure he'll ever not be protective. And even if he is, I then have to get past Jack. And Jim. And Jon, and Aiden, and Tink, and Iz. Basically, I have a whole army of people who treat me like a baby.

I've been attending daily physical therapy since I left the hospital and I've been working on regaining a bit of weight and muscle tone I lost while I was asleep. Ironically, I've now lost too much weight. I get tired a little easier these days but the doctors say that'll pass.

All in all, I'm feeling wonderful, despite a few gnarly scars left behind by the big night. They're my battle scars, and I'm okay with them.

At home, I couldn't be happier. The guys wait on me hand and foot, and I won't lie — it's kind of nice. Jack's been a model student, his grades perfect nowadays, his training spot on, and his protective streak a mile wide.

Bobby says that Jack will be fighting again soon and we're all pretty excited for that. I was devastated when I realized Bobby missed his big fight, essentially forfeiting and losing his title. The other guy, Thomlassen, won by default, but nobody wants to win like that, so they were quick to start organizing a rematch.

Bobby hasn't left my side much at all since I left the hospital, always there to help me, attending most of my physical therapy sessions and researching stretches and stuff to help me with at home.

I haven't been back to work yet, but intend to start back in March. My boss has been wonderful, assuring me my job is safe and to come back when I'm ready.

As far as we know, Rita, Chris, Renee, and Timms are all still behind bars and are expected to be sentenced in a few months. Lieutenant Stephens tells me he's confident of lengthy sentences and that they won't be a problem for us anymore. Fortunately, I rarely think of them. I try and focus on the more positive aspects of my life—I have plenty of those to keep me busy.

That brings us back to it being Lila Royale day today, and I've just finished in the shower and now I'm getting ready to go out. I can feel Bobby as he enters our bedroom; it's as though his body has this effect on the air around me, and I can always feel when he's nearby. I continue poking around the closet, looking for an outfit for tonight when I feel him place his large hands on my hips, my underwear the only barrier between me and the hardness he presses between my butt cheeks.

Unfortunately, we haven't been intimate since before the hospital.

Bobby is scared to touch me, terrified of hurting me. The first few weeks were understandable. Hell, I could barely stay awake anyway, so it was no big deal, but now I'm more than ready to go. If he doesn't fuck me soon, I might explode. I'm about ready to climb him like a tree, whether he likes it or not. I have a plan though — if he doesn't make a move soon, I figure I'll just sit on him. I mean, what are the chances he'll say no if I'm already on and he's in?

Exactly!

Smiling at my deviousness, I push back a little, pushing myself further into his hands and my back against his warm chest. I lay my head back and he lowers his, running his nose and tongue along my neck. "Mmmm. I love when you do that."

"Mmm, I just love you. Period."

I smile at that. He never, ever, misses an opportunity to tell me he loves me. And I love it. I love him. We have this solid connection, so much love for each other, one that I never worry will dim. It just couldn't; it's not possible. What we have is just too …. deep.

I know, I know. Cheesy as fuck. But it is what it is. Whatever it is we have, it's so powerful that the energy we give and receive back feeds us. It's vital to us to live and neither of us will let that go. Fine by me.

I look back toward my closet, eyeing a lavender dress, a favorite of mine, and decide that's what I'll wear tonight. If I pair it with boots and a coat, I'll be plenty warm enough.

"I'm almost ready. Just getting dressed then I'll be out. Ten minutes, tops."

"That's okay, baby. No rush. Are you excited for tonight?"

"I'm so freaking excited! Do you think we'll get to party with her after?" I'm joking, but kinda wishing it were possible.

"I don't know. You'll get to meet her, but maybe she won't like you, you know?" He laughs as he teases me. "Try not to go all fangirl and blubber all over her. Be awesome and she might want to hang out."

"Shut up!" I turn in his arms and smack his chest. "I'm awesome, she'll love me. What's not to love?"

"That's what I've been saying all along," he whispers, running his nose along my neck as goosebumps raise all along my mostly naked body.

Yep, I definitely have to force his hand soon. My hormones are about ready to boil over.

Less than an hour later, we're driving to the venue. The arena is in the city, about an hour drive for us, so I settle in for a relaxing ride. Bobby's driving and I turn slightly in my seat, my shoulder and back partially resting against the door. I study his profile—something I do often as I catalogue his handsome features.

It still sucker punches me that he chooses me. He's so … beautiful. He's just so damn handsome. I'm determined to never take him for granted, to never become desensitized to his looks or his personality, his kindness, his compassion. He's perfect in every way and I won't let myself become complacent or spoiled.

"What?" he asks, his sexy bow lips lifting in a smirk. "Like what you see?"

"Yeah, I definitely do."

He chuckles. "You're making it very difficult to drive right now. Your staring is distracting me." Despite his words, I know he doesn't mind. "What are you thinking about?"

"Climbing you like a tree and riding your face," I tell him neutrally, as though I were discussing the weather.

Bobby starts choking and the car swerves to the left. I just laugh and patiently wait for him to recover. I also enjoy watching the zipper on his jeans steadily lift and fill out. My mouth waters thinking about what we could have if he'd just stop being so damn stubborn.

"Jesus Kit! Don't say shit like that, I'll crash the car."

Lifting my shoulder, indicating my care factor — zero — I answer him, "Eh, it's the truth, especially because I know you agree." I place my hand on his leg and slowly move upward, and he sucks in a rattling breath. Poor guy; now I'm just being cruel. I know he's just as desperate as I am.

"Babe." he groans. "You're killing me."

"We don't have to wait anymore," I argue. "I'm all better."

"I'm trying to be a gentleman. I don't want to hurt you, baby."

"Don't worry about it," I dismiss the subject. "I'll just take the decision out of your hands."

"What do you mean?" he asks, pulling into a multilane as we approach the city. I wait until we stop at a red light before I answer him.

"Would you feel violated if you woke up already inside me? Like, if I were on top. Or maybe I could use my mouth …"

He doesn't answer verbally, he just leans forward and bangs his head on the steering wheel. "She's going to kill me," he mutters to himself. "I'm going to die a horny man."

Laughing again, I lean toward him and smack noisy kisses on the ball of his shoulder. "I'm sorry, Bobby. I'll stop. By the way, the light's green."

He looks up, then shakes his head and mutters as the car starts moving forward.

"Hey Bobby?"

He looks over at me cautiously. "Yeah?"

"I love you."

~*~

"Okay, so we get to meet her quickly before the concert, then we go to our seats to watch, then we get to hang with her for a few minutes after. Sound okay?"

Walking through the parking lot, Bobby takes my hand and leads me past the long lines of people waiting to collect tickets. I'm giddy with excitement that we have VIP tickets and don't have to line up.

"Yes! I'm so excited. I can't believe I get to meet her today! Case is so pissed she can't come." The day I told her I was bringing Bobby and not her, she almost ended our friendship there and then. Not really, but I think she was tempted.

"Yeah, she had a few words for me too when she found out. Poor neglected Tink," he laughs.

We approach a large man who appears to be security of some sort and I worry that we must stop. Buuuuuut no! Adding to my excitement, Bobby does a fancy pants bro's handshake and greets the guy like they're old friends.

"Mike! Good to see you man!"

"Bobby, good to see you too! It's been a long time. You don't strike me as a *Royal* though, B." Mike laughs, mocking those of us who are in fact *Royals*.

"I'm anything my girl wants me to be," Bobby says with a smirk. "Mike, this is Kit. Kit, this is Mike. Mike and I used to go to school together, a long ass time ago."

I put my hand out to shake his, but he pulls me in for a hug. I tense up, worried that he might squeeze and hurt my sometimes-tender ribs, but he holds me gently and drops a soft kiss on my cheek. "It's nice to meet you, Kit. If you're a friend of his, then you're a friend of mine."

"That's kind. Thank you." I smile, genuinely touched by this nice giant.

"How's the baby, Mike? How's Becky?"

Mike beams with pride. "They're good, man. We had a little girl last month. She's so beautiful. And tiny. We named her Caroline, after my mama. And Becky was so amazing! Not that I was ever in doubt, but watching my girl give birth, just..." he shakes his head and looks at us dreamily, "... just, wow."

The way this gentle giant speaks of his wife and baby girl puts stars in my eyes. I kind of love Mike, after only knowing him for three minutes.

Bobby puts his arm around my shoulder, securing me to his side and kisses my temple before answering. "Congratulations Mike. I'm so happy to hear that. I can't wait to tell my mom, she'll be psyched to hear."

"Ah Bobby, she already knows. Your mama's always in the know. You'll have to thank her again for me; she sent us some flowers and clothes."

"I will. And I'm not surprised." Bobby laughs.

"Listen, Becky and I would love to have you, and Kit of course, and all the boys over for dinner sometime."

"Awesome, we'd love to come. I'll text you."

"Alright man. We'll make it happen." Mike turns and opens the door and stands aside. "It was a pleasure to meet you, Kit. Enjoy the show."

Bobby keeps his arm slung over my shoulder and leads us down a dim hallway. There are people everywhere, rushing around, chattering into earpieces and arms overflowing with stuff ... clothes, fruit, water bottles, folders, phones. Lining a lot of the space are clothes racks overflowing with sparkly outfits, and I'm feeling star struck because I recall a lot of these outfits from film clips and You Tube clips of Lila Royale's previous concerts. I can't believe I'm this close to meeting her. Hell, if this were all I was getting, just to be at her concert, to be able to see the outfits, it would be enough.

"This way, baby." Bobby nuzzles my hair as we walk.

"How do you know where to go? Wait. Have you met her before?"

"No, I haven't. But I was given written instructions with our tickets. We have to go to her dressing room, which I believe is at the end of this hall. Are you ready?"

My heart bangs violently against my ribs. I'm so nervous. God, I hope I'm not a total weirdo and embarrass myself. "Oh, my god. Oh, my god. Oh, my god," I chant as I begin to hyperventilate.

Bobby stops our procession, and moves us to the side of the hall so we aren't in anyone's way. "Baby, relax. She's just a person. Just like the rest of us. And by all accounts, she's actually a really nice person. Just relax, please, before you hurt yourself."

I know he's worried about me. He hasn't stopped worrying since all that shit in December.

"We don't have to go in if you don't want to. We can just go out and watch the show. Or we can go home. This is your party, baby, tell me what you want."

"I'm sorry. I'm just nervous. If I don't go in, I might regret it for the rest of my life. I mean, how many chances will I get to meet Lila Royale? It's okay, let's go in. Quick, before I chicken out."

Bobby just laughs at me, not at all nervous about meeting the musical pop star. Must be nice to be a babe and confident in his hotness.

"I'm glad you said that." He nods toward a door just over my left shoulder. "Because we're here."

Oh, my god. Oh, my god.

Before I have time to freak out any more, Bobby knocks loudly and my heart trips with every booming thud. Jesus, get a grip, Kit!

Less than thirty seconds later, the door opens and we face yet another large man. He looks like he could squeeze our skulls in one hand, and I figure he's head of her security.

Note to self: don't attempt to kidnap Lila Royale.

Before we have a chance to speak, the man smiles and puts his hand out. "You're Bobby Kincaid, and I'm a fan. I'm Shane."

Bobby shakes his hand, his face splitting in a huge grin. "Thanks man. Yeah, I'm Bobby. This is Kit. We're here to meet Ms. Royale."

"Yes, of course. We were expecting you. Come on in."

We walk in, and I'm surprised the room is so big and bright and lush. A couch lines one wall, then a dining table full of flowers and fruit baskets sits six feet away. Along the far wall is a vanity mirror with stuff spread all over it and bright lights surrounding it. There's a second door which must lead to another room or maybe a bathroom.

"Ms. Royale will be with us in a moment."

I expected to be disappointed she's not here, but really, I'm thankful for the extra minute to get myself together.

"I was sorry to see your fight didn't go ahead."

Bobby squeezes me as a stab of guilt slashes through my belly. I know I shouldn't feel guilty — it wasn't my fault that I got hurt, and Bobby's told me a million times not to feel guilty, but still, I do. How could I not? I date a professional fighter for less than a year, and his first fight since we met, he had to forfeit. Because of me. The guilt burns.

"Yeah, it was too bad. But we're organizing a rematch, so no worries."

"You are? When?"

"Yeah, Thomlassen contacted me almost immediately and our people are talking. I'm not sure when, depending on the rest of the fight schedules, but I think sometime around May?"

"Sweet! I'll wait for an announcement."

"Cool. It's always nice to meet a fan. You train any?"

"Yeah, a bit. Haven't graded in anything though. I've tried my hand at BJJ and MMA. Sort of a requirement for my job, you know?"

"Yeah, I get you. Well, if you're ever in our neighborhood, drop by my gym. We'll be happy to have you."

"Will do, thanks man."

A noise behind the second door draws our attention, then it swings open and a petite little woman walks though. She reminds me of a chihuahua, though I forget about her immediately as a very beautiful, very sparkly woman walks in behind her.

Lila Royale is more beautiful than I even realized, and I almost pass out from excitement. She walks straight toward us, straight past the Chihuahua and Shane and stops in front of us. "Bobby Kincaid. Hi! I'm so excited to meet you. And you must be Kit." She turns toward me and leans in, and her sequined top makes jingling noises as she hugs me. "It is truly a pleasure."

She's a lot taller than I expected; about my height, but taller right now because her shoes are a hell of a lot taller than my boots. She pulls back but keeps her hands on my arms, as though she wants to stay close. "I'm very happy to have you here. I'm told this was a birthday surprise, so happy belated birthday, girl."

"Thank you, Lila… Ms. Roya … Shit what do I call you? Shit, I can't believe I said shit in front of you."

She just laughs at my awkwardness, and Bobby squeezes me tighter.

"You can call me Lil; all my friends do." Leaning back from me, she looks at Bobby. "Bobby, seriously, I'm a fan. I had tickets to your fight."

Ouch.

He smiles. "Thank you. It's a pleasure to meet you too."

"Okay, listen," Lila frowns at my guilt-ridden face, "I know what happened to y'all. My security does a background check before I get to meet with anyone, plus I genuinely am a fan, so I was interested to know. I know you were in the hospital, and I know why Bobby forfeited. I'm truly surprised that Bobby's people kept the media attention as low key as they did. The information is out there, but only when you search for it."

I'm starting to feel sick, hating that the whole world could know the private details of my life and the reasons behind the forfeit.

"Kit, I can see your face right now, and you need to stop that. You must know none of it was your fault. You didn't ask to get hurt, and you didn't ask Bobby not to fight. He did it because he loves you. Don't dwell on the negative, babe, just treasure the fact you have a man so willing to sacrifice for you."

She's right, I know she is.

"Anyway, come sit down and chat with me. I have about twenty minutes till I have to go, then y'all can go find your seats. I really hope you like the show."

~*~

The show is set to start in about fifteen minutes, so we find our section and sit down, my excitement simultaneously speeding time and slowing it down.

I watch as the seats around me quickly fill, the noise and excitement tangible. I worried that Bobby would be bored, thinking that he's probably not actually a fan, but I look at him and he seems as psyched as me. His eyes meet mine and he leans into me, kissing his way down my temple. "Are you excited?"

I don't bother answering him verbally, because I'd have to yell anyway. Instead I just nod my head and grin. His smile is dazzling in return.

A few minutes later, the lights start to dim and the crowd noise reaches ear-splitting levels. The excitement runs through my blood.

The opening notes to one of her songs begins, and Lila greets the fans, but the crowd is so loud, I can't discern the words. My eyes move from the live stage to the large screens, undecided which one I want to watch more. She walks out onto the stage and the crowd roars, enjoying their first view of her tonight.

After some brief hello's and thank you's, Lila starts into one of her hit songs, bouncing around the stage and singing her heart out. I've never seen her perform live before, but I'm thrilled that her live singing is as good as her studio recordings.

Launching into a second and third song, I decide I've never had so much fun in my life. To be able to share this with Bobby has been the topping on an already wonderful cake. When the current song ends, the bass line to *Blood Bonds* starts and my own blood starts thrumming.

Lila stops her stride across the stage and shields her eyes as she looks into the crowd. My adrenaline spikes before I even realize what's happening. "My next song, I'm told, is a favorite of a friend of mine. So, Kit, where are you, babe?" she smiles and winks when she finds me. "This one's for you."

I think I could die from excitement now. She's singing a song for me. She's belting out the lyrics and Bobby sits beside me with a smile on his face and his arm over my shoulder.

"Okay, okay, okay," Lila laughs as she waves the crowd down. "Now that I've primed you all ..." the crowd roars at her, emphasizing her point, "... now that I have you all primed, I want to say a few things. Thank you, thank you, I love y'all too," she says, answering a thousand declarations of love, "... thank you. Okay, so I want to thank y'all for coming out tonight. Thank you for loving me enough, for buying tickets and albums, for supporting me. It means a lot to me and you have no idea how thankful I really am.

"Now, the reason for interruptin' your evening—what kind of friend would I be if I didn't help a buddy out? Right? So, I have some special guests here tonight. Kit and Bobby, please stand up. Stand up guys and just say a quick hi."

Lila laughs as my face turns horrified. This is too much for a girl who enjoys anonymity. Bobby even looks nervous, and I can't say I've ever seen him nervous before.

It's … weird!

"Stand up guys!"

Bobby takes my hand and we slowly rise, the cheers building, especially from those closest to us when they realize they're close enough to touch two of Lila Royales' *personal friends*.

"Give 'em a wave guys!" She laughs and seems to enjoy our nervousness. When we comply, she continues speaking, "Okay, these two hotties are my good friends, Bobby and Kit. They're a couple of lovebirds who're out, belatedly celebrating their birthdays. Can everyone say hi?"

When the whole crowd cheers and says hi, I almost die, but she seems to be having the time of her life.

"Alright, I'm almost done embarrassing you Kitty Cat, but first I'm going to need you to come up here."

Instantly my body fails me. I sit down in my chair, hard, winded. This can't be real. It's just a birthday gift. Why would she interrupt her show for this? Bobby must have paid a lot of fucking money for this treatment, although when I look at him, he seems as scared as I am.

I'm screaming inside, terrified and nervous, but also so excited, I might wet myself. Within seconds, a big security guy is in front of me. Not Shane and not Mike; another big dude, and he holds his hand out for me.

"Take his hand, Kit, I want you to join me up here."

Slowly I stand and take his hand, then latch my free hand onto Bobby's, refusing to let him get out of this. He looks like he might be sick, but that's just too damn bad. If I have to do this then so does he. That's love, right?

It takes us a few minutes to reach the stage and Lila talks to the crowd to keep them entertained. I know the fans mean well and are just excited, but the enthusiastic back pats and touches are actually starting to hurt me, my ribs starting to ache, my body tensing.

Bobby must notice, because he transforms from nervous wreck to protector, stepping in close and shielding my body with his. God, I love that man!

Finally, we reach the stairs and I concentrate on each one, terrified of tripping in front of this crowd. That would be such a Kit thing to do. Thankfully we make it to the top and Lila is there, waiting for me, her hand reaching out to take mine. She pulls me in again for another hug, but I can tell she's being gentle with me.

"You good?" she asks, as she passes me a microphone.

Oh god! She wants me to speak?

"Kit, welcome! Look at all these beautiful people here tonight!" She gestures to the cheering crowd in front of us. I try to look but realize I can't see a thing — the rest of the room is too dark, the lights shining on the stage too bright. If it weren't for the camera flashes and fake candles – and the noise – it would almost feel as though we were here alone.

"So, Bobby has requested a song for you."

Lila busts up laughing when I whip my head his way. "He gave me full artistic freedom to choose which song, with the sole condition that it have a happy ending. Which kinda makes sense. Bobby, in five words or less, why did you request a song for Kit?"

Someone passes him a microphone and his face pales. "Ah …" he hesitates. "Um, because I love her?"

The whole crowd *awwww's* and *ohhhhh's* at his declaration, and Lila laughs. "Right. I thought you might say that. So, onto your song request. I took my time deciding, knowing not all mine end well, and I wanted to pick the perfect song for you. So, in the spirit of friends, new and old, I decided to invite yet another friend of mine along tonight."

She turns toward the crowd, pumping them up for her announcement. I look toward Bobby, who appears to be in the dark too, because when Lila announces, "Everyone, please welcome to the stage, my good friend … Teddy Diego!" Bobby shouts, "no fucking way!"

… into his microphone …

…making the crazy cheering crowd, and Lila, and Teddy-fucking-Diego, stop and laugh.

Teddy walks to Lila and hugs her, then toward us with a huge smile on his face and laughter in his eyes. His dimples are adorable, and I struggle between wanting to swoon, and wanting to pat his hair.

He shakes Bobby's hand first, then takes me in his arms, gently squeezing me then placing a soft kiss! … on my lips! Teddy Diego kissed me! Oh… my…. gawd.

In his adorable accent, he tells me he's happy to meet us, then laughs at Bobby when he (Bobby) tells him (Ted) to 'keep his fucking lips to himself.'

Ted walks back to Lila and they start chatting with the crowd, hyping them up, asking what song they should sing, but I already know what song they chose. Of course, I do! It's *their* song.

Lila turns toward us but speaks to the crowd. "Alright, since Teddy's here, I think we all know what we'll be singing tonight. So, please, Kit take a seat." I look to my left and find someone placing a bar stool a few feet away—bless their cotton socks. "And Bobby, you stand here," she says, manhandling him and placing him so he stands behind my sitting form. "Okay folks, strap in and enjoy!"

Someone runs out and hands the singers a guitar each and Ted strums his, testing I guess, then speaks into the microphone in front of him. "Kit, this one's for you. Because … he loves you."

Well damn. I think I might cry right now.

Teddy strums his guitar and begins crooning about knowing his one true love, and Lila joins in in a sweet low harmony.

I want to turn and hold Bobby, or more accurately, I want him to hold me, but I'm frozen to the spot, unable to take my eyes from the singers, knowing they're Bobby's proxies, and they're telling me he loves me. Obviously, I already know this, but fuck if I can turn away from them right now.

I sit with tears in my eyes as I mouth the words to a song that's been a chart topper for the better part of a year, but I don't dare sing out loud. I don't want to miss a single lyric, a single cord that the real singers gift me with. The four minutes or so that the song takes feels like I'm in some alternate universe. I completely forget I'm on a stage and in front of thousands of people. Tens of thousands? A hundred thousand? I just watch the magic and take every word to heart, imagining they're from Bobby. I can feel his chest against my back, his hand gently resting on my left shoulder.

Ever since the … incident … it's as though he always gravitates toward that side, as though he's declared himself protector of my weak side.

A single tear drips onto my cheek and I smile. It's not a sad tear — it is a very, very happy tear. The song ends with a flourish, the lights shutting off, and after long applause and whistling, the crowd silences. I can still feel Bobby behind me, his hand still on my shoulder, so I don't worry. I assume this is all part of the show.

Lila starts speaking even while the lights are still out. A spotlight swings around the crowd, highlighting random groups. "I hope y'all enjoyed that. Since we seem to have developed a theme to tonight's show, I want to talk about friends again. They can be family, or they can be randoms you found in the street. We have some of each here tonight. Are you still with me Kit?"

My heartrate spikes, nervous that she's making me talk again. Now that the main lights are out, we're no longer blinded and I can see more of the crowd than I could before. I lift my microphone and clear my throat. "Ah, yeah, I'm here."

"Good, I'm sending someone over to grab you. Relax, we won't let you trip, I promise. I want you to come over here. I have one more surprise for you."

I can feel someone near me as they grab my hand and pull me from my chair. The hand is small and soft, a woman's hand, so I hold on and let her lead me wherever she wants me to go. The whole time, I wonder if I'm holding the chihuahua's hand.

She, whoever she is, leads me a few feet in the direction Lila and Teddy were standing moments ago, so I prepare my 'I'm not a weirdo and I can be cool around superstars' face. I'm not sure it's convincing though. I probably just look like I have gas.

"Okay, we better hurry. I'll probably get in trouble if we leave the lights out too much longer. It's probably a safety issue, you know. Alright, so Bobby told me that your BFF wanted to come tonight but you didn't have enough tickets. But first, I'm not judging okay, whatever floats one's boat. But Bobby tells me her name is Tinkerbelle. Is that real? Who would name their daughter that?"

I crack, the hilarity of the situation too much. Casey will murder him for this. I try to pull myself under control, wiping invisible tears from my eyes. I feel another hand reach for mine, and I know this one, easy. It's the non-fairy in the flesh. She must be my last surprise from Lila.

I pull her in and hug her tight, then I bring the microphone back up. "Her name's actually Casey."

"Okay, well, just so the rest of us know what's going on, she's here tonight, and I assume you realize that's her hand you're holding right now. Surprise!"

"Yeah, I'd know her anywhere. Thanks for bringing her along. She was pretty mad at me when I decided to bring Bobby instead."

The crowd laugh at my words and I jump with surprise. Jesus, I guess I don't sound as flustered and nervous as I feel.

"Well, it was my pleasure. Anyway, I hope y'all enjoy the show. Umm, person in charge of the lights, could you switch them back on now, please?"

I'm blinded again when the lights come on, rendering the suddenly screaming crowd invisible to me, but as my eyes adjust I see faces—many faces, many familiar faces.

I scream when I recognize Jimmy's smoldering chocolate eyes right in front of me. He smacks a wet kiss on my lips and slaps my ass as he walks by, then Aiden and Jon next, hugging me gently and kissing my cheek. I start to cry when Jack steps up next, then Nelly, then Iz, each giving me a big kiss and soft squeezey hugs.

Nelly takes my hand, her tears running as freely as mine when she points to the front row. I follow her gaze and burst into tears when I see George—my dad's sweet friend George is here, as are Jack's friends Michael and Calum, then next to them is my boss and his wife, then a couple coworkers that I really like. There are other familiar faces from the gym, some I don't even know by name, and I'm touched that all these people came here tonight anyway. I wave at everyone, but stop short again when the crowd goes ballistic. What next?

I look up to my friends, but they're pointing behind me. My blood sizzles and I turn slowly, already knowing exactly what I'll find. Bobby kneels about ten feet away, looking at me nervously as his knee bounces with pent up energy. I guess I know now why he was so nervous earlier.

He's holding a ring between his thumb and forefinger in one hand, and in the other, a microphone. "Baby? Come over here a second?" His voice is liquid sex, sending the crowd into a swooning frenzy.

I already know the answer to the question he hasn't yet asked, but what does it say about me that I'm excited about leaving this place and taking him home? How could I not be excited about making love to my future husband with the sexy voice, and the sexy body?

He clears his throat nervously. "So … you probably already heard, I love you."

I nod and wipe away my tears. "I love you too, babe."

He smiles and shoves his microphone in my face. "Sorry. I didn't hear that."

I repeat myself so the whole stadium can hear. The look on his face is pure male satisfaction. Yeah Bobby, I love you, and the whole world can know.

He takes a deep breath, fortifying himself, then pushes on. "Kit, I want to spend the rest of my life with you. I want to protect you, I want to support you, I want to be your everything. Because you're mine. I want to sleep in the same bed with you every night, I want to wake up with you every day and I want to make blue-eyed babies with you. I want you to take my name. I promise to never stop courting you, even when we've been together forever and our skin sags. I'll never forget how wonderful and beautiful you are, and I won't let time and comfort let me become complacent. I won't ever take you for granted, and I promise, with everything I am, I'll make you happy. I'll never hurt you, and I'll never let you hurt … I want to be the man your dad would approve of. I'm sorry I couldn't ask him myself, but I hope I can be what he would want for you. I promise to try every day to earn his approval."

I'm crying, surprised by how much this moment makes me miss my daddy. I don't mean to dwell on the negative, especially in such a happy moment, but I've just realized my dad will never know my husband, and he'll never meet his grandchildren.

I'm devastated the two most important men in my life will never know each other. But I know, without a doubt, my dad would approve of Bobby, because Bobby loves me unconditionally, and that's all that he would want. It's as though they're both my protectors in life, and Bobby came to me when my dad couldn't any longer. They tag teamed.

"So, in an effort to do the right thing, by you and by your dad, I asked Jack for his approval, for his permission …"

I look toward Jack's glowing face, his smile the biggest I've ever seen it, even bigger than the day he won his first fight. He walks forward and places one arm around my shoulder and takes my microphone with the other. Placing a soft kiss on my cheek he says, "I authorized this," in a deep, serious voice, and his silliness makes me, and thousands of others, laugh.

Jack steps away and Bobby looks up at me seriously. "So, Catherine Maree Reilly, I love you with my whole heart. Will you marry me?"

I have no words. I can't force anything past the emotion clogging my throat, so I just nod, hoping my smile, my happy tears, and my actions convey just how truly happy I am. The smile on his face tells me he understands, and as he stands he asks, "Yeah?"

"Yes, I'll marry you Bobby. I would marry you right this second."

He moves toward me, in my face in half a second, and our microphones drop to the floor. "I love you so much, Kit. I promise to make you happy." He slides the most beautiful ring I've ever seen in my life on my finger.

"I love you too, Bobby. You already make me so happy. I promise to love you forever."

He smiles, then leans forward and kisses me, his tongue loving, caressing … hungry. I can't hear anyone around us anymore, I can't see anything except him. His arms move from my shoulders, running down my ribs then onto my ass, then he lifts me, and my legs automatically wrap around his waist.

Time is irrelevant. And I don't even care that we're on stage in an arena. Nor do I care that my future mother in law is standing near, or George, or my brother or brothers in law. I don't care because all I want right now is to ensure Bobby knows I love him.

"Whew," Lila dramatically fans herself as Teddy laughs. "Did somebody turn on the heat? Alright, let's get this show going again. Here's an oldie but a favorite of mine."

The opening notes to a new song begins, and I unwrap my legs and slide down Bobby's body. He holds me against his chest securely as we turn to watch Lila strut around the stage, singing and dancing and belting out the lyrics to her song. Our family is standing a few feet away, watching the show, but laughing and chatting with Ted Diego as he stands beside them holding his guitar. The scene is just surreal. To see my family having a laugh with superstars, is just … weird.

Bobby continues to nuzzle my hair the way he does, and I stare at the beautiful ring he gave me.

"Are you happy, baby?"

Nodding, I answer him while turning in his arms, "Yes. I'm so happy." I place a kiss on his lips, employing mountains of willpower to keep it light. "Can we go home now?"

His brows pinch instantly. "Huh? Why?"

"I'd really like to … you know … right now," I tell him with a smug smile as I watch his eyes warm and turn liquid. I feel him growing against my stomach and I'm thrilled that I get to stay with him forever. "Let's go do that. Then we'll go get married."

The End

Continue the Rollin On series here:

myBook.to/FindingVictoryEFinn

In loving Memory.

***

This book was for my dad.

Although, it's probably a good thing he didn't get to read it.

The sex scenes would have certainly gotten me grounded.

E, you were the best dad a girl could ever ask for!

I swear, I didn't really mind the fru fru dresses,

I was just thrilled I got to hang out with you at

every possible moment.

I'm sorry about my sixteenth year. I feel pretty

awful about that now.

I wish to god you got to meet my kids.

B & E know about you, though. You won't be forgotten.

I hope you're at peace.

I love you.

I miss you.

Love, your baby girl.

xx

To everyone reading this, I want you to know every single good thing I said about my dad in this book — it was all true. He was a wonderful man, and he's very dearly missed.

PS: He did the immature things also.

And yes, we needed to buy a new

vacuum after that day at the lake.

If you made it all the way to the end, wow. THANK YOU!! Thank you for reading Kit and Bobby's story.

This one was a labor of love, I hope you enjoyed it.

The Rollin On series is now complete, and you can pick up the next book at your favorite retailers.

Book 2 - Finding Victory (Bobby and Kit again – don't skip this one! Trust me! You'll wanna know what happens.)

Book 3 - Finding Forever (Jimmy's book)

Book 4 - Finding Peace (Aiden's book)

Book 5 – Finding Redemption (Jon and Tink's story), and

Book 6 – Finding Hope (Jack!!!)

I hope you read on and enjoy the ride that is the Kincaid's.

I want to shout a huge thank you to my Beta readers, Dana Hart, Amanda Deans, Debbie Berne and Jenelle O'Shea. You girls are the best! Xx

I want to thank Sloane Johnson for coming to my rescue and wrapping my books oh so pretty. I love my covers. Thank you.

I have a bunch of blogger friends now, and although I can't name them all, I want to shout out to Abri and Elaina from Real Talk Book Talk. You've been amazing and are wonderful mentors. Thank you!

To my real life Bobby – I love you. Thank you for being my constant support and my loudest cheerleader.

If you want to connect with me, please find me on facebook at the links below. I LOVE hearing from you guys.

My author page: https://www.facebook.com/EmiliaBFinn/

Join my reader group here:
https://www.facebook.com/groups/therollincrew/

Thank you so much for reading.

Emilia x

What's next?

Finding Victory

After an attack that almost claimed her life, Kit wakes from a three-week coma to find her boyfriend and the love of her life standing at her back, ready and waiting to sweep her up and make her life as smooth as possible.

She wanted an easier life, she wanted to nix the drama, but Bobby's caring for her threatens to smother her. He means well, but Kit craves independence and the satisfaction of knowing her earlier enemies won't take anything more from her.

With a wedding to plan and a career changing fight Bobby needs to prepare for, the Kincaids are rocked by a secret that tears their tight-knit group apart. Despite the volatile undercurrents hurting those he loves, Bobby must train and win, or risk losing everything he ever worked for.

Can Bobby let go of the reins he so desperately clutches to and let Kit take care of herself, or will he lose it all for the sake of control?

****

Reviewers are giving Finding Victory 5 stars!

"Once again, Emilia Finn ripped my heart out, stomped on it and then came to hug me. This woman just keeps on making me cry, swoon, laugh, fall in love and cry some more. The feels with both stories is amazing. It felt real. It was real."

Finding Forever

This is the third installment in the Rollin On Series and follows the Kincaid brothers through the cage and into their hearts.

She was his from the beginning of time, despite the fact that her brothers would kill him for even looking at her. Best friends since before kindergarten, they grew up together, secretly in love with the other.

Too bad they both kept their secrets until it was too late.

Bad choice's result in an unexpected pregnancy and a stolen future. Will she be able to find happiness - with him, or with the father of her baby?

Come on a rollercoaster ride with the Rollin crew; they're guaranteed to keep you on the edge of your seat - Again.

Finding Peace

Tina Cooper is running from a dangerous past, haunted by choices she made when she was young and naive. Now she and her three-year-old daughter are drifters, skipping from town to town in search of peace from the nightmares that follow them.

But her ex won't ever let them go. Till death do they part.

Aiden Kincaid is just a regular guy. A fighter, but without dreams of fame and fortune. He's happy to stay in the shadows and to meet women that expect nothing more from him than he does of them. A fun night. No strings attached.

Evie Cooper is the only exception. Sweet and sassy and all things lovable, she belongs to the mysterious Tina, who Aiden is still yet to meet. Tina is an enigma. But her daughter has already stolen his heart.

What happens when Evie's world is threatened? Can he save her when her mama is set on running?

Finding Redemption

Jon Hart clawed his way out of hell. He sat in the fire for the first fifteen years of his life but he finally escaped with his baby sister and as few scars as he could get away with.
Jon swore his poisonous bloodline would die out with him.

That was until he met Casey Irvine, the one woman in the entire world that has him wishing things could be different.

He refuses to set into motion that same cycle from his past, but the thought of letting her go is just as impossible.

She'll want more. Of course she will. She's beautiful and perfect and deserves the world. Friends with benefits can only work for so long.

What painful secret has Jon been holding onto his entire life? A secret no one knows, not even his brothers or best friend.

Not all is at it seems though; Casey has her own secret, a secret big enough it might ruin their world and any chance they might have ever had at happiness.

This is a story about friends. Lovers. Enemies. Casey is all three for him, and so much more.

Finding Hope

Professional fighter and undisputed champion, twenty-five year old Jack Reilly is back for the final instalment of the Rollin On series.

Dealing with more grief than any teenager should have to by his young age, Jack's life finally started to make sense when he stepped into the Rollin On gym. He found a whole new world and a family he never in his wildest dreams expected to love him back.

A new focus. A new goal. Jack was dubbed to be a champion long before he ever stepped into the octagon.

With his sweet girlfriend Stephanie by his side, Jack's world was picture perfect. But then grief and chaos strikes again, tearing him down and thrusting him into a pit of despair he couldn't possibly hope to escape. There's only so much pain a man can take in one lifetime.

Will this be the year Jack finally breaks?

Long awaited and eagerly anticipated, the boy we met five books ago is finally a man.

63111210R00307

Made in the USA
Middletown, DE
04 February 2018